FILTHY RICH
VAMPIRES

Second Rite

FILTHY
RICH
VAMPIRES
Second Rite

GENEVA LEE

Entangled Publishing, LLC
644 Shrewsbury Commons Ave., STE 181
Shrewsbury, PA 17361
rights@entangledpublishing.com

Amara is an imprint of Entangled Publishing, LLC.

Visit our website at www.entangledpublishing.com.

Edited by Yezanira Venecia
Cover art and design by Geneva Lee
Stock art by Elizaveta/Adobestock, Gluiki/Adobestock, tussik/Adobestock
Interior formatting by Britt Marczak

ISBN 978-1-64937-644-2

Manufactured in the United States of America

First Edition February 2024

10 9 8 7 6 5 4 3 2 1

ALSO BY GENEVA LEE

For my mate

At Entangled, we want our readers to be well-informed. If you would like to know if this book contains any elements that might be of concern for you, please check the back of the book for details.

CHAPTER ONE

Thea

"You have to get out of this place," Olivia announced as she stepped inside my mom's room. She was still dressed for rehearsal with a pair of knit boots pulled over her tights. In her arms, she carried a bouquet of fresh flowers.

"Is it Sunday?" I asked, trying to figure out where Friday and Saturday had gone.

"Yes! That proves my point." She busied herself, taking out the old, limp flowers and replacing them with fresh ones. She fluffed a few of the blossoms, then turned and smiled at my mom. "Hello, Mama Melbourne."

My mother didn't respond. She couldn't. Not while she was in a coma. Olivia always said hello anyway.

My roommate took a chair next to me, tucking her knees against her chest. "Seriously, Thea. She wouldn't want you to sit vigil like this. You need to get out. See the world."

I winced. I'd been doing just that when I got the call something had happened to my mom. In the past four weeks, I hadn't seen much past the inside of this room. A month had passed since I'd left Julian in Paris. I'd been at the hospital pretty much every moment since I'd stepped off the plane in San Francisco. The days were starting to blend together, but I wasn't ready to admit that my friend was right.

"Okay, poor choice of words," she said quickly. "But, honey, you're not the one in that hospital bed."

"I know that," I snapped. Guilt rushed through me instantly. Both Olivia and Tanner had been here supporting me through this whole mess, and now I was being a bitch. "I'm sorry. I just wish she would wake up."

"Me too, honey." She squeezed my shoulder, and for a moment, I was reminded of Jacqueline. My heart ached at the thought of my lost friend, but that was a different life. One that had cost me too much.

"I wish I hadn't gone," I confessed. "I shouldn't have left her to follow some jerk I barely knew to Paris."

"Well, you did," she said impatiently.

I turned a surprised look on her.

"Sorry." She sighed. "It's just that beating yourself up over it isn't going to change anything."

"I know. That's why I'm here now."

"There's nothing you can do for her, Thea. Not while she's like this. You know what the doctors said."

The trouble was the doctors hadn't said much. Whatever'd happened to my mother was as much a mystery to them as it was to me. Not that we only had a coma to worry about. Nope, that would have been simple. No one could figure out why she wouldn't wake up, and I was determined to be here when she did. It had happened while I was gone—how was I supposed to leave her side again?

Before I could remind Olivia of that, we were interrupted by a businesslike rap on the door. Dr. Reeves, the physician in charge of Mom's case, strode in with a chart, flashing a blinding smile when he saw I wasn't alone.

Olivia shifted in her seat, putting her legs down and straightening up. "Good afternoon, doctor."

"It's nice to see you, Olivia." He nodded to the fresh flowers. "You're such a good friend. You're lucky to have her, Thea."

"I know." I barely resisted the urge to roll my eyes. Olivia had taken one look at Dr. Reeves and memorized his schedule. Most days, she popped in when she could to deliver me fresh clothes or coffee, but every Sunday, she was here like clockwork to flirt with the attending physician. Not that I could blame her. In fact, it was almost like my own personal rom-com.

"I was just trying to convince Thea she needs to take a break," Olivia said, fluttering her lashes.

"I take breaks."

"Bathroom breaks do not count," she informed me, still staring at Dr. Reeves. "Do they?"

"I'm afraid she's right," he said to me gently. "I want to rerun some of the scans we did on your mom last week. Maybe you two could grab lunch."

My eyes darted between them. "Did you two plan this?"

"Desperate times." Olivia got to her feet and tossed me my coat.

I caught it with a frown. I must have looked really pathetic if the doctor was kicking me out. "How long will the tests take?"

"A couple of hours," he said.

"And if she—"

"We will call you immediately if something changes," he cut me off.

Yep, they'd orchestrated the whole thing. I got to my feet grudgingly and walked over to Mom's bedside. Carefully avoiding the tubes and wires attached to a dozen machines monitoring her pulse, heart rate, oxygen levels, blood pressure, and who knew what else, I kissed her forehead. "I'll be back soon."

I turned in time to see Olivia's worried expression. Quickly, she plastered on a smile. "Let's get you out of here."

Olivia looped her arm through mine and directed me out of the hospital room, marching us toward the elevator with a clear sense of purpose.

"We could just grab something in the cafeteria," I suggested. Technically, that qualified as getting me out of the room.

But she groaned. "Nope. You are all mine for the next two hours."

I opened my mouth to argue, but she held up a hand.

"You heard what he said. She won't even be in there. Besides, there's a new burrito place on the corner." She hit the button for the lobby, still arm in arm with me. I suspected she'd labeled me a flight risk.

It felt strange to step through the hospital's sliding glass doors and onto the sidewalk. San Francisco was suffering a cold spell by Californian standards. I hated that it reminded me of Paris. Or maybe the weather just matched my heart, broken and cold. I buttoned my coat, nearly bumping into a passing couple.

"Sorry," I muttered as they darted out of the way.

The man looked annoyed, but his girlfriend smiled. "It's okay. Happy holidays."

I couldn't quite muster a response, so I nodded. But they were already on their way, their arms laden with paper shopping bags full of their Christmas purchases. The man paused to take the packages she carried. He looped them on his other arm and took her hand. A hollow pang rattled the broken pieces of my heart, and I turned away only to realize the entire street was full of couples and families out to do their holiday shopping.

"Let's get that burrito," I mumbled.

Olivia offered me a sympathetic grin as she tugged me down the street. "Finally. Let's eat our feelings."

· · ·

My feelings tasted pretty good with a side of guac and sour cream. By the time we'd finished our massive burritos, I felt better. I wasn't about to admit that to Olivia, though. She'd want to make a habit out of this. But I needed to stick around the hospital. I needed to be there for my mom.

"Thanks," I said as we stepped outside the restaurant. "I guess I better—"

"We still have an hour," she informed me. "Don't even think that you're heading back yet."

"Fine."

It was growing colder by the minute, and we huddled together as we walked. Across the street on the corner, I spotted a man watching us. Even from here, his eyes seemed too dark. Had we attracted the attention of a vampire?

Or did I just wish we had? For the last month, part of me had fantasized I'd be dragged back into the world I'd run from. How would Julian react if he heard I'd been attacked by one of his kind? Would he even care? If he'd been telling the truth—that it was better for me to stay out of his world—he might. But as the days passed without any contact, I'd begun to realize that he didn't care. It had been an excuse. If he'd been telling the truth the last time we spoke—that I wasn't meant for his world—he might. But as the days passed without any contact, I'd begun to realize that he didn't care. He was right; I wasn't meant for his filthy rich world.

Across the street, the stranger continued to stare as we drew parallel to him. From here, I could see two black voids where his eyes should be. A nauseating thrill shot through me.

He *was* a vampire.

"Thea, what do you say?" Olivia interrupted my thoughts with an insistent tug on my arm that tore my attention from the vampire for a split second.

By the time I whipped back around, he'd vanished.

"Let's go in." Olivia pulled me toward the shop we were passing.

I glanced at its battered door in time to read the peeling vinyl lettering. It said *Madame Lenore*, and under it, *fortunes told* with an illustrated hand beneath. There was no way I was going to get my palm read by some stranger while a vampire roamed the street outside.

"Wait!" But it was too late.

Olivia called a cheerful "hello" to the cluttered room.

An old woman poked her head from behind a beaded curtain, an unlit cigarette dangling from her mouth.

"Come in!" Madame Lenore called in a heavy Eastern European accent. "Take a seat. I will be right there." The beaded curtains tinkled as she vanished into the back.

It took care to navigate the maze of oddities stuffed into the tiny shop: a haphazard collection of chairs from various time periods, a cabinet stuffed with tarnished silver, and books in every language piled and scattered everywhere. The fortune teller floated back into the room in an array of colorful silks and pointed to a worn table nearby. We arranged ourselves around its layers of lace tablecloths while Madame Lenore lit a fresh cone of incense, waving the rising smoke to fill the room. Sandalwood filled my nostrils, and I coughed as its heavy perfume hit me.

"Your palm," Madame Lenore said as she held out her gnarled hand.

"Oh, not me," I said quickly. "This was her idea."

Olivia obediently dropped her hand into the old woman's, her eyes glinting. "Will I be rich?" Olivia giggled and looked at me.

"If you want to be," Madame Lenore told her carefully, "or you can be happy."

I bit back a smile, turning away before Olivia spotted it. Apparently, Madame Lenore didn't mind delivering tough love.

"What's the difference?" Olivia asked.

"Money doesn't make people happy," I said without thinking. Red painted my cheeks when I realized what I'd said.

But if I'd stolen Lenore's line, she didn't seem to mind. "Your friend is wise. I see two paths."

My attention rapidly waned as she recounted an increasingly generic fortune for Olivia. By the end, my roommate was completely deflated and I was checked out. Lenore's vision of a normal, simple life wasn't what Olivia hoped for.

"Your turn." Lenore turned to me.

"No, really. We should go." It was stupid to be so cautious about sharing my palm with the woman. She was probably just some old lady who told people whatever popped into her head. But I knew something Olivia didn't.

Magic was real. Or it had been. And while it was probably a cry in the dark to think this old woman had a magical bone in her body, how could I be sure?

"Just do it, Thea!" Olivia pushed. "For me."

"Fine." I laid my arm across the table. My cheeks burned as I presented my palm. The last time anyone had been this interested in it had been...

I swallowed, refusing to let my thoughts go down that path. This was about my future, right?

"Will she meet a tall, dark stranger?" Olivia asked with another giggle.

Lenore stayed silent as she studied the lines on my hand. Then she spoke softly. "It seems she already has."

I whipped my hand back like she might bite it.

"We should go," I said shakily.

"Don't you want to know the secrets I see?" she asked.

"I thought you were going to tell me my future." I stood up—not wanting her to tell me either.

"What is your future but a secret, Thea?" A cryptic smile danced on her face. "When you're ready to learn the truth, find me."

I dug a few twenties out of my purse—the proceeds from selling the Chanel bag I'd bought in Paris—and tossed it on the table. "Thanks."

I made it out of the shop in record time. Olivia burst through the door a second later. "Okay, so that was weird."

"It was nothing," I said firmly. "Just some old con lady. I need to get back."

"I'll walk you."

We started toward the hospital as clouds moved overhead, shadowing the street. When we reached the corner, I turned to find Lenore's heavily lined eyes peering through the shop window. Then they disappeared. I tried to shake it off as the crosswalk sign changed, and we dashed across the street toward the hospital.

"I'm so sorry," Olivia said at the door.

"It's okay." I gave her a quick hug.

"It's not okay. She made you think about *him*." Olivia refused to use Julian's name.

I shook my head and lied, "She was harmlessly creepy. Next time, can we just get coffee?"

"Deal," she promised.

"Be careful!" I called after her as she started to head in the direction of our apartment.

Olivia flashed a smile and then turned the corner.

I took my own advice and got fresh coffee before I headed back up to my mom's room. No matter how hard I tried, I couldn't quite shake the uneasy feeling churning inside my stomach.

And when I reached my mom's hospital room, I discovered why.

CHAPTER TWO

Julian

"N o."

I stared at the bartender, waiting for an explanation. She wiped out a glass and placed it under the absinthe fountain but didn't turn the tap.

"Need I remind you I own this whole block?" I snarled and reached for the glass.

"You already have," she said, sounding unimpressed. "Fire me. Bite me. I don't give a fuck, but you're cut off. You need to get out of here."

I stalked back to the private room I'd taken three or four nights ago. Stepping over a few bodies, I sank on a cushion and vanished into the shadows. Judging by the moans, the bodies littering the floor weren't all unconscious. I was pretty sure they were all alive, though.

Sebastian's head appeared, followed by his bare chest. He extricated himself from a mass of naked limbs and sauntered over. The fly to his jeans hung open, revealing a thatch of hair I'd rather not have seen.

"I thought you went for more drinks," he said, sinking onto a tufted cushion across from me. He wiped some blood from his lip before picking up an opium pipe from the table.

"She refused to serve me," I said bitterly. A hopeful, and completely nude, woman crawled toward me, but I shooed her off.

Sebastian raised an eyebrow. "I'll talk to her," he said before tipping his head toward the orgy happening in the corner. "You'd feel better if you joined us."

"You're not really my type," I told him.

"Look, you aren't going to get Thea out of your system by drinking her away—not with absinthe, at least." He leveled with me. "Getting laid—"

"I'm not interested in any of these women," I growled.

"I've got a few men if you think you want to try something new," he suggested.

I rolled my eyes and rose to my feet. I'd lost track of the days and the amount of absinthe and opium I'd consumed. But even when the drugs were working, I'd had no desire to jump into Sebastian's all-hours sex-a-thon. Since my brother had never met someone he didn't want to screw, he found this difficult to understand.

He sighed. "Vampires are sexual creatures. It's okay to act on your instincts."

"Right now, my instincts are telling me that if you don't stop talking, I should rip your head off." I placed a hand on the wall, surprised to feel the soft touch of velvet. I ran my fingers over the patterned wallpaper, wondering when I'd taken off my gloves.

"I can see why Layla cut you off." He held out the pipe. "Have some opium."

I shook my head, which hurt more than it should. Opium would fix that. It would also result in me sitting in the corner, watching Sebastian mount everything with a hole for the next few hours. The real trouble was that once the high started to leave a vampire's bloodstream, it was gone in a matter of minutes, and it usually left me in whatever state my body would have been in if I hadn't just clocked out on life in favor of drugs.

Pain shot through my gums, my fangs aching to descend. I didn't know how long we'd been in here, but I knew it had been days since I fed myself anything other than an escape.

"I need to feed," I told him.

"There's plenty here—"

"Clean blood," I cut him off. "I'll see if Layla has any bags."

"Ask nicely," he called after me, but I was already walking toward the bar.

Layla sighed as I approached, her heavily lined eyes tracking each step. She placed a hand on her ample hip, her breasts swelling over the top of her boned corset. My eyes traveled from them to the gentle pulse at her neck. I'd never seen her ingesting any of the substances she slung.

"Can I help you?" she asked, sounding like she'd rather not.

"Blood bags," I said, tearing my eyes from her neck.

"We don't serve that. Look around. There are plenty of humans. Ask nicely and someone will share."

"Would you rather I drag some innocent off the street?" I challenged her. "I'm not touching anyone here, unless you're offering."

I had no interest in Layla other than getting rid of the violent headache that intensified with each passing second.

"You have some nerve," she hissed. "You think because you're a Rousseaux, you can take whatever you want?"

"I think I can do that because I'm a vampire, sweetheart." I stepped closer to the bar and placed a hand on it. "I know I can do it because I'm a Rousseaux."

She muttered something in French. I only caught two words.

Dégoûtant and *pur-sang*.

Well, she wasn't wrong on either count. Using my planted palm, I leaped over the bar. Or I tried to.

A moment later, I hit a wall.

"Is he causing problems?" a brutish vampire asked Layla, wiping his hands together as he glared at me.

I remembered why I was barehanded: No one wore gloves here. It was too easy to distinguish myself as a pureblood by wearing them. *Le Poste de Nuit* didn't cater to the upper rungs of vampire society, even if there were always a few purebloods hanging around the place. Tucked in the basement of a strip club in Pigalle, it mainly attracted turned vampires. I hadn't felt so much as a spark of magic since Sebastian had dragged us here. These weren't vampires who relied on tradition or cared about bloodlines.

But we had one thing in common. We were all here to escape something.

Or they were. I'd come for an entirely different purpose, and glaring back at the vampire who'd tossed me across the bar, I knew I'd finally found my solution.

"What's it to you, *switch*?" I stood, dusting myself off. Heads turned toward me, shocked to hear anyone use the vulgar term in a room full of turned vampires.

"Alek!" Layla scrambled around the bar, trying to step in front of him, but he was already stomping toward me.

So the brick wall had a name. That would make it easier for me to press his buttons. I just needed to keep Layla from spoiling my plan.

"Let the men talk, sweetheart," I called over to her.

A few more vampires got to their feet. The only thing worse to vampires than a bigot was a misogynistic bigot.

"Alek," Layla said, sounding panicked, "he's a Rousseaux."

My shoulders slumped as she outed me. So much for finding one final escape. But Alek brushed past her. "I don't care if he's God himself."

"That's the spirit, Alek." I flexed my fingers. "Care to dance?"

A wicked grin split his face. "I was hoping you'd ask."

"Then, let's dance." I wagged a finger, beckoning him closer.

Before either of us made a move, Layla's voice boomed through the den. "Outside!"

Both of us straightened and started toward the door. I nodded to her as I passed.

"What are you doing?" she demanded, grabbing my sleeve. "You know what will happen."

Her money was on Alek. That boded well. I hadn't picked the fight accidentally. Alek looked like he could handle me.

"I do," I said, feeling oddly cheerful at the prospect. "If the Council comes sniffing around, tell them I started it. My brother will vouch for it. Alek will be fine."

"If you think they'll just overlook a turned vampire killing a pureblood—"

"Tell you what," I cut her off. "I'll make sure it looks like self-defense."

I didn't wait around for her to argue with me. I had an appointment.

A few more vampires followed me as I climbed the stairs leading from the cellar. I could smell the blood rage blossoming among them. That would definitely speed things along.

So would this.

As soon as I reached the top landing, I threw myself at Alek. I caught him around the middle, and we crashed through the back exit of the strip club and stumbled into the crowd. People scattered from their seats, shrieking, as I tossed Alek onto the stage. I jumped up next to him and stepped to the side as a dancer fled, her hands pressed over her breasts as she ran.

"Filthy pureblood, you think you're above all the rules," he spat at me, gesturing to the club. "She said *outside*."

"I interpreted 'outside' more loosely." I shrugged. "Now, stop stalling and let me kick your ass."

"I don't care who the fuck you are." He crouched, squaring his shoulders as he prepared to pounce. "I'm putting your head on my wall tonight."

"We'll see, *switch*." I took a fighting stance as if bracing for impact. The slur tripped his final button, and he lunged for me. At the last moment, I relaxed, closed my eyes, and waited to die.

But death was a bastard.

A loud crash shook the space, but nothing happened. No impact. No fingers tearing into my neck or chest. I propped open one eye and found Alek on the floor, looking dazed. At the other end of the stage, a beautiful blonde adjusted her leather gloves before delivering a reproachful frown to me. She looked like she'd just left a five-star restaurant in her red cashmere coat and matching heels.

"You have terrible timing," I said.

"That depends on who you ask," Jacqueline said sweetly. She

turned a fraction of an inch as a vampire careened toward her. She caught him around the neck and lifted him into the air. "Naughty boy. Where are your manners?"

She launched him at the others who'd followed hoping for a fight. Vampires scattered, overturning chairs and tables in their hurry to escape. Two pureblood vampires shifted the odds considerably in our favor.

"What are you doing here?" I asked. I'd been carefully avoiding my best friend for weeks. The fact that she hadn't tracked me down before now told me she hadn't forgiven me for breaking up with Thea.

"Saving your ass." She clenched her jaw as she looked me over. Reaching into her coat, she pulled out a blood bag and another pair of gloves and tossed them to me.

I caught both with a sigh. I shoved the gloves in my pocket and tore open the blood bag. After sucking it down in a few gulps, I threw the empty plastic on the ground.

"Better?" she asked.

I wasn't sure how to answer that. I was still alive, which wasn't what I'd hoped for, but my headache was gone. So there was that.

"How did you find me?" I stalked past her, jumped off the stage, and headed for the door.

Jacqueline followed, leaping gracefully to the ground. As we reached the entrance, a group of young men stumbled inside. Their eyes widened as they looked around at the havoc we'd caused.

"Club's closed," Jacqueline purred. They stared at her like they'd never seen a woman before in their lives.

Owing to what was undoubtedly a high blood alcohol content, one leaned closer to her. "Where are you headed? Can we come?"

"Oh, you sweet, simple boys, you can't handle me." She directed her gaze at them. "Go home, sleep the night through, and help your mothers tomorrow."

They blinked with confusion but slowly turned and headed back to the streets of Paris. As we stepped out of the club, we watched them part ways, each talking about their respective mothers.

"They never stood a chance," I said drily.

Jacqueline rounded on me so quickly I didn't react until her palm collided with my cheek. I fell back, rubbing the sting of her slap.

"Neither did you," she accused. "What were you thinking? If Sebastian hadn't called…"

"When did you two become best friends?" I continued to massage my cheek. Despite her recent display, I'd forgotten how damn strong she was.

"We have a common purpose: keeping your stubborn ass alive." She grabbed my jacket and shoved me forward. "I'm taking you home."

There was no point arguing with her, even though home was the last place I wanted to be. What was the point in telling her what she already knew?

That everywhere I looked, I saw Thea.

That I swore I could smell her still.

That I'd nearly ripped the place apart trying to erase her from it.

Jacqueline wasn't blind, but that didn't mean she'd been terribly understanding for the last month. She'd made her opinion on my decision clear when she collected Thea and helped her pack. Nothing had swayed her stance since.

We walked in silence as the sun began to rise. Now that I'd had a little blood, I felt better physically—except for the gaping hole where my heart should be. No matter what I did, nothing filled that. It was a festering wound no one else could see. Every breath, every step, every moment—I felt it.

Her absence.

Hughes met us at the door to the house, already dressed for the day. His lips pursed as he took in my appearance, but he didn't say anything.

"Morning," I greeted him stiffly. I shrugged off my wool coat, which was ripped in several places, and passed it to him.

"Should I…" He looked over the coat and seemed to decide it was beyond repair. "I'll have a new one delivered."

I started toward the stairs, but he called out, "Your room is as you left it, *per your request*."

Fan-fucking-tastic. I couldn't wait to hear what Jacqueline said about this. I stripped off my shirt as I climbed the remaining stairs with her at my heels.

She said nothing as we walked into the bedroom—or what was left of it. Chairs were shredded, paintings flung on the floor, the bed wrecked. In a fit, I'd tried to vanquish Thea from the space, but she wasn't in the objects. She was in the walls, the floors, the very air. I couldn't escape her. No matter where I went. I'd learned that after wasting time in Pigalle.

But here, I not only couldn't escape her. I couldn't ignore her.

I sank into the remnants of a chair, picking up a scarf still holding her scent. Balling it into my fist, I waited for my best friend to break her silence.

Jacqueline opened her mouth, took one steadying breath, and turned a furious glare on me. "I worked really hard on this."

I hadn't thought of all her efforts. "Sorry."

"What are you doing?" she asked, attempting to take a seat near me. She gave up and hovered over me. "You ended things with her."

"I know," I said bitterly.

"If you still have feelings for Thea—"

"She's my mate!" I roared.

"I suppose that's a confirmation you're not moving on." Her nostrils flared as she crossed her arms. "So, what's the problem? Your family? The virginity thing?"

"To start."

"Sometimes, I wish you had an imagination." She shook her head. "There's a way around that. You just have to look."

"I can't," I said through gritted teeth.

She clicked her tongue. "You mean that you *won't*."

"I mean I *can't*," I said loudly. "Every last bit of me wants to go to her. I'm not sure how much longer I can resist."

"So, what's your plan? Get yourself killed so you won't be tempted?" she demanded.

I lifted my face to hers, my answer written across it.

Jacqueline stumbled a few steps, her anger giving way to

devastation. "How? Why?" She shook her head to clear her thoughts. "How could you just give up? How would Thea feel if she found out you'd rather die than be with her?"

"Do you think I have a choice?" I whispered. For some reason, that idea seemed worse.

"What happened?"

"The Council paid me a visit. They gave me one chance to save her life. It only cost me her."

Her eyes widened, but she shook her head. "Do you really think they'd kill her?"

"The term 'execution' was bandied about."

Jacqueline loosed a weighty sigh. Her eyebrows nudged together as she studied me. "So you killed her instead?"

"I saved her," I roared.

"And at what price to her? What's the point of living if you're empty inside?"

I hung my head. "I didn't have a choice."

"You did. You still do."

"What are you talking about?" I muttered.

"*Julian.*" She heaved my name at me. "Get your ass to California."

CHAPTER THREE

Camila

Monday, I received the call I'd been waiting for since the night of the opera. A month had passed since our attack on the privileged vampire elite, and in that month, Julian had done... nothing.

It was pathetic.

But now, if my informant was to be trusted, my darling twin was finally going after his human. Our family's private jet had filed a flight plan from Paris to San Francisco.

He'd held out longer than expected, given the rumors I'd heard. It seemed he was practically tethered to the pathetic creature. So I'd been shocked when he'd pined for her instead of claiming what he so clearly wanted. She was a human. She was his for the taking, and he'd just let her go. Maybe he was getting soft. It looked like my whole family was—and that was the problem.

It was time for a wake-up call.

I parked across the street from his Paris home and waited until a car arrived to take him to the airport. Trust Jacqueline to convince him to take action. Talking my brother into things was really all she was good for.

Julian left with nothing more than a small leather carry-on. He looked worse than he had that bloody night at the Paris Opera. Then, he'd been lethal, taking out several of my comrades. But he'd also been feral, driven by bloodlust—a mistake that had nearly cost him his life and forced me to intercede.

I might hate my family, but no one else was allowed to kill them.

But killing him would keep me from finding her, and she was the prize I was after. He had made no contact with his human since she'd left, which had kept me from tracking her down myself. Without knowing her full name, the creature had simply vanished. Even the vampires who'd met her seemed to barely recall it. It was odd for a human to leave so few traces behind. No one seemed to know much about her, but the rumors sparked my interest. I wanted to meet her before I decided her fate.

My phone rang as I watched my brother get into the car on his way to his private jet. I answered with a terse, "Yes?"

"Bad timing?" a slick voice asked.

I grimaced. "What do you want, Boucher?"

I didn't trust the beady-eyed vampire, but he'd been more than willing to sell us information. All he'd wanted was to return to Paris from his exile. Now that clemency had been granted, he was in our debt. That didn't mean he was loyal. It just meant he came with a low price tag.

"I had contact from one of our associates in California," he said slowly. "But if now is a bad time…"

"You won't make yourself more useful to me by dangling carrots over my head," I snapped. "Tell me what they found."

"A human leaving a fortune teller," Boucher told me. "She matches the description of Thea. The old witch who runs the parlor wasn't eager to share what she knew, and she clearly has a ward against compulsion."

"Pay her," I ordered.

"No need to waste the money. My associate is very persuasive. She didn't know much, but she confirmed the woman was linked to a vampire."

"Have someone follow the trail and keep an eye on her." Maybe

I could beat my brother to his girlfriend. Wouldn't that be a reunion? But there was something I needed to do first. "I need to go."

Boucher stopped me. "There's one more thing."

"Yes?" I asked impatiently.

"The witch said she reeked of olibane."

"Olibane?" I paused as this information hit me. Trust Boucher to save the important details for last. I couldn't stand the man. He didn't have ideals. He just hated playing by anyone's rules. He was as likely to aid us as he was the purebloods if it suited his whims. But he always had one more card to play.

"If that's true, it means—" he began.

"I *know* what it means," I hissed. Julian's car drove off, and I saw my opportunity. I'd waited too long for this moment to be distracted now. I had work to do. "Good work, Boucher."

I hung up before he could make any more slimy comments. I grabbed a canister from the passenger seat of the Mercedes, got out, and started across the street. A driver screeched to a halt, shouting out his window until he saw me. Pathetic human males were so easily distracted. Another time, I might have paused for a bite, but there was something much more delicious waiting for me inside Julian's house.

I rang the bell and waited, tightening the belt on my black trench coat. The door opened, and Hughes appeared, looking put out to receive a visitor with his master gone.

"May I help you?" he asked.

It wasn't a surprise he didn't recognize me. It had been a couple of decades, and while neither of us had aged, I wasn't the female he remembered. I lifted my Chanel sunglasses so he could get a better look at me.

His stalwart composure faltered, and he inhaled sharply.

"Mistress Rousseaux," he greeted me with shock. Yanking the door open, he stepped to the side and allowed me into the house. "I'm afraid your brother isn't here, but he only just left. I can call him back."

"That's not necessary." I looked around the entry, impressed with what I saw. Then again, like me, Julian had grown up with money and privilege. He knew how to use both.

"But he'll want to know. He's under the impression that..." Hughes trailed away.

"Yes?" I prompted. I wanted to hear him say it.

"That you died. We all thought..."

"Is that the pretty story they spun about me?" I asked with a laugh. "I guess I'm not surprised."

"I don't understand, but please let me call—"

His words died along with him.

I dropped his head to the ground as his body crumpled to the marble floor.

"Sorry, Hughes. Nothing personal," I said to his body as I closed the front door behind me. Killing him was easier than working around him, and I had things to do.

I didn't bother to tiptoe. Sneaking would imply that I cared about getting caught.

I didn't.

The long fingers of my right hand trailed along the oak banister as I mounted the staircase, which wrapped around the foyer and led to the second floor.

An arsonist knows where to start a fire. It's a matter of instinct, born to their blood, like a sickness. My husband was an arsonist— when he was alive.

An attic or basement concealed the flame longest. Although, an attic, if caught quickly, could be put out with only minor damage to the rest of the house. A basement was a bit like leaving a burner lit on a stove. Left without supervision, the inferno would char the whole building to a smoldering ruin. But I wasn't interested in concealing my devastation any more than my footfalls. The plan was to send a message. I tightened my hand on the canister I carried. When starting a war, preparation was often rewarded. When lighting a fire, gasoline always helped.

I coated the stairs as I went. Fumes burned my nostrils, and I greedily inhaled the promise of liquid destruction. His bedroom was on the top floor, below which waited another two stories; and below that, the extravagant living spaces bursting with his treasury of collected lifetimes: antiques, books, art. I'd passed a lovely Renoir in the entry. My brother had had such exquisite taste once.

And now he was pining for a fucking human.

Disgust seeped into my blood as I stepped inside his room. It looked like it had been ransacked. A cracked mirror was tipped on its side, shattered glass all around. The bed had been flipped over. I could smell his human everywhere. My eyes darkened. If she were here, I would drain her. I would make him watch—make him face the pathetic modern vampire he'd become.

That was the key to breaking Julian—to breaking my whole family. Once they gave in to their true natures, they would beg to join us.

And once one pureblood family fully fell, the rest would follow.

I moved to a bedside table covered in letters and books. Several had been ripped apart.

"What were you looking for, little brother?" I asked the empty room, but then I spotted it.

A folded letter, yellowed and brittle, lay on a stack of old notebooks. I picked it up and perused the contents. The harried scrawl was hard enough to read, and the stupid thing was a strange mix of French and Latin. I snorted when I saw the name assigned to it—the only sound to flit through the yawning silence of the empty estate. Had he kept it for vanity or sentiment? The fact that it was still sitting near his bed hundreds of years later meant *something*.

I dropped it on the bed, then collected the various pages he'd stripped from the books. I crumpled them and added them to my pyre. Taking out my only match, I struck it on the headboard, and a flame burst from it with a crackle. I allowed myself a moment to admire the way it lapped the air in its desperate fight for life. Then I flicked it onto the pile, the old paper and their ideas a ready tinderbox.

"Happy housewarming, Julian," I said as the fire unfurled across his bed.

From here, the fire would spread, its tendrils reaching in every direction until the whole house was engulfed in its embrace. New paint couldn't make up for old French bones. I took my time as I made my way out of the house, enjoying the growing heat on my back. But I didn't stop to survey my work until I stepped over Hughes's body and paused. I knew how to destroy a vampire: strike the heart and burn the body. Admittedly, I was doing things a bit backward. But now that I knew where Julian's precious human was, I'd carve her out of his life—after I discovered what secrets hid in her blood. Maybe then, he'd finally open his eyes. For now, I left the burning house and everything and everyone in it—a message to my brother and our filthy rich family.

But I did take the Renoir.

CHAPTER FOUR

Thea

The doctors couldn't explain it. One minute my mother was comatose, and the next she was awake. I'd walked in from the disastrous palm reading to find her sitting up like nothing had happened. I didn't know whether to laugh or cry, so I pretty much did both on repeat while they ran dozens of tests.

"I can't believe I wasn't here," I muttered as I cuddled next to her on the bed.

My mom smiled even though she looked like a human pincushion. "You're here now. That's all that matters." She paused and took a deep breath. "I suppose you might need to leave, though."

Her words twisted my heart, and I forced myself to shake my head. "Nope. This is where I belong, and it's where I'm staying."

"So, it didn't work out?" she asked. "This mysterious job you took?"

I'd been avoiding this conversation since she woke up, but I knew I couldn't hold it off for much longer. We'd barely spoken while I was away. She'd been livid at my decision to take a sabbatical so close to graduation. At the time, I'd done everything in my power to keep her from knowing why I was dropping everything and leaving for Paris. We'd always been close, but she was still my mom. What was

I supposed to tell her? That I'd fallen head over heels for a vampire?

"I think I just wanted to do something reckless," I admitted to her, hanging my head. "It was stupid."

"Maybe," she said softly, "but, darling girl, you've never done anything reckless. Perhaps it was time for an adventure."

I peeked up at her. That wasn't the response I'd expected. "Wait. Now you're okay with it?"

"Facing one's mortality puts things in perspective." She pulled me closer to her, hugging me with her free arm. The other was attached to too many wires and tubes to be of much use. "I don't want you to spend your whole life waiting tables and trying to get by. I'm glad you went." She glanced over at me. "Are you?"

A lump formed in my throat. I'd spent the last month beating myself up for my decision to leave. It was easier than accepting the truth.

Julian had hurt me. He'd broken my heart. I'd given up everything to follow him on some insane trip around the world that had ended before it really started. I should hate him. I should feel stupid. Part of me did. But if someone offered me the keys to a time machine right now, I wouldn't change a minute.

Memories tingled on my skin just thinking about him. Sometimes, I almost swore I still felt his hand pressed against mine. I balled my hand into a fist, brushing my fingertips over my bare palm, and recalled the tender ache that had consumed me the moment he took my hand. He'd left me my virginity that night and seized my heart instead.

"I see," Mom said quietly when I remained silent. "So this job was …"

"Complicated." My voice cracked on the word, betraying my pain. "It was very complicated."

"Thea, are you—"

Before she could finish her question, Dr. Reeves poked his head into the room. "How is my favorite miracle today?"

Mom flushed and sat up a bit straighter, shoving the pillow behind her back. Apparently, Olivia wasn't the only one with eyes for the handsome doctor. I didn't see what about him worked them both up. Then again, I wasn't exactly emotionally available.

"Wonderful," Mom gushed, "but when will I get to go home?"

"Already ready to leave me?" Dr. Reeves stepped inside and leaned against the doorframe. He tucked a pen inside his lab coat and smiled.

"Of course not," she said, "but I'd rather get out of these clothes."

"We're just waiting on the results of your CT scan. Once we have those, you are a free woman." Reeves glanced over at me. "No more Sunday flowers, I suppose."

I rolled my eyes. I'd borne witness to the perpetual flirting between him and my roommate for weeks. "I'll give you her number."

"Oh, that's not—" He sounded slightly panicked.

"Trust me. It's okay. I'll ask first."

I pulled out my phone to text Olivia, and my stomach plummeted. I had a missed call from a French number. Before I could excuse myself to listen to the voicemail, a stout woman rapped on the door, clipboard in hand.

"May I speak with the patient?" she asked, already halfway into the room. "I'm from the billing department." She pointed to her name badge, which read *Marge*. Below it, the word *billing* appeared in bold blue letters. I nearly threw up. "I need you to sign a few things, Mrs. Melbourne."

"*Ms.*," my mother corrected her proudly. "I'm not married."

"Oh, my apologies." But Marge was already shifting pieces of paper around as she strode over. "It will only take a moment."

"I'll check in later," Dr. Reeves said, ducking out to give us some privacy.

I wished I could vanish, too. This was the part I always hated. Eventually, the billing department always showed up to review repayment options. I didn't blame Reeves for leaving. I couldn't imagine what it was like for a doctor. He'd worked so hard to save my mom's life, all the while probably knowing the debt would drown us. I'd known it from the moment I got the call. At least the hospital had waited until Mom was awake. No one had bothered me about the bill until now.

"Let me," I said, reaching to take the clipboard. "I can sign anything. I have power of attorney."

"Thea, you don't have to," Mom said gently. "This isn't your burden."

"Like hell, it's not," I muttered. My mom was the only person I could always count on at the end of the day. She was all I had, and vice versa. The last thing I wanted was to stress her out now that I had gotten her back.

I shuffled through the paperwork. We'd already owed the hospital a small fortune. They'd been kind enough to put our prior balance at the top to remind me. The debts from a month in the ICU just added to the total. I watched the numbers build with each itemized procedure and mounting dread to match—and then I reached the last page.

"I don't understand," I said with confusion, staring at the last line. Above the zero, a minus symbol decorated an amount well into the mid-six figures.

"There may be some final adjustments. We were informed earlier this month that the bill would be taken care of privately, but I still submitted all the claims," she explained to me. "Your husband was quite insistent that we didn't need to wait for your mother's insurance company."

"My what?" I stuttered. My mouth went dry, and my heart began to race. I rubbed a hand absently over my chest. "I'm not married."

"Thea, what's going on?" My mother craned her neck, trying to see the paperwork.

"A mistake," I said quietly.

"He was quite clear." The billing representative moved closer and checked my mother's hospital bracelet. "Yes, he paid the bill for Kelly Melbourne. You are Kelly Melbourne, right?"

"Yes." Mom looked between us like she needed confirmation. "But I don't understand. Who paid my bill?"

I was torn between screaming and tears. I couldn't decide if I should be happy, angry, or cautious. Maybe it was a mistake. Perhaps someone had said the wrong name. Perhaps some random billionaire had walked in and started paying hospital bills, driven by guilt over his bank balance.

But I knew it was none of those things.

"I'm sorry. I assumed he was your son-in-law. He seemed very *familiar*," Marge said. I blanched at her choice of words as she studied me more closely. "You aren't married?"

"No," I said firmly.

"It must be your lucky day." I didn't miss the judgmental edge or head-to-toe she gave me as she spoke. Apparently, when a man showed up and started paying off your debts, everyone assumed you were an escort.

But I didn't care what she thought about me. Instead, I thought about the phone call I'd missed. Was that him? Had he called to tell me he would pay off the bills? I wasn't sure what was more surprising. That he had honored our broken arrangement or that he'd remembered at all. Not after he'd been so clear in Paris that I meant nothing to him. I was just an unwanted human. By now, he'd probably found himself a pretty little witch without any pesky virginity issues.

My heart tripped at the thought as though it saw the lie that it was.

Julian had loved me. I was sure of that, but I couldn't let myself believe that's why he had paid off the debts. Not when he hadn't even bothered to call to check in on me since I left him.

"I'll sort this out," I said to Mom. "Don't sign anything."

"It's all finalized," Marge told us. "If I were you…" She trailed off when I shot her a sharp look. "I'll come back later."

No doubt she planned to wait to accost my mother when I wasn't there. Marge was right, of course. It was ridiculous to refuse the payment, but I needed a minute to process this turn of events.

"Thea, do you know who paid these bills?" Mom asked when we were alone.

I couldn't bring myself to look at her. After a minute, I nodded. "I think so."

The silence extended between us. The lack of any reaction

was almost deafening despite her mute shock. But there was no disapproval when she finally asked, "What did it cost you? What did this man take?"

"Only my heart." I closed my eyes, wondering how it was possible to feel so much pain from absence. "He didn't take anything else. He didn't want anything else."

"Somehow, I doubt that," she said carefully. "Oh, darling, I feel like there's more to this story I've missed."

"There is," I mumbled.

Mom reached up and took my hand, squeezing it fiercely. "Do what feels right to you."

"I can't make them give back his money—I won't." I shook my head. "But I can pay him back."

"What?" she gasped. "How? Not—"

"Nothing like that," I said quickly, realizing she'd gotten the wrong idea. Seriously, did everyone think I had a sugar daddy? "He gave me a cello—an expensive one. I can sell it."

It hurt to consider. The cello was all that remained of my relationship with Julian. There hadn't been time to sell it. At least, that's what I'd told myself. But now, as I faced the prospect of losing the last tangible proof of our relationship, I wanted to cry. A cello had brought us together. A cello would sever whatever ties still bound me to him.

It was fitting—almost operatic, in a way.

"Maybe you should talk to him first," she suggested. "Call him. Give him a chance—"

"He's in Paris," I cut her off. I'd made my decision the night I left there. I wasn't running back to Julian Rousseaux. I deserved better than that. He'd made his choice, and I'd made mine. A phone call wasn't going to change any of that. "And there's nothing to explain. It was a temporary bout of insanity for both of us."

"You love him," she said sadly. It wasn't a question. She just knew. Of course she did. She was my mother.

Still, I shrugged. "I did." I stood, feeling a bit lightheaded. "Excuse me. I missed a call earlier."

She nodded and released my hand as I stood. "I'm not going anywhere."

I leaned down and gave her a tight hug. Thank God for that.

Stepping into the hall, I looked at the missed call on my phone. My fingers fumbled as I swiped the notification, and I dropped the phone. It landed with a nerve-racking crack.

"Good job, Thea," I muttered as I bent to pick it up. I could already see a crack in the screen.

Long, elegant fingers brushed mine as I reached for it. A shock of recognition sparked where his bare skin met mine. My knees buckled, but before I suffered the same fate as my phone, Julian caught me and steadied me before backing away.

It felt as though my chest might crack open and spill all the turmoil churning inside me. I couldn't bring myself to look at him. I wasn't sure I could survive it. Instead, I pinned my gaze on the OUT OF ORDER sign hanging from the hallway water fountain. My brain churned until I thought I might need a sign of my own. His touch alone had sent my body into an anxious frenzy. Why wasn't he wearing gloves? I tried not to read too much into it, even as every ounce of my being wanted to fall into his arms and take whatever precious moments I could.

But my brain wasn't on board with this plan. There was too much for me to comprehend at once. Too much pain. Too much hope. Too much love. Too much anger.

I clutched my phone, my thumb slicing open when it caught on the crack. I winced and glanced down to find blood blooming along the cut. I shoved it into my mouth before I accidentally incited a blood-rage incident.

"Are you hurt?" he asked, his voice full of concern as he stepped toward me.

I backed away, shaking my head.

"Let me see, pet," he said gently but firmly.

Without thinking, I held out my injured finger for his inspection. Julian took it, his bare hands cradling mine. It didn't mean anything. I knew that. He'd ended things. He'd broken my heart. He'd rejected me. Maybe he was high-fiving strangers about it—bare-handed. I should be numb or furious.

But maybe it was because I'd never expected to feel the touch of his hands against mine again. Still, I couldn't cling to reason or logic or even the fury boiling under the surface of my confusion. All that mattered was that his hand was touching mine.

So, naturally, I burst into tears.

It was such a stupid, *human* thing to do.

He reached for me, but I sidestepped him.

"Why are you here?" I demanded, unwilling to accept pity from him.

"I needed to pay a bill," he said in a clipped tone. His jaw tightened, drawing attention to his carved lips, reminding me what waited beyond them. I felt a subtle throb in my thigh where he'd bitten me, as if my body was thinking of his fangs, too.

"You didn't have to do that. Our arrangement—"

"I don't give a shit about some stupid arrangement, Thea," he muttered. "I'm not going to let you sit in a hospital and worry about bills."

"I don't know why you care," I shot back.

He flinched, anguish blazing in his blue eyes. "I deserve that."

"Maybe you—"

Before I could ask him to leave, Dr. Reeves appeared. "Is everything okay, Thea?"

"Yes," I said, but Julian stiffened. "A friend dropped by."

Dr. Reeves looked unconvinced. He turned to Julian, oblivious to the fury vibrating off him. "I'm afraid that visiting hours are over for the day. Only family—"

"I am family," Julian cut him off. My stupid, traitorous heart thrilled at his claim.

"I was under the impression Kelly only had one child, a daughter," Dr. Reeves said, glancing at me for confirmation.

"Um." I chewed on my lip. "Julian is—"

"Family," he said again, turning an intense glare on Reeves. "You have to go check on a patient now. One on another floor."

Dr. Reeves nodded, a puzzled look flitting over his face. "Excuse me. I need to see if test results are back for Mrs. Grant."

I groaned as the doctor headed in a daze toward the elevator. "Why did you compel him?"

"We weren't finished talking," Julian said casually, but I noticed the darkness lingering at the edges of his retinas.

"Yes, we were." I lifted my chin, ignoring every instinct to go to him. "I can arrange to sell the Grancino, or you can take it. That should cover most of the bill. The rest—"

"Stop," he growled. A few passing nurses nearly jumped out of their skins. He moved closer and lowered his voice. "I don't want you to repay me. I didn't come for money or to fight with you."

I swallowed, hoping my voice didn't tremble as he backed me against the wall. "What do you want? Why did you come back?"

He angled his head to my ear. It was the only thing I had to give him and the last thing I should ever trust him with.

"You," he murmured. "I came back for my mate."

CHAPTER FIVE

Julian

Mate.

The word hung in the air between us. It wasn't news to either of us. We'd finally faced that reality in Paris, and then I'd colossally fucked things up. Eventually, I would tell her the truth about why I'd pushed her away. I didn't have a choice. I'd acted rashly that night in Paris and told myself I was protecting her. I'd thought I could live without her—that she would be better off without me. But now I understood my mistake. I should have fought for her. I should have told her the truth then. Instead, I'd told myself I'd spared her. But judging by the tired, bluish circles under her eyes, I hadn't spared her anything.

I'd failed her when she'd needed me the most.

There was no knowing what the Council might do when they learned I'd defied their new law. For now, it didn't matter that I might be placing both Thea's and my life in danger. It didn't matter that our relationship was impossible. None of it mattered—as long as she still wanted me.

Her chest rose and fell, matching her shallow, quiet breaths. "I need to get back to my mother."

I wanted to drag her off so we could work this out, but that wouldn't win me any points in the mating department. I jerked my head in understanding. "Of course." I paused. "May I come with you?"

"You're actually asking?" she asked drily, displaying the no-bullshit attitude I'd come to love. "That's novel."

"And that's not an answer, pet." One step closer and I could kiss her. She wouldn't be able to run. She wouldn't even try to resist. I glued my feet to the floor. I was going to do this the right way. Mating bonds lasted for life, and Thea was human. The longer she stayed pissed at me, the less time I had to make her happy. I didn't want to waste a second.

She took a deep breath and released it slowly. "I guess."

But she didn't move toward the door. After a few seconds, she cleared her throat and angled her head. I was blocking her path, and she wasn't going to risk so much as the slightest contact between us by pushing past me. My lips lifted in an obligatory smile as I moved out of her way.

"After you," I said in a strained voice.

She walked a few steps but stopped before she reached the door. "Did you…"

I raised an eyebrow, waiting for her to finish the question.

"Did you tell the billing department you were my…family?" She chose the word carefully.

She already knew. The woman who'd helped me must have told Thea. I studied her, looking for a clue as to how she felt about my claim, but she was doing a damn good job of keeping me in the dark.

"I told them I was your husband," I said smoothly.

Thea's eyes rounded, and her jaw unhinged.

"Is that a problem for you?" I asked as if I didn't notice her reaction.

"We aren't married," she said slowly.

"I'm aware." I picked a piece of lint from my sleeve.

"You can't go around telling people you're my husband."

"Why?" I asked, seizing the chance to move closer to her. "You are my mate."

"Unofficially," she grumbled. Lifting her chin, she stared me down. "But mates and husbands are different."

I frowned.

"Right?" she tacked on, suddenly sounding uncertain.

"A mate is much more serious than a spouse. Lots of vampires are married."

"But not to their mates?" She pressed a hand to her stomach like she was sick. "How could they do that?"

I didn't have to ask her what she meant, because I felt the same way. Just the thought of tying myself to another while Thea existed sounded like hell. It wasn't that way for others. It wouldn't be unusual for a married couple to have lovers in the human or vampire world. My own parents were proof. That was usually how it worked. Mating, it turned out, was completely different. "Mating is *unusual*. It's very rare for vampires to mate."

This time Thea's shock wasn't from surprise. She was furious. I wasn't quite sure why. It was one of the many mysteries about my mate I'd have to solve.

"Let's be clear." She jammed a finger into my chest. "You aren't my husband."

I nodded, then added, "Yet."

So much for being on my best behavior.

"What the…" Thea threw her hands in the air.

I bit back a grin at how adorably flustered she looked.

"Don't use that boyfriend smirk on me," she ordered.

"Would you prefer I used a husband smirk?" I asked, feigning innocence.

But she wasn't amused. Not even a little bit. "You cannot just walk back into my life and act sweet and declare yourself my husband. That is not how this works."

"I know," I said solemnly. "There's usually a ring and a wedding. Don't worry, pet; we'll get there."

Thea released a strangled cry of frustration, stomped one foot, then turned toward the hospital room. I was only a step behind her when she swiveled with narrowed eyes to face me again. At this rate, her mother would die of old age while we hashed trivial details out in the hall. "No husband or mate talk in front of my mom," she ordered.

"Fine," I agreed. I might have been enjoying watching Thea squirm a bit too much. Mostly I was just enjoying being this close to her again. Right now, I would be thrilled to watch her eat a sandwich. She didn't know it, but at the moment, she could talk me into anything—I was determined to make this work. But I wouldn't make the situation with her mother more stressful, especially since I intended to impress Kelly Melbourne. Stealing her daughter away to Paris hadn't been a great start. Returning her with a broken heart probably hadn't helped. I was all too aware that I had more than one woman's favor to win back.

And if I couldn't—if Thea didn't want me—I'd find a way to let her go. But I wasn't giving up without a fight this time.

Thea stepped inside, holding a hand up to keep me from entering behind her. "Mom, I have someone I want to introduce."

Thanks to my preternatural hearing, I caught her mother's response. She sounded cautious, as if she knew her daughter's absentee boyfriend was on the other side of the door. Maybe I should have waited to pay the bill until after we'd been introduced. It looked like I was trying to buy my way into their good graces. If Kelly was anything like her daughter, she wouldn't relish that idea. I wondered how the two of them would handle the other news I planned to deliver.

Thea stepped inside and waved me in. "Mom, this is my friend Julian Rousseaux."

I moved beside her, slipping my hand into hers. Thea glanced down, her mouth forming an *O* shape before she composed herself. It wasn't the behavior of a friend. I'd probably get an earful about it later, but I wasn't going to hurt Thea by hiding behind half truths again.

"*Friend?*" her mother repeated, zeroing in on our clasped hands.

"Boyfriend," I said firmly.

Thea sighed, clearly torn between relief that I hadn't said husband or mate and annoyance that I'd taken matters into my own hands. "Fine. This is my boyfriend."

Kelly stayed quiet for a minute. Then she leaned back against the pillows, propping herself up in bed, and crossed her arms. "In my day, we just called guys like you 'shitheads.'"

"Mom!" Thea yelped.

I chuckled half-heartedly and tipped my head. I deserved that, and everyone in this room knew it. "In my day as well."

"I doubt that," Kelly muttered mysteriously. Her beauty nearly matched Thea's. She had the same auburn hair that leaned more copper than brown, with a few added streaks of gray. She was petite but not quite as short as my mate. Kelly's green eyes flashed, the lines on her face deepening as she assessed me.

But there *was* something else about her—something I couldn't quite put my finger on—an otherworldly quality Thea shared. It wasn't the same familiarity I'd felt when I first saw Thea playing her cello, but it bore the same markings. It felt oddly similar and entirely different.

I felt a small alarm go off in the back of my mind, but I ignored it as Thea continued. "Julian isn't a shithead."

I snorted when she said it. I was a shithead. I had nine hundred years of proof, culminating in the spectacularly stupid move of nearly losing Thea—just another addition to my dossier of idiocy.

"You aren't," she said firmly, elbowing me. "But you are important to me."

Fuck, it felt good to hear her say that. It wasn't a solution to our problems. It wasn't a commitment to forgive me, but it was a start. I couldn't ask for more than that. Not yet.

"It seems that you aren't in Paris after all," Kelly said to me.

"No."

"Mom," Thea said softly. "Maybe we can save the interrogation for later?"

"It's fine," I told her. "Your mother can ask me anything she wants."

Kelly's gaze lit up, and she seemed more than okay to take me up on the offer, even as Thea shifted nervously beside me. "You paid the hospital bills?"

"I did."

"Out of guilt?" she asked. "For hurting my daughter?"

I blinked, processing the turn we'd taken. Apparently, Thea came by her bluntness naturally. Kelly was every bit the spitfire my mate was. That made me like her.

I got the impression the feeling wasn't mutual. Yet.

"No. I know better than to think I can buy Thea's forgiveness," I said and meant it. "Neither of you should carry this burden when it's easy for me to take care of it."

"Thea wants to pay you back. She mentioned selling some cello you gave her. Do you always shower young women with life-changing expensive gifts to convince them to run away from their lives?"

"No." I didn't dare say more. Despite my intentions, I was on the verge of saying something I might regret. Thea's mother was determined to see the worst in me. I couldn't blame her for that.

"What do you do, then, Mr. Rousseaux?" she murmured, more a thought than a question. Before I could answer, she continued. "How old are you?"

"Older than Thea," I said simply. Aging slowed when a vampire reached their prime. To her, I must look twenty-eight or thirty. It wouldn't be a worrying age difference by modern standards, but Kelly was clearly concerned. There was something else gnawing at her that she was keeping at bay. I could compel her and find out what she really thought. I could force her to like me. If only it could be that easy.

My phone rang in my pocket.

"Should you answer that?" Kelly asked.

She wanted me out of the room so she could demand answers from Thea. The call cut off, and I shrugged. "I'm sure it can wait."

The fucking thing started ringing again.

"It seems it can't," she said like she'd won the lottery.

"Excuse me." I squeezed Thea's hand before releasing it. "I'll only be a minute."

Striding out of the room, I whipped out the phone and nearly crushed the fragile thing as I accepted. "What?"

"Things going well in San Francisco?" Sebastian asked.

I didn't bother to ask how he knew where I'd gone. If my brother knew I'd left to find Thea, it wouldn't be long before the rest of my family found out. The threat of what would happen to me might encourage their silence, but eventually, the news would reach the Council. I would have to come up with a plan to win over Kelly and win back Thea—and fast. "Did you call to chat, or is there a reason you're bothering me?"

I checked my Rolex, which was still set to Paris time, and saw it was just after midnight there. Maybe I'd missed one of the sodding galas and someone had noticed.

"Do you want the bad news or bad news, brother?"

"Spit it out," I growled.

"Hughes is dead."

"What?" I blinked. Of all the things I'd expected him to tell me, that wasn't on the list. "How?"

"Murdered." Sebastian sounded serious now.

"Who did it?" Had the Vampire Council paid a visit in my absence and meted out a punishment for my departure? It was hard to imagine anyone would want to kill the old butler. He wasn't an obvious target.

"Probably the same person who burned your house down," he told me. "Firefighters found his body. There's not much left of the building, but they put it out before it spread."

I swore under my breath. There was a time when I would have raged over the loss of my books and art and personal papers, but that was before I knew what true loss was—before I'd lost Thea.

Still, Hughes's death rattled me. That definitely wasn't the work of the Council.

"We're looking into it. I'm doing my best to keep it quiet."

"The made vampires I pissed off at the absinthe bar?" I guessed. The assholes were lucky I wasn't there. They wouldn't have gotten as far as lighting a match.

"Maybe, but there's a certain flair here. If I had to guess, it was someone who has a real reason to hate you."

That was a long list.

"When will you be back in Paris?" he asked.

My eyes sought the hospital room door. "I don't know."

"Well, hurry up. When this leaks—and it will—they'll know you're gone."

"Call Jacqueline," I gritted out. "See what she thinks."

"Already did." There was a pause. "Watch your back, brother."

I ended the call, wondering how much attention this would draw. I'd known I wouldn't have long to fix things with Thea. Now I had even less time. The house didn't matter. I had others. But someone had killed one of my men. Someone had invaded my home. Sebastian was right. This wasn't the work of some angry stranger. This was personal. That knowledge rested heavily on my shoulders as I turned back to the hospital room. I stopped when I heard the argument going on inside.

I did my best to block it out—to give them privacy—but blocking Thea was almost impossible while in the throes of the mating bond.

"You don't understand—"

"Mom, it's complicated." Thea sounded tired. I suspected she'd been spending all her time by her mother's side. "But I need to hear him out."

"No!" Kelly shrieked. "You have to listen to me. You have no idea who he is."

The alarm in my head went off again, and I reached for the knob instinctively.

"I know it's happening fast, but you have to trust me. I love him," Thea added softly.

My relief and joy at her words was short-lived. I opened the door to say them back as Kelly grabbed Thea's arm and whispered in a pleading voice, "You can't love him. You have to run. Thea…he's a vampire."

CHAPTER SIX

Thea

I'd heard her wrong. My mom's nails dug deeper into my arm as Julian reentered the room quietly. One glance at his face, and I knew he'd heard what she'd said. I forced a laugh, hoping its uneasy tone sounded like disbelief.

"Are you feeling okay?" I managed another a laugh as I gently pried her fingers from my wrist. My mother didn't know about vampires. She *couldn't* know.

She collapsed against the raised head of her hospital bed and closed her eyes. "You knew."

"Mom, how do you…" I started, but I couldn't bear to ask the question. How could she possibly know about his world?

She finally reopened her eyes and broke the silence between us. "Are you a vampire?"

For one terrible second, I thought she was asking me if I'd been turned. Then, I realized she was scanning him.

Julian paused, a muscle beating in his jaw. "Yes, I am a vampire."

Maybe I was dreaming. Maybe I'd fallen asleep next to my mom's bed and dreamed everything that had happened since I'd visited the palm reader with Olivia. Julian wasn't here. He hadn't come back. My mom was still in a coma. She didn't know about vampires. She hadn't just asked him that question, and he hadn't confirmed it. I'd expected we'd have to lie to her to keep her safe, and it would drive us apart like secrets always did…but she knew *some* and would now want to know *everything*.

The truth wouldn't set Kelly free.

It was still a surreal nightmare. I pinched the inside of my wrist and winced.

"Pet," Julian said in a soft tone, "don't do that."

"Is that what she is to you?" my mother demanded. "A pet?"

His lips quirked, biting back whatever angry response waited on his tongue.

"She is not my pet." His whole body was taut from his effort to remain calm. A muscle in his neck stretched like a rubber band about to snap. His shoulders remained set in a rigid line. I sensed the blood rage boiling in his veins. Any more of this, and he would explode.

"What is she, then? A game?" Mom continued, sitting all the way up in her bed. She winced as she brought her legs over the side.

"Mom, stop," I said, rushing to keep her from getting up.

But she ignored me. "What will you do when you're through with her? Compel her? Kill her?"

I froze, realizing she didn't just know vampires were real—she knew a lot about them. How had she kept this from me all of these years?

Why had she?

"I will never hurt your daughter," he said stiffly.

"You already have," she murmured, the words rich with accusation. "It's not as if you can help it. Your kind never can."

"You don't have a very high opinion of vampires." Only his mouth moved. The rest of him stayed in place like a statue. He was a monument to self-control.

But for how long?

I tried to coax her back into the bed as my brain tripped over what was happening. Could things get any worse?

She turned on me, brushing off my attempt to calm her. "Has he fed on you?"

It could get worse—*so* much worse.

"No." I swallowed, but she caught the slight hesitation.

"You've always been a terrible liar." She shook her head, tears leaking from the corners of her eyes. "Oh, my darling, you have no idea what you've done."

"I love him." I kept returning to that. Not that it had swayed her before. Maybe my feelings weren't the key to helping her understand. "And he loves me."

She collapsed against the bed with disgust, turning her body away from mine. "Vampires don't love."

"You're wrong," Julian said. Murder ran through his quiet words. I whipped toward him, shaking my head. I didn't want to hear him say this. I didn't want to feel any more confused than I already did, but his words continued. "I love Thea more than you can imagine."

"You barely know her." She didn't bother to look at him. Instead, she stared at the monitors beeping steadily next to her. Her shoulders slumped in her thin gown. "Release her from whatever compulsion you've placed her under."

"Mom, I'm not compelled." Now I was starting to get annoyed. "I'm not a child. I know what I'm doing."

"You couldn't possibly," she scoffed.

A dam burst inside me. All the feelings I'd pushed away while I'd sat beside her bed and begged for her to wake up came flooding through. "Believe me, I do! I've been to a freaking blood orgy. I have watched vampires rip the heads off other vampires." I kept the fact Julian had been the one ripping heads off to myself. "I made it through an ancient ritual that involved snakes crawling up my body, *and* I've survived *his mother*."

"You're in his thrall." She acted as if she hadn't heard me at all. "You would never let this *thing* feed on you if you weren't."

Rage bubbled in my core, but before I erupted, Julian broke in. "She is not in thrall. I cannot compel Thea."

"What?" we both said, our heads swiveling toward him.

He turned to me, apology welling in his eyes, but then he spoke to her. "Thea is immune to my compulsion."

"Vampires must be getting weaker."

I was shocked at her smugness. It was just another surprise in a night full of them. It was like a stranger had taken her place.

"No." He said nothing else.

"You expect me to believe that my daughter, who has spent her entire life working to have a chair with the symphony, just threw it all away?" Barbs covered her laughter. "Maybe she doesn't know what you can do, but I do. Tell her the truth. Tell her that you forced her to leave."

It was strange. At that moment, I'd never been more confident that Julian was my mate. He hadn't compelled me. I knew that. Like I knew the sun would rise tomorrow and the world would keep spinning. He had never forced me to do anything I didn't want to do. Even after he'd broken my heart, I'd been the one to leave, and he hadn't tried to change my mind. But leaving hadn't altered that fundamental truth. I didn't know what to expect tomorrow or next week or even a minute from now. But I knew that as long as I breathed, he would be mine, and I would be his.

I spoke before I could think twice about it. "Julian is my mate."

"No!" Her mouth widened with a horrified gasp. She shook her head. "Tell me you didn't bind yourself to this creature."

Julian opened his mouth. No doubt he planned to set the record straight. If my mother knew so much about vampires, she'd probably learned a thing or two about mating.

"I did," I said before he could say anything. "That's why he told billing he was family—because he is."

"A few hours ago, you were crying over him," she pointed out.

"Yes," I admitted, flushing that she'd revealed this to Julian. "And I'm still hurt. I'm still angry. But that doesn't change the fact that he's my mate. Nothing ever will."

"You can't know—"

"I know," I stopped her. I didn't dare look at him as I confessed this, but I felt his anxious energy swelling in the room. Was he upset I'd admitted the truth to her? Was he having second thoughts?

Her face crashed, taking my heart along with it. A ragged sob escaped her. "You have no idea what you've done."

But I had questions, too, and now that I was past my initial shock, I wanted answers. "How do you know about vampires? How did you know he was one?"

"I know a monster when I see one."

I balked at the hatred in her voice. This wasn't my mother. Kelly Melbourne planted gardens every spring, even though she inevitably killed all the plants within weeks. She'd volunteered at the children's library to keep her mind off her chemo treatments. My mother had always found a way to pay for my music lessons even when we couldn't afford them. This woman was a stranger.

"Talk to me," I pleaded with her. "Tell me how you know about vampires. Tell me anything. I don't want to keep my life from you."

"You didn't tell me he was a vampire."

"I didn't want you to think I was crazy." I lunged at my opportunity to help her see where I was coming from. "If you would just give him a chance—"

"I will never trust a vampire." She pinned her sights on me. "I can't believe you do. You can't be with him."

Fire burned inside me. "You can't stop me. I'm an adult."

"Then get out."

"What?" I choked.

"I will never sanction this relationship, so it's either him or me."

"You can't make me choose." I stared at her. She was calling my bluff. She had to be, but she didn't even blink. "I only want to know why you've kept this from me. Maybe we should talk later, after you've calmed down."

That was the wrong thing to say. She straightened, blistering fury burning in her eyes.

"I will do whatever it takes to keep you safe from their kind. I always have," she added, the words cutting. What was she talking about? "If you want answers, you will end this *now*."

The world spun around me, and I took a single faltering step before Julian was at my side. He wrapped an arm around my waist and steadied me.

"It's okay," he murmured. He didn't try to plead his case. He didn't ask me to choose him. "I'll leave."

"No." I held on to him.

How had it come to this? My mother was right. A few hours ago, I'd been crying over my broken heart—a heart that hadn't yet mended from the hurt he'd caused. My mother'd comforted me. She'd held me. And now she was asking me to choose a fragmented life. Either way, I would lose. There was no way to win.

I turned to face her, too tired to offer anything other than a soft, "Please."

"Him or me," she repeated.

I closed my eyes. The thorns of her ultimatum shredded me. She had given me everything. We'd survived so much together. I couldn't imagine my life without her. She had made me who I was today. She was my childhood, my dreams, my whole life.

Until him.

"I love you," I whispered, unable to say it more loudly. I placed a hand over Julian's, an unspoken request to leave before I broke down entirely.

"Thea!" Her voice pitched in panic. "Don't go with him. You can't trust him."

"And I can trust you?" I challenged her. She'd lied to me, and I didn't know how deep that lie went. The realization softened her expression.

It only lasted a moment before it hardened again. "I will tell you everything, I swear, but end this now before it's too late."

"There is no ending this. I already tried." I felt like I was falling. I clung to Julian, afraid of what would happen if I let him go while my world was spinning in opposite directions. "You want me to choose? I choose him. I'll always choose him, even when he's been a shithead."

He snorted quietly as if agreeing again.

"You will change your mind. You'll see what he truly is." Her hands fisted in her sheets.

"I won't," I said firmly. "But when you need me, I will always be here."

I waited for a second, half hoping she would say the same. But she turned away.

"Come on." Julian took the lead. He gathered my coat from a hook at the door and helped me into it in the hall. Then he steered us in the direction of the elevators. I was dimly aware of other people. When the elevator doors opened, Julian nudged me inside and held out a hand to a doctor. "Catch the next one."

I didn't know if Julian had compelled the doctor or scared him. I didn't care—it worked.

Julian hit a button on the panel before wrapping his arms around me. I melted into him and began to sob. He stayed silent, but he stroked my back with his palm as he let me cry. When we reached the parking garage level, he took my hand. Heat prickled where our skin met as if to remind me I'd chosen him for a reason.

We reached his BMW, and he opened my door. He slid into the driver's seat before I was done buckling my seatbelt.

"Home?" he asked, reaching for my hand. I stared blankly at him, so he clarified. "Your apartment?"

The last thing I wanted was to explain any of this to my roommates.

"Where were you going?" I asked, my voice cracking on the raw ache throbbing in my throat.

"I didn't think further than finding you," he admitted.

"I don't care." And I didn't. He could drive us off the Golden Gate Bridge and I wouldn't say anything. "Take me with you."

He must have come up with a plan, because he pulled onto the street with a speed that suggested purpose. I didn't ask where he was heading. I didn't care. The only thing that mattered was the hand holding mine. He was my anchor. He was all I had now.

When he finally slowed, I stared out my window at a fortress of a building. For a moment, I thought he was taking me there, but then he pulled into a nearby private garage. I didn't bother trying to race to beat him out of the car. After unbuckling myself, I found my door open and his hand extended. He paused to close the garage door, and I looked around, wondering which building was his. He tugged me toward the fortress. I stayed rooted to the spot.

"Where are we going?" I asked. Like most natives of San Francisco, I'd seen The Armory before. I just didn't know why we were here.

"To my place," he said like we weren't walking up to something that looked more like a fortified castle than a home. It had never occurred to me that someone might call The Armory home. "I bought it when the National Guard put it up for sale. Don't worry. I rent most of it out."

"Good. I'd hate to have to scrub all these toilets," I muttered. At least taking it all in was a distraction. He bypassed the large entrance and headed for a small side door. He pressed his thumb against a panel, and the steel door buzzed open.

"Tomorrow, we'll add your fingerprint so you can come and go."

I swallowed, trying to process not only that tomorrow would come, but that he would be in it.

"Are you tired?" He led me into a narrow entry banded by a slatted staircase. His hands went to my shoulders, drawing off my coat. I shook my head. "Hungry?"

I twisted around and grabbed hold of the lapels of his jacket. Perching on tiptoes, I yanked him down. Julian growled softly as our mouths clashed. A thrill barreled through me at the primal sound. In a split second, he'd lifted me off my feet entirely and started up the stairs, his tongue sweeping hungrily over mine as he climbed them.

Tomorrow, we would fight or talk or whatever needed to happen. Tomorrow, we would untangle ourselves from this mess. Tonight, we'd erase our pain with fingers and lips and skin.

"Want a tour?" he murmured, breaking our kiss when we reached the second floor.

I bit his lip and dragged his mouth back to mine. A snarl erupted from him, and with dizzying speed, I found my back pressed against a cool glass window. I flattened a palm against it, steadying myself as Julian's head dipped to my neck. A fang dragged across my throat. Goosebumps rippled over my skin as my breath caught.

"Go ahead," I breathed, remembering the night at the opera when I'd climaxed from his fangs alone. "It's yours."

He stilled as if considering my offer. "Don't test me, pet," he warned, "or I might lose control and have you against this window, and it's a busy street below."

"I wouldn't mind," I purred, dropping my hand to stroke the bulge straining through his pants. "I'm your mate. It's all yours."

"Thea." My name was a warning on his lips.

I heard it. I understood the risk. But I didn't care.

"Take me," I demanded.

He straightened, restraint leashing his face. But his eyes—those blue eyes that had once stared murderously at me across a crowded room—were absolutely *feral*.

"I'm yours." The words ghosted from my lips. He started to turn his head, but I brought my palm to his cheek. Lightning flashed through me where our skin met. "My blood. My body. It belongs to my mate. It belongs to you. *Now claim it.*"

CHAPTER SEVEN

Julian

Her hand burned on my cheek—my mate's touch was more potent than any magic I'd ever felt. I couldn't breathe. I didn't dare. Not with that offer on the table.

There were a million reasons why I had to say no tonight. But the number one reason—her current emotional state—would make it harder for her to accept rejection.

"I can't," I said, leaving no room for her to question me. Thea drooped in my arms and began to worm her way out of them. I held her fast against the window. "Hear me out instead of running off."

"Are all vampires so talkative, or did I just get lucky?" she grumbled.

"That's not what this is about, and you know it. It's not the right time."

"It's never going to be the right time," she said miserably. "Put me down."

It was better to respect her wishes. Not only because I respected her but also because it was hard to resist her offer when she was pinned against my body. I twisted and set her on her feet. Instead of continuing arguments, she started to walk toward the stairs as though to leave.

"Where are you going?" I followed behind her.

"To take care of this," she announced. "There's gotta be a bar around here, right?"

I went absolutely still, not trusting myself to move or speak. She wouldn't actually...

I'd pitched the idea in Paris: if Thea took another man to bed, if she gave him her virginity, we could move forward. We could mate properly. I just had to find a way to be cool with the idea that another male had touched her. I wanted to believe I could be. I wanted to believe I was more than the primitive beast prowling inside me.

Thea started down the stairs, and blood roared in my ears. I wanted to stop her. I wanted to beg her, but I stayed put—even though every instinct I possessed wanted to go after her.

She paused three stairs down and turned her head to look at me. "It was your idea," she reminded me. "Have you changed your mind?"

I didn't say anything. I had to let her go. I had to let her choose.

I had to stay right where I was and not throw her over my shoulder and haul her into my bed. I couldn't tether her. I wouldn't do that to her. No matter what it cost me—it would cost her more.

She shrugged her narrow shoulders. "Since you don't seem to mind and you aren't interested in sealing our mating bond, I guess I don't have a choice. I'll see you later."

Her soft footfalls continued down the stairs, but when her hand reached for the front door, I was standing in front of it.

Thea blinked, jumping back. "I'm never going to get used to that."

"You will." I didn't budge.

She glared up at me. "Are you just going to stand there?" She crossed her arms over her chest and waited, foot tapping a beat on the wooden floor. "I don't see the point of stringing this out any longer."

"You can't do this," I said in a strangled voice.

"That's news to me." She arched an eyebrow. "You were the one who suggested it."

"I know." I must've been suffering a temporary bout of insanity, or maybe I'd just never expected her to go along with the ridiculous idea.

"I guess I'll see you later." She pushed toward the door, but I caught her around the waist. Spinning her against it, I leaned in, caging her with my arms.

"Don't do this," I said in a soft voice.

"You're not leaving me a choice," she whispered. The angry attitude faltered. All that remained was a gut-wrenching sadness.

"There are things we need to discuss," I said. I had to buy time. I had to help her see it was a mistake to act emotionally right now and live with regrets forever. "You're upset. You're not thinking clearly."

Fury rippled over her petite frame and grew until I could practically hear the rage bubbling inside her. "I'm acting emotionally?" Her gaze pierced me harder than any stake. "Is that what you're saying?"

That had been the wrong way to handle it. I saw that now. "What I mean," I said quickly, "is that a lot has happened. I don't want you to look back on this and feel like you made a mistake."

"Would you consider it a mistake to mate with me?" she whispered.

I didn't answer.

"That's what I thought," she murmured. "Why do you think it's any different for me?"

"Because I'm still trying to figure out what I did to deserve you," I confessed. "Once we're fully mated, that's it. I'll never be able to let you go find someone...worthy."

Because I did not deserve her. I wasn't certain I ever would. I'd done terrible things in my past. She'd only glimpsed some of the darkness I carried inside me. I'd learned to control it, but it didn't excuse who I'd been once.

"Is that what you're worried about?"

I gritted my teeth and nodded. "I'm not worried about it. I know it. Thea, I've been alive for hundreds of years, and if you knew the things I've done, the lives I've claimed—"

"I don't have hundreds of years to waste. I chose you, and I will keep choosing you. You're all I have. You are my family."

"But if you're tethered—"

"You know what I think?" she exploded. "I think this tethering thing is bullshit. You can't compel me. You told me so yourself. Something's different. Maybe it's the mating, maybe it's me." She lifted her eyes to mine. "Maybe I'm different. Maybe that's why my mom knew you were a vampire."

It was the first time she'd mentioned her mother's revelations about vampires. I seized on it. "Exactly. We need to find out more. Don't you want to know how your mother knows? Aren't you curious?"

"Of course I am." She let out a frustrated huff and turned. I sighed with relief when she started up the stairs. At least she wasn't going to make good on her threat to share her body—even if only for one night—with another male. I would have let her go, but I wasn't sure how I was supposed to stand by, how I was supposed to ignore the pain it would cause her to pretend she didn't mind. She had waited for a reason—even if that reason couldn't be me—and we both knew it. I reached the top before she did, and she shot me an annoyed look.

"Is there any food in this house?" she asked.

I doubted it. "Are you hungry?"

"No, not really," she mumbled, moving into the kitchen anyway. She opened the fridge and found it empty. "I eat when I'm stressed. It's a human thing." She moved to riffle through the cabinets and seized something. She turned with a bag of coffee in her hands. "This is probably stale."

"I'll get fresh," I offered. "I would never keep you from your caffeine."

She walked over to the Italian coffeemaker and began making it anyway. "If all I've got is stale coffee, it's better than no coffee." She didn't speak as she went through the motions of filling the machine, except for a few curses here and there. Finally, she sighed. "Is everything you own smarter than me? It's just a coffeemaker. Why does it need to have half a computer attached to it?"

"Here. Let me."

"Why do you have a coffeemaker anyway? I thought someone always served you."

"Not here. I assume my mother had it delivered," I admitted.

"When I came home from the island, she'd refitted the entire house with gadgets and technology. You should've seen how long it took me to adjust the thermostat."

That earned me a smile. I tucked it away to keep my hope alive. After a few tries, I finally got the fucking thing to work.

"Vampires aren't really coffee drinkers," she said. "Why would she think you needed…" She trailed off, putting two and two together. "She expected you to find a familiar—a mortal. That was the whole point in bringing you home, after all."

"It worked out," I said as lightly as I could, given the circumstances. "Because I have a fancy machine and a mate who loves coffee."

"You have a girlfriend who loves coffee," she corrected me. "I've decided you can't call me 'mate' any longer."

I whipped around to face her. "Fucking you isn't going to change anything between us. You are my mate. You said so yourself."

"No, I'm not," she said defiantly. "I'm just your girlfriend—and I'm really not even sure I'm that. I'm not your mate or your wife or *anything*."

"Then let's get married."

Whatever defiant comment was poised on her lips to hurl at me next fell away as her mouth hung open. "You aren't serious."

"I *am* serious." I stalked toward her, backing her against the kitchen counter. Her hands fumbled as she hit its edge. She looked like she was on the verge of falling over. "Marry me."

CHAPTER EIGHT

Julian

"I'm not sure what to say," she said, blinking rapidly.

"Say yes."

"You sound like you're trying to compel me."

"We both know I can't do that." Thank God I couldn't. If I could compel her, we wouldn't be standing here right now fighting or proposing or whatever the hell was going on. I would've forced her to walk away from Valente that night, and I might never have seen her again.

She studied me, and I hoped she was considering the proposal. "Do you wish you could? Compel me, I mean? Is that why you didn't tell me about this before?"

"I didn't tell you about it because I didn't understand why," my answer strained from me. Of course, that's how she would see it—me biding time until I learned how to "fix" it. "I didn't realize what it meant. Or maybe I was just trying to ignore it."

"Go on."

"Keeping secrets is second nature to me. My very existence is guarded. I'm still learning how to talk to you. I should have told you before tonight. But telling you meant forcing myself to admit that mates can't compel each other—if old wives' tales are to be trusted," I admitted. "I should have seen it before. I think I didn't want to see it."

"Because I'm just some pathetic human?" Ice chilled her voice. But despite her frosty demeanor, her lower lip trembled.

That's what she thought? No, that was what *I* had made her feel. I'd inflicted this damage. Now I had to start making it right, beginning by letting her know just how wrong she was about my feelings for her.

"Because you are fragile and fleeting and everything I've ever asked for. And I am so scared this world will take you from me or break you that I didn't want to accept what I knew from the moment I met you," I confessed.

Thea didn't move. She just stared back at me, her face blank and her eyes somewhere else. For a second, I wondered if she'd even heard me. Finally, her throat slid as if swallowing the truth I'd delivered. "That was a terrible proposal, by the way."

It wasn't the reaction I'd expected. Casual. Flippant. She was hiding behind the criticism to avoid giving me an actual answer.

"It wasn't planned," I admitted. "But if you need proof that this bond between us can't be broken, I'll give it to you. Marry me."

One eye narrowed as if annoyed at receiving a second shitty proposal in one evening. "And then what? A sexless marriage?"

She might be poking holes in my offer, but she was also asking questions. It was a start.

"A compromise." My mind raced in the background of our conversation, putting together an alternative I hoped she would accept. I had nothing to lose by offering her that.

"I'm listening," she said quietly.

"Six months." I pressed closer to her. "In six months, marry me, and then I will make you mine in every way imaginable."

But she shook her head. "That's too long."

"Are you negotiating with me?" I asked carefully. Negotiation was dangerously close to an agreement. I decided to play along. "Five months."

"Six weeks," she countered. "That will give us time to get answers about my mother and deal with this mess."

"Three months to plan a proper wedding," I said, continuing

quickly when she opened her mouth to counter again, "and I'll compromise on one more thing."

Thea waited, holding her breath expectantly. My gaze zeroed in on the lovely blue vein that ran down her neck. A human would barely be able to see it, but it called to me. Each pulse, each beat of her heart—a silent siren song I'd tried to ignore. I reached over and brushed my finger along it, tracing the path down until it disappeared at her breastbone. My finger lingered there. "You offered your blood."

She released her long-held breath and sucked in another one. Finally, she nodded, her eyes as round as the moon hanging behind her in the window. She still didn't speak, so I proceeded with my offer.

"It would be my privilege to feed from my mate," I purred. Venom pooled in my mouth at the thought. My fangs lengthened as my body prepared to take the pleasure I'd denied myself. "Feeding from the same person repeatedly changes body chemistry. No one will doubt what we are to each other when they catch our scents."

"It isn't mating, though," she said carefully.

"It isn't," I agreed. "But I've never shared a feeding bond with a lover."

"You've never bitten someone during sex?" She sounded unconvinced.

"Oh, I have." I laughed darkly, and she hissed with displeasure. "It's a hard instinct to control. But I've never sustained a feeding relationship with another person. It always felt too...*intimate*."

"Why?" she tested me. "You said no before. Why change your mind now?"

But that wasn't the question she really wanted to ask. "You think I'm trying to distract you from the mating issue."

She lifted a brow. "Are you?"

I leaned in, forcing her to look me point-blank in the eyes. I refused to let her see anything but the naked truth in what I was about to say next. "In three months, when you are my wife *and* my mate, I will fuck you and feed from you every fucking hour. I will enjoy my mate in every way possible. But for now, I don't think I can wait another minute to taste you."

She planted her palm against my chest, holding me back, and delivered one more ultimatum. "If I say yes, then I want mine to be the only blood you consume."

"Pet," I started to argue.

"Take it or leave it," she stopped me.

I wrapped my hand gently around her throat and angled my face over hers. Brushing my lips over her mouth with a dangerous kiss, I continued down before planting a kiss on that tempting vein. She inhaled sharply, and the aroma of melon drenched in honey filled the air. First, I would enjoy the sweetness of her blood. That would be my second course.

"I'll take it," I said softly, accepting her condition.

She stretched her neck in invitation, but I chuckled.

"I appreciate your enthusiasm," I said, my voice as shattered as my vision was becoming. "But it's considered bad manners to feed from the neck if it's someone you respect."

Her head straightened to reveal a glare. "Any more rules I should be made aware of instead of embarrassing myself? I mean, where will you feed from?"

I refrained from reminding her that she already knew the answer.

"Some vampires feed from the wrist." I lifted her hand to my mouth and pressed a kiss against the veins pulsing there. "But I am not fond of that, either. I don't want others to see my marks on you. Those are for only me to enjoy."

Given how our bodies pressed together, I was already hard, but my balls ached as I remembered the two small puncture wounds I'd left in her delicate flesh. She might regret her own condition when she realized how often I'd want a taste of her.

She shivered at the shadows and smoke hiding in my words. But despite my desire to spread her legs and sink my teeth into the forbidden veins there, I offered an alternative. "There are several more discreet places that I can feed from if you disliked last time, or, if you prefer, there is always bloodletting."

"Bloodletting?" she squeaked. "Like they used to do…?"

I stifled a laugh at her reaction and shrugged. "The downside of having healing powers is that humans sometimes mix up the 'how' with the 'what.' Bloodletting was often practiced by vampires in exchange for healing. Our food source lived, we fed, and easily compelled humans believed what we told them to believe. When human doctors took up the practice, changes had to be made so they didn't kill their patients. It's one of the reasons that it's illegal these days to heal a mortal's wounds in exchange for a drink of their blood. After the Council enacted the new law, doctors hoped just letting out some blood might do the same trick vampires could," I explained. Once again, history had it entirely backward. "Bloodletting by vampire standards is quite painless. A small, precise incision and a cup, or a needle, tube, and blood bag. Some humans prefer to avoid the fangs."

"I want the fangs." The ownership in her voice wrapped around me, squeezing my heart as it sent a primal message barreling to my cock.

"In that case," I said, gritting my teeth to restrain myself from taking her immediately, "I can do things to make the initial pain more bearable."

"Like at the opera?" she breathed.

The world was black as night when I nodded. My vampire instincts wanted to seize control with our new agreement on the table. "Yes, like that. I think you'll find it enjoyable."

"Okay." Thea reached for the button of her jeans. Clearly, she was coming to the end of her own patience, too.

I caught her wrist. "There's no need to rush. Every moment that you make me wait reminds me of what's to come."

"I'm done waiting," she said impatiently, stamping her foot a little.

"A defiant, beautiful woman—how could I resist?" I smirked and lifted her off her feet. But I didn't take her to the bedroom. I headed straight for the dining room table. I laid her across it, and her legs fanned open, beckoning me to claim my willing mate.

"I'm going to feast on you," I rasped, and she moaned. "So this seemed more appropriate than the bed." I reached to unfasten her jeans. Her teeth sank into her lips as I dragged down the zipper. I drew the jeans a few inches down her hips. "About my other question."

Her head popped up from the table, triggered out of her daze. "Ask me later, and make it less sucky."

I snorted at her choice of words and brushed my thumb across the flat plane of stomach I'd exposed. "Are you sure?"

"This is worse than compulsion," she grumbled.

I threw my head back and laughed. "We'll do it your way," I agreed after my amusement subsided. "But I might take my time."

"Take whatever time you need—but take my pants off *now*," she demanded.

I drew them another inch lower. "Maybe you need a lesson to remind you about boundaries."

The honeyed-melon scent grew so thick I could almost taste it in the air.

"Maybe later," I promised darkly, yanking her pants off and lowering onto one knee. "Maybe I'll ask you like this—with you spread like a banquet before me."

She whimpered as I brushed my palms along the insides of her thighs. I paused. "What you said before—say it again."

I heard her swallow, her arousal growing stronger with each second. She knew what I wanted to hear. "I'm yours. My blood. My body. It belongs to my mate. It belongs to you. Now claim it."

I dragged her ass to the end of the table and dropped onto my other knee. "Gladly."

CHAPTER NINE

Thea

I dreamed of teeth, flashes of sharp white fangs invading my sleep.
But I didn't run from the monster in my dreams. I welcomed him.
And in my beautiful nightmares, there were no rules. No boundaries.
Nothing was off-limits.

I writhed and rode and offered myself again and again. But every
time my body clenched, anticipating release, the dream shifted and
left me unsatisfied.

I woke, drenched in sweat, to find Julian smirking down at
me from the foot of the bed. He had a tray in his hands. I startled,
forgetting for a moment where I was until it came rushing back to
me. Not all of the teeth had been a dream, I realized with toe-curling
giddiness. He was here, and he was real. And unlike my dreams, he'd
left me satisfied five mind-blowing times.

"Dreaming about me, pet?" he asked, his grin widening as he
raked his gaze shamelessly down my body.

"Somebody has a high opinion of himself." I yanked the sheets
over my breasts, blocking his view.

"It must have been all the times you confused me with God last
night." He moved around to my side of the bed and tutted. "Sit up for
me."

I pushed up, still clutching the sheet over my naked body, and rested my back against the leather headboard.

"I made you breakfast." He placed the tray over my lap, cursing as he tried to get its wooden legs to cooperate.

A raw ache crept into my throat as I took in the plate of eggs, toast, and fresh fruit. Steam streamed from a small silver pot wrapped in a linen towel. The food looked delicious, but it was the smell coming from the pot that I couldn't resist. I picked it up, my eyes rolling back as I inhaled the rich, earthy aroma of fresh coffee.

"Should I leave you two alone?" he asked.

My gaze flicked up to him. "Take your clothes off, and you can join us."

His low laugh skittered along my skin and settled in places only he had traveled. But Julian walked over to a chair by the window and took a seat. "You need to eat. Your blood sugar is low."

I wrinkled my nose. Another unfair advantage my vampire boyfriend had was that he could tell way too much about my bodily functions through my scent. Not that I could complain, if it meant he'd deliver breakfast to me. I poured some coffee into the bone china mug. Taking a sip, I closed my eyes with pleasure.

"Do you like it?" he asked. "I picked it up from the market down the street."

I nodded, opening my eyes to give him a smile. "Thank you, but you didn't have to do all this."

"I couldn't sleep," he informed me, shifting to stretch his long arms over the back of the chair. Thick bands of muscles strained against his T-shirt's sleeves. "It must have been all the caffeine you consume."

I choked on the sip I'd just taken. Grabbing the napkin, I coughed, then dabbed at my mouth. "Are you saying that my blood…"

"Is like a triple espresso with a few extra shots," he said wryly.

I lifted a shoulder and took another sip. "I guess if you don't like it…"

"Like it?" he repeated darkly. "I'm almost ashamed of myself. I could have nibbled on you all night, pet."

I swallowed his words along with the drink I'd just taken. Both landed hot in my stomach and spread, warming me to the core. "I don't have plans today," I said suggestively. "Feel free to do that."

A growl rumbled from him, and his fingers sank into the arms of his chair. "Stop tempting me and eat," he bit out.

I dutifully picked up a piece of toast and took a big bite of it. Maybe I was starving, or maybe food just tasted better on the other side of our separation, but I polished off the piece in two more bites. Reaching for my fork, I spotted two pills next to a small glass of water.

"What's this?" I asked, picking one up.

"Iron supplements," he said, clearing his throat. "I thought it might be a good idea if you want me to continue…"

"Feeding?" I finished for him, lifting a brow. "Wait. Are you changing your mind? Was it the caffeine? I can quit drinking coffee."

"No," he answered quickly. He shifted in his seat, his knuckles white from clutching the armrests. "I didn't want to assume that you enjoyed it as much as I did. Are you sure it's what you want?"

His words settled on my chest and wrapped around my heart. I popped the supplements into my mouth and swallowed them with a gulp of water. "Does that answer your question?"

His throat slid dangerously. "Keep eating."

I got the feeling I was going to need my strength. I dove into the eggs as he watched me. When I pierced the last blueberry on my plate, he flashed to my side and lifted the tray. I popped the berry into my mouth and held out the fork. Julian placed the tray on the bedside table. Now that I was fed, did he expect to eat as well? I shivered at the thought and let the bedsheet fall away.

His eyes tracked its movement as I shoved it off me. There was a wicked glint in his eyes as he took me in, but when he licked his lips, he turned away. "I'd like to check on the spots where I bit you."

Spots. The word turned me molten. Most of last night was a blur of skin, sweat, and teeth. I'd felt more than one bite, but I had no idea how many places he'd marked me.

"Are you sure that you don't want breakfast?" I said meaningfully.

"I'm nine hundred years old, Thea," he said in a strangled tone.

"I only require blood every few days."

"Oh." I bit my lip. "And last night?"

"I fed enough to last me a month." His jaw tightened from his confession, and I found myself reaching out to soothe him.

"Last night was different," I murmured. "We needed that."

He bobbed his head in a detached way, and I knew he wasn't going to listen. Not until he'd proven to himself that no harm had been done. Bare fingers ghosted over my breast, and I moaned instinctively.

Julian coughed. "Pet…"

"Sorry," I said sheepishly. I couldn't help it if my body responded to his touch. He traced a thumb over my nipple, and I clamped down on my pleasure.

"Can you see them?" he asked quietly.

I peered down where his thumb continued to circle, doing my best not to forget *why* he was touching me. Barely visible on the inside of my left breast were two moon-shaped dots, the pearly color of scar tissue.

"They're healed," I said with surprise.

"Nearly," he said. "I didn't want to leave you with open wounds."

I stared at the proof of his intimate kiss. "Will they scar?"

"Yes," he said quietly. "I should have warned you of that."

"Will I scar every time?" I asked.

"It seems so. Some skin is more prone to scarring." He lifted his head and studied me, his own face unreadable. He'd leashed his feelings on this, waiting to hear mine. "Does that bother you?"

"Not really." I shrugged, even as my heart raced at the idea of scarring. "Does it bother you?"

He ignored the question. "Your heart is pounding. Tell me how you really feel."

"It…it excites me," I said, pulling my lip between my teeth.

Julian's mask slipped, revealing his surprise. "You like the idea of my marks on you?"

I hesitated before nodding.

"Even when they leave scars?" He sounded as if he didn't believe me—*couldn't* believe me.

"Why wouldn't I?" I challenged him softly. "I love everything else about you. I'm proud to carry your marks. It means I belong to you."

"I think it means *I* belong to *you*," he corrected me. His voice dropped so low that it scraped a red-hot line between my legs as he added, "Because my marks on you are the hottest thing I've seen in my nine hundred years."

My mouth went dry as his eyes shadowed, his stance becoming predatory. Half of me expected him to pounce. All of me wanted him to.

His hand skimmed down, pausing to push the sheet off my hip so he could study my bikini line. "And here," he pointed out, tracing the small scars with the tip of his index finger. "There are two here." I forced myself to breathe as his hands continued down and pushed apart my legs. "And then here."

When he touched the scars there, a bolt of electricity shot through me, and I gasped.

"There's another thing you should know." He kept rubbing the scars, and each rotation of his fingertip made me dizzier and dizzier. "Unlike a normal wound, a vampire bite heals differently. Do you see how your skin looks like moonstone where I bit you?"

I glanced down again. He was right. The scars were practically shimmering. "Yes."

"Some of the magic remains, or whatever it is that nourishes a vampire, along with some of the venom." He pressed harder on it, and a tremble shattered through me. "It makes the spot sensitive."

"Each time?" I breathed, trying to focus on what he was saying instead of his clever fingers.

"Yes."

I peeked over at him. "Are you saying every time you feed from me, it's going to feel even better?"

"If I feed in the same places, yes."

I sucked in this information with a deep breath. "Are you positive you don't want breakfast?"

Julian laughed again, the sound coiling my stomach into knots.

"That's my gorgeous, greedy pet," he purred.

His fingers continued up, sweeping past my folds as they hunted for the button ticking between my legs.

"Greedy?" I repeated. I pushed him away from me. Julian didn't resist when I shoved him onto the mattress and crawled onto his lap. "I can be very generous."

"Oh?" His lips twisted into a grin.

"Yes." I rocked my bare sex against the bulge in his jeans. "Allow me to show you."

I shimmied off him, dropping to the bed beside him, and he frowned.

"I was enjoying that," he informed me.

"We could take your pants off, and then you'd really enjoy it," I pointed out. I didn't wait for him to respond. I already knew that he wouldn't bed me until we had answers. For now, I was delighted to show him what he was missing. Unbuttoning his jeans, I slipped a hand down his pants and wrapped my fingers around his shaft. Julian hissed with approval as I freed his cock.

"What are you doing, pet?"

"I'm still hungry." I planted a palm on the bed to keep my balance and bent over him. My other hand stroked him, enjoying how he stiffened more as I touched him. Slowly, I angled my mouth over him. I swirled my tongue around his broad tip and then gradually lowered my lips until I'd taken most of him inside me.

I lifted my gaze, mouth wrapped around him, and found him watching me with midnight eyes. I unleashed a moan to let him know that I enjoyed his taste as much as he enjoyed mine.

Julian dropped a hand onto my bottom and began to rub circles on my round cheek. Then he lifted his palm and smacked it. Sparks shot through my skin, and I groaned, my mouth still covering his cock.

"I love watching you suck me off." He traced a finger down my backside into my seam. Then slowly, he pushed it inside me. I gasped, the sound smothered. "You're almost as wet now as you were when I had my fangs in you."

Holy... I pressed my rear against his hand, urging him deeper. I was supposed to be tempting him.

"Someday, this will be mine." He pumped in and out of me leisurely, his finger hitting some invisible spot deep inside me that made my eyes roll back. "Just like the rest of you. Won't it?"

I bobbed my head faster, stroking him harder as he unraveled me with one finger alone.

"I'm close," he warned me as I continued to pleasure him. "Come with me."

I tightened around him, shattering as he spilled inside my mouth.

When he finished, I collapsed against him. Julian gathered me in his arms, kissing me softly on the forehead.

"Is this what happens when I bring you breakfast in bed?" he asked.

"Maybe." I peeked up at him. "Better do it again tomorrow."

His expression shifted, growing serious. "How are you feeling about other things?"

I knew he meant my mother. I shook my head. "I don't know. Can't we just pretend for a minute that we're normal people in a normal relationship?"

"If you wish, pet." He laughed, revealing his slightly elongated canines.

So much for that idea. Just the sight of his fangs, even if only the tips, sent my thighs squeezing together.

"We could stay in bed," I suggested, rolling over to straddle him. I felt him stiffen beneath me, and I resisted the urge to drag myself along his length.

"That might be dangerous." His words were thick, as if he was also preoccupied with the nearness of our nether regions. "We might never leave."

"Would that be so bad?" I asked, leaning down to kiss him.

Our mouths met, and suddenly, I found myself on my back. Julian lorded over me, a smirk slashing across his brutal, beautiful face. "If old vampire tales are to be believed, not being able to keep our hands off each other is a natural part of mating."

"Oh?" Every time he said the word, a thrill shot through me. "How long does it last?"

"I suspect we won't have a minute's peace until…"

I swallowed, nodding that I understood. "And when we do?"

"It will linger for months. Maybe years. Although"—his lips whispered a kiss over mine—"I can't imagine ever having my fill of you, so perhaps decades."

I closed my eyes and imagined how it would be to love him freely. Yeah, decades sounded more like it, except… "What about when I'm old?" I whispered.

It was a reality we hadn't faced yet. Other issues had seemed more pressing. But with a new agreement on the table and the reality that someday we would be mated, I couldn't ignore that there was one more decision we needed to make.

"Even then," he promised softly.

I brushed a finger down his corded bicep and forced myself to confront the fact that he was a nine-hundred-year-old vampire and I was a human. "And when I die?"

He went completely still, like he did whenever I brought up something painful.

"That's a long way off," he said, his lips barely moving.

But it wasn't. Not by vampire standards. "Julian, I'm mortal. I could die tomorrow."

"If you're trying to convince me to tie you to the bed and keep you here, safe and well-pleasured…" But the teasing tone he took didn't reach his eyes. They flashed as though he was already thinking ahead to some bleak future we couldn't escape.

I swallowed and forced myself to ask the question we both seemed to be skirting around. The question we were avoiding. The question our futures hinged on.

"Julian, will you make me a vampire?"

CHAPTER TEN

Julian

I hesitated. It was only a moment for Thea, but a lifetime for me. "You don't know what you're asking." I rolled my body off hers and sprang to my feet. "No, I will not."

"Seriously?" she said, scrambling up, the bedsheet forgotten.

I trained my eyes away from her, but she closed in on me. Her scent changed, and between that and the sight of her luscious body, it was all I could do to keep myself from taking her right then and there.

"Look at me," she demanded, "and give me one good reason."

I winced, shaking my head.

"Look at me!"

The room darkened as I turned to face her. Thea took a step back when she saw my eyes. Her gaze drifted down, taking in my rigid posture and the fists I kept tightly at my sides. One question had triggered my bloodlust. The wrong word might unleash me to act on it.

"What the hell…?" She staggered another step away from me, listening, but didn't go far. "We can't even *talk* about it?"

"Put. Some. Clothes. On." Each word took effort to launch from my lips. "*Please.*"

For once, she didn't argue. She grabbed the first thing she found on the floor and slipped it over her head. My T-shirt nearly swallowed her, but it had the intended effect, especially since it made her smell more like myself. The roar of my blood dampened and then finally quieted. Gradually, the world brightened to its normal shades.

"Was that bloodlust or blood rage?" she asked softly, still maintaining her distance.

"Lust. Maybe both." My head fell as relief relaxed my shoulders. The primal urge ebbed away, still present but less noticeable. I hadn't attacked my mate. I hadn't pinned her to the wall and done the things that had flashed through my mind.

I hadn't turned her the second she'd asked so that she would be mine forever.

She paused as if weighing her next question. "Why?"

But I didn't have an answer for her. The lust had seized me more violently than it ever had in the past. Even the night of the blood orgy, I'd felt more in control. It was the suddenness of it that gnawed at me. One minute, I was in control. The next, I had nearly lost it entirely.

Thea studied me, no doubt looking for signs of danger. "We have to talk about it sometime."

"We will," I gritted out, "but perhaps we shouldn't be in bed when we do. Now, put more clothes on before…"

Her face asked the question she didn't dare. *Before what?*

We stared each other down until she finally cleared her throat. "I'd like to take a shower."

One nod. It was all I dared move. "Over there. It should have everything you need."

"Care to—" She cut the question off quickly when my eyes flashed.

Thea vanished into the en suite bath, and I stayed in the same spot until I heard the water turn on. What the fuck had just happened?

Every time I thought I had myself in check, some primal urge overcame my self-control. If Thea had pushed or refused to cover herself, I suspected I would not only have bent her over the bed and claimed her sweet virginity in a brutally swift way, but I might have gone further than that.

Will you make me a vampire?

I hadn't answered her. I couldn't. My brain had stopped almost the second she'd asked the question, and the monster had taken over. It lurked still, pushing me toward the bathroom door, even as I resisted. I didn't trust myself to join her. I didn't trust whatever dark urge this was that I felt. The monster got as far as the bathroom door, which she'd left open a crack. Why had she done something so stupid after what had just happened? Was it a temptation? An offering?

Or worse, did she *trust* me?

I watched her through the opening. Her head fell back under the oversize showerhead. Water cascaded over her hair, down her breasts, and dripped farther.

I launched myself across the room to get away from her as darkness surged inside me again. The monster's grip loosened with the added distance, but I struggled to walk out the bedroom door. I closed it behind me, and the beast relaxed.

She was right. We would have to talk about this, but perhaps we needed to be on opposite sides of iron bars first. I would do whatever it took to keep her safe, even from myself. But I could only do that if I could manage some bloody restraint.

I crossed to the kitchen and started a fresh pot of coffee for her. By the time she was dressed, I would have a hold on myself. I would take her for a walk so we could discuss practical matters like the fact that my house in Paris—really *our* house, now—was a smoldering ruin, but only so we could decide where to go next. She might want to stay in San Francisco, but I couldn't allow her to keep living in her poorly secured apartment. The list of issues we needed to talk about grew with each passing second, and nowhere on it was her question.

Will you make me a vampire?

How could I answer her? I couldn't. I wouldn't. Being turned was entirely different than being born a vampire. That wasn't just down to social standing. She would be marked as a made vampire and treated differently, less than. But the real issue was that I couldn't stomach watching her suffer—and turned vampires *suffered* during their transition. The thought of Thea enduring that was too much to bear. How did I tell her that?

Especially when the thought of her death was even more painful.

I took my phone off the charger and called Jacqueline, not bothering to calculate the time difference. She would be awake. She never slept. Even after nearly a millennium of life, she hated to rest. She hated to miss out.

She answered on the second ring. "I've been waiting for you to call." She yawned, surprising me. "I assume you've been preoccupied."

I didn't miss the hopeful tone of her voice.

"I have," I said casually.

"Thank the gods." She sighed. "Tell me you made an honest mate of her."

"That's not why I called." I bypassed her question, paced to the window, and watched a man taking a leak on an abandoned building. I already missed Paris.

"I see," she said pointedly. "I salvaged what I could from your house, which wasn't much." She sounded disappointed. Considering the work she'd undertaken to oversee the renovations, I couldn't blame her.

"I'm sorry about the house, Jacqueline."

"Why are you consoling me? It was *your* house." But she sounded grateful. "The next one will be better. I think you should buy Thea an estate on the Riviera."

"Oh?" I smiled despite everything.

"Yes, she'll love it."

Translation: Jacqueline would love it, and she wanted to decorate it. I failed to point out I already had two houses on the Riviera— one on the Italian side and one on the French side. And a penthouse in Monaco. As far as I was concerned, she could do whatever she wanted with them—as long as it was okay with Thea. "I'll keep that in mind, but I didn't call to discuss real estate."

"What's up?"

"Something odd happened." I filled her in on everything from the hospital until the bloodlust incident, skipping over the more intimate parts of my reunion with Thea.

"It's likely the mating drive," she said, but uncertainty clung to her words. "Your body and mind and whatever we have that passes for a soul want to claim her. Just do it already."

"How romantic of you. There has to be a way around the tether. I just have to find it." Patience. That was the key.

"You aren't really going to wait three months, are you?" Something rustled on the other end of the line.

"I'll wait longer if I have to," I said, my mood souring.

"And what if you can't?" she pressed. "What if you hurt her? Turn her?"

"You act like I'm not considering those very questions." I pinched the bridge of my nose. If vampires could get migraines, she would have given me one.

"I know you are, because you're avoiding the real question, Jules. Will you turn her?"

"How can I even consider it without preparing her for what it means? And how can I prepare her when this fucking mating instinct keeps triggering bloodlust?"

"You're the one who said three months," she reminded me. "I'm sure Thea would be happy to move the timetable up."

"You sound like her."

"Yes, because we're females, so we're smart and know everything." I bit back a retort.

"I'll assume from your silence you agree." She continued: "Look, I'll talk to her about it. We've touched on the basics, but I'll answer all her questions. Maybe we can take a girls' weekend. If she says yes to your proposal, it can be a bachelorette party."

I swallowed a growl at the thought of having Thea out of my reach for an entire weekend.

Jacqueline laughed when I didn't respond. "I swear I can hear you brooding. Whatever it is, you'll get through it. Just help her take care of her mother and focus on getting her to say yes."

"Maybe. There's something else. Thea's mother—she knew I was a vampire."

A pause followed by surprise. "Did Thea tell her?"

"No. Thea seemed just as shocked."

"But how would she know?" Jacqueline asked. "Someone got sloppy and forgot to compel her?"

I'd considered the same possibility. "I don't think so. She seemed to know a lot about vampires. At least, she seemed pretty prejudiced against us. She forced Thea to choose between staying with her or being with me."

Jacqueline whistled. "And Thea chose your grumpy ass?"

"Why do I call you for advice again?" I asked.

"Because you love me and, as I already pointed out, I'm always right," she answered. "That's big."

"But that's not it." I pricked my ears, listening to make sure the shower was still running. I already had a laundry list of things I needed to tell Thea, but this was one item I needed to think over for a while before I did. "There was something familiar about her mom. It was like I knew her."

"Do you?"

"Not that I'm aware of." It wasn't like recognizing her, and it hadn't been the same as when I'd first seen Thea—a moment I understood now was colored by the mating bond reaching out to me. Still, there was something about Thea's mother that puzzled me. I needed to figure it out. It might be the key to mending the relationship between mother and daughter—one of the many things on my to-do list. I couldn't allow Thea to lose her mother over me. I wouldn't. I just needed to know what I was dealing with. "I can't shake the feeling that Kelly Melbourne isn't what she claims to be."

"What does she claim to be?" Jacqueline asked.

I heard the water shut off. I was running out of time to speak freely, so I kept my answer short. "Human."

CHAPTER ELEVEN

Thea

The BMW felt more cramped than usual. Julian hadn't said much since we'd left his apartment to head to mine to grab a few necessities. As we approached my street, his lips turned down with disapproval. He surveyed the graffiti and litter and shook his head.

"Since you're my mate..."

My heart thrilled to hear those words, especially after the weird turn our morning had taken.

"...I would prefer that you move in with me," he said.

"Move in?" I repeated.

His frown twisted into a wicked smirk. "Don't tell me that sharing an apartment gives you cold feet. You were ready to tether yourself to me a few hours ago."

And he knew I still was. It wasn't an oversight that he hadn't pointed out the other huge commitment I'd been considering: becoming a vampire. "You want me to move into The Armory?"

"If you wish to stay in San Francisco." He shrugged a broad shoulder, steering the car to an empty space on the street. "Or we can find somewhere that suits both of us wherever we wish."

"Paris?" I said softly. Before things had gone horribly wrong between us, I'd fallen in love with the City of Light.

"We could." His mouth tightened. "But we'll have to find somewhere new."

"What happened to the house?" I asked.

"It's a long story, but it's less of a house now."

"And?"

"More of a smoldering pile of ruin." Surprise must have flashed over my face, because he added, "*I* wasn't the one who burned it down."

"I think we have some things to talk about." Other than mating and marriage and my mortality.

"We do, but they can wait. I assumed you might want to remain in San Francisco near the university." He hesitated before adding, "and your mother."

Right now, all I wanted was to get away from all of this, and with the possibility of marrying Julian and mating on the horizon, putting an ocean between me and my mother seemed like a good idea. At least until she got over my choice long enough to act like a human being toward me. I'd called her a dozen times, but she refused to pick up. I couldn't believe she was actually shutting me out.

But Julian had a good point about school. "I hadn't thought about Lassiter."

It felt like a hundred years ago. Everything had changed when I met Julian. My eyes had been opened to a whole new world. I'd been so captivated by it, I'd walked away from my own.

"I only needed to finish this semester's courses." I sighed, considering starting them all over again.

"I'm sure something can be arranged," he said lightly, his blue eyes deepening with some sort of plot.

"You mean bribed?" I said drily.

His gaze softened. "I would never take your accomplishments from you, but if you wish to take your final exams and receive your degree, I'm sure something can be arranged."

"Finals are this week," I pointed out.

"Then, perhaps a little bribery," he said with a smile, "but you'll have to pass on your own."

"Most of them involve playing pieces I've hardly practiced." I twisted my fingers together. I could count on one hand how often I'd played since we'd met. But that had more to do with my mother being in the hospital than him.

"Then we better get your cello—unless you sold it," he tacked on.

"No." I rolled my eyes. "I sold all the clothes and stuff instead."

"Of course you did." He shook his head slightly but made no further comment about my choice.

Somehow I knew I'd find my closet restocked within the week. I wondered what poor employee would get stuck with the chore—probably Celia.

"Get your cello and this underwear you so desperately require," he said, referencing my reason for stopping by the apartment. He was of the opinion that underwear should be optional. "You can practice at my apartment, and I'll make some calls to Lassiter."

Part of me wanted to say no, but Julian was the reason I'd walked away from graduating with honors. As long as I was the one to finish things, I didn't care if he reopened the door for me. "I believe the last time I was playing, you didn't let me finish."

"That's strange." He licked the tip of his tongue over his teeth. "I remember you finishing *several times* that night."

I raised an eyebrow as if to say *exactly.*

"I will be happy to provide incentives for you to master your pieces," he offered.

"Like?"

The look he gave me in answer sent my toes curling inside my shoes.

"You'll be stuck listening to me play the rest of the weekend," I warned him.

"I love when you play," he said in a soft voice. "You were playing when I first saw you."

"You mean the time I caught you looking like you were going to murder me?" I asked with a snort. Apparently, we remembered our first encounter very differently.

"Indeed." He turned his attention to the steering wheel, acting nonchalant, but his voice was thick as he continued. "I suppose it looked that way. Every instinct urged me to spirit you away. I thought I wanted to kill you, too, but I think I would have just mated with you the second we were alone."

My mouth fell open at the harsh truth of it. Julian had mastered his primal instincts that night, but it was still a struggle. What if he hadn't? What if he'd...

"You look horrified," he murmured. I started to protest, but he cut me off. "You should be. Never forget what I am, pet. I can't."

I heard what he was really saying under those words. *Never forget what vampires are.* I'd asked him about turning me; was this his way of gently preparing me for his rejection?

A lump formed in my throat, but I swallowed, pushing the thought away. Nothing had been decided yet. In three months, we'd mate and figure things out from there.

"I should get my things," I said after a moment.

"Shall I join you?"

"Give me a minute to make sure no one's naked," I said, but the joke fell flat. I knew my roommates would be approximately as happy about our reunion as my mother had been. "But yes."

I hesitated before lurching across the console and planting a swift kiss on his lips. I noticed his hands were still wrapped around the steering wheel when I pulled back. He'd stopped wearing gloves around me, so he couldn't hide his white-knuckled grip.

How would we make it three months with him being this on edge? I forced a smile as I climbed out of the car and dashed toward the building. It took me a minute to find my key in my bag, and I swore the whole time that I felt his eyes burning into my back. When I finally made it inside, I left the door slightly ajar so he could follow me, knowing he'd attack any suspicious types.

I climbed the stairs slowly, trying to decide exactly how to play it if Olivia and Tanner were home. However they reacted, it would still be better than my mother's reaction.

That theory was disproved as soon as I walked through the door. Olivia jumped up from the couch, still in her pajamas, and rushed toward me. But there was no hug or relief to see me. Instead, she brandished a cell phone charger like a weapon. "Do you know how to charge your phone?"

I grimaced. "Sorry. I left it at the hospital."

"I know," she told me. "I know because they called me to come and get it."

"What?" I asked, taking it from her. "Why?"

"You weren't answering your phone, so they called your secondary contact, which is me, by the way." Olivia tightened her messy bun, fuming as she began pacing the room. "Your mom left all your things at the hospital when she was released."

"She was released?" The news hit me like a punch in the gut. I grabbed onto the back of the couch to stay upright. "So, everything is fine."

The tumors must have been benign. I focused on that instead of the fact she'd left without a word.

"I doubt it," Olivia raged. "Because they have tests they need to talk to you about, since they can't reach her."

"What do you mean?" I looked up at her, horror washing through me.

"Your mom left. The nurse wouldn't tell me, but I found Dr. Reeves, and he said your mom was distraught after she had a fight with you and some guy claiming to be your husband."

"Oh shit."

"Yeah, care to fill me in about that?" She planted a hand on her hip. "What the hell is going on, Thea?"

"I can explain," I said, but not quickly enough, because a knock on the door interrupted us.

Olivia glanced from me to the door, and I could have sworn I saw her brain actually implode. She stepped between it and me as if to prevent me from answering it. "Is that him? Did you actually leave your mom to run off with him again?"

Again. The word cut me to the core, and I gasped. We stared at each other, neither of us moving.

Finally, Olivia turned her head. "I'm sorry. That was a shitty thing to say."

"It's fine," I said, but I knew she meant it.

"So, he's here," she said flatly.

"Yes, but I didn't abandon her at the hospital to run off with him," I told her. "It was more complicated than that—she was mad."

"Why? Because some guy who *shredded* you walked back in like nothing happened?"

"It's not that simple." I hated this. I hated fighting with Olivia. I hated feeling like everyone wanted me to choose between the man— the mate—I'd fallen in love with and my old life. I hated that I couldn't tell her what he meant to me, how much more magical and expansive the world was, how it was full of creatures she'd only dreamed about. I hated that there had to be secrets between us, but what choice did I have? There was no way Olivia would believe me, and, even if she did, I wasn't sure that I'd be doing her any favors by making her aware that she didn't just need to worry about muggers and rapists, but vampires, too.

"Do you know where your mom went?" Olivia changed the subject, still blocking me from the door.

"Home? I don't know. She…" I swallowed. "She made me choose between her and him."

"And you chose him?" Olivia's voice peaked, letting me know exactly how she felt about that, too.

"I shouldn't have had to choose at all," I exploded. "So, yeah, I left with him because I needed to hear him out. Because it's my life, and I've given years of it, sitting in that hospital, praying she didn't die. Because he was there to pay the hundreds of thousands of dollars those years cost us. But mostly because he *didn't* ask me to choose. He let me decide for myself, even though I already knew my answer. Because every answer, every decision, every choice I have will always lead me back to him."

Olivia's eyes widened, but she didn't speak. I'd stunned her into silence. Julian knocked on the door again, and I swore I could hear him in my head.

I've been patient, pet. Let me in before I go crazy.

She didn't try to stop me as I brushed past her and opened the door. Julian lounged against its frame, his muscular body filling it. One look at his face told me he'd heard the entire fight.

"Bad time?" he muttered, then held up his phone. "I just got a call. Unfortunately, it can't wait. Do you want me to come back?"

I closed my eyes, wondering if we'd ever catch a break, and stepped to the side. "No, I'll only need a minute."

He stalked into the room, nodding at Olivia. She didn't so much as blink in acknowledgment.

"I just came to grab a few things." I held up the charger. "I'm staying with Julian for a few days while I try to take my finals." I didn't know why I was bothering to tell her any of this. But Olivia looked at me and bobbed her head once.

"I'll wait out here," Julian murmured. I paused, wondering if I should leave the two of them alone in the same room. Julian tilted his head as if reading my mind. "Go on."

A pissed-off best friend and a deadly vampire mate were a dangerous combination. Both wanted the best for me. They just had very different ideas of what that meant. As I left them to pack an overnight bag, I realized that for once, the vampire might have met his match.

CHAPTER TWELVE

Julian

I'd lived through a few showdowns in my day. Sebastian had even dragged me to the American West to play cowboy for a couple of months. I knew when I was staring down the barrel of a gun. Olivia might not be armed, but she was ready to pull the trigger. Her body vibrated with unspoken words, causing her adrenaline to spike in mouthwatering ways.

I suspected Thea would be pissed if I snacked on her roommate. I sank into a chair and braced myself. "Something on your mind?"

Olivia's eyes snapped wide, a string of Spanish—mostly curses— falling from her lips.

I smirked so she'd think I was an evil bastard. She had no idea. "I deserve that," I admitted.

Olivia paused, reassessing me. "You understood me."

"I'm fluent in Spanish." I didn't offer any further explanation.

"I forgot," she said, taking on a dramatic tone. "You're a billionaire CEO or something. I guess you had to learn a foreign language to give orders to the peasants you exploit."

"I enjoy other languages, and I'm not a CEO," I corrected her.

"That's even worse." She leaned against the wall with a huff. "Money without purpose."

"Oh?" This wasn't the attack I'd expected. I found myself both caught off guard and intrigued. "And you assume I have no purpose."

"All I know is that you showed up and started waving your wallet around and making big promises, and then my friend quit school and ran off to Paris with you."

"And you don't approve of Thea's choices?" I asked quietly.

The question needled her. "Of course I respect whatever Thea decides—"

"Unless it's to go away with me," I pointed out.

"She worked her ass off for years earning that degree while taking care of her mom. She loves the cello." She flung an accusing finger at the violet case sitting in the corner. "She didn't even take it with her."

"An oversight," I murmured. "I want Thea to keep playing."

"For you or for the world?" Olivia demanded.

Another unexpected attack, this time striking her target. "I want what she wants."

"Do you? Because asking her to leave meant she blew a fellowship opportunity. It would have allowed her to make an independent living from her music. Can you offer her that?"

I remained silent. She wouldn't like my answer. Olivia didn't want to hear that with me, Thea wouldn't need to make a living. "I'll never come between Thea and her dreams."

"You already did," she said, "and then you broke her heart, and now you've lost Thea her mom, so excuse me if I'm not thrilled she's shacking up with you."

"Noted." My fingers strained against the leather tips of my gloves. It was a good thing I'd put them on before I followed Thea, or I might have ripped holes in the arms of the shabby secondhand chair.

"I don't like you," she finished unnecessarily. That was clear. "And I don't trust you."

"Should I bother trying to change either of those opinions?" I lifted one brow.

"Probably not."

"You're a dancer," I said, changing the subject.

She glared at me. "So?"

"I'm only making conversation," I said simply. "I'd like to know more about the people in Thea's life."

"Why? You're going to take her away from here again, aren't you?"

I paused. There was no easy way to answer her. "My position requires me to travel. I would like Thea with me, but she can stay here if she chooses."

"She won't." Olivia shook her head. "I've seen the way she looks at you. She can't think straight around you."

I stood, hearing a bag zip shut in Thea's room. "The feeling is mutual." I paused and offered Olivia the only consolation I could. "I would never hurt Thea. She is free to make her own decisions."

"You already hurt her."

This again. I forced myself to stay calm. "It won't happen again." Olivia met my eyes and delivered one final blow: "Liar."

"You seem to think I'm using your friend," I said gruffly.

"Are you?"

"No." The clipped response was met with suspicion. "But I suppose time will prove it."

"And you're sticking around, huh?" Her unamused laugh scraped at my fraying nerves.

"I will stay until she asks me to leave," I said in a strained voice.

"And if she does?"

"I meant what I said. Thea is free to make her own choices."

"In that case, Thea would like to be taken to lunch now," Thea announced from the hall. A few bags were slung over her slight shoulders. I walked over and took them from her. "Chivalry, huh?"

"Still think it's dead, pet?" I murmured, studying her face for signs that she'd heard my argument with Olivia. "I'll get your cello and meet you in the hall."

I tipped my head to Olivia as I carried Thea's belongings out the front door. At least her glare was silent. Allowing the door to shut behind me, I groaned. I was zero for two when it came to winning over Thea's loved ones. I heard Thea mumbling a goodbye to Olivia and what sounded like an awkward hug. I tried not to, but it wasn't my fault the shitty walls were thin in the rundown building.

When Thea stepped into the hall, I trained my face into a blank mask. She sighed as she joined me. "Stop pretending like you didn't hear everything." She reached to take one of the bags, but I shook my head.

"I've got this, and I did my best to give you privacy."

"Do I need to fill you in?" she asked. "About my mom?"

"No," I admitted. I'd heard what Olivia had said. It would be harder to find answers if Kelly Melbourne had disappeared. But the fact that she had was a clue in and of itself. Was she afraid of me? And if she was, would she really leave her daughter in my clutches?

"I know she wasn't very friendly, but she doesn't know you. Maybe if we give it time…" Thea didn't seem upset that I'd overheard the news about her mother. Instead, she looked relieved. "I guess we should go and talk to the doctors."

"Whatever you wish."

She rounded, bumping into me at the bottom of the stairs. "Do you really mean that? Because I know what she said, and I guess I should stay away. But if they can't reach her and there are test results—"

"Yes," I cut her off, then continued in a soothing voice, "I mean it. Your mother might not approve of our relationship, but she is your family. That makes her my family."

Thea listened, the panic seeping away from her features, and then she snorted.

That hadn't been the reaction I was expecting.

"Sorry," she said. "I was just wondering if I could claim the same about your family."

"No one would blame you for not feeling the same. Vampire families are different." *My mother did cover you in snakes.* I refrained from reminding her of that particular trauma.

"Exactly," Thea grumbled as we left the apartment. It felt colder than when we had entered her building, and I wondered if she needed a warmer jacket.

"I'm fine," she said even as she clenched her sweater against the biting wind. "I mean, how am I supposed to act when she hates me that much?"

"Who?" I asked with a blink. I circled to the back of the car and opened the trunk.

"Your mom," Thea said. "I know I'm not a familiar, so I can't give her grandbabies or whatever she's hoping for."

The last thing she wants is grandbabies. I packed Thea's bags in the trunk, arranging them around her cello. When I closed it, Thea watched me, her fingers drumming on the roof.

I moved to open her door, but she paused as she climbed inside. "I thought that was the whole point—of The Rites, I mean. More vampire babies."

"It is," I said slowly, "but there's more to it."

Thea chewed on her lower lip as I shut the door. I didn't rush to the driver's side. I took my time, parsing what she'd said. When I got behind the wheel, Thea shrugged.

"It doesn't matter," she said.

"It matters to me." I turned on the car. "I don't want you to worry about what my family thinks of you."

"I could say the same," she said sardonically. Then she sighed. "I should be nicer to your mother. I know you tried with my mom."

At least your mom won't try to kill me. I couldn't say the same for Sabine.

Thea laughed. "I don't know. She might."

I slammed on the BMW's brakes several hundred feet short of the red light ahead. Rubber screeched behind us, and a car horn blasted. A moment later, a car whipped past us, the driver throwing a lewd gesture in our direction.

"Julian!" Thea shouted, clutching her chest. Adrenaline surged in her blood, turning the air around me sweet with temptation.

"Calm down," I ordered her.

"I will not." She rubbed the spot over her heart and watched the car ahead of us zoom away. "One of us is still mortal. What the…"

Fuck. That's the word you're looking for.

"I can finish my own damn sentences," she said testily.

Thea?

"What?" she demanded.

I'm not saying this out loud.

"What?" she repeated. This time she sounded confused. "I heard you."

Look at my mouth, pet.

Her eyes zeroed in on my lips.

Well, that pretty much proves it.

"Holy shit," she whispered. "What is going on?"

This time I opened my mouth to answer her. "I have no idea."

But whatever it was, it couldn't be good.

Thea nodded as if she'd heard me and agreed.

CHAPTER THIRTEEN

Thea

I played cello day and night. Not only because Julian might succeed in convincing Lassiter to let me finish my final semester, but because it was a way to drown out his thoughts. I didn't want to eavesdrop, exactly. I just couldn't help it. The new trick came and went like it had a mind of its own. I never knew when to expect it, and I had no idea if it worked on anyone else. So, I escaped into my music.

The acoustics in Julian's apartment were surprisingly good. Probably because it had the cavernous feel of a stage. Of course, maybe stage fright was to blame for my continual fumbling of a solo piece by Kodály. My bow slipped slightly, cutting off a note, and I grimaced. I paused, repositioned myself, and started again. I loved the piece. It was gentle but demanding. The notes swelled indulgently and then became a frenzy. It was unpredictable and erratic, beautiful and haunting.

It reminded me of Julian.

I felt each note like my love for him. It was deep and lovely and consuming—but so hard.

So very, very hard.

I closed my eyes, ignoring the sheet music, and played from memory. My fingers took over, darting and plucking over the strings.

Sweat formed on my brow as my pace increased to match the piece's strange energy. When I reached the strained final note, I slumped and inhaled deeply.

"Beautiful," Julian said softly behind me.

A shiver raced through me like an icy shot and combined with the lingering rush from the difficult sonata. It met the ache growing inside me as he circled around and leaned against the wall.

"You've been at it for hours," he said. It was impossible to tell what he thought of that. He'd grown quieter in the last two days. I couldn't decide if that was because he expected me to read his mind or because he was trying to keep his cool. Our leading theory was that I could hear his thoughts when he or I got upset. We couldn't figure out what had triggered it, though, and I found myself disinterested in learning more. What if I didn't like what I learned? There had to be a reason he'd been so careful around me...

"It feels good to play." He raised an eyebrow as if he knew that was only slightly true. It wasn't a lie. I did enjoy it. But Julian knew there was more. I could see it on his face. "Fine. I never hear your thoughts when I'm playing. The music drowns it out. Are you sure I'm the only one who reads minds?"

"You're a terrible liar, pet," he said with a feral grin. "That's all."

Can you hear me now? His voice tapped at my mind.

"Yes." I sighed, putting away my cello. Once it was tucked into its case, I swiped at the hair sticking to my damp forehead.

I like it when you're sweaty. It reminds me of how hot and bothered you get when my mouth is on you.

I swallowed, pretending I didn't hear him. If only so he would keep up the dirty talk.

Ignoring me? That's rude, and I was going to reward you for all your hard work.

I lifted my head to him with a grin. "Oh really?"

Yes. He moved closer and held out his hand. "But first, I have news."

"About Paris?" I frowned. It seemed like every day, some bit of bad news filtered in to us. I suspected there was even more that he wasn't sharing. When I pressed him on it, he told me I had enough to worry about.

"No word there. The authorities don't have any leads. The security footage was removed." He barely seemed angry about the loss. The only matter that upset him was the murder of Hughes. It was the only reason he was looking into it at all. "It's just a house."

"That's easy for you to say," I told him. "My favorite jeans were in that house." Joking about it helped me loosen the knot that formed the minute I thought about it. I couldn't shake the feeling that the fire had been a message meant for both of us. The truth was that the fire had stripped away the last of my pretenses that the vampire world wasn't every bit as dangerous as Julian had warned me.

"I'll put holes in these ones later," he promised, eying my casual apparel. "Celia is coming by this afternoon. She went shopping."

"I could have done that." Unlike him, I hadn't grown up with servants to meet my every whim and need. It still felt weird to have someone running my errands.

"But you wouldn't," he said.

I glared at him. He already knew me too well.

"And Celia didn't mind. She spoke with Jacqueline, so everything should fit."

It was like having two vampire fairy godmothers constantly using their magic to turn me from ordinary human into mortal consort to a god. I wondered if any of this would ever get less weird.

It won't.

I glanced up at him, surprised. "Did you hear me?"

"No," he said apologetically. "It's just all over your face, my love."

"Of course it is," I grumbled. I brushed past him and walked to the fridge. It had been stocked with every type of food imaginable. "What is all of this?"

"I didn't want you to get hungry," he said, moving behind me. He slipped his hands around my waist. "Did I forget anything?"

"The kitchen sink?" I laughed, taking in the packed shelves. "This is enough food for an army, Julian."

"You need your strength," he said tightly.

I didn't have to hear his thoughts to know what he'd left unsaid. I swiveled around and looped my arms around his neck. "Thank you." I perched on my tiptoes and barely managed to kiss him. "But I'll tell you if I'm feeling weak."

"Still, we should slow down."

According to him, he didn't need to feed as often as he'd been indulging since we'd agreed that I would serve as his only source of blood. That hadn't stopped either of us. I wanted his fangs inside me. I begged for them, and he was all too happy to comply in the heat of the moment. After? That was another story.

"I'll tell you to stop," I reminded him quietly. "Consider it part of the arrangement."

But this time, it didn't soothe the ragged fear on his face. "It's getting harder," he admitted, "to stop feeding and to…"

I bit back my standard response, knowing it would do no good. Whatever Julian's reasons were for refusing to seal our mating bond, he kept them locked away so that I couldn't even hear them in his head. It didn't matter that I was willing to be tethered. He wouldn't relent, and I was tired of pushing him on it. In three months, I'd hold him to his word. I knew he feared tethering me, but I trusted him. I hoped that when the time came, he trusted himself.

"I heard from Lassiter," he said, and a new panic rose inside me.

"Yeah?" I twisted around, suddenly grateful that he'd filled the entire freezer with ice cream. I grabbed a pint of chocolate peanut butter and peeled off the lid. I found a spoon waiting in his palm with a flash of movement.

"They can squeeze you in on Wednesday."

I nearly dropped the spoon. "That's two days from now."

"It's the best I could do." *I should have dangled another million.*

"Million?" I yelped. "Please tell me you didn't bribe them to let me graduate."

"I bribed them to let you take your finals. You have to pass them, pet." He waved off my concern with a pale hand. "They needed the money for a new student theater. They're so grateful that they wanted me to name it."

"The Rousseaux Stage is where I'll be auditioning?" I said drily, finally scooping a spoonful of ice cream into my mouth.

Try again.

I nearly choked. "You didn't."

He shrugged. "You're marrying money. Get used to it."

"Marrying, huh?" I did my best to cover the giddiness I felt. "I don't remember a proposal."

"I proposed. You demanded romance," he reminded me.

"I demanded effort." I snorted. "So, I'm not marrying anyone." I bit back a smile. We were getting good at this dance, and maybe by the time he actually proposed, my personal life wouldn't be such a wreck. Maybe my mom...

We'll see about that.

I pushed the spoon around the pint of ice cream, working up the courage to ask about the other subject weighing on my mind. "Have you..."

"There's been no word from her. She hasn't been back to her apartment."

I ate a bite, letting it melt over my tongue until my mouth felt as cold as my blood. I was trying not to worry, trying not to let her sudden disappearance eat me alive. I was trying to give her the respect she should have given me. "Dr. Reeves left another message," I confessed. "I think I have to call him back."

Julian only nodded. He'd been neutral on the situation with my mother in terms of how he felt, but that hadn't stopped him from hiring someone to find her. "That might be for the best."

"Is it?" I asked him sincerely. "What if he's calling to tell me she needs more tests or something? I don't know where to find her."

"We will keep looking." He hooked a finger in the waistband of my jeans and drew me to him. "We'll find her."

And then what? I kept the question to myself.

"Do you think..." I hesitated. "Do you think she'd know why I can read your thoughts?"

"Maybe."

The room went eerily silent, and I realized I'd been trying to hear his thoughts—and Julian? He'd been actively stopping me from doing so.

"Tell me what you're thinking," I said.

"So it worked." He smiled. It was a low-cut, arrogant smirk that made my heart flip.

"What worked?"

"I called an old friend. A familiar I met years ago. I told him someone kept trying to get into my head, and he had some helpful hints." The smirk slid away when he saw my expression. "I didn't think it would bother you."

I rearranged my face quickly. "It's good," I said. "I don't want to feel like I'm being nosy."

"You couldn't help it," he murmured. "I only phrased it that way to him to respect our privacy." He brushed a kiss over my forehead. "I don't mind you being in my head most of the time."

"Most of the time?"

"I'd rather you didn't know how many hours I wasted thinking about you naked," he teased, but shadows clouded his eyes. There was more he'd kept hidden, and I wasn't sure if I wanted to know why.

My fingers itched for my bow to bring relief. Now that my audition was back on my radar, turning to music felt less like the refuge it had been.

"I should practice more," I said, casting a defeated look at my cello. "I only have a couple of days."

I'd never be ready to perform in time, especially with everything weighing on my mind.

"I'll make you something real to eat." He took the pint of ice cream from me and returned it to the freezer. "You're going to make yourself sick."

And I knew he wasn't talking about practicing too much or subsisting on ice cream. "A familiar helped you," I said, deciding not to hide from the fear his words had provoked. "Does that mean what I'm doing is magic?"

Julian paused, his face obscured by the refrigerator door. Each second he stayed quiet was torture. Finally, he closed it empty-handed. "I think it is."

I gasped before getting ahold of myself. I could face this—whatever this was. "I'm a witch?"

He bit his lower lip, and I noticed his fangs had extended. When had that happened? "I don't know. I don't think so…"

"But you aren't sure?" I whispered. When he didn't respond, I closed my eyes. "That's why you want to find my mother."

"I want to find her to put your mind at ease. You're barely sleeping." He took a step closer and wrapped his strong arms around me. I buried my face against his hard chest and breathed in his spicy, intoxicating scent. "But finding her might also give us answers, pet—or shorten the search for them."

"I know." I just wasn't sure I wanted those answers.

"Worry about your final performance," he said roughly, "and I'll worry about all this."

That was easier said than done. But he was right. Music could be my escape from this for now.

"And, pet, feel free to practice naked if it helps."

I lifted my head, my eyes narrowing. "How would that help?"

"You were sweating earlier." He feigned innocence. "I'm only thinking of you."

"Sure. You'd be willing to suffer through watching me play naked, huh?"

"If I must." He grinned, and the sight shook my heart free from the fear surrounding it.

"And you'll be able to keep your hands off me and let me practice?"

"I never said that," he admitted.

"Good!" I tugged free of him, feeling considerably lighter but infinitely more distracted. Julian caught my hand as I turned, clasped it, and…

I ripped it away, clutching it to my chest as my brain tried to process the electric spark still tingling on my skin. Julian was frozen, his now empty hand still outstretched. He stared at it like he was trying to understand what he'd just felt, too. My mind groped around for a thought—*any* thought from him to fill the stunned silence in mine. His mind remained blank, but not because he blocked me from it—we'd both found the same question to ask. He was just the one to break the silence.

"What the hell was that?"

CHAPTER FOURTEEN

Thea

"This way." The teaching assistant sniffed as she looked me up and down. Thanks to Celia's shopping prowess, I wasn't in a worn gown for my final performance at Lassiter University. This dress was by a designer—some Italian name I couldn't pronounce—and I couldn't imagine what it had cost Julian's bank account. Not only was it a luscious silk blend, but it also made me feel invincible. I'd known it was the dress I wanted to wear as soon as I saw it on the hanger. Not only was it gorgeous, but I could actually perform in it. Apparently, that was at Julian's request, because he proved it by dropping to his knees, shucking its long skirt to my waist, and giving a performance of his own.

And an encore.

It wasn't winning me any points with the TA, however. A last-minute addition to the schedule must have been annoying at best. If she knew I'd basically dropped out over a month ago, she had every reason to act like a condescending bitch in my privilege's direction. Something she was doing quite well.

We paused at the door to the student stage, a small black box theater reserved for recitals and exclusive performances. Today it was where I would end my undergraduate career and turn the page on the next chapter of my life. I just hoped this chapter ended happily.

The door opened, and a dark-haired girl stepped out carrying a flute case. I'd had a couple courses and workshops with her, so despite my nerves, I said, "Veronica, I hope that went well. It's good to see you."

"Thanks..." She paused, a friendly grin registering on her face. Her eyes widened, and she looked me up and down. "Thea?"

"New dress," I said, trying to sound casual.

"To say the least." She laughed. "You look hot. Giving your final performance?"

I nodded, my anxiety returning at the reminder. I held my cello case tightly to keep my shaky hands from dropping it.

"I guess I thought for some reason that you'd left school. I'm glad you didn't," she added quickly. "More stuff with your mom's health?"

"Yeah, and some family business," I lied. "But they're letting me do my final performance. Hopefully it's enough to let me graduate."

"You'll be fine. Break a leg."

She swished away happily, free from any stage fright she'd felt half an hour ago. I was jealous as I watched her leave.

"They're ready for you," the TA told me, holding open the door.

I shot her a tight smile as I made my way inside. It was a traditional black box: small, dark, and square. Seats were lined around an open space in the middle. Most of them were empty, except for one row. An elegant woman sat closest to me, making notes on an iPad. I didn't recognize her. In the next two seats, two professors I'd had for various theory classes were chatting about something in hushed voices. But the man at the end had stood. Professor MacLeod beamed at me. He tucked his phone in his tweed jacket and ambled over to me.

"Miss Melbourne," he greeted me warmly. "I'm so glad that you were able to return and finish your semester."

"Me too," I murmured, accepting the handshake tentatively. Since the spark that had nearly fried me alive, I'd avoided contact with anyone's palms, even Julian's. But as I took Professor MacLeod's... ordinary hand, I relaxed a little and dredged up a genuine smile.

"And thank you. I know this is a favor."

"I would have done it without the generosity from your fiancé," he said under his breath, "but we're still happy to take his money."

My cheeks burned. At least Julian wasn't still telling people he was my husband. But I didn't correct Professor MacLeod. "He is very generous."

"And congratulations," he added. "I suppose this explains your sudden sabbatical."

My lips pressed into a thin line as I nodded. This conversation wasn't doing anything to help the rapid churning in my stomach.

"Mac," one of the others called over. "I think Diana is finally ready."

The woman lifted one bemused eyebrow and inclined her head. "I am."

I started as I recognized her. Diana James was a prodigy-turned-impresario who played no fewer than five instruments, including the cello. She'd performed on stages around the world. I'd seen pictures and videos of her performances, but I was surprised to discover how young she looked in person.

"Before Thea begins, since this is her final performance at Lassiter before romance whisks her away"—I cringed a little at the implication of Professor MacLeod's words—"that Miss Melbourne is a singularly gifted cello player. It's been a pleasure to see her natural talent develop over the last four years despite considerable adversity."

Diana's eyes flicked down my expensive gown as if questioning the truth behind his words. Maybe I should have worn the washed-out old dress I'd kept for moments like this. But nothing registered on her regal features. Let her think what she wanted. I'd paid my dues, and I would prove it with my final performance.

"Thank you," I said softly.

He tipped his head, and I made my way to the seat. I removed the cello from its case, and there was a slight murmur of surprise amongst the panel. I blushed, remembering this wasn't just any student cello—or even one many professionals could ever afford. The professors must have realized, too. They whispered amongst themselves, but

Diana remained still. Her face was an impassive mask. Given her level of fame and multi-instrument split-focus, I doubted she was very impressed by expensive cellos.

My hands shook as I placed my sheet music on the stand. I didn't really need it. I'd practiced so much that I could play the pieces in my sleep, but there was something comforting about having them there. I'd chosen two of my three pieces to showcase what I'd learned while studying here, and one simply for sentimental reasons.

I led with Schubert. I'd refused to let Julian come with me, but playing this piece first made me feel like he was here. It was easy to slip under its hypnotic spell. Each time I played it, it buried itself a little deeper into my soul. By the time I reached its final haunting notes, I was completely relaxed. I didn't bother to change my sheet music. I simply paused and began Bach's Cello Suite No. 1. Its tranquil pace was broken by bobbing, fragmented chords that echoed inside me like the urgency of desire. The piece was slightly shorter, and it ended too quickly. I closed my eyes and took a deep breath, hoping I hadn't made a mistake with my final selection. Kodály wasn't exactly a classic choice, but that drew me to him. The unearthly music vibrated through me as I played. The notes veered and snagged, so unlike the smooth, lovely pieces that I'd played first. When I reached the dramatic end, I gasped for air, unaware of how long I'd been holding my breath.

There was a moment of stunned silence, and then Diana began to softly clap.

"You weren't lying, MacLeod," she said to my mentor. "She has a true *gift*." The last word lingered on her tongue, and a warning thrill shot up my neck.

I swallowed and pushed the unnerving sensation to the back of my mind. "Thank you. I'm honored."

"As are we," MacLeod jumped in and began singing my praises. "It's been a pleasure to teach you."

I couldn't speak—emotion swelled in my throat, blocking my words—so I nodded. They made notes as I packed up my instrument and music. It hurt a little. This might be the last time I played on this stage—maybe any stage. I didn't even know if I'd ever play for others again. Something told me that life as Julian's mate might mean avoiding the limelight for his sake.

Professor MacLeod continued to congratulate me as I stood to leave, but Diana met me at the door.

"I meant what I said." Her nostrils flared slightly as she studied me. "Your performance was...magical."

My blood turned to ice at her choice of words, and I fought to act normally. "That means a lot coming from you. I've always admired you."

She tipped her head, graciously accepting a compliment she'd probably heard a thousand times before. She glanced over at MacLeod, whose barrel chest was puffed with pride as he spoke to his colleagues. "It's sweet of you to let him think he had something to do with it."

"He did," I said slowly. "I learned a lot at Lassiter."

She lifted one shoulder like she'd allow my lie, but I wasn't lying. What was she implying? Diana glanced at my case. "That's some cello for a student."

"It was a gift." I met her eyes.

"I'd be careful what price you pay for such an expensive gift," she said in a measured tone.

"You don't pay for a gift," I pointed out, ice filtering into my voice.

She sniffed the air again. "Don't you?"

If she was responsible for determining my collegiate fate, politeness was the way to go. "Thanks for the advice." I was suddenly glad I'd agreed to meet Julian for dinner. If only because it provided an excuse for me to get away from this interaction. They did say never talk to your idols... "I should go. Someone is waiting for me."

"I'm certain he is, if the stench hanging all over you is any indication."

My mouth fell open. I'd known what she was getting at. It was pretty hard to miss the big "you're messing with a vampire" red flags she'd been waving seconds ago. Even though I hadn't expected the insult.

"Sorry. I have overly developed senses," she said, not sounding apologetic in the least. "It helps with the music, but you already know that."

"What do I know?" I asked.

Her eyes narrowed, and then she laughed softly. "That's why I didn't notice until you played. It's all there, though. I can hear it singing in its sleep."

It took effort to force a response. I only managed a single word. "What?"

Her answering smile terrified me.

CHAPTER FIFTEEN

Thea

Diana cocked her head a little farther, the angle almost unnatural. Her eyes swept over me as that terrifying grin widened. "You really don't know?" She paused. "You smell like a vampire. I assume you know about our world."

I glanced over my shoulder at the professors. They remained near their seats, still deep in discussion and completely oblivious to us. "Are you a familiar?"

"I'm a witch." The smile slipped and hardened into an angry slash. "Not all of my kind are enslaved sycophants. Many of us reject vampires and relationships with them."

"Oh." I couldn't think of anything else to say. I reeked of Julian, according to her. I doubted she thought very highly of me. Squaring my shoulders, I looked her dead in the eye. "I don't know much about that. I've only been part of this world for a little while. My mate is a vampire."

"Mate?" The word echoed on her plum-stained lips. "I suppose that explains the Grancino. May I ask the family name?"

"Rousseaux," I said, uncertain I wanted to give her more info.

She snorted, her eyes dancing. "Let me guess. Julian?"

I hesitated. "Yes."

"Good luck," she said. "He's a grumpy bastard, and his family..."

I didn't need her to tell me why I might need luck where they were concerned. "It's complicated. They don't exactly approve, since I'm not a fam—" I cut myself off before I used the term again. "Uh, witch."

I waited for her to tell me that I was wrong. I waited for her to confirm the suspicion that had been growing inside my mind since Julian's thoughts had found their way into my head. Since that spark of what had to be magic passed between our hands.

"Maybe not." She shrugged her leather tote higher onto her shoulder. "But there's magic in you, and if there's magic in you, it has to come out."

"I thought magic was gone."

"Yes. No. It's not what it once was. True magic is rare, but it sleeps in the veins."

"Even in humans?" I asked with a dry tongue. "I thought that faded long ago."

"Magic is life, so yes, even human blood still has a spark of whatever created us. Vampires still drink blood, right?" she asked me bluntly as if she worried these were things I hadn't considered—or hadn't been told.

Jacqueline had been honest with me, but even she'd admitted there were lots of things that neither species understood.

"I guess I must have a little more magic than most humans," I said.

"Human?" She giggled at me. "You're not human, honey."

"But...I'm...not...a...witch." I forced each word out. "You said..."

"I said *maybe not*," she corrected me. "You obviously have no magical ties, or you would know. Your mother would have told you. But I think you are right. I don't think you're a witch. It doesn't feel right."

My heart constricted so painfully that I thought I might be dying. I wasn't human. I wasn't a witch. I'd thought my life would be simpler when I returned to San Francisco, but I found myself waist-deep in a muddy mess and couldn't be freed.

"I should go," I blurted out. I needed air. I needed to breathe. I knew she was telling me the truth, but truth without answers was somehow worse. At least until I knew who I was.

"I've upset you," she murmured, shaking her head. "I didn't mean to do that. If I had known that you were…"

In the dark? An idiot? A freak? I thought of a million ways to finish that sentence.

"Magic is a gift," she finally said. "Don't be afraid of it. But be careful. Messing with magic you don't understand can tear you apart."

"You're wrong," I said quickly, making up my mind. "If I had magic in me, someone would have sensed it. Julian. Or his mother."

"All magic is the same to vampires," she said with a wave. "Yours is faint, but it grew louder when you played. I'm sure Julian's felt it a little, although if you recently mated… His mother would definitely sense it. She's very intuitive." She spoke as if she knew Sabine; judging from Diana's downturned lips, she wasn't a huge fan of the vampire matriarch.

"You think she'd be happy I'm her son's mate," I said bitterly.

"Pureblood vampires want magic, but they need to control it. They pretend other witches don't exist. They act like they protect us. But the truth is that you are something new. Something *other*."

"What am I?" The question was a knife to my chest.

"I don't know," she said softly, lowering her voice further as the professors began walking toward us. "Maybe there is magical blood in your veins. Witch families have died out over the centuries. It's possible one of your ancestors was a witch. But…"

"But?" I pressed.

"How do you control what you don't understand?" Her eyes flickered to the approaching men, and she smiled warmly, holding up one finger. Their footsteps paused. "It's possible you aren't something new. Maybe you are something forgotten."

She smiled at the men once more, and they started toward us again. I made awkward small talk with them as we left the theater. I promised to visit Lassiter and check in with MacLeod, and I could have sworn I heard an imperious voice whisper in my mind.

Liar.

Diana and I walked together but didn't speak until we reached the exit. I followed her into the parking garage, wishing that I hadn't insisted on driving here by myself. I wasn't sure it was safe to be behind the wheel while my mind was consumed with the thoughts Diana had planted in my head.

"I'm this way." She pointed to a row farther down. "It was nice to meet you, but be careful with that vampire and his whole filthy rich family. Purebloods are ruthless. Stay vigilant."

I nodded, but not because I appreciated the warning. I trusted Julian. His family? Maybe not so much. But we would figure that out. It was clear Diana held no love for vampires. She walked a few feet away, and I called out, "How? How do I figure out what I am?"

She walked back toward me after a brief hesitation. Slipping her bag from her shoulder, she withdrew a thin, linen card. "I would start with your family. Ask them."

"I don't have family, really," I said sadly. "It's just my mom and me."

"Start there. She might know something, even old stories about weird family members."

I stared at her, warmth draining from my face. My mother did know something—something about vampires. "My mom—"

The lights in the parking garage went out, cutting me off mid-sentence. The afternoon sunlight trickled in from a few rows over, but the winter sun couldn't compete with the swallowing darkness of concrete.

"Shit." I heard Diana fumbling in her bag. She turned on her cell phone flashlight and then froze. "Thea, walk toward me slowly."

I hesitated a fraction of a second, surprised by the odd request.

"Thea!" she snapped, jerking me into action.

I was halfway to her when a dark-haired woman stepped out of the shadows and into the light cast by the phone. Her glossy hair swept the shoulders of her leather motorcycle jacket. Her features were sharp and brutally feminine. Her body, while slender, wasn't skinny. The cropped shirt under her jacket showcased defined abs, and her tight black pants revealed strong quads. She sauntered closer, her movements too graceful to be human. *Vampire*. Dread sluiced through me.

"Come here," Diana ordered.

"Come now, sister." The vampire clicked her tongue against her teeth. I couldn't see them, but I knew her fangs were out and ready. I sensed it. "We're not enemies. You're not a familiar. We have no quarrel. I'm here for her."

As she spoke, I spotted a red scar rising past the neckline of her shirt. It reminded me of the masks the other vampires had worn during the attack. I swallowed against my swelling fear and pushed it back down. "I'm afraid we haven't been introduced."

"Interesting," the vampire said in a bored tone. She circled around us, studying me from other angles. "Julian's pet has fangs of her own, but I doubt you're brave enough to bite."

I backed closer to Diana. Not for my own protection but to shield her. "Try me."

"And she's brave, too, but I smell that fear on you, mortal." She paused. "And something else. Hmmm, what's hiding underneath your skin?" She stalked closer, and Diana grabbed my arm. There was a jolt where our skin touched: her magic. "Should I peel it off to find out what you are?"

"Let's google it instead," I bit out, trying to buy myself enough time to think.

"It must be torture for him to put up with you. So young and inexperienced." Her nostrils flared as she took a deep breath. "Is that why he hasn't bedded you?"

I froze, but slowly my fingers fumbled, feeling for the zipper of my cello case.

The homicidal woman was having too much fun to notice. "You can tell. His smell is there but not joined with yours. I suppose the rumor that you're his mate is untrue."

"Why would you care?" My thumb snagged on the zipper pull. "Let me guess—you were hoping to bag a Rousseaux brother during the season?"

Her barking laugh bounced against the concrete. She flung a finger at Diana. "You, leave. Tell no one."

I twisted to find Diana staring at me with apologetic eyes. Her body tried to move, but she was fighting it—trying to resist the compulsion.

"It's okay," I murmured. "I can handle this."

She backed away, dropping the card in her hand. Diana cast a look at the vampire, who snarled.

"Run, witch!"

Diana dashed away, disappearing down a row of vehicles. The vampire chuckled darkly. The sound skittered down my spine, and I waited for any opportunity to make a move.

"Your friend left you a card," she said in a mocking voice. "Pick it up."

My body snapped forward, compelled to move, and my cello case dropped to the ground. I prayed it did its job. My fingers closed over the card, and I saw my chance. Lunging for the case, I yanked open the zipper and grabbed my bow. Standing, I brandished it like a sword.

The vampire stared for a moment before bursting out laughing. "What are you going to do? Play me a symphony?"

"It's wood," I said simply.

Her eyes narrowed, but she didn't seem afraid. Just annoyed. "Brave and stupid. Terrible combination. Do you really think you can stake me with it?"

"Do I really have a choice?" I asked.

"Is that any way to treat family?" she crooned. "After I came all this way to meet my brother's new *mate*?"

I hated the way it sounded so much that it took me a second to realize what she'd said. I nearly dropped the bow. Brother? But Julian only had one sister. It couldn't be… "Camila?"

"You sound so surprised." She shot me a feline smile. "I announced I was coming. Didn't you get my toasty housewarming present? I left it in your bed."

I blinked. "Paris? You started the fire?"

"What better way to warm a house? Pity you weren't in it," she purred. "Now, come with me, *pet*. I hear that's what he calls you. I have a message for my brother that only you can deliver."

I locked my knees, refusing to move, my cello bow still extended between us. My feet tried to go anyway, and I buckled, falling to my knees. It took every ounce of effort I had to resist her demand.

"Stop being such a stubborn bitch," she demanded. "I'll make it quick. A lovely little kiss. I'm sure you know how well vampires kiss."

No. No. No.

My body lifted, my hands pushing me up into a crawling position. My legs tangled in my skirt as I started to move. The delicate fabric tore, and my knee scraped against the cement. I clawed forward, throwing every ounce of energy I had into resisting her compulsion. But I couldn't. It hooked me through the middle, urging me back toward her. She was going to kill me, and Julian... What would he do when he discovered what had happened? When my death delivered the news she was alive?

"Come here," she ordered with a vicious snarl, and I felt myself start to rise—start to move toward her.

A piercing squeal cut through the air, and I whipped my head toward it, Camila doing the same, to find blinding lights barreling toward us.

CHAPTER SIXTEEN

Julian

I rechecked my Rolex. I'd expected Thea to return to the apartment nearly an hour ago. Outside, the afternoon sun faded to orange along the horizon. As the holidays approached, winter stole more and more of the day. I paced the windows that overlooked the street below, watching for the BMW to appear, hoping she hadn't wrecked it.

It wasn't that I didn't trust my mate to drive my car. I didn't care about it. I could easily buy a new one. But Thea? The longer we were separated, the more I began to worry, especially since she'd planned to come straight back after finishing. Or maybe she was fine but the performance had gone poorly? I should have driven her myself. But she hadn't wanted me there.

A distraction. That's what she had called me. I'd been offended and flattered.

I took my phone out, hoping to see a missed call or message. But my screen was blank, as it had been the last ten times I'd looked at it. I decided against calling and risking actually distracting her. She would be here any minute. I scanned the room to make sure everything was in place.

The candles I'd lit drooped with spent wax, puddling on the wood floors beneath them. I suspected the rose petals I'd carefully sprinkled from here to the door weren't as fresh as they'd been an hour ago. I'd picked them up from the florist on the corner a few minutes after Thea had kissed me goodbye.

I slipped my phone back into my pocket, feeling it knock against the velvet box that was beginning to feel like a lead weight.

Romance. She wanted *romance*. I would give it to her.

But the longer I stood waiting, the stupider I felt. Was this romantic or just some cheesy copy of stuff they did in movies? Thea might want romance. I just wanted my ring on her finger. It was a stupid, human impulse. My own parents had married on a whim with no grand gestures. Every few decades, I'd be invited to a vampire wedding, which was more about showing off new alliances than love.

I'd never wanted a wife or a wedding. And now I wanted both. I wanted to see Thea in a white dress, walking down the aisle. I wanted to take her to bed after and claim her as my mate. It was fucking old-fashioned, and I didn't care. I was old-fashioned. Thea wanted romance. She wanted a fairy tale, even if she'd fallen for the villain instead of the prince. And all I wanted was to make her happy.

But the chances of that wedding were almost nonexistent. Neither of our parents would want to attend. We'd be lucky to avoid action by the Vampire Council, a wrinkle I'd purposefully forgotten to mention to Thea. Not that I could avoid it much longer. By now, word would have spread that I'd missed more than a few social events. My absence would be noted and investigated. Jacqueline might think they were bluffing, but I wasn't sure.

And then there was the issue of Thea's magic. I didn't understand it any more than her. I wouldn't bind her to me in any way—by mating, tethering, or even marrying her—until I had answers for her. She deserved to know who she was before I asked her to make me part of that identity. If I had to wait my whole life, living off scraps of our love, I would.

Fifteen more minutes passed while I brooded, asking myself if my ring was good enough, then if I deserved to have her wear my ring at all. When my phone vibrated, I sighed, grateful for the interruption and relieved to hear from her. But it wasn't Thea calling.

"Yes?" I answered in a clipped tone.

"Where are you?" Benedict asked. "Did you really leave Paris?"

I understood why Thea was constantly rolling her eyes. Had my family always been this dramatic? "I think you already know the answer."

"I wanted to hear it from you," he said flatly. "Please tell me you didn't go after her."

"I think you already know the answer to that," I repeated.

Benedict cursed, and I heard ice tinkle against crystal. "Do you have any idea the mess I'm dealing with here?"

"You?" I fingered the velvet box in my pocket. "Why do you need to be involved? Jacqueline is handling it."

"Your best friend doesn't play nicely with authority figures," he reminded me. "Did you forget Rome?"

I didn't bother to answer him. I'd never forget Rome. Rome would never forget Jacqueline. Even after all this time, the incident followed Jacqueline like a shadow. "It's just a house."

"You think I'm worried about the house?" he roared.

I didn't say anything. I couldn't. Benedict never lost his temper. It was why he handled the family's relationships with other bloodlines. But he was angrier than I'd ever heard him.

"You defied a direct order from the Council."

"The Council exists to guide, not govern. I should have told them that when they tried to enact their stupid Rites into law," I snarled. "Regardless, I'm losing patience with their constant interference."

"You know what your duty is," Benedict groaned. "You can't avoid settling down forever. It's time to take a wife."

"I'm not avoiding anything." My fingers closed on the box. If only he knew the truth. "I'm in the process of settling down right now."

"You can't honestly be planning to marry her," he said, then I heard him gulp whatever he was drinking.

"She's my mate," I said. "I won't marry anyone else."

"If you put a ring on her finger, you might as well draw a target on her forehead," he warned me. "The Council made it clear—"

"That they would kill her?" I finished. "They'll have to go through me."

"You really think you can stand against vampires who are thousands of years older than you?"

"Since I've fought most of their battles over the last few centuries, I think I have a fighting chance," I said drily. "I haven't seen many of them on the battlefields."

"Be reasonable. Is she worth dying over?" he asked in a strained voice.

"Few things are worth dying for, but love will always top the list."

He paused, and I knew he was thinking. Benedict did nothing without calculating its consequences. Every decision he made was perfectly tuned to his or the family's needs.

"Have you ever been in love?" I asked him softly.

"What?" Another pause. "No, I suppose I haven't."

"Then you'll have to take my word for it. I've chosen Thea. I will not change my mind." I left it at that, hoping he wouldn't argue.

"But family duty—"

"She is my family," I cut him off, disappointed.

"And us?" he pressed. "Will you choose her over us?"

"I don't want to, but I will." Just like Thea had chosen me.

"If you do this, they will hunt you down—both of you. You won't stand a chance without the family behind you," he pointed out.

"Then I hope the family stands behind me, but if you don't accept Thea as a Rousseaux, she and I will stand alone."

He let out a string of curses, using words in so many languages even I was surprised. Finally, he sighed. "I'll talk with everyone. See what I can do."

"Brother, you don't have to be in the middle of this."

"Trust me. When Mother finds out that you went to America for the human, it will be better to be on a separate continent. She might rip your head off herself."

"Indeed." My lips pursed. "I suppose I shouldn't bring Thea around for a while."

"No," Benedict said thoughtfully. "I think you should join us.

Staying away only makes it look like you're hiding. There's safety in numbers. The Council is less likely to take action if you're amongst us, not undermining them or The Rites, even if you're not participating the way you were supposed to. Returning to the season might be safer than staying away, and it will give me time to work my own magic."

"I'm not sure you're capable of swaying the Council or our family to accept Thea. I won't place her in harm's way."

"Julian, you already did when you brought her into this world. Did you think you could return to the humans and keep her safe? The best place for both of you is in our world."

"Unfortunately, my house is a large pile of ash."

"Paris is over. The season is moving to Corfu," he told me.

"Greece?" I said with surprise. "In December? It will rain the whole time."

"Not in the quarter. Anyway, it's something to do with the next Rite," he said. I could almost hear him shrug.

So we hadn't missed the second one. More bad news. "And you think we should come?"

"I think that if you want your family behind you, you need to ask us. In person. Any fight brought to our door because of you will be personal, brother… We'll be in Corfu by the end of the week."

I considered it for a moment. It was stupid to go, but it was suicide to stay. I glanced at the candles, which were nearly spent. I wanted a life with Thea. If Benedict was right—if I could get my family on board—we stood a chance of swaying the Council to our perspective and living a life *not* on the run. It felt like a long shot, but it was the only one I had. "We'll be there. I'll have Celia find us a place to stay."

"No," he advised. "Stay with the family. It will be safer."

"Do you really believe that?" I asked, but he had already hung up.

I busied myself cleaning up the petals and candles. As much as I wanted to see my ring on her finger, it was a bad idea to make things official before we met my family in Greece. Sabine would see our engagement as a threat to be problem-solved. It was better to play the game as Benedict suggested and win them to our side first.

If that was even possible, which I very much doubted. Walking into the bedroom, I took the ring box out and placed it back into my drawer. It would have to wait for a better time. I slid it shut as my phone rang. Relief washed over me when I saw Thea's name on the screen.

"I was beginning to worry about you," I admitted as I took the call.

But it wasn't Thea's voice that answered.

CHAPTER SEVENTEEN

Julian

"Miss me?"

The voice curled softly around my memories like a housecat. But under the friendly warmth ran a dangerous current. I froze, staring out the window at the misty twilight now hanging over the city. The thick fog blurred the world and made the city lights dance in and out of view. A dozen disturbing realizations hit me at once, but three seemed the most relevant.

Camila was alive.

It had been my sister I'd seen attacking purebloods at the Paris Opera.

And she had Thea's phone.

"I've been trying to reach you." She continued in a bored drawl. "I even sent a gift to your home in Paris, but you've been so preoccupied with this mortal of yours."

She was responsible for Paris.

She'd burned down my house.

She had killed Hughes.

And if she was willing to do that… "Where is she?" Cold fury ran through my blood and found itself in my words.

"Your little pet? Darling nickname, by the way," Camila said, and I stopped breathing. "She's around here somewhere."

"Tell me where she is!" I roared. "Or I will—"

"Kill me?" she interrupted loudly. She *tsked* into the phone. "It turns out I'm not easy to kill. Am I?"

I didn't care that she was my sister. My twin. I didn't care that I'd spent the last three decades thinking she was dead. I didn't care if every question swimming in the back of my brain went unanswered. Because there was only one thing that burned brighter than the grief that had nearly consumed me for all those years. A driving instinct that placed Thea above all else—above my own family, even Camila. "If you touch my mate, I will rip you apart. Now, *where is she*?"

"Julian," she cooed, "you know the rules. She isn't your mate. Not until you *fuck* her. I wonder. Why haven't you? Fucked her, I mean? She's pretty enough for a mortal."

"That's none of your business," I said through gritted teeth. I clenched my phone so tightly I heard it crack. Camila had been at the opera. She'd been with the people attacking the vampires. But she had saved me. Why? I might have thought it was love, but there was nothing but bone-chilling hatred in her voice.

"But you'll fuck anything that moves. All of you boys did. It's the only thing you have in common. You must get it from our faithless father." Her spite stung more because it was true. I'd never denied myself the pleasure of a woman before. Neither had Sebastian or Benedict. Or any of my brothers.

Camila, on the other hand, had married as a virgin. She'd been tethered to a husband who took full advantage of that.

"There was nothing we could do. We tried. We all tried."

"And you all failed," she snarled. "But nothing leashes me now, Julian. You could have saved me, and you didn't."

And there it was. The truth no one in our family had been able to admit. We had tried over and over again, but we had failed her. Camila had died bound to a cruel man who twisted their bond to suit his whims. Then, I'd gone to sleep, unable to face a world without her. Until Thea, my twin had been my other half. Watching what she went through had nearly destroyed me. I'd never forgiven myself for her apparent not-death.

It seemed Camila hadn't forgiven me, either.

But I couldn't allow my mistake to put Thea in danger.

"This isn't about Thea. Whatever happened," I said, feeling more strained with each passing second, "wherever you've been, leave her out of this."

"Hell," she said in a soft, cold voice. Behind her, a foghorn bellowed faintly. "I went to hell, and they made me their queen."

If only she could see—if only she could remember—how hopeless the situation had been, how different this was. "You didn't have a choice. You were tethered."

Another foghorn bellowed, sounding slightly louder than the first. I glanced at my watch. Two blasts so far. The second hand ticked as I waited for the third—and confirmation of her location.

"I'm free now," she hissed. "No thanks to any of you."

"We're your family. We tried to intervene. If we had known you were alive, we would have come for you." Any second now.

"What a lovely excuse for failure." Laughter pealed through the line, unearthly and dangerous. The sound clawed against my frayed nerves. "For hundreds of years, I was the good one. The pure one. The most valuable bartering chip in the family collection, and when it was time, I was traded for an alliance. But now, everyone cares about feelings and is cool with you shacking up with some mortal because you claim to be mates."

The third foghorn sounded. The pattern was familiar; timeless, in a way. I'd listened to the Golden Gate sing its warning song to ships off and on for over a century. She couldn't be far from there, judging by its volume in the background. Not much to go on, but it was something. I couldn't stand here and argue. Not if she had my mate.

"You clearly haven't talked to our family," I said, striding toward the door. "They aren't *cool* with anything, especially Thea."

"She has no family name, but her magic isn't enough to please Mother? She reeks of it. She's fertile, you know." A pause. "Is that why you won't bed her? You always hated children."

I stopped in my tracks. There was magic inside Thea, I was certain of that, even if I couldn't explain it. But I had never considered…

"Thea isn't a witch. She can't bear my children any more than a werewolf could."

"How would you know? There are things the Council keeps from you. Things I could help you understand." Her icy anger slipped for a moment, becoming something that sounded strangely like desperation or a startling invitation. But when she spoke again, the rage had returned. "She's not human. Don't tell me otherwise. You've tasted her. I can smell that much. You're feeding on her like a buffet!"

"Camila, what do you want with her?" I asked quietly. "Just tell me how to make this right, and I will, but…please, *please* don't take her from me."

She ended the call.

Blind panic surged through me, and I lunged for the door. Throwing it open, I remembered I'd sent the car with Thea. I fumbled for my phone, trying to think of who to call. Celia would answer, but she was on the other end of the city. It was twenty minutes in light traffic to the bridge at this time of day.

My fist flew, punching a dent into the steel door and cracking open my knuckles. I smelled the blood, but I felt no pain. I couldn't feel anything else. I was a void. An abyss. I should never have allowed Thea to go to that performance without arming her. I'd told myself my smell would protect her. It might have with anyone else, but I hadn't known Camila…

No, I hadn't wanted to *believe* Camila could be alive and that she'd chosen to hide that from me.

I'd chosen to believe I'd been mistaken about seeing her, and now it would cost me the only treasure I couldn't live without.

My mate. Thea. We'd had weeks. I wanted lifetimes. The moments we shared were stolen, restrained, confined by my own fear. I'd told myself it would be enough—that whatever scraps I could have of her were worth more than a life without knowing her. And now, standing at the precipice of losing her too soon—too fucking soon—I saw all the lies I'd told myself.

I wanted her. I wanted her in every way. As my mate. As my wife.

As my partner.

I didn't care what she was, witch or human or something else. I didn't care what magic ran hidden in her veins.

I didn't care if she was tethered to me, because facing the loss of her, I knew I would never abuse that bond.

And now?

It was too late.

CHAPTER EIGHTEEN

Thea

I clutched the cup of coffee in both hands, my fingers splaying over its warm porcelain. Heat soaked into my skin, reminding me I was no longer in that damp parking garage. My eyes skittered to the scrapes covering my hands. I couldn't imagine what the rest of me looked like or what Julian would say when he saw me. Outside the diner, night crept across the sky, black erasing the foggy gray day. Night calmed me. I didn't fear it. Not when my mate wore darkness with such graceful ease. Soon, I would be in his arms. First, I needed to collect myself, which was why I'd taken Diana up on coffee instead of immediately calling him.

"You're thinking of him," Diana said with a cautious smile.

I blinked, staring at her over my cup. "How did you know that?"

"It's one of my family's gifts—to sense emotions," she explained. "It used to be stronger—or easier to wield, at least." She picked up a pink sugar packet and shook it. She tore it open, then dumped it into her own untouched cup. "It's different for each of us. I usually sense strong emotions. It's why I love music."

"Oh?" I lifted an eyebrow, grateful for the momentary distraction.

"I feel the emotions that went into the composition, and when I play, it's like all that magic is at my fingertips." She paused as if considering what to say next. "I felt it when you played in a way I don't with most musicians. Maybe you have some of our bloodline in you."

"I don't know much about my family," I admitted. "My dad was out of the picture before I was born. Mom never talked about him or his family. And if my mom has any magic in her, she never used it. She's been sick for years. Cancer." I bit my lip, realizing that I'd just dumped half my life story on a stranger.

"Cancer?" Diana repeated. Something flashed in her eyes, but she continued breezily past the subject, as if sensing I didn't really want to wade through family tragedies at the moment. "Your love almost sounds like music. It's lovely. *Real*."

I smiled, sighing as I nodded. "Yes, it is."

"I can't say I condone a mortal linking herself to a vampire. Those relationships usually get messy, but if he feels the same—"

"He does," I interjected. It was no longer a matter of debate in my mind. The mating bond might not be complete, we might not be tethered or married or joined, but there was absolute certainty in our love that gave me peace. I clung to it to keep myself from freaking out over what had happened in the garage.

"And the vampire who came after you—did you know her?" Diana hadn't pressed me for any information since she'd saved me in the garage.

I shook my head. "Not really."

"That's *not really* an answer," she pointed out.

"I don't understand it, myself. I think she planned to hurt me to send Julian a message." It wasn't that I distrusted Diana. I didn't really know her. But telling her what I knew would only lead to more questions, and right now, my head was swimming with them.

"It's dangerous to be in love with a vampire." She took a sip of her coffee and grimaced.

If it was bad, I couldn't tell. I was still too numb. I only cared that it was hot. "I know, but I don't really have a choice."

"You can't outsmart fate. If he is truly your mate, you never had a chance."

I swallowed. "He says that it's rare. I don't think... I don't think either of us understands it."

"Comprehension always fails men when their dicks get involved," she muttered, shaking her head. "It used to be more common, if the family grimoire is to be believed. There's a spell in ours that is supposed to aid in finding one's true mate."

"A spell?" I knew so little about witches that I found myself fascinated, and the distraction soothed my nerves. "Does it work?"

"I think every woman in my family has tried it, but no luck so far." She laughed. "Most of the spells don't work. Only a handful still have any potency, and they mostly rely on earth magic."

"And true magic? Do you know what happened to it?"

"There are stories. Some believe it's dead, but it's still inside us. Sometimes I feel it scratching at my bones. Still, very little true magic remains accessible, and using it comes at a cost." Her face darkened, and an icy finger traced up my neck. I didn't want to know the cost, judging by her reaction. "Being around vampires often stokes magic. It's why so many familiars, as you call them, take vampire partners."

"I thought it was for protection and"—I blushed at the thought—"babies."

"I'm not sure I should speak so freely," she admitted. "There are things my kind doesn't reveal to vampires. It's safer for us."

I nodded, understanding where she was coming from. "I'd like to tell you I wouldn't share it with anyone, but if Julian asks…I usually tell him the truth."

"Good," she said, surprising me. "You should. Honestly, though, I don't care. My family doesn't approve of relationships between species, even though some claim that a vampire partner helps stir the blood. Or the magic in it, at least."

"But then why wouldn't you…?"

"It is a cost we choose not to pay," she explained, reminding me of what she'd said moments before.

"But not the only cost you can pay?" I guessed.

"No. There are other ways. Some dark. Some light. My family chooses the light."

"So, I won't be running into you at any of the season's parties?"

I asked drily.

"For more reasons than one." She snorted. "I'm much happier away from a life filled with other supernatural creatures. Luck brought me to you."

A spark glinted in her eyes, and I heard her voice in my head. *Or maybe fate.*

I looked down quickly, red coloring my cheeks.

"You can hear me when I *speak to you*," she said quietly. "I thought you did back there, but I wasn't sure. That's rare magic. Can you speak back?"

My mouth fell open, and I shook my head. "It just started. I thought it might be a mating thing."

"Maybe," she said but didn't elaborate. "Whatever you are is a mystery."

Camila's words resurfaced. *Should I peel it off to find out what you are?* A tremble racked my body. I had questions about what was happening to me, but if it took extreme measures to find out what I was, I'd rather not know.

"Thank you," I said after a moment. Diana's forehead wrinkled in response, and I clarified, "For coming back for me. It must have been hard to fight the compulsion."

"It was easy." She shrugged. "She told me to leave, to tell no one, and to run. I did all of those things. She didn't tell me not to hit her with my car." Diana's mouth curved into a wolfish grin.

I flinched, remembering the wet crunch Camila's body had made as she hit the hood of Diana's Subaru. Camila had flown across the garage, hit a cement column, and crumpled to a heap on the ground. When Diana yelled at me to get inside her car, I'd done it without thinking. All I cared about was getting out of there, because I knew the truth. "She's not dead."

"No." Diana shook her head. "I imagine that she's already on her feet, but she'll need a few hours to heal. I think I broke a few bones." I didn't miss the pride hiding in her words. "You should expect her to come after you again."

Diana might not know who had attacked me, but she was smart

enough to know it was personal.

"Then I should get home and tell Julian." I couldn't avoid it any longer, and he had to be getting worried. I hadn't given him an exact time on when I would be done with my performance, but he hadn't called. "Of course, the car is in the parking garage."

I fished my hand into my bag, searching for my phone to call an Uber, but came up empty.

"What's wrong?" Diana asked when my eyes closed in frustration.

"My phone." I heaved a breath and dug deeper into the bag. "I think I might have dropped it back there."

"I can take you to his place," she offered.

"Like you said, she might come after me again." I couldn't risk Diana's life one more time.

"Strength in numbers."

It was sweet to say, but we both knew that the homicidal vampire who'd come after me had let her go. "The longer you stick with me, the more danger you're in."

"I think I can handle another twenty minutes." She picked up her bag and stood, then her eyes landed on the cello case leaning against my side of the booth. "At least you had your priorities straight. A new phone is easy. A new Grancino is harder to come by."

I mustered a small smile, knowing she was trying to distract me. "You're sure that it's not a problem?"

"As long as you know the address."

"It's The Armory," I said quietly.

Diana rolled her eyes, muttering something about billionaire vampires, and then tilted her head toward the door. "Let's get you home."

• • •

She dropped me off in front of the brick fortress, making me swear to go straight inside and lock the door. I had no problems with those conditions. The weight on my shoulders eased as soon as I pressed my thumb to the biometric scanner. The heavy steel door clicked open, and I waved at Diana before slipping inside. Leaving my cello by the door, I turned toward the stairs. My thighs hurt just looking at them.

I'd taken a quick trip to the restroom before we'd left and done what I could to minimize the damage, but there was no hiding my torn dress or scraped knees. I'd thrown myself hard to the ground when Diana came around that corner in her car and scraped the skin off one cheek in the process.

I touched it gingerly, wondering how long I'd have to live with it before I'd be able to cover it with makeup. I groaned as I took the first step, my thighs burning from some pulled muscles.

Thea?

Julian's voice whispered in my head. Tentative but wild. Desperate. Broken. It shattered any resistance I felt toward those stairs. I needed to reach him. *Now.*

And then a shadow fell across the staircase. I glanced up and found him at the top, staring down at me with white-faced horror.

Did I look that bad?

Before I could ask, I found myself in his arms. My mortal brain didn't process a single movement. One second, he was standing all the way up there. Then, he was with me. Warm and strong and real. Wet heat prickled my eyes as I tucked myself against him. Salt stung the wound on my cheek as tears fell.

For one terrible moment, I'd faced my death. At that moment, I'd only cared about one thing: that I would never see him again.

Julian cradled me to him, clutching me tightly as if I might slip from his hands. Finally, he pulled back and studied me. The whites of his eyes darkened, blood rage taking hold. For once, I found it oddly comforting.

"What happened?" he growled. "Did... Are you hurt?"

I didn't know how to tell him. I bit my lip and shook my head. "Bumps, scrapes. I'm fine."

He released a reedy breath. "I thought you were gone. I thought I'd lost you."

"I'm right here." I placed my palm on his cheek. "But there's something I have to tell you...about who attacked me."

"I know," he said hollowly. "She called a few minutes ago. She had your phone. I thought…"

My mouth formed an *O* shape, horror cascading through me. She had made him believe she'd killed me or hurt me, and I'd been out having coffee. Then an even darker thought hit me. "Wait, did you already know Camila was alive?"

A pause, followed by a shake of the head. "No. I thought I saw her that night at the opera, but I told myself it was the chaos. A mistake. Until today, I believed she was dead."

And he had mourned her. I believed him. I'd seen the grief that wrote itself across his features when he mentioned his sister. I couldn't imagine what this was doing to him—how this was tearing him apart.

"I'm so sorry," I whispered. "There was a witch, and she helped me. I didn't know I'd lost my phone, and I left the car at…the scene."

"I don't give a shit about the car," he roared, his arms tightening around me.

"Have you seen how much overnight parking costs in San Francisco?" I said weakly, but the joke didn't land.

Instead, Julian's eyes bored into me, returning to the piercing blue that always took my breath away. Even in the dim light of the stairwell, they seemed to glow that unearthly color. I realized then how rigid his shoulders remained. His body was stiff, clinging to some determination he'd made before I'd arrived.

My stomach twisted, sensing things were about to get very serious. I forced myself to hold his gaze. "What is it? What are you thinking?"

He paused, and I swore I lived an eternity waiting for him to speak.

"I'm thinking," he said slowly, his words halting but unyielding. "I'm thinking that I've changed my mind about us."

CHAPTER NINETEEN

Julian

I wasn't thinking at all. I was acting. I was giving in to instinct. I didn't know what else to do.

Thea went still in my arms, her breath catching as she hung on my words. I realized instantly how it sounded to her, especially after everything we'd been through.

"Not that, pet," I murmured, leaning down to brush a kiss across her lips. I smelled the blood on her, and my nostrils flared. But it wasn't lust I felt. It wasn't the sweet, beckoning scent that greeted me when her blood spilled freshly on my tongue. It was dry and dead, devoid of the essence that gave it flavor. Someone had hurt my mate. No. Not just someone.

My twin had hurt my mate.

Fury burned through my veins as I considered what I would do when I caught Camila. I wouldn't enjoy killing my twin in the way I might if Thea's attacker had been someone else. But I would end Camila for what she'd done, and I would end her thoroughly this time.

A palm settled over my chest, and I felt a slight jolt. I snapped back to the moment and looked down at Thea's hand in surprise. My eyes traveled up to her, but there was no shock. Only a sort of tired resignation at yet another twist for us.

"I felt it, too," was all she said.

I studied her, wondering how she could be so small and yet so strong. It radiated from her. "Later, I want to hear what happened," I said carefully. She nodded once, biting her lower lip. She seemed to understand what I didn't say. I wanted to know the details when I was calmer. Once I'd had a chance to appreciate that she was safe. Telling me now might result in sending my blood rage into overdrive, and I wasn't sure I'd be able to stop myself from instantly hunting Camila down. Anything standing in my way... I took a deep breath. "I have a question to ask you, but first, I need to tell you a story."

"Okay." She offered me a loving smile that loosened some of the anger gripping my heart.

I carried her from the private entry iupstairs to the apartment, pausing to lock all the doors. It seemed impossible that anyone could get past the biometric security system. Still, considering that Camila was back from the dead, the unthinkable was now on the table.

"Bed or couch?" I asked.

"Do you want to talk or..." Thea teased, and I knew she was trying to put me at ease.

It might have been a joke, but I realized she was right. After this evening's events, the bed was probably a dangerous option. I wasn't certain I'd be able to stop myself from claiming her—and I knew she damned well wouldn't stop me, either, once she knew... "Good point, but if you would be more comfortable... Or do you need to rest first?"

She groaned, craning her head to kiss me. "Julian, I am fine. I will tell you if I need anything."

"So, I shouldn't ask if you want a glass of water or some coffee?" I managed a painful grin as I leaned down and placed her on the couch.

That earned me another eye roll. She folded her legs under her and grabbed a throw pillow. "A glass of water, please."

You're just trying to make me feel better, I thought halfway to the kitchen, allowing my mind to reach out like my friend had described.

"Maybe," Thea said from the couch, sounding amused.

I got her the water anyway. I took it to her and then disappeared into the next room. I dug around in the bathroom, searching through the human necessities that Celia had acquired per my request. Finally, I found a small first aid kit.

Thea watched me as I returned to the living room. The glass of water remained untouched in one hand, her other arm coiled tightly around the pillow. Under her quiet strength, I felt something else stirring. Fear. Concern. But one look in her eyes told me those were all secondary to the emotion churning in her core. It was curiosity.

"I can heal you the slow way." I waved the first aid kit. Then I swept my tongue over my teeth. "Or the fast way."

"I think the slow way is fine," she tried to sound casual—tried to make it sound like nothing had happened. Did she know I wanted to rip my sister apart for what she'd done? Was she trying to defuse me before I detonated? "I'm not sure it's even necessary. I washed them after."

I ignored her resistance and knelt before her. Unzipping the pack, I took out a few bandages, some alcohol pads, and a small tube of antibiotic cream. Reaching for her hands, I examined them, doing my best to remain calm as I took in the raw pink flesh and newly clotted scratches. She was right. They weren't medically serious.

They were very serious to me.

"What story do you want to tell me?" she asked as I set to work.

"One without a happy ending," I said quietly as I dabbed an alcohol pad over a large patch of road rash. "Although, maybe it has no ending at all."

She winced from the sting of the alcohol but didn't say anything. I picked up the cream and began to apply it. "My parents had nearly given up on pureblood children when my mother became pregnant with my sister and me. She says they waited—that there were too many wars after they first married. Maybe it's the truth. My father can't seem to stay away from a battlefield." My mouth curved a little, thinking of how many times I'd been dragged along. "They were considered quite old when they had us and had been married for some time."

"How long?" Thea asked softly.

"Nearly two thousand years," I answered. Her eyes widened a bit, but she remained silent for me to continue. "They met around the founding of Rome. My father was helping sack the Sabines, and my mother tried to free some of the women they took as slaves."

"Sabines?" she repeated.

"She took her people's name after that. It reminded everyone, even my father, of where she came from. She hated living in Rome, hated the reminder of what they did to her people, so she took that name to remember and to warn that she might have chosen a Roman, but she was her own person."

"That sounds like her," Thea murmured. Despite her strained relationship with my mother, she smiled a little. "What was her name before?"

"She claims she doesn't remember." I doubted that, but I'd never pressured her to tell me. "My father claimed it was love at first sight. She claimed he'd kidnapped her."

Thea's lips pressed into a thin line, her eyes sparkling, and I knew she was thinking of her first encounter with me.

"It runs in the family, I guess," I admitted. "But despite both being young vampires from ancient bloodlines, no children came."

"I thought they waited," Thea said.

"Maybe, at first, but my father tells the story differently. He told me once how she wept for decades when no children came. It nearly tore them apart. He wanted to make a family, believing she would find joy in choosing and turning new children. But she refused. So, they remained childless until we came along. After that, they hoped for more born children but began to concede to creating a family. When I was still very young by vampire standards, I got my first brother and another and another and another until Mother decided it was enough. I think my father wanted to build his own army."

"But no other sisters?" she prompted.

I shook my head. "My sister was the family jewel. As beautiful as my mother but with a mild, sweet nature. She was so unlike other vampires. Camila was always self-possessed and graceful. Most young vampires can't even handle being around animals without hunger getting in the way, but not Camila."

"You loved her," Thea said, putting words to what I'd left unsaid.

I nodded, my throat closing for a moment. I adjusted a bandage on Thea's right hand and reached for her left. "I mean, it was annoying to be compared to someone so perfect. But none of us really minded. We couldn't. We all adored her. So they filled the house with rowdy boys to protect their daughter. But as she grew older, my mother changed. She kept Camila home when we were given leave to go off on wild sprees or to war with our dad. I never really considered Camila might resent that. She never showed any sign that she did."

There had been only once. Camila had begged to go to a party with us, and my mother'd refused. I recalled my sister standing at the door to our Paris home, watching us leave. She never spoke of it. She didn't fight our mother's refusal. "I should have made her go into the world more, but things were changing. Magic became forbidden. Dangerous. Witches were hunted, vampires became legends, and the old gods died, replaced by new ones. Human women did not have the freedom vampire women did, so when my mother expressed concern...we all just fell into line. No one would risk Camila, not even Camila herself. And then at the beginning of the nineteenth century, The Rites were announced."

"Your first Rites weren't until then?" Thea sounded surprised.

"They'd happened a few times, but we were too young. Vampires consider anyone marrying before five hundred to be too young," I explained, earning a bemused smile. I wondered if she was also thinking about my marriage proposal. She tipped her head like she'd heard my thought, and I laughed. "Okay, nosy, little pet. Remember, it's all relative. A five-hundred-year-old vampire is like a human exiting their teenage years."

"Then you aren't really an old man." Laughter glinted in her eyes, and I couldn't help smiling.

"I am very much in my prime," I growled, nipping one of her fingers playfully. Thea shivered, but she didn't pull away.

"So, they called The Rites, and Camila ...?" She trailed off, prompting me to return to my story.

"She was older than me by a few minutes. I suspect most of society thought we would both be on the market, but I wasn't interested in marriage. Our mother didn't mind. She was obsessed with making the right match for her only daughter."

"Some things never change," Thea groused, and I nodded.

"Now I see how much worse it was for Camila," I said thoughtfully. "She wasn't just marrying a male. She was marrying a family, and there were expectations. They had to be wealthy, powerful, and one of the old bloodlines. That knocked a lot of males out of contention. We'd just gone through several revolutions. Everyone—mortal and vampire—was turning their attention to America. Camila's marriage was an opportunity to strengthen the family position."

"How romantic," Thea interjected. I met her eyes, finding them wary and conflicted.

"I know I'm not selling you on my family, nor am I attempting to gloss anything over," I admitted, "but I need you to understand what happened. I should have told you before, but…"

But I'd been afraid. Afraid not only of how a modern mortal woman would react to very traditional vampire values, but also afraid of facing the past. I should have been more vocal during the last Rites. My silence had cost my family.

Delicate fingers wrapped around mine, and I realized she'd heard my thoughts. Thea squeezed encouragingly.

I swallowed, my tongue feeling thick in my throat. "From the beginning, Camila was sought after, but one suitor stuck out. Willem Drake. He was the eldest in a line of powerful vampires."

"A vampire?" Thea's voice piqued.

"The Drakes were considered quite scandalous. They'd begun intermarrying with familiars long before any treaties or arrangements. Their blood was—*still is*—potent. Willem was the most eligible bachelor, and Camila was the prize. Everyone watched them. Their wedding was the event of that season. And Camila was utterly in love, charmed by his attentions, his flattery, his looks."

I was done with her hands, but I stayed on my knees before her.

I didn't trust myself to move. Not before I reached the story's tragic end. Not before I faced what had happened. I felt a spark of magic pass between us as though Thea held my hand—not just for comfort but to give me strength to get through this. I closed my eyes and reached for that tiny ember, allowing it to guide me out of the dark memories.

"After they were married, things changed. At first, Camila's visits with us were shorter. She seemed quiet. When we asked about her and Willem, she lied. I knew it," I said darkly. "I sensed it, but I didn't understand. And then the visits stopped altogether. Mother said they were newlyweds and it was to be expected, but soon the letters stopped, too. When he moved her from Paris to England without a word, we all began to worry.

"It took a while to get word, and when letters came, they were strange. Distant. There was none of the gentle, kind Camila in them. They felt…fake. Wrong. We received word that they planned to move to America, so we invited them for a visit." I closed my eyes, recalling the painful details. "They'd been married a couple of decades." I peeked at Thea, but she didn't comment. "And it had been years since we'd seen Camila. She was a shell. She smiled at the right times. She laughed. She talked and danced. But she wasn't there, and we could all see it. Willem was as charming and flattering as ever, so my mother decided Camila was upset over the lack of a baby. Camila wouldn't talk to her about it, but Sabine cornered one of her maids. The maid told my mother the truth about Willem…about the beatings and the punishments and the orders."

"Oh God," Thea gasped.

I forced myself to continue. "We all tried to talk to her, but she refused. She would admit nothing, but she said one thing to me…" I still recalled the haunted ache in her eyes as she spoke those words. "'*I can't tell you. He won't let me.*' And that's when we realized she was tethered. That Willem controlled her completely. He'd made her a prisoner inside her own body, bound to him with no hope of mercy. And that," I said, looking to Thea's pale face, "is why I refused to sleep with you and seal our mating bond."

Thea stayed silent, so I drove the point home. There could be no more ambiguity. She had to know the truth. She had to know why our love was doomed. "Thea, that's why you're still a virgin."

After a minute, she lifted her chin, looking a bit like a queen, and asked, "Now, what was your question?"

CHAPTER TWENTY

Julian

y lips threatened to tug into a grin, but I resisted. "I love when you're imperious, pet. We're getting there, but I'm not done with my story."

Her eyes narrowed, annoyance simmering along with her curiosity.

"But your mother must have known," Thea said, anger coating her tone. I didn't know if she was mad about our past choices or where those choices had left us. But I understood why she was upset. "If Camila wasn't allowed to have a social life before The Rites, she must have known she was a virgin."

"She did, but it was common then to save one's self for marriage. Especially among pureblood females, because it made them more marriageable."

"Don't you mean more manageable?" Thea grumbled.

I tipped my head, agreeing with her. "Most couples saw being tethered like the mating bond—mating was extremely rare even then. It ensured that whatever alliance the marriage formed would remain."

"Did your family stay allied with the Drakes?"

"At first," I said, shame washing through me. I continued quickly when I saw her horrified expression. "We thought that it would help us get her help. But you cannot break a tethering bond. Only death can sever it, and if the tether is disobeyed or threatened…" I shuddered. "And then new wars came. Terrible wars. My family was scattered across the world fighting. Willem and Camila remained in America. She gave birth to a baby. We received word through a telegram with instructions not to come. Our alliance with the Drakes ended then. My mother went to the Council, and new guidelines were enacted, warning of the dangers of tethering. She spent decades reforming old attitudes about it. Now, it's not only frowned on, it's almost forbidden. Vampires can be tortured, even executed, for bedding virgins if complaints are made. It turned some families away from the traditions and from the Council, including the Drakes."

"I see," Thea said carefully. "I had no idea your mother did that—or why."

"I think she felt responsible for what happened. We all did." I hung my head. "But it was too late to save Camila. We reached out again and again and were turned away. In 1984, we received word that she'd died in a fire with the rest of her family—her husband and her children. Everyone died." I nearly choked on the guilt I felt. "We all wondered if there was more. If she set the fire or he had—but it didn't matter. She was gone. We never freed her. We all coped differently. Mother forbade any of us to speak her name."

"That's cruel!"

"I think it hurt her too much. The loss had been long and painful, and she never gave up hope that she could free Camila. Not until the day she died. My father started having more affairs. Sebastian had rock music and cocaine. Benedict threw himself into politics. Lysander and Thoren just disappeared. They only pop up now and then. And I…"

"Went to sleep," she finished for me.

"Yes. I hid."

"You were grieving." Her voice was soothing, but it did nothing to calm the pain ravaging my guts.

"I told myself that I would never marry," I confessed, "but I swore to my family—along with my brothers—that we would never tether another soul to ours. We would never inflict that suffering on a partner. None of us has ever broken that vow."

Thea remained quiet after I finished. For a long time, we sat without speaking. Finally, she broke the silence. "And I asked you to break that promise." I shook my head, but before I could say anything, she continued, her voice breaking. "I tempted you. I pushed you. I made you face that pain over and over again. Julian, I'm so sorry."

"Don't," I stopped her. "You did nothing wrong. I should have told you her story, but I couldn't face the idea of losing you."

"But in three months," she said, sounding strained, "nothing will have changed. You will still have made that vow. The Council could still punish you. Your family—your mother—will know you broke your promise. I won't ask you to do that."

"You don't have to," I said quietly. "I've known for weeks what needs to be done."

Tears streamed down her face as her lower lip quivered, but she didn't turn away. She didn't hide from the pain she saw coming. It was how I knew I'd made the right choice.

"There is magic inside you, Thea. We both know it. Magic neither of us understands," I started. She swiped at her tears, confusion blinking on her face. "You deserve to know who you are—what that magic is that runs in your veins—before you bind yourself to me forever. I thought I might find a way around the tethering while we looked for answers."

"We will," she said fiercely.

But I shook my head, my lips turning up in a sad smile. "We've been down this path. My family and I. It's a long shot. At first, I told myself I would get you out of my system. I didn't recognize the signs of mating until Jacqueline pointed them out. I believed it was a myth until I felt it. And then, I told myself I could share you for just one night." I shut my eyes against the darkness that yawned awake at the thought. "One night in exchange for a lifetime seemed fair."

"I can do it," she offered with a forced confidence that made me love her even more. "One night. But maybe you should be in another country."

A hollow laugh slipped from me. "I can't," I confessed, and she blanched. "Any male—man or vampire—who touched you... I would kill him. I know that. I won't place that guilt on your shoulders. So I decided to give those answers to you and buy myself time. I told myself I would find a solution while we looked for the truth about your magic. But it wasn't just about preventing a tethering bond. I wanted you to know who you are. I've had nine hundred years to learn who I am. You've had twenty-two." One more confession remained—the one I needed to admit most to myself. "Once we learn the truth— once you know what you are—what if you don't want me?"

Thea inhaled sharply. She didn't move for a second, and then she sank to the ground next to me. Reaching out, she took my face in her shaking hands and forced me to look at her. "That isn't going to happen. Julian"—she said my name like a lover—"I will always want you. I will always stand by you. There is no part of your past I can't forgive. There is no moment in your future I refuse to share. You told me to run once, and I refused because I'm not scared of you."

I huffed, pretending to be offended, even as her words wrapped around me and began to weave a magic all their own. "Thanks a lot."

"Your darkness called out," she whispered, "and mine answered. You are my mate. You are mine. Nothing will change that. Not in three months. Not when we get answers. Not ever. What happened to Camila was terrible. I wish I could take that pain away. I know I can't, but..." She hesitated, and my heart twisted. "...I can respect it, and to hell with what everyone thinks. I'm your mate as long as you want me. We have nothing to prove."

"I will always want you," I said fiercely. I brushed a hand to her face, wiping away the lingering dampness of tears. "Always. But tonight I faced a world without you, and even a few minutes was too long. I will find answers. I will protect you. And I will propose *in a more romantic way*," I couldn't stop myself from adding, "but three months from now..."

Thea swallowed, nodding as if she understood. Her gaze dropped to the floor, her hands falling away from me, and that's when I realized she wasn't in my head. She couldn't hear my thoughts.

"...is too long," I finished, and her head lifted, her eyes flashing. "You are my mate. You are mine. I won't put us through the pain of you taking another male to your bed. I won't wait for some miracle that isn't coming." I swallowed hard and gathered the courage to ask her the question that might destroy me. "I won't allow my past to rob us of our future. Now you know everything. Now you know why I couldn't take your virginity. Now you know the risk of accepting the mating bond fully—of consummating our relationship. And maybe I'm selfish and stupid, and you have every right to tell me to go to hell, but I cannot wait three months to take you as my mate. When you walked through that door, it took every ounce of restraint from claiming you against it then and there. I want you now and every minute for the rest of our lives. But one word and I will walk away. I will never ask this sacrifice of you again. I will stand by you as long as you will have me and never ask for more."

Thea began to breathe heavily, her pulse speeding up to match the heart racing in her chest. I heard every beat of it, each more precious than the last to me. The beat of my mate's heart. I would protect it until my dying breath no matter what she answered now. Maybe that's what gave me the courage to finally ask the question I'd forbidden myself to ever utter.

"Thea, may I take you to bed?"

CHAPTER TWENTY-ONE

Thea

The apartment was dim save for light streaming through the cracked bedroom door. Night had swallowed the room, the moon no match for its darkness.

"Thea, may I take you to bed?"

My eyes flickered to that light in the bedroom. It seemed to call to me, beckoning me to take his hand and his offer.

But I stared at him, waiting for the catch. There was always a rule—always a boundary. As soon as I answered, a new uncrossable line would appear as if summoned into existence by the mere question. Even though I clamped my mouth shut, there was a tug in my chest. I felt the gentle but demanding call to action, but I wasn't sure if it came from him or me.

Julian's brilliant eyes flitted over my face. Was he checking for more injuries or looking for clues?

A car honked on the street outside, and I snapped my attention to the window. Its glass panes muzzled the sound, but my mind flashed to screeching tires, blinding lights, and the deafening, unrelenting blast of a car horn. I inhaled sharply, closing my eyes to ward off the memories.

"Thea," he murmured as if afraid to startle me, "it's okay. You're safe."

Somehow he knew. Despite not being able to read my mind, he always knew what I was thinking. I swallowed, realizing how dry my throat was, and forced myself to look away. I reached for the forgotten glass of water he'd brought me. My fingers shook as I lifted it and took a sip.

"I'll get you more," he suggested gently as he pried it from my hand. "Are you hungry? I could order something."

And just like that, he'd switched gears like he hadn't just asked me the biggest question of my life.

His head dipped as he moved to stand, but I grabbed his hand before he could.

"I didn't expect that," I whispered, struggling to put a sentence together. "I thought you were…"

"What?" he prompted darkly.

"Ending things." I forced myself to say it—forced myself to face the fear that had gripped me since he'd started his story. "When you said you knew what you needed to do…I thought you meant leaving me."

His throat bobbed, and he glanced away. Shadows clouded his features, and I knew he was fighting one of his more primal instincts. I suspected if he opened his mouth, his fangs would be visible.

"A moment ago, when you told me how you felt," he began, his voice strained, "you said nothing would change how you felt."

I nodded. That was true. Nothing would change my feelings for him. Nothing could even come close.

"But the entire time, you thought I was preparing to end things?" The words were as taut as his body.

I bit my lip and forced myself to nod. I already knew it was unfair. I saw that now. But I wouldn't lie to him, even about something so small. Not with so much at stake for both of us.

"Why do you think my feelings are different for you?" he asked roughly. He pressed his index finger to my chin and turned my face to his again. "Tell me."

I knew why. We both did. "Because you pushed me away. I still hear your rejection," I confessed, "and the pain I felt…it lingers like a ghost. Sometimes I nearly forget it's there, but I always sense it. You said you're afraid I won't want you when we find the truth about my magic. Well, I think part of me is scared you will leave again—that you will change your mind again, removing my choice."

A muscle tightened in his jaw, but he didn't look away. Finally, he blinked and sighed. "There is something you should know about that night and why the Council visited."

Something he'd kept from me. I'd suspected as much, but when he'd come to San Francisco, I didn't ask questions. Probably because I knew that I didn't want his answers.

But things were different now. We weren't in bed carefully circling our boundaries. We weren't caught in the heat of the moment. But more than anything, we weren't clinging to the fantasy that someday all of our problems would vanish. We were facing the truth. We were at a crossroads. I licked my lower lip. "Go on."

"The Council demanded I take part in The Rites," he said carefully, "and they made it clear that there would be consequences if I refused."

"Torture." I repeated the word he used earlier. "What will they do to you?"

He winced and drew a deep breath. "Not to me. To you. They threatened to execute you."

"Execute?" I said, trying the word out. It tumbled out of my mouth like it was the first time I'd ever spoken it. It might actually have been, come to think of it. I pulled away from him, dropping back onto my heels. A stream of moonlight fell between us like a barrier.

"I should have told you."

I nodded, feeling numb. "And were they going to execute you, too? Or was removing me going to solve whatever problem they have with our match?"

"I would not have allowed them to touch you." His nostrils flared, and I knew what he was saying. The mating bond might not be sealed, but Julian would have protected me. He...

"You would have died." It wasn't a question. I knew, because I felt the same way.

"I thought it was a bluff, but then I saw my mother's face," he said, surprising me. "I saw something I've never seen before there."

"What?"

"Terror," he said softly. "I have never seen fear like that in my mother."

I understood. Sabine Rousseaux might not be one of my favorite people, but I respected his love for her. I understood why he couldn't put her through that. "So, you changed your mind. After your sister, you couldn't hurt her that way."

Julian huffed, a frustrated smile tugging at the corners of his mouth. "That's a generous interpretation. I wish I could say that I wouldn't hurt my family that way. A few months ago, I might have even believed it. But no. When I saw her fear, I knew they were not bluffing. I knew the Council would kill you then and there unless I swore to end things." He paused, and his eyes found mine in the darkness. "I was ready to die. I would have killed *anyone* who tried to attack you."

I didn't miss how his voice snagged on "anyone," and I knew he meant it. I knew he would have torn them apart, even his own mother, if they came after me. I tried to breathe, but it became difficult. Air rasped over my dry lips.

"I don't want you to die for me," I blurted out. My fingers twisted together, trying to dissipate the panic I felt at the thought of his death.

"I could say the same," he said softly. "In fact, that's what I decided that night. I've lived a long life. You've had twenty-two years. I would have died for you, Thea, but I wasn't willing to let you die for me. Not when I could save you."

My scarred heart, still tender and newly healed, ached.

"So, I broke your heart to save your life," he finished.

I didn't know how to feel. Angry? Yeah, that was definitely in the mix. Sad? There was some of that, too. Hurt? Confused? There were too many emotions vying to take control of me, so I focused on something rational instead. "And now?" I asked matter-of-factly. "What changed?"

"Our time zone," he said.

Nothing had changed. The Council's threat remained. They could appear at any moment to take action.

"So, they could show up to execute me?" I expected to feel some fear when I said it, but none came.

A bob of his head was all I got.

"And you didn't think to mention this before?" I crossed my arms.

"I should have stayed away." His eyes shuttered as if he was digging into whatever deep well of self-restraint he relied on for more. "I'll leave."

"What?" I burst out, annoyed. I groaned so loudly that his eyes snapped open. "Did you learn *anything*?"

He didn't say a word, which was probably smart.

"Let's be clear. No more secrets," I demanded, "even if you think I'll fight you on something. It's not fair, and it makes me feel like some dumb, young mortal."

His head tilted as his eyes narrowed further. "That was never my intention."

"Just don't do it, okay?" I waited for him to nod slowly. "And stop trying to solve all of our problems on your own. I can help."

"But if it's dangerous…" he began.

"Then we face it together. Teach me how to protect myself." I ignored the sharp thrill of fear I felt at saying those words, but I couldn't ignore that choosing Julian meant becoming part of his world. "But no more talk of sacrificing your life for mine."

He snarled at this demand. "No one will—"

"We go together," I cut him off. "Do you think for a second that I would choose my life over yours?"

"It's hardly fair." A dangerous edge sharpened his tone. "I've lived many lifetimes."

"I get it, old man, but you and me?" I whipped a finger between us. "We're ride or die."

"Ride…or die?" His eyes sparkled, losing some of the frantic despair he'd worn since I returned from my fateful afternoon.

"Ride or die," I repeated firmly. "We're in this together. Got it?"

Julian tipped his head in silent agreement. He waited for me to deliver more ultimatums. When I didn't, he seized his chance. "There is still the matter of the Council and marriage…and *mating*."

And the question he'd asked me.

"No decisions need to be made right now," he said, reading my face, "and I still have to find a romantic moment to propose. I suppose this doesn't count?"

I snorted and shook my head. "Definitely not."

"I don't know. I found the ride-or-die bit rather romantic," he said drily. "I suppose I'll just have to hold on to your ring a little longer."

"Ring?" I repeated, and everything got that much more real.

He shrugged but wore a wicked smirk. "Another time."

"Maybe after the Council decides not to kill me?" I offered.

"About that." He took a deep breath, and I knew I wasn't going to like whatever he said next.

CHAPTER TWENTY-TWO

Thea

"What if instead of waiting for the Council, we went to them?" Julian finished.

I raised an eyebrow but stayed silent. The shadows in the room deepened as he spoke. The noise from the streets outside the apartment's floor-to-ceiling windows had faded as the hour grew later. I fidgeted, trying to get comfortable, but my legs tangled in the ruins of the long gown I still wore. Finally, I managed to sink against the couch. The expensive leather cooled my skin, which, despite the change in conversation, was still heated from his earlier question.

"Back to Paris?" I asked cautiously. I'd fallen in love with that city, but now it was tainted by memories I wasn't quite ready to relive.

Julian shook his head. "The season is moving to Greece—Corfu—and then likely to Mykonos from there. I think we should join them."

"Why wait for the enemy to come to us?" I guessed. "But why do vampires go to sunny Greece, anyway?"

"Most vampires believe we originated in Greece, but no one knows. The belief persists, so we always wind up there. But Corfu can be rainy, and no one stays there long." I felt his blue eyes watching me as he spoke, trying to get a read on how I felt. "The parties generally move to Mykonos following The Second Rite."

I flinched, sure I felt a snake's scales on my skin. Now I understood why he'd hesitated. I didn't have fond memories of the First Rite and its slithering guests. "Another Rite?"

"I'm afraid it is Rites, as in plural, my love," he said gently.

"So you want to walk into the lion's den?" I felt a little sick as I considered returning to the vampire world. The last event we'd attended had ended in bloodshed. I closed my eyes as my brain called up images of thick, black blood pooling on marble and blank masks hiding unknown enemies. For a second, I swore I could hear the screams echoing through the opera house. I swallowed and opened my eyes to find Julian had moved closer, as if to protect me from my own mind. "Is that…safe?"

"My family will support us." He twined his hand with mine and rested them on my knee.

I stared at him, waiting for him to explain his newly discovered optimism. When he didn't, I blurted out, "They will?"

"Things are different now. You are not human," he reminded me, "and whatever you are, there is magic in you. The Council will be forced to reconsider, as will everyone else."

"Everyone else" meant his mother and brothers, and we both knew it. I got the impression that his father didn't care one way or the other as long as I didn't piss off his wife. But Julian was placing too much faith in our new discoveries, especially when we knew so little about my magic.

"But we don't know… I don't know how to even use magic," I admitted.

"Most familiars can barely whip up a spell from the family grimoire," he said with a shrug that sparked surprise inside me. "Magic is magic."

For a second, I wondered what Diana would say about that. Or my friend Quinn, whom I'd met during the first orgy I'd attended. The magic I'd experienced didn't feel as ordinary and harmless as he made it out to be. But it wasn't the idea of my *magic* knotting my stomach. "What happens at the other Rites, or are you all sworn to secrecy?"

"There are rumors, and I've heard a thing or two." He met my eyes and sighed, signaling he knew about as much as I did. "The first two Rites are for everyone called to participate. After that, it changes. Once a couple announces their intentions, they continue to attend all the parties. But they also begin facing the rest of the Rites. Some are tests. Others are rituals."

"More snakes?" I asked faintly.

"Unlikely," he promised with a faint laugh. "Some we will attend together, and I promise to take care of any and all snakes. But others we face alone, like when you faced the First Rite."

"Why do you bother? What's the point of all of this?" I shivered at the thought of facing the next terrible test someone like Sabine cooked up without Julian by my side.

"Vampires don't divorce. Marriages are legally binding until death," he said meaningfully. "That's not a problem for all of us. Many couples just take on their own lives and appear in public when necessary. But there have been some unions that ended badly. It's best to make sure both parties are committed to some type of agreement and not just caught up in bloodlust."

He spoke like this was completely normal, and maybe it should be. At least the bit about being sure. Humans rushed into marriage all the time and wound up divorced. How many people would marry if there was no way out? "I see."

None of that changed my desire to marry Julian, but it was good to know how these things worked.

"Mostly, though," he continued, "it gives the families time to discuss dowries, mergers. That kind of thing."

"Dowries?" I barked, laughter seizing me. "Do I need to bring a goat or something?"

A smug grin curved across his face. "Sometimes you are so delightfully *human*, pet," he said, the smile growing. "The male provides the dowry in vampire marriages."

I couldn't think of anything to say but, "Oh."

"If it matters to you, I can tell you about the substantial dowry you'll receive for accepting me," he said wickedly, tacking on, "after I find a romantic way to propose, of course."

"Of course," I echoed, feeling a bit faint. I shook my head. "But a dowry?"

"It's considered the beginning of the male's vow to protect his wife," he said in a quiet voice. "We consider it our sacred duty to guard and serve her."

"Serve?" I licked my lower lip.

His gaze tracked the movement of my tongue and lingered. "What a dirty mind you have, pet. Traditionally, it means respecting and carrying out her wishes as head of the household, but I will be more than happy to serve you *in every possible way*."

My toes curled at the suggestion in his words. I'd be more than happy to let him, as long as I got to return the favor. "I don't need you to give me a dowry. I want us to be equals."

"Such a radical." He brushed his thumb across the back of my hand, and goosebumps shot down my arm. "My mother will love you once she gives you a chance."

"Doubtful," I muttered. "I might be magical, but...I'm a virgin, remember?"

There was a painful pause. Lightning chased shadows in his blue eyes, his voice tightening as he spoke. "Yes, there is that."

But thrumming under those careful words, I heard his hunger. We might be reconsidering our plans, but I sensed his earlier offer remained on the table. He was ready to put aside all his concerns and all his past promises.

Was I?

"You said some of The Rites are tests," I started, tracing my thumb along his. "What if we fail one?"

"We will not fail." His determination left no room for any other possibility. I couldn't help but believe him.

"Will..." I hesitated, butterfly wings beating rapidly in my chest. I had a question that needed an answer, but I also knew that asking would make him hopeful. "Will being mates give us an unfair advantage?"

"Perhaps." The strain had returned to his words. His gaze raked down me as if he were already contemplating the advantages he planned to enjoy. It nearly undid me to see him prowling along the cage he'd built himself. He could break free of it any time he chose, but he didn't. Instead, he'd given me the key.

Was I ready to use it?

"I wouldn't want to cause trouble." I bit my lip, and this time I knew exactly what button I was pressing.

He swallowed so hard that I heard it. "Since I've known you, you've been nothing but trouble, pet." I started to protest, but he ignored me. "I think maybe you enjoy trouble."

It was almost impossible to resist his smirk or the barely restrained need humming from his body. My own felt it, too. *Desire.* It was a live wire stretched between us. All it would take…

"Will there be trouble if we show up in Greece fully mated?" I whispered.

"Probably." His mouth twisted.

"And what if we're tethered?" I forced myself to ask.

"Definitely, but I think I might have a way around that."

My head whipped back at his revelation. "And you're just mentioning it now?"

"It's an untested theory. We won't know if my idea will work without…" He paused, allowing me time to process what he was implying. There was only one way to test it. We would have to be tethered.

"Why didn't you tell me before?" I asked.

"Because I will not allow you to make this decision based on nothing more than hope and wild ideas," he bit out. "There is every possibility that we will be permanently tethered. I didn't want to risk you saying yes because you believed there was a solution. I only wanted you to consider the worst-case scenario."

I blinked, studying the grouchy, obstinate, perfect mate the universe had gifted me, and then I threw my head back and laughed.

"I'm not sure how to take that," he said gruffly.

Tears filled my eyes as I turned my joy on him. "I'm sorry," I said between peals of laughter. "It just hit me—you worry about everything…you are going to absolutely suck at finding a romantic way to propose."

"Probably." The cocky grin I loved reappeared. "Maybe I should call Jacqueline."

"Good idea," I said with a final giggle before the feeling inside me shifted. It was a different kind of happiness than any I'd ever felt. My joy heated and spread, wrapping itself around my heart and then working deeper. I felt it in my bones, my blood, my very soul.

I reached out slowly, my fingers grabbing a handful of his shirt. Julian's eyes dropped to my hand before shifting back up to mine. But he didn't move. He didn't even breathe. And I knew why he remained still, just like I knew what he wanted from me.

Something he would never take.

Something he'd fought to resist.

Something that could only be given.

It was up to me. It had always been up to me. I saw that now.

This brutal, strong vampire could command any room he entered. I'd watched him. I'd seen how others responded to his power. I'd witnessed him use it. He could take life. He could give it—he'd certainly changed mine.

I hadn't spent all these years waiting for the right man to take me to bed. I understood now why it had never felt right before. I was never meant for a man.

I'd been waiting for a god. I'd been waiting for him.

The energy inside me sparked, and I gave in to it. I felt it flow through me, felt it surge toward the hand that still held his. Julian remained silent as I gave in to my magic, but his gaze locked with mine as I felt it pool in my palm before seeping into his. And then something brushed back—something dark and beautiful and powerful. *Him*.

His magic.

Julian's eyes narrowed slightly as if he hadn't expected it, but he didn't pull away. Instead, his grip tightened, accepting me as I accepted him.

I saw past the cage he'd built to the leash he kept on himself. Not only to restrain his nature, but to hide his own power. He would have denied his own magic—his own instincts—to the point of madness to give me my choice.

And my choice? It would be him. Over and over and over. Him. Always him. So, I didn't hesitate when I tugged on him—both physically and mentally—and drew him closer. His movements were stiff and controlled as he angled his face over mine. What did a tether matter between our souls? I was already his completely, and he was mine.

And with three simple words, I unleashed him.

"Claim your mate."

CHAPTER TWENTY-THREE

Thea

Julian paused, meeting my eyes with a fierce gaze as something primal rumbled in his chest. Goose bumps rippled down my neck, and I opened my mouth to repeat myself. Before I could, he dropped my hands and cupped my face in his palms. My heart thumped several times as he lowered his mouth over mine with such agonizing purpose I thought I might die for wanting him.

His lips met mine with a tenderness that brought more tears to my eyes. I tasted his love. I feasted on it, parting the way for his tongue to sweep against mine, for his teeth to nip my lower lip, for his breath to become my own. The dark magic he'd freed filtered into my skin where his palms held me. It shuddered and yawned and grew, wrapping silky tendrils of midnight around my throat. When he gently pulled away, I reached wildly for him, and he chuckled. The low sound of it warmed my core, stoking the fire inside me into an inferno.

"I've waited nine hundred years for my life to begin," he murmured, his lips dancing over mine as he spoke. "I've waited nine hundred years for you. I'm going to take my time."

I swallowed a whimper, the edge of it escaping, and the eyes watching me danced like the flames burning deep inside me. "Take all the time you want," I murmured. "Just take me. Tonight."

I didn't have to ask again. Air whipped around me, and I found myself in his arms as Julian carried me swiftly to the bedroom. I braced myself for him to throw me on the bed. Part of me wanted it like that—wanted him to hike my skirt to my waist and take me hard and fast. It was some desperate part of me that wanted this behind us before something tore us apart again. But Julian placed me on my feet and guided me gently away from him. The rough pads of his fingers brushed my hair over one shoulder. His lips pressed to my exposed neck as he began to unzip my dress.

"I have imagined this moment since the night we met," he whispered as he gently slid my sleeves down. My breath caught as he kissed my bare shoulder, his hands peeling my dress from me. Between his touch and the cool air, my nipples beaded under the delicate lace holding my breasts. "I've imagined this perfect body under my palms."

He cupped my breasts, and they responded to his touch—his magic. They grew heavy, swollen with desire as his fingers circled their pebbled tips until I cried out. He shifted, moving his hands away from the wicked game he'd started. One slipped lower, pushing my gown off my hips as the other wrapped itself around my throat. His thumb rested on my chin, and he turned my face to the side to lower his mouth to kiss me.

I understood what he meant as I melted into him, wanting more even as I lingered. I wanted this night to never end. I wanted it to last forever.

I reached up and grabbed his shirt, holding him in place as he kissed me until all rational thought gave way to senseless, undeniable desire. The hand on my hip dipped lower. Julian's massive form curved around me as his fingers explored lower and lower. One finally found its way to the slick want between my legs, and he responded with a guttural, primal groan as he felt my wetness.

Julian's mouth moved, his teeth catching the shell of my ear. "May I taste you, Thea?"

I sensed that his hesitation was a check—a way to keep himself from succumbing to the beast inside him. I'd unleashed him, but he was still in the cage, pacing along its bars to stop himself from feasting, but the hunger in his words was palpable. I didn't know if he was asking for my pleasure or my blood, but I felt that longing as much as I heard it—the strain, the desperation—and my voice trembled as I spoke. "I belong to you. All of me."

He snarled as though I'd turned the key he'd given me.

Carefully, I opened the lock. "Put your mouth on me."

I was on my back a second later. A blast of cold air hit me as my lacy underwear snapped. Julian's rough hands pushed apart my thighs and slid down, spreading me open as he dropped to the floor. He dragged his tongue clean up my center before pausing to circle the point of my pleasure. I cried out as he devoured me, and then I felt a finger dip slowly inside. Magic pulsed in it, and I felt it swirling there. My hips rocked, trying to give him more access. Blue eyes flashed up to me, and I moaned, seeing him there between my legs, taking what was always his. But it wasn't enough. It wasn't what I wanted.

"Please," I called to him, my thighs clamping around him to stop him. He stilled, his mouth still buried against me. "Please. I'm ready. I want *you*."

Julian drew back, pausing to kiss my thigh. He pushed me farther onto the bed so he could stand. His eyes never left mine as he reached back and yanked his shirt over his head. I drank in the sight of him—his broad shoulders, the powerful stack of muscles honed over centuries. All of it was mine. All of him was mine. I dragged my lower lip into my teeth to keep the almost hysterical joy inside me from bubbling over.

He reached for his pants, but then he paused. "Are you certain, my love?"

I smiled at the concern in his voice, knowing he was worried he might hurt me or that I might have second thoughts. How could we ever have worried about being tethered to each other? I was meant for him as he was meant for me. Every beat of my heart was his, and I knew he would die to protect it. I let my legs fall open again in silent answer. His gaze raked fiery coals over me, the slide of his throat saying more than words ever could. He lifted his eyes to mine and held them. I moaned when I heard his belt unbuckle, fighting the urge to look away as I heard his zipper next.

A trembling need broke out across my body. I reached behind me with quivering fingers to undo my bra and found I barely could.

"Let me," he said softly. Leaning over me, he slipped a hand behind my back and undid it smoothly. Julian drew the bra off me strap by strap. He tossed it over his shoulder, his mouth tugging into a boyish smirk that set my heart racing again. A heavy heat settled on my belly, and I went molten when I realized it was him and that there was nothing left between us but a single moment. One final act.

But he didn't move to press between my legs. Instead, he traced a finger along the side of my face, gazing at me with such love that it consumed me. "There is something I would like to do with your permission." His lips parted to reveal a fang.

I inhaled sharply before turning my head to offer him my neck. The only other bit of me left to claim.

"Always so eager to have my fangs in you," he said lightly, his words making me feel dizzy. His index finger pressed to my cheek and drew my face back toward his. "Someday very, *very* soon, I want to sink my fangs into you, so I can enjoy the taste of my mate coming on my cock. But this time—the *first* time—I would like to make it a little more pleasurable for you if I can."

"I trust you." I swallowed, suddenly remembering that this was the part that scared me. Not choosing Julian. Not giving myself to him. But the pain I'd come to expect from years of being primed for this moment.

"Just a drop of venom. Not enough to affect you," he murmured, "but enough to dull…"

The pain. He didn't need to say it. We both knew that my body wasn't exactly prepared for what was about to happen. As much as I wanted this—wanted him—I couldn't deny the anxiety twisting my stomach. I nodded my grateful, official permission.

He moved onto the bed, kneeling between my spread legs, and slid his hands under my hips. Lifting me to meet his lowered head, he kissed my seam once. Twice. Three times. Then, his tongue slipped past it and licked greedily up my entire length. Warmth spread through the spot, followed by a tingling sensation that made the ache inside me deepen until I thought I might burst.

When he finally lowered me back to the bed, the whites of his eyes had darkened. He closed them as the black seeped into the blue of his irises. Anguish contorted his face, and without thinking, I placed my palm over his chest, to where his ancient heart beat slightly faster than usual. The agony vanished, and he opened them again, looking at me with the brilliant blue eyes I loved, even if I'd never minded when they shifted to midnight.

"Say it again," he said through gritted teeth. *Give me permission.*

I kept my hand on his chest, opening myself to him again, and I gave in. Not just to the magic but to the love, to the need, to the desire. I offered it all to him. I felt it spark and flare. "I am yours," I whispered. "All of me. Claim me, Julian. Claim your mate."

He convulsed on a groan as he moved lower, seating himself between my thighs. His strong arms bracketed me, holding his crushing weight carefully over me. He brushed a kiss over my lips. "And I am yours. I will protect you. I will serve you," he promised. "You—*my mate*—above all others. It is my privilege to be your mate. It is my honor to love you."

A tear rolled down my cheek at the realization that this moment meant more than any public wedding vow or whispered promise. We lingered in it, on the edge of forever, until I reached between us to where he rested heavily against me. Gripping his length, I guided his crown to my entrance, more tears falling now as I realized his own lashes were wet. Julian rocked his hips, nudging the broad tip of his cock against the barrier of my virginity. It smarted, and I flinched, my breath snagging, before his venom chased away the discomfort, turning it from awkward pain into exquisite torture.

Julian released a ragged breath as he breached me, but he didn't push in farther. Instead, he reached for the hand still on his chest. He clasped it and drew it up over my head, then the other. His muscles strained, shoulders and biceps coiling into thick ropes as he held himself over me with our hands clasped together. There was a brush of his dark magic against mine, and I welcomed it.

"For eternity," he swore, a tear spilling onto his cheek.

I couldn't find words. There were too many feelings crowding inside me, so I raised my legs to frame his body. I wrapped them around his waist, flowering open farther where he remained pinned shallowly in me. Finally, I found my voice, thick with happiness. "I am your mate, Julian. I am yours."

I reached out through that magic flowing between us and opened his cage door. Julian lifted his head and roared, plunging inside me deeper, deeper, deeper. I cried out as he sheathed his soul inside my own. My entire being cracked open as he began to move. His face dropped, his eyes wild but still clear as he thrust and claimed, destroyed and remade, took and gave.

My fingers tightened against his as my magic cooled and darkened. No longer my own but *ours*. His eyes flashed to our joined hands as he continued to roll his hips in punishing, torturous strokes that left me moaning even as our magic spread past our hands. It wrapped itself around our arms as the muscles tightened, coiling around our chests as we climbed and climbed. When it reached my heart, I heard his own pulse thundering inside me, slowing and speeding until, as we reached the edge, our heartbeats matched and we went over it together.

As mates.

CHAPTER TWENTY-FOUR

Julian

Midnight hung like a portrait in the window, the moon shining brightly in an unusually clear sky. Thea's petite body was tucked against me, my own body shielding her like a cocoon. Neither of us had spoken since we'd finally untangled ourselves, only to immediately find each other's arms again. My face pressed into her hair, kissing her absently and drinking in her scent. It had altered slightly. Her candied violets were edged in smoke and her honeyed-melon now spiked with clove; under it, something new that was herbal and timeless. Because it was no longer her scent—it was *ours*.

I suspected it wasn't the only change our mating had caused.

"What are you thinking?" she murmured, brushing her thumb over our joined hands. Neither of us had let go of each other completely since we'd forged this new life. Instead, we lingered in the bed, our bare bodies entwined.

"You smell different," I admitted to her.

"Like you?"

"Are you reading my mind, or can you sense it, too?" I smiled into her hair and gave it another kiss.

"I sense it," she said slowly, laughing slightly. "I think I short-circuited whatever magic helps me read your thoughts."

That's unfortunate.

She snorted. "Well, that was loud and clear. Maybe I was just too caught up in the moment."

"I rather like the idea of short-circuiting you with orgasms," I confessed. I allowed the hand I kept on her hip to drift to her belly. I drew shapes across the soft skin in teasing strokes.

But she didn't laugh again. "I feel different," she whispered.

"I know. I sense that, too," I said, doing my best to act casually. This was new territory for both of us, but I'd picked up on another transformation while we lay together.

Her heartbeat. Before tonight, I'd memorized its rhythm—its normal human speed. I'd cherished it. Now it was slower, nearly half what it had been before. It had changed in the final moments of our mating. Mine had as well, but it was beating faster. Twice the average rate of a vampire. I told Thea what I'd noticed.

I heard her swallow, and a second later, she released my hand and twisted to face me. "I felt it happen," she said softly. "Did you?"

I nodded. "I thought I was just caught up in the moment. I expected it to be temporary."

But it seemed it wasn't. We'd been lying here for an hour at least.

"They match," she said. "They beat together."

"'And the two shall become one,'" I recited. "Apparently, quite literally in this case." A frown captured my mouth as I considered what this meant, but I banished it swiftly. Just not swiftly enough.

"What?" she demanded, catching me out.

There was no point in hiding it from her. Not only could she probably dig around in my brain for an answer, but it was something we'd have to confront sooner rather than later.

"There will be no hiding that we're mates," I said carefully.

Her body stiffened a bit, defiance sparking in her eyes. "Did you plan to deny it?"

"No! I just…" How did I put this without upsetting her? "I might have liked to announce it, rather than…"

"Show up to your family's vacation home with the same smell and heartbeat?" she asked drily.

My mouth curved, unable to resist her sarcasm. "Something like that. On the other hand, we'll make a hell of an entrance."

"Maybe if we go in separately," she suggested, and I chuckled.

"It definitely won't be that easy." I shook my head. It was something we had to face. There were no other options except... "If we could harness your magic, we could try a glamour."

"What is that again?" she asked.

"Like *Île Cachée*," I reminded her. "The island uses a glamour to remain hidden, but the spell can also make someone appear other than what they are. It can be used to shield appearances, scents—"

"Heartbeats?" she added. "I wish I could, but I have no idea what my magic even is."

Given that I'd just mated with her, I had a few ideas. Of course, I might be biased.

"There's another possibility," she said, sounding unaccountably shy. I lifted an eyebrow. She took a deep breath before plunging on. "We could use your magic."

I remained silent even as something flared where our palms met. I wasn't certain if the spark came from her or me.

"You've been holding out on me," she continued. "You told me why you wore gloves, but I didn't realize there was actual magic inside you."

I stared into her eyes, wondering how she could be looking at me but still so blind. "Neither did I. Not anymore."

"What?" She blinked, pulling away slightly. "But you told me... the gloves..."

"It's tradition more than anything. But my bloodline is very old, and both of my parents remember the ancient magics. My mother has a little prophecy, even if it comes out mostly as riddles and she seems to see things others can't. There were times I felt something when I was much, *much* younger." Thea giggled. "But the only magic I've felt for centuries belonged to others. A witch gave me some of hers the night of the opera, but it was nothing more than an ember with no source to feed it."

"I see." Thea just stared at me for a minute as if digesting what this implied—that I'd felt another creature's magic. "And your father?"

"I honestly don't know, but there's probably something. Vampires don't share their magic often. It's not only rare—it can be dangerous. If someone finds out about your powers, they might try to take them."

"Take them?" she repeated. "You don't mean…"

"I told you this was intimate." I knitted our fingers together. "Explaining it more deeply didn't feel terribly pertinent. Humans have never carried magic in their hands. Only familiars and vampires. We learn to guard our magic—no matter how weak—from the time we are very young."

"You wear gloves."

I nodded. "Plus, it helps to stop us from shredding things with our nails."

"Remind me not to let your hands near my vagina again." Now she looked horrified.

"Don't worry, pet. It's generally fangs coming out to play, not claws," I murmured, drawing the tip of my tongue over my teeth. "And my fangs are always out for you."

"How romantic," she teased, but her throat slid in promising ways, as if she liked hearing this tidbit. "So, when you hold hands?"

"It makes our magic vulnerable to be stolen or claimed."

Her eyes widened, and she gulped. "I didn't…accidentally…"

"No." I grinned at her concern. "I think rather the opposite. Magic can be given." I told her about the familiar at the opera and others who had passed me their magic over the centuries. "It's unusual, but it happens."

"Julian." My name danced on her lips. "What is your magic?"

"I don't know. I've only felt sparks before tonight," I confessed. "I assumed it was inside me. Occasionally, I felt it stir, like when the witch gave me hers, but it's never acted like that. You felt it, didn't you?"

"Yes." Her hand squeezed mine. "I think maybe I saw it, too."

Interesting.

She nodded. "I still feel it—*inside* me."

I'd been too preoccupied with her to do a thorough inventory of my own changes. The scent. The heartbeat. Those had been too obvious to ignore. I paused and turned my thoughts inward, searching for that dark magic I'd felt as I'd claimed her. It stirred as I discovered it, rousing as I poked at it and willed it to reach out through our clasped hands. The magic extended, beating inside me, and as it begrudgingly answered, I felt something else: a pure, golden warmth tucked under its dark wings. My mind reached for the light, and the creature inside me rumbled, baying at my audacity. Claws scratched a warning against my chest. I grunted, the dark magic wrenching away from my call.

"Fuck," I bit out. I rubbed my chest with the back of our entwined hands. "Yeah, you're in there."

"You don't sound very happy about that," she pointed out.

"That's because my magic seems to be guarding yours like a dragon," I said, noticing it was a little hard to breathe.

Thea's mouth pressed into a thin line, and I sensed she was holding back laughter.

"It's not funny. It hurt."

A giggle escaped her. The creature calmed at the sound and settled back around its prize. "Sorry, but you basically just told me you have a grouchy dragon hoarding treasure inside you."

I raised an eyebrow, waiting for the punch line. "And?"

"And you can be a little grumpy," she said carefully.

"Grumpy? I have grumpy magic?" I repeated. "I think you might be confusing me with how you are before coffee."

Thea gasped, her eyes narrowing. "I am nev—"

I rolled on top of her, cutting off her protest. "I love you, but it's true."

She glared at me, but a smile tugged on her lips. I shifted my weight, allowing my erection to brush against her. Her eyes rolled back.

"Not fair," she panted, curling a leg around my waist. She closed her eyes as if searching for restraint. "Do you mind?"

"Mind?" I asked, kissing a path down her neck. "Do I mind what, my love?"

"Having it inside you—my magic or whatever it is?" she whispered.

I drew back and regarded her for a moment. "Do I mind carrying a bit of my beloved mate inside me?" My throat bobbed as I tried to keep control of the instincts that roared inside me to show her just how little I minded by taking even more of her. "No, I do not mind, Thea. Do you?"

She shook her head slightly, wrapping her other leg around me. "I will never have enough of you."

"Then you want more?" I asked darkly, reaching between us to position myself. I slid in a fraction of an inch, the resistance less this time, although she was still so tight that my balls clenched as I anticipated what was to come. "How much?"

I pressed in farther, her gasp of pain shifting to a slight moan as I stretched her. Finally, she opened her eyes and stared up at me with those priceless, glittering emeralds. Then, she unleashed me with one word. *"Everything."*

CHAPTER TWENTY-FIVE

Thea

It was an unusually bright morning for San Francisco in the winter. That was, if the sky outside the kitchen window could be trusted. I huddled near the sink, jealously guarding the bowl of cereal I'd just made myself. I'd lost track of how long I'd been in bed with Julian. We couldn't seem to get out of it, save for the occasional bathroom trip. Every time I started to tell him I needed to eat, he'd look at me—and that was that.

We couldn't keep our hands off each other.

I was pretty sure this was the second morning since we'd finally gone to bed and mated properly. I seemed to remember seeing the sun between sleep and pleasure, but I couldn't be sure. All I knew was that I was hungry enough I was already planning my second bowl.

I'd only gotten a few bites in when Julian appeared at the bedroom door.

He spotted me and grinned wickedly. Rubbing a hand through his tousled hair, he sauntered toward the kitchen in nothing but a loose pair of silk pajama pants. I closed my eyes and scrounged up what little restraint I still had.

"Don't come any closer," I warned him, shimmying over a few inches so there was an entire counter between us. I shoveled more cereal into my mouth.

"I wouldn't dare. Stake through my heart, I swear." He slashed a cross in the air over his heart, but the wicked gleam remained in his eyes.

My knees buckled, my entire body aching to go to him. That was the problem.

"I'm going to starve to death," I said, my mouth still full.

There was a blur that made me blink, and when I opened my eyes, he was on the far side of the living room. His shoulders were a straight, rigid line, his posture equally stiff. Muscles ticked in his neck, and his hands were balled in fists at his side. He opened his mouth but didn't speak for a few seconds before he finally grunted, "Sorry."

"Whoa." I started to put down my spoon, but he growled.

"Eat."

I took another bite before he exploded in front of me. I chewed it loudly, hoping it would soothe him. My mind reached for his, but I couldn't hear anything. I felt something, though. It tightened around my chest like an anchor and then vanished. It wasn't my chest at all. It was his.

"It was a joke," I said softly. "Relax. I'll finish this."

He closed his eyes, and his shoulders settled into their normal, broad set before his eyelids opened again. But Julian didn't move any closer. He tracked my every movement as I finished the bowl. When I finally put it in the dishwasher, he approached me slowly.

"Was that enough? I can cook something," he offered.

"I'm fine." I studied him, noting the tightness that clung to the corners of his eyes and his controlled movements. "What the hell was that?"

"I haven't been taking care of you." He looked away, a muscle straining in his neck. Anger rippled over him, but I knew it was all directed inward. "I've just been having my way with you."

I snorted with laughter, quickly smothering my mouth when his eyes flashed. "I'm sorry, but seriously?"

"My mate starving to death isn't funny to me," he muttered.

"It was hyperbole, and stop acting like you tied me to the bed. I've been just as bad as you." I tossed a kitchen towel at him. I meant for it to jolt him out of this sudden mood swing. Instead, it landed on his head, covering his face—except for a deeply etched frown.

He whipped it off his head. "I'm serious."

"So am I." I didn't back down. "I will tell you if I need to eat from here on out."

"Promise?"

"I promise," I mimicked, crossing my heart like he had a few minutes ago.

He exhaled, reaching up to rub the bridge of his nose. "I guess that's the tether." He peeked out at me, grinning half-heartedly. "I'm sorry if I was being... What did you call me the other night? Grumpy?"

I swallowed, digesting this development, and nodded. "So, we are tethered."

"It felt like it," he said, sounding gloomy over the prospect. "You said that you needed to eat or you might starve, and something just snapped inside me. It shoved me away from you and wouldn't let me move until I saw that you were fed."

"That sounds...terrible," I admitted after a second.

"It wasn't great." We stared at each other for a minute. In the bliss of our mating bond, we'd ignored the possibility that we'd also been tethered. We'd been far too busy screwing each other on every flat surface in the apartment for the last two days. Now, it was time to face facts.

I cleared my throat. "You had a theory about tethering," I said carefully, uncertain what might set him off. "You thought we might have a way around it."

"I'm not so sure after that," he said with a hollow laugh. He planted his hands on the marble counter, hanging his head. "Fuck, I'm sorry."

"For what?" I asked. "I knew what I was getting into when we slept together."

Didn't I?

"For watching you like some primitive freak while you ate a bowl of cereal," he said, his honesty disarming any lingering tension between us.

"Maybe we should test this whole tethering thing," I suggested, and he tensed again. "Just to see how it works. So, for the male, you need to protect and care for me, right? And in return…I'm supposed to do whatever you tell me?"

"Something like that," he said through gritted teeth, and I knew he was thinking about his sister, about how Willem had abused the tether and cared for her in the loosest, cruelest sense of the term.

"Okay, no big deal." I tugged at the shirt I'd swiped from his closet, pulling it down to cover more of my backside as I straightened. "Tell me to do something silly."

He lifted an eyebrow. *Seriously?*

"Yes. How else are we going to figure this out?"

"Fine," he said with a resigned sigh. "Hop on one leg."

"Really?" I put my hands on my hips, rolling my eyes at his choice. Nothing happened.

"Touch your nose," he said, earning another eye roll.

I shook my head. "Nada. Maybe I'm immune, just like with compulsion."

"You are only immune when I compel you, my love," he said, frustration grating in his voice. "Don't forget that."

Something clicked in my head like my brain had taken an actual note. "Wait," I said slowly, "I think… Tell me to do something but really, really mean it."

He paused, a wrinkle forming between his brows as he considered. The gleam returned to his eyes, a smirk carving across his broad mouth. "Take off that shirt."

My hands grabbed the hem of the overlarge T-shirt, and I ripped it over my head. I narrowed my eyes, the shirt balled in my hand. He chuckled.

"Throw that on the ground," he demanded.

I tossed it on the floor.

"Well?" he asked me. "Was that just your newly discovered

wantonness or…"

"You think I'm wanton?" I shrieked, crossing my arms over my bare breasts.

"Drop your arms," he said. They immediately fell to my sides, and I groaned.

"Yeah, I'm tethered," I grumbled. "I had no idea it would be so…"

"Humiliating?" he asked softly.

I shook my head. "Irresistible, I guess?"

Somehow I hadn't believed he'd be able to control me. Not after he'd been unable to compel me.

"Do you…regret it now?" he asked roughly, pain shadowing his eyes.

"No," I said without hesitation. "Because it's you. I trust you. I meant that. I will never regret being your mate."

"Unless I tell you to jump off a cliff," he said humorlessly. As soon as it was out of his mouth, he sprang between me and the door as if he might have triggered me to do so.

"Nothing," I told him. "I think it only works when you mean it."

"You were only joking about the cereal earlier," he pointed out, rubbing the back of his neck.

"I was a little serious," I said. "I really meant it when I said I was hungry."

"Oh." His handsome face collapsed into a frown. After a second, a corner of his mouth lifted. "On the other hand… Come here."

I groaned as my body instantly responded. I walked toward him and stopped. My eyebrows lifted. "You rang?"

"Touch yourself." His low voice sent a shiver up my spine.

I brushed my palm over my other arm and smirked. "Happy?"

"Between your legs," he ordered. "Pleasure yourself."

"I don't really…" But my fingers were already moving to the aching need pulsating there. I slipped a fingertip between my folds, and his eyes followed. "I don't really know how," I whispered.

Embarrassment flushed my face. He already knew that I'd never made myself come. He'd figured it out when we first met.

"There is no shame between us," he murmured, then circled around me, placing his hand over mine. "I want you to know how to control your pleasure, even without me."

His finger aligned with mine and began guiding it in strokes around my swollen clit. I moaned, freed from any restraint I'd felt a moment ago. A new heat coursed through me as Julian showed me how to work my fingers: swirling and pausing and circling my way toward release.

"That's right, pet," he murmured in my ear, nipping it slightly. "You are so beautiful when you come. In my nine hundred years, I have never seen anything as beautiful as your face when you orgasm. Keep touching yourself until you come."

His hand withdrew. My eyes closed, my entire being focused on the need building inside me. Julian stayed close enough that I felt his heat and heard his shallow, hungry breathing as he watched me. My muscles tightened, my own breaths growing frantic. I could feel it waiting for me. Any stroke might push me over the edge. I whimpered, realizing how close I was—how much I wanted it, not just for myself.

But for my mate, who'd demanded it.

"Put your fingers inside yourself," he growled.

I pushed two of my fingers into my slick heat.

"Pretend it's me. My fingers. My tongue. My cock."

I choked on the pleasure his words sent barreling through me. My hand moved faster until I clenched around my fingers, spilling open with moans and cries. My legs shook as I came, and before the last tremble of pleasure left me, Julian pressed against me from behind. He grabbed the hand still between my legs and carefully spun me to face him.

"Open your eyes," he demanded.

My eyelids lifted automatically, and my gaze met his jet-black eyes. Julian clasped my hand and lifted it to his lips. Slowly, he brought one finger to his mouth and sucked it clean. Then the next. I held my breath as I watched him lick each one.

"You taste so fucking good," he snarled. "That was unbelievably hot."

I was barely standing up, but I had to agree. If this was how he planned to use the tether on me, I was game.

"One more thing," he said as if he was thinking the same thing. I bit my lip, bracing myself for the next pleasure he'd deliver. Julian stared at me, his eyes returning to normal but still flashing. "You will never blindly do anything I ask again unless you want to."

I blinked and stared.

"Never take another order from me," he roared.

I fell back a step like his words had pushed me. Shaking my head to clear it, I finally looked at him. *"That was your big plan?"*

"It's worth a shot." He shrugged. Then he turned his flaming eyes on me. "Bend over."

"No way." I snorted. "I'm done with this game." I made a show of squatting to pick up my shirt. *Bend over!*

But inside me, love spread, warming every inch of my body. I'd chosen to take a risk. I'd chosen to trust him. And maybe it wasn't a perfect solution, but he'd found a way to give me my freedom. He could have abused the tether, like Camila's husband. Instead, he'd been selfless. Because he wasn't my lord or master. He was my mate.

"Drop that," he demanded coldly, but I glared at him.

I shook my head. "Say please."

A wide grin split his face, and he exhaled deeply.

"Were you really trying at the end?" I asked. It couldn't be that simple. Julian had not just managed to find the easiest way around the tether ever. Had he?

"With everything I had," he said, his grin deepening. "But really, please, keep the shirt off. I have other plans for you."

"Oh really?" I considered the request. "So you can't boss me around anymore?"

"Nope." He looked too pleased.

"What about you?" I asked quietly, twisting the cotton T-shirt between my fingers. I couldn't release him from his end of the tether—from that primitive drive to provide for and protect.

"Who cares?"

I knew he meant it. No, it was more than that. I knew he believed it. But it didn't sit well with me. "I don't want you worrying about me all the time. It's not fair."

"Thea"—he said my name with flat amusement—"I would be worrying about you with or without the tether."

"Are you sure?" I couldn't stop myself from asking. "Do you regret it?"

"Never." He grabbed hold of me, lifting me off the ground. A second later, my back was against the marble counter. "It will always be my privilege to serve my mate."

"Is that so?" I fanned my legs open for him, smiling sweetly. *"Show me."*

Something primal tore through his eyes as he lowered his head toward me. My back arched off the counter when his hot tongue lashed up my swollen seam. I cried out as his mouth claimed me. My eyes rolled as he showed me exactly how he planned to serve me.

"No," I called. "I want you. *Please.* I want my mate."

Julian straightened, one hand freeing his cock. He moved to press inside me and froze. I strained to sit up, half pinned by him. "What is—"

The front door opened.

CHAPTER TWENTY-SIX

Julian

Maybe it was the delicate position we were in, or maybe it was the unexpected intrusion, but instinct overrode rational thought. I'd been distracted by Thea and the issue of the tether—so distracted that someone had breached my private entrance. By the time I heard her footfall on the stairs, I'd picked up her scent.

It wasn't an enemy breaching our unofficial honeymoon. It was a friend—and it didn't matter.

In the split second after the knob turned, I'd tossed Thea my T-shirt, shoved my cock back in my pants, and made it across the apartment. I lunged as she stepped inside.

"Julian!" Thea screamed, but I already had Celia by the throat.

I slammed her into the wall over my head. Celia sputtered, staring down at me with a mixture of surprise and annoyance. I snarled in response. Her nostrils flared, her eyes widening as she processed what was happening. She threw a leg around me. I bucked it, but it was a distraction that cost me.

Her hand chopped the crook of my elbow with enough strength that I lost my grip. She ducked around me and hooked an arm around my neck.

"If this is going to happen every time you ask me to run an errand for you, find a new assistant," she hissed.

"Then knock," I said, both words sounding choked by her hold on me.

"If I let you go and stay away from her, can you get control of yourself?" she whispered.

Rage vibrated inside me, but I managed a terse, "Yes."

Celia dropped her hold on me and flashed across the room. She stopped, her back to the wall, now as far from me as she was from Thea. She knew exactly what was going on and knew it was safest to stay away from me and my mate.

I whirled around to where Thea stood in the kitchen. She was dressed again. My T-shirt swallowed her petite frame, but she held its hem firmly down. My shoulders relaxed as my rational self took control back from the tethered male running the show.

"Celia, you remember Thea," I said, pausing before I added, *"My mate."*

To her credit, Celia barely flinched at this development. She must have smelled the change in our scents and the beat of our hearts. "It seems you left a few things out of your recent messages."

"You are the first to know," I said quietly. We'd been too caught up in lovemaking to speak to anyone else. But I realized then that I didn't want this news to be delivered over the phone—not to the people we cared about. I wanted them to be with us to celebrate.

"Might I suggest that you refrain from attacking anyone else you plan to tell?" she deadpanned.

"I apologize for that," I said through gritted teeth, stalking over to join my mate in the kitchen. "I suppose I'm feeling a little protective."

Celia wisely said nothing. Instead, she looked at the woman at my side.

"Thea, it's lovely to see you again," she said smoothly, tucking a strand of silver hair behind her ear. The smile she added was genuine, but probably only because it was directed at Thea and not me.

"Y-y-yes," Thea stammered. Her eyes met mine, and I spotted the silent rebuke in them.

I know I overreacted.

She raised one eyebrow as if to say *you think?* Then she took a deep breath before turning toward Celia and saying in a composed voice, "We weren't expecting company."

Celia glanced at me and crossed her arms. I cleared my throat. "Actually," I said, "I knew she was coming by today."

"Seriously? And we were..." Thea groaned, gesturing wildly to the kitchen counter we'd been christening a few minutes ago. "Why didn't you tell me?"

"It slipped my mind." That was the hazard of being newly mated. I'd planned to tell her about Celia's visit. I was on my way to do just that when I'd come into the kitchen. One look at her wearing nothing but my T-shirt and carrying the scent of our lovemaking had driven it from my mind.

"Perhaps it is time to remove my access to your home," Celia suggested gently, drawing our attention back to her. "Especially if Thea will be staying here."

I started to agree with her, but Thea cut me off. "Absolutely not. He needs to get his caveman under control. He can't attack everyone who comes within thirty feet of me."

Celia's lips pressed into a bemused smile. "That might be difficult. I've always heard that mated males are intolerable for the first few decades."

"I'll do better," I promised Thea, leaning to kiss her forehead, "and it's good practice."

"Practice?" Celia interjected.

"For when we tell everyone else." I shot her a look that dared defiance.

She rolled her eyes and ignored the boundary. "If you're smart, you two will find a private island somewhere and get this out of your systems before you make any announcements."

There were a lot of reasons that wasn't going to work. Most of them had to do with my family and the Vampire Council, but there was also the issue of Thea's mortality. My mate seemed to reach the same conclusion.

"But you just said this could last decades," Thea said softly.

"Vampires don't adapt as quickly as humans," Celia explained.

Thea swallowed and looked between us. "I can't spend decades waiting…"

"I know," I said quickly.

"It was just a suggestion," Celia offered, but I knew she believed it to be the best course of action. It was certainly the easiest if we could ignore all the problems. She shifted on her heels and pointed at the door. My gaze tracked her movement and landed on a number of bags. "I picked up the items you requested. There are a few more things downstairs."

"What items?" Thea asked.

"The rest of your wardrobe for the season," Celia said with a pointed look at me. She had expressed her apprehension when I'd messaged her my plan to return to finish the social season with Thea by my side. Now that she knew we were mates, she must think I'd lost my mind.

"I don't need anything else," Thea scoffed. "You already bought me so much."

"That was before Greece was on the agenda," Celia said, bypassing her concern with the breezy indifference of a vampire with a few centuries behind her. "And there was also the other issue."

"Other issue?" Thea repeated.

"May I?" Celia asked, gesturing to the shopping bags.

"Of course," I said, the words rough around the edges.

"Don't act like I'm being unreasonable," Celia advised me, edging across the room. "You nearly took off my head."

I was going to have to buy her something very expensive to make up for that.

"Yes, you are," Thea murmured, and I realized she'd heard my thought.

Celia rounded toward us, clutching a bag, and smiled sweetly at me. "May I approach?"

"Oh, this is ridiculous." I held up my hands.

She nodded toward them, and I realized they were bare.

I growled softly. "Give me a second, and yes, you may go near her. Braid her hair for all I care. I'll be right back."

I prowled into the next room to find some gloves. It took me a few minutes. I'd grown used to having my hands uncovered around Thea. Given that we hadn't left the apartment in days, I had no idea where I'd left a pair. More than that, I liked keeping my hands bare. Finally, I found a few pairs tucked into a dresser drawer. My eyes snagged on the velvet box that held Thea's engagement ring. I'd almost forgotten about my plan to propose to her. It seemed both silly and desperately important now. Like us, it was a study in opposites.

I yanked on the gloves and returned to the kitchen, where Celia had just finished showing Thea a few purses.

"They're beautiful," Thea said genuinely, admiring the couture bags. Later, she would claim she didn't need them, but my mate was going to have to get used to having the finer things in life.

Celia's gaze darted to me, nodding subtly as she opened a large red bag. I braced myself for what was about to happen. I had no idea how Thea would respond to this addition to her wardrobe. I wondered if having Celia here was a mistake. Perhaps I should have been the one to present her with these purchases. But it was too late, and with our trip to Greece only a few days away, we were running out of time.

"What's this?" Thea asked as Celia passed her a beautiful silver box. She plucked the black bow tied around it and let it fall away. "I really don't need more jewelry."

"It's not jewelry, pet," I said, my words thick. I cleared my throat. "But I hope you will like them."

She raised her eyebrows, a familiar curiosity on her face, as she lifted the lid and gasped at what she found inside.

CHAPTER TWENTY-SEVEN

Thea

I wasn't certain what to say. Celia excused herself quietly to get the rest of the bags she'd left downstairs. As she moved away from the kitchen window, a bright shaft of sunlight fell across the contents of the box: a pair of exquisitely tailored red gloves. I picked them up with hesitant fingers, smiling slightly when I felt the buttery-soft leather.

Julian hadn't moved—hadn't so much as released a breath—since I'd opened the box. Apprehension tightened his shoulders as he waited.

"Pretty," I murmured. Holding them in my hands, I knew they'd been custom-made. How he had managed that, I didn't know. Then again, as I lifted my gaze to him, I was reminded that I knew his body like my own. I took a deep breath. "I suppose I need them now."

"Whether you wear them is up to you." A fierce determination coated his words, and I knew that if I refused, he would not only respect my decision, but he would support me if it became an issue.

"If I don't, will my magic be vulnerable?" I didn't expect him to answer. It was a question I needed to face. "I just never really thought about it. It seems so…restrictive."

"I imagine it does," he said carefully.

Was he fighting his tether? Did that primal force binding us want me to wear them? Or did it want to respect my wishes, damn the consequences? There was only one way to know.

"Do you want me to wear them?" I asked him directly.

He blinked. A hint of shock flashed across his face, but it settled into a sweeping grin that made my stomach flip. But his answer skirted my question. "It's not a decision for me to make. My feelings don't matter."

"No, it isn't," I agreed. I took a step closer, shortening the small gap between us. "But I still want to know how you feel. My mate's feelings always matter to me."

His eyes shuttered for a moment, his shoulders taut with lingering tension. "Have I told you how much I love you yet this morning?"

"You showed me," I whispered, pressing onto my tiptoes to attempt a kiss. I was still too short, but his face lowered to mine. His lips brushed mine softly like a prayer. But despite its relative chasteness, my body heated in response.

A breeze ruffled my hair, and I opened my eyes to find Julian on the other side of the counter. He winked even as his chest heaved twice.

"I don't think Celia wants to find us on the kitchen floor," he explained with a lopsided smirk, but pain edged his voice. He didn't want to risk what would happen to her if she interrupted us again. He gripped the counter, his knuckles straining against the gloves he'd put on after Celia's arrival, and I knew he was anchoring himself to the spot.

Something told me that Celia would be more careful about announcing herself in the future, but I appreciated his position. Besides that, we weren't through discussing the gloves. If we gave in to our mating instincts every time they flared inside us, we'd never finish a conversation.

"How do you really feel about them?" I studied the gloves, marveling at their neat stitching.

"I don't wish to hide your magic," he said roughly. He paused and cleared his throat, and I saw the battle waging inside him.

"Even from the Council?" I asked.

"Especially from the Council. They can have no objections to our match once it is revealed."

I carefully slipped my right hand inside the glove. I'd worn velvet gloves in Paris, but these were different. I realized the material was thicker but no less flexible as I wiggled my fingers. They'd been crafted with care by someone who knew what they were doing. The glove fit like a second skin, stopping just above my wrist with a notched cuff. "And your family?"

"Will get over it," he muttered.

I thought of Celia's reaction to his announcement. She'd scented the changes between us, and her blasé response hadn't entirely covered her surprise.

"Celia handled it well," I said as I began to put the other glove on.

He nodded, his eyes following every movement of my hands.

"Why didn't you tell her about us before she came over? That we're mated?"

He tore his attention from my hands and met my eyes. "It didn't occur to me."

"It slipped your mind?" I frowned. Sealing my mating bond with Julian was the most important moment of my life—by a mile. How could he have forgotten?

Julian chuckled darkly at whatever he saw on my face. "No, being your mate completely preoccupies my every waking moment. It slipped my mind that she was coming over. But I'm glad I got to tell her in person. It feels more *real*."

I understood that. Since the first time we'd made love, I'd felt like I was living in a dream. I'd cherish those beautiful moments for the rest of my life, but there was a different joy that came with sharing our happiness with the outside world. It was too bad there were so few others who would accept our new commitment. "I imagine telling your family is going to make it feel *very real*."

"We might want to strategize that," he admitted, his shoulders relaxing a little even as his eyes kept darting to my gloved hands. "Maybe tell them one at a time."

"Or we could just rip the Band-Aid off all at once?" I giggled at his confused look, realizing that vampires probably had very little personal experience with bandages. "If we tell them all at once, it will be over faster."

"Faster?" he repeated. "I just wonder if it will be bloodier that way."

"Bloodier?" I emphasized the final half of the word. "Are we expecting bloodshed?"

"When it comes to my family, always expect bloodshed." He hesitated, his eyes shifting to the window. "But no one will touch you."

He wouldn't allow it—with or without the tether.

"I'd rather not see you get hurt, either," I pointed out, knowing it made no difference. I held up my hands. "They fit perfectly. Do you like them?"

Julian's throat bobbed slowly before he answered. "Very much."

"Why?" This was about more than protecting my magic or falling in line with a magical tradition. He remained silent, so I pressed harder. "How do you feel about me wearing them?"

"Knowing your magic is safe means a great deal to me," he said slowly, "but that's not the real reason I like seeing them on you. Part of me..." Frustration twisted his mouth, and he shook himself loose from it before he could finish. "Part of me wants to keep your magic for myself. The same part of me that needed to claim your virginity despite knowing the consequences."

Julian wrestled with that part of himself. I suspected he hated it. I just didn't understand why. "And what is wrong with that?" I demanded. "Do you think I want to share my magic with everyone or anyone else? Or that I would ever choose to go back and sleep with another man to make things easier?"

He swallowed thickly before shaking his head.

"Then what is the problem?" I asked.

"You are not my possession," he snarled softly.

I started a little at the ferocity behind his words. "But I belong to you..."

"As my mate," he said. *"As my equal.* You have every right to choose whatever path you wish, but I find myself struggling with how to control my feelings for you."

Love swelled inside me as I processed what he was saying. He wanted me to wear the gloves so that no one else could touch what we shared. He'd told me once that holding hands was more intimate than sex for a vampire. Now that we'd been to bed, I somewhat disagreed. How could anything mean more than staring into his eyes while he filled me—completed me? But Julian had worn gloves for over nine hundred years. I'd worn these for minutes. It wasn't the same. It might never be the same. But he had taken his gloves off for me and only me. That knowledge wound itself tightly around my heart. "I will wear them." I held up a hand when he started to protest. "I want to wear them. This is *our* magic now. It belongs only to us."

His eyes were wild, but he nodded. His body tensed, coiling as if he might spring over the counter and claim me. I had half a mind to lift my index finger and beckon him to do just that. But before either of us could make a move, Celia stomped her way into the room, knocking into the entry table before throwing bags on the ground.

Julian leaned against the counter, regarding his assistant with a smirk. "That was quite an entrance."

"Better safe than sorry," she said. "Do you want to look over the rest of the items?"

They both looked to me for an answer, but I shook my head. "I'm sure it's all perfect. Thank you again."

"They suit you." She nodded to the gloves. "There are several more pairs. Louis wanted you to have options."

She had to mean the glove maker.

"Send him my thanks," Julian told her, "and tell him they are nearly as beautiful as the woman wearing them."

"That will go straight to his head, and his prices are already outrageous," she warned him. "Regarding that, I have his bill and a few other matters to discuss."

"Of course," Julian said. "Shall we settle it now? I have a few more matters to see to before we depart."

"Yes." Celia cast a sidelong glance in my direction, and I realized she wanted to speak with him alone. "Or we can wait…"

"You can discuss any matter in front of Thea," he said sharply.

Maybe he felt that way, but it probably wasn't as easy for her to trust someone she barely knew. I turned on my brightest smile. "Actually," I said loudly, "I should shower while there's someone here to distract you. Maybe I'll even put some clothes on."

Julian growled his disapproval softly but tipped his head. "As you wish, my love."

My heart constricted on those final words, but I found myself speechless. Probably because it still thrilled me to know I was his and he loved me as much as I loved him. Still, it hadn't escaped my notice that he'd chosen them more and more the last few days. Part of me missed being his pet.

I excused myself to the bedroom, closing the door behind me to give them privacy. Instantly, something tugged inside me as if my body resented even being in a different room from my mate.

"Have a little pride," I ordered it. As much as I might like the idea of spending endless hours in bed with Julian, we were going to have to reintroduce ourselves to the rest of the world sooner or later. With Greece on the horizon, sooner seemed like the better option. When we got through these stupid Rites, and it was behind us. After we dealt with his sister and handled his family, then maybe I'd convince him to find a private island for us, like Celia had suggested.

I tugged his T-shirt off and threw it in the hamper, smiling as I considered how long we could extend a vampire honeymoon. Carefully, I took off my gloves and laid them next to the bathroom sink. Turning on the shower, I stepped under it as my thoughts shifted to a different question—one I'd actively resisted asking myself.

Now that we were mates, would Julian turn me? I hadn't dared bring the subject up again. Not given how he'd reacted to it. But things were different now. Calling ourselves mates and being mated had changed both of us. I suspected we'd only scratched the surface of those changes. Something dark stirred inside me as I considered the natural companion to my question.

Did I want to be a vampire?

Dark magic thundered in my chest as I asked myself that question. His magic seemed to have an opinion on the matter. If, according to Julian, my magic felt like a warm treasure, his was something beastly, powerful. It had claws and fangs. Most of the time, I felt it slumbering inside me, like a guardian creature, content to rest at the foot of its master. But now, it roared and paced as if waiting for a threat.

"Calm down, grumpy," I whispered as I turned off the water. I reached for a towel, smiling as I felt it slow. Now wasn't the time to worry about another big decision. Not while we would soon face the consequences of our mating bond and the tether between us. Once this danger was behind us, I would bring it up again and let Julian have his say. His magic settled as if it approved of this plan.

I wrapped the towel around me and padded into the next room, catching slightly raised voices in the kitchen. A moment later, I heard his voice inside my head.

Give us a few more minutes, my love. I'll tell you later.

That didn't sound good. He must have heard the shower stop. I decided to take my time getting ready. I flushed when I saw myself in the mirror. Even with wet hair streaming down my shoulders, I saw proof that I was no longer the girl I'd been when I met him. My eyes snagged on the pearly scars where he'd fed from me. My lips, even now, looked swollen from the hours they'd spent exploring his. But underneath those subtle changes, I saw myself looking back at me. I was still Thea, but now I felt more like myself than ever before. Maybe because he'd completed the missing parts of me.

I grabbed some clothes, sighing at the number of gowns and fancy outfits that had found their way into the closet. Soon, I would be on his arm as we faced the remaining Rites and all of vampire society for the rest of the social season. I pushed down the sickening dread I felt over returning to face The Rites—and, if I was being honest, his family. The dresses were simply a reminder that our time alone was rapidly coming to an end. For now, I was sticking to jeans and sweatshirts.

As soon as I was dressed, I grabbed my new phone off the charger. Julian had managed to compel some poor soul to deliver a new one and restore most of my contacts and settings with a single call. But the fancy new phone didn't feel like my own, so I'd almost forgotten about it. So far, the most I'd done was send a quick message to my friends with the new number. I winced when I saw half a dozen new messages, mostly from Olivia.

Bracing myself, I read the first, but it was nothing more than a quick check-in. The next sent my heart into my throat. It was a message from Lassiter—just a generic announcement that final grades had been posted. The rest of Olivia's messages were a string of increasingly agitated requests to know if I'd seen the final grades, how I had done, and if I was ignoring her.

"It doesn't matter," I told myself as I logged into my email and spotted the official report among a handful of unread messages. But I couldn't lie to myself. It did matter. Even if everything I'd thought I once wanted had changed. It mattered to me. And I'd nearly thrown it away entirely. I deserved to fail. I knew that.

So, I opened the email and faced the consequences of my actions.

CHAPTER TWENTY-EIGHT

Thea

I didn't stop to think. I just ran into the next room, wet hair soaking the back of my T-shirt. As soon as I spotted Julian lounging in a club chair by the window, I remembered he'd been speaking to Celia. I glanced around the spacious apartment, but there was no sign of her.

"Did she leave?" I asked.

Julian looked up from the drink he nursed and nodded. "She's gone."

An ominous current ran through his words, and I tamped down the excitement bubbling inside me. "What's wrong? What did she need to speak with you about?"

"Nothing. Security issues. Rumors. Most of it doesn't make sense *yet*." He beckoned me with a curled finger. His gloves were gone, which was a relief, considering I'd forgotten to put mine back on. When I moved to him, he patted his lap. I sank onto it, burrowing against his muscular chest.

"What does *yet* mean?" I murmured.

"It means I'm trying to figure it all out." He kissed my forehead. "I told her about Camila."

"How did that go?" I couldn't control my surprise.

"She needed to know. Anyone connected to me should know," he said absently. "She was upset and a little bit confused. But now she's aware of the threat."

"Do you really think Camila is a threat?" We'd avoided talking of her since the day she attacked me.

"Yes, I do," he said quietly. "The woman who called me wasn't my sister. She was a stranger."

"She saved your life," I reminded him.

"And tried to hurt you." His lip curled with disgust. "Camila is a threat. I'm just not looking forward to telling the rest of the family."

"I know." All the joy I'd felt a few minutes ago flattened. I tried to shove my new cell phone into the pocket of my jeans, but Julian noticed.

"What is it?" he asked quietly. "Did you hear from your mother?"

I shook my head, my stomach twisting. My mother had been on the list of people I'd reached out to with my new phone number, along with instructions to ignore any calls or texts from my old number. She hadn't responded to me yet—probably since I hadn't texted the exact words she wanted to hear.

"No. It's not important." I leaned to kiss him, but he moved away.

"Tell me."

"I received word from Lassiter. I graduated." It felt so silly and inconsequential given what we were dealing with, but Julian wrapped his arms around me.

"I knew you would," he beamed.

"With honors," I added. "I can't believe it. Not after I missed so much coursework." I swiveled to face him. "You really didn't bribe anyone to let me pass?"

"I only bribed them to reverse your course withdrawal for the semester. You did this on your own," he said firmly. "When is the ceremony?"

"I'm not going," I said with a laugh that earned me a frown.

"Why not?"

"It's not important to me." I shrugged. "And it's on Sunday."

"Would you have gone to your graduation ceremony if you hadn't met me?" he asked.

"Probably, but only…" I swallowed as tears thickened my throat. "…only because my mom would have wanted to go."

"I see." Julian remained silent for a moment. "I would be honored to watch you graduate. I will leave it up to you if we attend."

I nodded. "Actually, Olivia asked me to go out tonight to celebrate. I told her I would ask you."

"To go out?" He lifted an eyebrow.

"If that's okay, but you can come if you like."

"Why do you need to ask me if you can go out?"

I blew a thin stream of air through my lips as I tried to think of the best way to remind him that he had a tendency to go a little caveman every now and then. "With everything going on and your sister…"

"There is that," he said bitterly. "But if you take my driver, I can discreetly have some of our men follow you. You'll have no idea that they're there unless there's trouble."

"Our men?" I repeated. "Like, your family's security?"

"Like, *our* security," he said. "That's one of the reasons Celia needed to speak with me. After what happened with Camila, I'm bringing in a team. Most of the older families have security—you saw them at my mother's party. As a bachelor, I never felt the need to keep bodyguards."

I heard the implication in his words. He could take care of himself. He still could, but now he wasn't a bachelor. "But are you sure about this? Can we trust them?"

"Yes. Don't worry about that." He paused and forced a smile, but it didn't reach his eyes. They remained shadowed even in the bright afternoon light. "I would feel better knowing they were nearby with Camila out there."

"Or you could just come with me?" I wrapped my arms around his neck.

"Go have a night with your friends."

Before I take you from them.

I wasn't sure if he'd meant for me to hear the last bit or if it had slipped past the barriers he'd managed to build between our minds. But he was right. Soon we'd be off to Greece. The next ten months would be spent jumping around the world, following the social season. It wasn't like I'd never come back to San Francisco, especially with my mom here. Someday she'd be ready to speak to me again. And Julian had a home here. His family did as well. But it wasn't the same, and he didn't have to say it for me to feel it. Something had already changed. Even now, San Francisco felt more like my past than my future. Without realizing it, my life had divided from the moment I met Julian. My future was with him. Tonight wasn't just a celebration of my accomplishments. It was a farewell to the life I'd had before.

"If you're sure…"

"Not only am I sure, but allow me to arrange the evening for you." He narrowed his eyes. "Will Tanner be joining you?"

"Yes. Is that a problem?" I held back a giggle, remembering the first time he'd found out about my male roommate.

"Just asking." But a muscle tensed in his jaw. I wondered what primal instinct he was fighting.

"No one will mind if you come," I said quietly. I wasn't certain if I was worried about how he felt or how hard I might find it to be away from him.

"I have some matters to attend to," he said. "This will give me a chance to deal with things."

"Because you're too distracted when I'm around?" I guessed happily.

"Exactly," he teased. "But I will only be a phone call away. Ring if you need anything."

"I will." Even with a security team on standby, I felt better knowing I could reach out to him.

"Just promise me one thing." His blue eyes pierced me. "Promise me that you'll be in my bed tonight."

I licked my lower lip, already knowing I'd find myself in his bed sooner than that, and nodded. "My love," I said, borrowing his new pet name, "I promise I'll be in your bed every night."

• • •

A few hours later, I managed to drag myself away from Julian long enough to get ready, but only after kicking him out of the apartment. On my first attempt to leave the bed, I'd made it as far as the bathroom before Julian innocently tried to finally get dressed. One look at his naked backside had been enough for me to forget what I was doing. We'd lost another half an hour on the bathroom floor and even longer when we'd attempted to shower together. Maybe it was his vampire stamina, or this was just how it was between us. Either way, I never wanted it to end.

Thanks to Celia, it was easy to find something to wear for the evening. Julian had been vague on where he planned to send us to celebrate, but he'd warned me to dress up a little. In the end, I'd bypassed the sweeping ball gowns and expensive ensembles purchased for the social season in favor of something sexier.

I was just throwing my phone and wallet into one of my new purses when Julian stalked through the front door. He caught sight of me and stopped in his tracks.

"What is it?" I asked when I spotted the pain on his face.

"Maybe I should go with you," he said through gritted teeth as he took in the velvet dress I'd chosen.

If the dress had been any shorter, it would have been considered a shirt. He raised a finger and twirled it. I spun around to give him a glimpse of the full package. It hugged my hips and stopped only an inch past the curve of my rear. The front dipped low enough to nearly show my bellybutton, and it was held in place by a panel of beaded mesh. The back crossed over my shoulders but was otherwise bare.

"What do you think?" I asked him as I stopped spinning.

There was a black edge to his eyes that matched the darkness in his voice as he answered me. "I think we better get you out of this apartment before I change my mind and keep you here all night."

"As if you could stop me," I said lightly and started toward the door.

Julian didn't follow for a minute, and when he did, I heard his gruff response, even though I had no idea if he said it out loud or thought it. "I'd enjoy trying."

And just like that, he crooked his arm and guided me into the night.

CHAPTER TWENTY-NINE

Thea

Despite my objections, Julian had secured one of the family limousines for our use this evening. He'd effectively silenced my concerns by reminding me that his own car was still in the parking garage at Lassiter. I squirmed in my seat as we drove across town to pick up the rest of the party.

"Are you sure you don't want to come?" I asked as we turned down my old street. Even in the dark, everything felt familiar, from the cars parked bumper-to-bumper in all available space to the trash littering our building's sidewalk. But it wasn't where I belonged anymore. It was strange to know I'd never feel like this place was my home again.

"I can occupy myself," he said seriously. "I'm not crashing your party."

"You aren't crashing any—" A squeal outside the car cut me off.

A moment later, the driver opened the door, and I spotted my friends. Olivia ducked inside the limo and beamed at me—until she spotted Julian.

"Oh. *He's* coming."

"I am merely delivering you," he said calmly.

Olivia's eyes cast daggers at him, but before she could say

anything else, the rest of the party joined us.

"Alexia!" I said brightly, spotting one of Olivia's close friends from the ballet program. Like Olivia, she was wearing a sophisticated but sexy black dress. Her dark hair hung in loose waves past her shoulders, freed from its usual bun. She was shorter than Olivia but had made up the difference with a pair of dangerously high platforms. "It's good to see you."

"You too!" She nearly fell in my lap, trying to hug me in the cramped quarters. Julian blinked next to me like we were under attack. "Congrats! And this must be your fella."

After Tanner got in, I introduced her to Julian, noticing that Olivia hadn't said another word.

Tanner and Alexia kept up a steady stream of chatter. Tanner even poked his head out of the roof, but nothing seemed to break through Olivia's icy demeanor. I'd given up by the time we reached downtown.

"Wait!" I gasped and squinted out the tinted windows. "Are we going to...?"

"You're celebrating, my love," Julian said smoothly as the limo pulled to a stop in front of one of the Bay Area's five-star hotels. It cut a striking figure in the night, but it was the glass box perched on the roof that drew the eye up. In this evening's clear ink-black sky, it stood out amongst the shorter buildings around it—as if to prove its own importance.

The restaurant situated on the top floor of the San Francisco Eaton Hotel was one of the most exclusive spots in the city. It was called The Penthouse for obvious reasons. Its prices reflected its exclusivity, so naturally, I'd never been there, and neither had my friends.

"We're going to The Penthouse?" Tanner asked with a wide grin. Even Olivia looked mildly impressed despite her commitment to giving Julian the cold shoulder.

"I asked around. I was told it was the place to be," Julian said with the casual ease of someone who had never had a door closed to him before. He also sounded every bit his nine hundred years. "Is this okay?"

I leaned over and kissed him, murmuring, "You didn't have to do this."

"You only graduate from college for the first time once," he said.

Alexia didn't bother to hide her excitement at all. Instead, she nudged Olivia in the ribs before looking at Julian. "This is really cool."

But Olivia's eyes were narrowed on my mate. "What do you mean, 'for the first time'? How many times have you graduated?"

"Liv," I snapped, annoyed at her determination to spoil the evening.

"I have more than one degree." Julian brushed something off his sleeve and shot her a wolfish smile. "Perhaps Thea will someday, as well."

I made a mental note to ask him how many degrees he had when we were alone. I imagined he was talking more than a master's.

"Is she allowed? Will you let her stay in one place long enough to pursue her dreams?" Olivia pressed.

I felt his body tense next to me, and I was grateful for the dim lighting in the back of the limousine. Something about the rigid set of his shoulders told me his eyes had darkened despite his attempts at restraint. "Her dreams are my own dreams."

"Do you really—"

"That is so romantic," Alexia cut in, glaring over at Olivia. "Thea, you're very lucky."

Olivia slumped in her seat, and I was torn between annoyance that she wouldn't let her dislike of Julian go and concern that we were ganging up on her. Before I could choose which side to come down on, the door to the limo opened.

"I *am* lucky," I said, wanting to be sure that Julian knew exactly how I felt. I placed a hand over his. "Are you sure you don't want to come?"

"No," he said softly. "Have fun with your friends. The car will be available whenever you require it—*as will I*."

I wondered if I'd imagined the wicked implication of his words for a second. Then he turned his hand over, knitting our fingers together, and brought our clasped hands to his lips. A tendril of dark magic seeped into my skin, and I bit my lip as my whole body warmed. Julian smiled and kissed my hand.

"I will see you later *tonight*." I didn't care if he'd bought out the whole of San Francisco for our graduation celebration. There was only one place I cared to end this evening: his bed.

The others had gotten out of the car. I moved to join them, but Julian slid to the open door and stood smoothly before offering me his hand. Meanwhile, I wiggled over, trying to keep my skirt down as I maneuvered the limo's short seats. I took his hand, and he guided me onto my feet. His other palm moved to the small of my back and rested there.

"Change your mind?" I asked hopefully.

His eyes darted to Olivia, and he shook his head with a smirk. "Just saying goodbye." He angled his body, lowering his face to mine. But right as our lips were about to touch, he paused. "I love you."

"I love you, too," I said breathlessly. Was "love" even a strong enough word for what I felt for him? His mouth brushed mine, the kiss relatively tame, considering that I felt as if I'd melted into a puddle at his feet.

Someone will come if you signal, but be careful.

I smiled at him and tipped my head ever so slightly.

"Oh, come on." Olivia groaned and started toward the door, where a uniformed attendant smiled dutifully and opened it for her.

Alexia and Tanner gave me sympathetic looks as we started to follow. When we reached the door, Tanner looked over his shoulder and paused. "I think he has something to tell you."

Olivia groaned again.

I turned slightly and raised an eyebrow when I saw Julian still standing by the limo's open door. The driver had already gotten back in the car.

I want to make sure you get inside safely.

I closed my eyes once to show him I understood and stepped into the lobby. When I looked back to the limo, the door was closing with Julian already out of sight.

"Did he just wait for you to get inside safely?" Alexia asked, looking like she might clutch her chest and swoon on the spot. "Where did you find him?"

"By chance." I wished I could tell her that there was a handsome, overprotective vampire waiting to take her as a mate. I wished I could tell my friends that as well. Judging from Olivia's unwavering disapproval, I wasn't sure she would celebrate if I did.

"At some party for rich assholes who buy whatever they want, women included," Olivia said as if to prove my point.

Something snapped inside me, and I rounded on her. "What is your problem?"

"What's *your* problem?" she demanded, drawing curious stares from others entering the lobby. She ignored them and plunged ahead. "I haven't forgotten how much he hurt you. How can you forgive him after that?"

"That doesn't matter," I said, keeping my voice down. "I've forgiven him. Why can't you?"

"Because I don't trust him, and I don't think you're thinking clearly." She threw off Alexia's subtle attempts to stop the argument and glared at me. "I think you lost your virginity to him, and now you can't see straight."

Tanner's mouth fell open, but he collected himself quickly. Stepping between us, he nodded to the small audience we'd attracted. "Let's discuss this in private."

Olivia ignored him and craned her head to see me. "You slept with him, didn't you? There's something different about you. I know it has to do with him."

My heart thundered in my chest, aware that people watched and waited for me to respond as though my intimate life was entertainment fodder. Whatever fracture had formed in my friendship with Olivia splintered deeper. I knew she was worried. I knew she cared about me. But right now, all I could see was my mother demanding that I choose between her and my mate, regardless of my feelings. I could hear Sabine's mocking reminders that I would never be good enough for her son. And something broke inside me.

But there were no tears. I felt no sadness. Instead, dark power slipped through my new cracks. My heart beat so rapidly I swore it was wings battering against a cage. I felt his darkness filter through my blood, erasing any doubt of who I was or what I wanted, and it was all I could do not to throw back my head and roar.

Instead, I let that power form a protective skin around me. I allowed it to soothe me with its midnight presence. I'd never been afraid to fight my own battles, except for when it came to those I loved. Olivia was right. I had changed. I didn't want to lose her, but I wasn't going to apologize for the person I'd become.

I stared her down for a long moment, that dark power flapping its mighty wings inside me. With one word, I could set it free, but I didn't need to prove anything. I didn't need to explain myself. Although I would gladly tell her all the juicy details if she asked. Without a word, I shifted away from her and walked toward the bank of elevators, heading directly for the one marked *The Penthouse*.

When I reached it, I stopped with my finger poised above the UP button on the panel and threw a look over my shoulder. Alexia and Tanner were only a few steps behind me. Tanner's eyes were wide, but he didn't say anything. Alexia gave me a small thumbs-up.

But Olivia remained where I had left her. I turned around, lifted my head, and extended a rather brittle olive branch.

"Are you coming?"

We glared at each other for a minute before she stalked toward us. The crowd that had been watching us moved away slowly with disappointed faces. I pressed the button as Olivia joined us, daring one more glance at her. She didn't say anything. She didn't have to.

I knew her well enough to know that this fight was far from over.

CHAPTER THIRTY

Julian

I'd never spent this much time in a hospital, but I could see why humans hated them. The fluorescent light overhead flickered every thirty seconds. Its low hum was almost as off-putting as the sharp antiseptic smell tainting the air. I walked down a corridor in the ICU, wondering who thought it was a good idea to paint every wall a flat, soulless gray. Between the bad lighting and lack of windows, the paint only made the place feel more like a cage. As I rounded a corner, a tired woman in alphabet-print scrubs frowned.

"Sir," she called over, "can I see your visitor badge?"

I hadn't bothered getting one from the security guard I'd compelled at the front desk. I stopped and turned a disarming smile on her. She froze, her mouth falling open as she dragged her eyes up and down my body.

When it became clear she'd been rendered speechless, I said, "I don't need a badge. I'm here to see Dr. Reeves about a patient."

Maybe she'd been pulling a long shift, or maybe her blunt attraction helped, but I barely had to compel her.

"Let me page him." She didn't hesitate. Instead, she snuck glances at me as she picked up a nearby phone to call the doctor.

"Thank you," I said after she hung up.

She leaned across her desk, her lashes lowering. "Is there anything else I can help you with? Perhaps you'd like to wait somewhere more private?"

The invitation was clear. There was a time when I might have taken her up on the offer. I couldn't be less interested now. Thea occupied my every thought. She was the reason I was here. I shook my head, ignoring how the woman's face fell. "That's not necessary." I jerked a finger to a waiting area. "I'll be over here."

She frowned and made a show of returning to the paperwork she'd been processing when I arrived.

I stood by the wall, out of the way of physicians and nurses moving busily from room to room. Every once in a while, I caught the chirp of a monitor or a groan of pain, but I did my best to block out the sounds. It was strange to be around so much pain and death. Vampires left the world quickly and brutally. But humans? They clung to life, even when it couldn't possibly be better than the release of oblivion.

"You paged me?" Dr. Reeves called to the nurse still working at the desk. She pointed to me, blushing a little when our eyes met briefly.

The doctor paused, his eyebrows furrowing as he tried to place me. He studied my tailored wool coat, tilting his head to see past my upturned collar. I considered him in turn. Thea'd mentioned Olivia had a crush on him. Most of my interactions with Olivia suggested she didn't like anyone, especially me.

On the surface, it was easy to see what caught her attention. By human standards, Reeves would be considered handsome. He had a strong jawline and a straight nose, but he was lean and pale from the hours he worked. He didn't smile as he strode over. Judging by the wrinkles in his scrubs, he'd been on this shift for a while. Hardworking and good-looking—that's what Olivia wanted.

"May I help you?" he asked after a long minute.

"I need to speak with you about a patient," I said quietly. "Kelly Melbourne."

Recognition lit across his face. "You're Thea's friend."

"Her boyfriend," I corrected him, even though calling myself her boyfriend felt entirely wrong. I wasn't her friend or her boyfriend, but I couldn't expect a human doctor to understand the significance of mating. And Thea refused to allow me to say I was her husband or fiancé, since, technically, I was neither. Something I planned to remedy as quickly as possible.

"I believe you told billing that you were her husband," Reeves said pointedly, proving he remembered me better than he'd initially let on.

"It is surprisingly difficult to pay someone's hospital bill." I picked a piece of lint off my sleeve. "It seemed easier."

"Well, since you are so close to Thea, you must know her mother is no longer here." He said her name with too much familiarity. Between that and being separated from her, I was beginning to lose patience.

"I'm aware." I dialed into my compulsion and spoke again. "We should speak somewhere privately."

Reeves blinked, a bit dazed, and nodded. "Room eight is available."

"Excellent. And I would like to see Kelly's file," I added.

"Of course."

I wasn't proud of resorting to compulsion, but I was desperate. Not only had my own investigators failed to find a clue as to Kelly Melbourne's connection with supernatural creatures, but they'd also failed to find any trace of her. She hadn't returned to her apartment after her release. Her neighbors had been no help. Most of them remembered her and Thea, but no one seemed to know them. Any hope I had of tracking her down before Thea's graduation dwindled more by the second.

The doctor paused at the nurse's desk and asked for Kelly's file, but I continued to the room when I realized I'd somehow attracted the attention of the entire nursing staff.

"We've been trying to reach Kelly for a few days," the doctor said, stepping into the room and closing the door. "Has Thea been in contact with her?"

I shook my head. "She's worried about her mother."

I held out my hand for the file, but he hesitated.

"I really shouldn't," he said.

"Thea has power of attorney, and she gave her permission," I told him, knowing that was all he needed to hear.

"That's right," he said absently and handed me the folder.

I flipped it open and scanned its contents. There was hardly any information about the woman here, either. No information on family members, even her parents. No indication that her life existed beyond Thea or the time she spent in treatment. But it was the test results that puzzled me. Earlier this evening, I'd admitted to having more than one degree. In truth, I had over a dozen, including in medicine. But despite my background, the results made no sense. "I thought she'd gone into remission."

If I was reading the information correctly, Kelly had been in remission until a few days before her mysterious accident. Tests run only a week before showed no sign of cancer. Now it was an entirely different story.

"She was," he confirmed. "I've never seen such an aggressive tumor regrowth. It's as if none of her tumors were ever treated. Not only that, but there are twice as many. She really needs to be seen."

I closed the folder and leveled my eyes with his. "Will it make any difference if she starts treatment?"

"There's always a chance," Dr. Reeves said.

But I didn't want the reassuring lies most loved ones swallowed. I wanted to know what was going on. "What would you say her chances are?"

"Maybe ten percent if we treat her aggressively as soon as possible," he said softly, but his eyes told me this was another lie.

Kelly Melbourne was dying, and if I'd questioned that there was more to my mate's mother than she let on before, I knew I was right now. The cancer wasn't just aggressive. It was *unnatural*.

"I've never seen anything like this," the doctor admitted. "Do you know if she was exposed to anything that might cause this? Asbestos? Something like that?"

If asbestos was the most help the doctor could be, we were finished here.

Before I could dismiss him, he added, "It's like something is eating away at her from the inside."

"Magic," I murmured, my thoughts turning to the power hiding within Thea's own veins.

"I'm sorry?" Dr. Reeves lifted his eyebrows. "Did you say—"

"Nothing," I cut him off. "I said nothing." I passed the file back to him with a forced smile. "I appreciate your help."

"If you get ahold of Kelly, please have her call."

"I will." But I was beginning to see that Kelly hadn't just vanished because she was upset about my relationship with Thea. She was hiding. But where and why?

"You should also prepare Thea," he added more quietly. "She should know that her time with her mother might be very short."

And thanks to me, she might not even get to say goodbye. I had to find Kelly, and quickly. I thanked the doctor again and stalked out of the hospital room. There was nothing that could be done. I'd seen the tests. The doctor had said as much. My mate's mother was dying, and any chance I had of helping her depended on knowing where she was. But Kelly Melbourne lived the life of a ghost. She had no real friends. No one knew much about her. Even her daughter, it seemed.

I stepped into the cool night and pulled my coat closed against the wind. The air suddenly so heavy with fog that I couldn't spot a single star. Not that I ever could in the city. That was the price I paid for being around so much life. What price would Kelly pay for avoiding her own? Just then, another terrible realization hit me so hard that my knees nearly buckled. If magic was slowly killing Kelly, was it the same power that ran through Thea's veins? Would it steal her from me in a few short decades?

My stomach clenched, the world darkening around the edges as blood rage took hold of me. I had not lived centuries to find my mate and lose her like this. I wouldn't.

That only left one option—an option I'd refused to consider. Did I have any choice but to turn Thea into a vampire? Not that it was up to me. She had to be the one to choose, and she had to know what she was getting into. And until then, I would give her as much of a normal life as I could. We would celebrate her graduation. I would find a romantic way to propose. I would take her as my wife. I would prepare her for becoming a turned vampire in a pureblood world.

But first, I needed to find her mother and heal the rift I'd caused between them before it was too late.

I pushed through the foot traffic on the sidewalk and lumbered toward the limo. Tonight, I would keep all of this to myself. Thea deserved one night of happiness before I delivered the latest blow.

As I reached the limo, I slid into the back seat, not bothering to wait for the driver. I slumped against the leather, my fingers kneading my pulse, and called up to the front, "We can go."

The engine continued to idle.

I tried the intercom again, searching for the driver's name and finally landing on it. "Han?"

Nothing.

I pressed the button to lower the barrier between our seats, and the sharp tang of iron hit my nostrils. I could make out Han's profile, but there was no movement. Not even a hint of breathing. I inhaled deeper, recognizing the scent filling the cabin.

Death.

"Fuck," I grunted, lunging for the handle a second too late. The back passenger door opened...and my sister slid in beside me.

CHAPTER THIRTY-ONE

Thea

As soon as we stepped off the elevator, a man in a charcoal suit stepped in front of us. "Miss Rousseaux?"

Olivia flinched out of the corner of my eye, but Alexia giggled. Meanwhile, I resisted the sudden urge to bang my head into the wall, but I refused to show any sign of nerves.

"That's me," I said, not bothering to correct him. What was the point? But Olivia had heard that, and no doubt, she'd made a mental note I hadn't set the record straight.

"I'm Jax, the manager of The Penthouse. We're delighted you've joined us. Please follow me." He guided us through the crowd. Along the way, people turned and stared at us. They were probably trying to figure out what made us so special. When we reached a private alcove, set off from the main dining room by sliding doors, I understood why. The spot screamed V.I.P.,

Inside, the private dining room was like something out of a fairy tale. Rose-colored lights were dimmed to cast a romantic hue over a large, round table. Rather than individual seats, two curved velvet couches with low backs and dozens of cushions awaited. In the center of the table, a flower arrangement that had to be taller than me was filled with roses in full bloom and long tendrils of ivy. Petals spilled elegantly over the gold-flecked marble tabletop. But it was the view that stole my breath.

Rather than walls, floor-to-ceiling windows enclosed the space on all sides, allowing a sweeping view of downtown San Francisco. As we stepped in, Jax motioned to one of the windows, through which we could see what The Penthouse was really known for: its rooftop bar.

We settled onto the seats, Tanner next to me and the others across from us. Olivia positioned herself opposite me and continued to glare.

"You are welcome to come and go as you please." Jax touched a glass panel, and it shifted open, revealing that the side wasn't a window at all. It was a door. "Your tab has been seen to, and my staff is prepared to meet your every request." As he spoke, two servers entered, each carrying a bottle of Dom Pérignon. "Mr. Rousseaux wished to provide you with a celebratory toast to start your evening."

"Of course he did," Olivia muttered, still looking gloomy, but Alexia and Tanner remained in mute shock.

"May we?" Jax asked, and I nodded. A little social lubrication might be just what we needed.

The servers popped the corks and poured champagne into our flutes. We each took them, eyeing one another nervously as they placed the open bottles into a huge silver urn filled with ice. When they finally left, we all burst out laughing.

Except for Olivia.

I ignored her and raised my glass. "What should we toast to?"

"To making it out alive," Tanner suggested, waggling his eyebrows.

If he only knew. I bit my lip and plastered a smile on my face.

"Barely," Olivia said softly.

It was getting harder to ignore her subtle jabs on top of the not-so-subtle ones. I suspected that was the point. She wanted to finish the fight we'd started downstairs. Instead, I tapped my glass against Tanner's. "I'll drink to that."

We each took a sip. Across from me, Alexia's dark eyes popped open. "Oh my God, that is good. It's like fizz from heaven."

"Agreed." Tanner downed his glass and reached for the bottle. "Shall we drink more?"

"They're already open," I said lightly.

"And the bill is paid, right?" Olivia added.

I hesitated for a moment before I placed my champagne flute on the table and stood up. "Let's go, Liv."

Silence fell around the table.

"Where?" she asked.

"Bathroom? Out there? I don't care, but we need to talk," I demanded, planting my hands on my hips.

She stood and pointed to the door.

"Are you sure?" Tanner asked, glancing at the rooftop. "I don't love the idea of you two fighting on a roof."

"We're not fighting," Olivia said.

"We're arguing," I finished.

He shared a glance with Alexia, but neither of them spoke.

"Just don't get us kicked out," Alexia said, holding up a small menu. "I'm starving, and the food looks amazing."

My own stomach growled as though to remind me that I'd spent more time in bed with my mate than eating. I couldn't fault Alexia's priorities, but I wasn't going to sit and take shit from Olivia all night.

"Order for us," I instructed Tanner and Alexia.

"What do you want?" Alexia asked.

"All of it," I said smoothly. "Order it all. We're *celebrating*." I threw the last word at Olivia.

Her lips pinched together, and she strode to the hidden door, pressed the panel, and stomped outside. The one glass of champagne felt hot in my belly, but it did little against the chilly night. Most of the people at the bar were wearing coats, and I could see why. Wind whipped my hair into my eyes. I shoved it back, spotting an outdoor heater, and pointed to it.

Olivia followed me without a word, even though I knew she had to be cold, too. The heater had been turned to its highest setting, and I could have wept when I felt the heat radiating around it. Now that I wasn't going to freeze to death, I turned on my best friend.

"Yes," I said.

Olivia blinked, anger shifting to confusion. "Yes, what?"

"I slept with him," I said, my heart jolting into a frantic pace. I couldn't tell her everything. How exactly was I supposed to explain that Julian was my mate? By all accounts, it shouldn't be a big deal to tell my human friend that I'd done a completely normal human thing.

But somehow, at this moment, it felt like a really big deal.

"When?" she asked flatly.

"A few days ago," I admitted. "I should have told you."

Olivia's eyes zeroed in on my face. "And how did you get that bruise? What happened to your phone?"

"This?" I sighed as I reached up to touch the lingering injuries from Camila's attack. "I was mugged."

It wasn't exactly a lie. My cell phone had been stolen. It made sense.

"And you slept with him before or after that?"

I wasn't sure where she was going with this, so I decided to be honest. "After."

"And where was he when you got mugged?" Something about the way she said it told me she didn't believe my story.

Part of me longed to come clean to her. I hated keeping secrets from her, but I couldn't tell Olivia about vampires without putting her life at risk. And would she even believe me? I hadn't even believed it when Julian told me. I could have him show her his fangs, but telling Olivia meant revealing a world I wanted to protect her from. "He wasn't with me. It was after I performed my showcase. Someone attacked me in the parking garage at Lassiter."

"And you didn't tell me?" Past the bitter coating of her words, I heard pain.

"It was just a mugging, and I was okay," I said weakly. "I didn't want you to worry."

"And when you slept with him? Why didn't you tell me then?"

Annoyance reignited inside me at what was beginning to feel like an interrogation. "It was only a few days ago. You still had finals, and we've been...busy."

"Busy?" she repeated. "You mean you've been screwing?"

I opened my mouth, trying to think of a clever retort, but all I found was the truth again. "Yes."

Olivia stayed silent for a second. Finally, her eyes locked on me. "I saw your mom a few days after he came back into town."

Oh.

"She made me choose," I reminded Olivia. "It wasn't fair."

"She said that he's dangerous." She waved an arm around us. "Look around. You went from a college student pulling two jobs to having everything you could ever want. Trips to Paris, expensive cellos, champagne flowing like water."

"What's your point?" Inside me, Julian's dark magic grew more agitated by the second.

"Do you know what you're getting yourself into?"

I laughed. If she only knew, she wouldn't be asking. "Yes, and Julian isn't a bad guy."

Not really. He only ripped apart people who deserved it.

She looked unconvinced. "What does he do?" she demanded. She waited for a second while I tried to dream up an explanation for his wealth that didn't involve money laundering or being a secret royal. "Well, Thea? Do you even know?"

"Investments," I snapped.

"Remind me to ask him for market advice." She rolled her eyes.

"His whole family is rich." I shrugged. "It doesn't matter to me."

"No," she said, shaking her head. "Don't lie. You don't go from having nothing to being filthy fucking rich and not care at all."

"I'm not rich," I reminded her, but it sounded like a lie even to my own ears.

"You sure about that?" she pressed.

"It's his money, not mine."

She finally smiled. "I'm glad to hear you say that, because you know this isn't going to last, right?"

"What?" I asked slowly.

"This." She pointed to the restaurant. "You two don't know each other. I don't want to see you fall apart when things don't work out, and I don't want to see you burn too many bridges for him. You quit your job, the quartet; you barely graduated."

I paused, digesting the truth, not her tone. Olivia wasn't upset that I'd slept with him. She was worried, just like my mom had been, that I was being used for my virginity by a rich asshole who would discard me like I was nothing. But I'd been able to tell my mom the truth because she knew about vampires. Even then, she hadn't accepted Julian as my mate. No one else in my life knew what was really going on, and it left me disconnected. I felt like a balloon that had gotten away from its string. There was nothing holding me to my old life. I was floating alone in this strange new world, and while Julian was there to tether me—quite literally—everything still felt surreal.

And she was right. Not that things wouldn't work out between us—since the mating, I was more sure of Julian than I was that the sun would rise every morning. She was right that I was in danger. Not from vampires or his family and especially not from him. I was in danger of losing the people that meant the most to me. How was I supposed to be part of his world and still be me?

"You didn't correct that guy when he called you Miss Rousseaux," Olivia finally said when the silence had stretched to a thin line.

"I'm getting used to it," I admitted.

"Getting used to what?"

"The name," I said softly. I knew what I had to do.

"Thea," she said in a strangled voice. "Please tell me you didn't elope."

I laughed and shook my head. "We're not married," I told her, and she sighed with relief until I added, "yet."

Olivia went completely still as what I meant sunk in. "Has he asked you?"

"Yes. No. It was a shitty proposal." I dredged up a smile and met my best friend's wide round eyes. "But we're getting married."

"You don't even know him!" she shouted, her voice carrying over the noise of the bar.

"I know him. He's my mate." Just saying it erased the tightness in my chest. The dark magic in me didn't object. Instead, it seemed to puff its chest and then settle down happily for a nap. Of course it responded that way. Julian wanted to shout the news from the rooftops. His magic must feel the same.

She shook her head, confusion clouding her face. "You're what? What does that mean?"

"My mate," I repeated to my shocked best friend. "It's what his world calls it."

"What do you mean *his world*?"

I took a deep breath, my decision already made, and told her, "Julian is a vampire."

CHAPTER THIRTY-TWO

Julian

Everything about her had changed, and yet everything was the same. She shut the door, blocking out the noisy city outside, and smiled at me. Her eyes—the same shade of blue as mine—observed me, and although her lithe body appeared relaxed, I knew she was on edge. How? The same way I'd always known. Even now, after everything that had happened, I felt the palpable connection between us. The same twin bond that had sent me racing after her in Paris.

Camila reached for a bottle of whisky from the limo's stocked minibar, uncapped it, and took a swig. The last time I'd seen her, she'd been dressed in Victorian finery. Tonight, her hair was chopped into a slinky black bob that dusted the shoulders of her tight leather jacket. She stretched her legs, showcasing a pair of chunky motorcycle boots with enough straps to make a dominatrix blush.

She held the bottle out to me, but I kept staring until the vehicle began to move. My eyes darted to the front seat, where a stranger dressed in all black steered the car into the San Francisco traffic. I'd been so distracted I hadn't even noticed.

"Don't worry about him." Camila leaned over and pushed the button, raising the barrier between the driver and us.

My shock snapped, and I snarled at her. "I should kill you."

"How dramatic." She rolled her eyes as she reached into her pocket. A second later, she tossed me a phone. "I came to return your mate's phone." Camila paused and inhaled deeply. "It seems that's what Thea is, finally. No longer playing house, huh?"

"Stay away from her." Even hearing Thea's name on her lips sent fury boiling inside me. The dim lights of the limo's back cabin darkened as blood rage took hold of me. The fragile phone in my hands shattered, pulverized nearly to dust. I wouldn't be able to stay in control much longer. Blood rage was the cousin of bloodlust. The two were often linked together, but now that I was mated, the need to protect my mate consumed me to the point of madness. It was only the fear that acting prematurely might endanger Thea more that kept me in check. I needed to know what Camila was up to—before I ripped off her head.

"Look at it this way," Camila said as though we were still just catching up. "I did you a favor. You finally fucked her, didn't you?"

I lunged for her, grabbing her by the throat. Camila only laughed. It was a strangled, unsettling sound, but her amusement twinkled in her eyes. Staring at me, she choked out, "Do it."

I wanted to. Every instinct in me roared to take her head off and remove whatever threat she posed to Thea. But Camila's words twisted inside me. She meant it. She wanted me to kill her. So, I loosened my grip instead and delivered a warning. "You will not speak of my mate that way."

"The birds and the bees are a fact of life," she said, her teeth gritting together. I let go of her completely, and she sucked in a deep breath. "But we can drop it. We have other matters to discuss."

"Like what?" I adjusted my gloves, trying to remain focused on the situation developing here and now, but my thoughts strayed to Thea. If Camila had caught up with me, was Thea safe under my protection? She had to be. I'd arranged the security myself. No one could touch her. But I'd let my guard down. I'd been too distracted leaving the hospital, considering what to do about Thea.

"War is coming," my twin said softly. "I'm here to give you a chance to join the right side."

"And that side is…?" I taunted her.

"Don't pretend that you agree with the Council," she hissed before taking another swig of whisky. "I know they threatened to execute Thea. And I'm here to tell you that was not an empty threat."

"The Council isn't an issue."

"Why? Because she's got magic in her? Do you think they care? You disobeyed them. Even now, they're voting on whether or not to take action against you." Camila's upper lip curled to reveal a fully extended fang.

"The Council won't get near her," I said in a low voice, adding, "and neither will you."

"Fighting words." She chuckled. "We both know that's not true. I already got to Thea."

My blood rage built to a crescendo, and I fought to halt its swell. "And you never will again."

"If I'd wanted to kill her, she would be dead," Camila reminded me flatly. "So simmer down before your head explodes."

My breathing was hard and ragged, but she made a fair point. Even though Thea claimed the witch had saved her, I knew that if Camila had wanted to hurt either of them, she could have.

"You don't trust me," she said.

"Why would I? You let us believe you were dead—you let *me* believe it."

"I might as well have been. I felt dead. My life traded for an alliance, my children another way for Willem to control me, and Willem…"

"I know," I murmured. "I know what he was."

"*Is,*" she corrected me.

"What?" I stared at her. "And the children?"

"Dead," she said flatly. "Willem's last gift to me. Burned alive in the fire he set to *cleanse* our home."

Despite her chilled response, she couldn't hide the truth from me. My heart stuttered, feeling her pain like it was my own. Somewhere inside me, golden light spread in soothing tendrils. Thea's magic wrapped itself around my heart protectively as if to tell me I wasn't alone.

"I'm sorry." The words were too little too late.

"You never even met them," she said mostly to herself, her eyes lost to some distant place.

"And you? You're still tethered," I added.

"No, I died that day with my children. I passed beyond."

I didn't say anything. Vampires, as a rule, didn't believe in heaven or hell. Our kind had lived long enough without seeing proof that such concepts seemed silly.

"Do you want to know what lies beyond?" she asked, and I found myself nodding. "*Freedom*. It only took a minute. My soul passed into this great, beautiful oblivion, and then I was yanked back. A servant healed me. I never found out how. When I opened my eyes and discovered the nightmare I'd returned to, I killed her. I think she was a witch," she added thoughtfully.

Camila had died. That much was true, but it didn't explain where she had been all this time.

"Why didn't you find us?" I demanded.

"Why would I?" she seethed, turning on me. "You left me to rot."

"You can keep telling yourself that, but it's not true. Do you know that every year Mother shopped for you and filled a closet for you, hoping you would visit? Every year until your death. She kept a room for you. She kept a room"—my voice broke—"for your children. Her grandchildren. She changed laws. Benedict followed her lead. Sebastian tried to drown himself in cocaine. And every war our father fought in the last two hundred years was driven by his hatred of Willem."

"And you?" she asked pointedly. "Where were you? Where was my twin?"

"I tried." I couldn't tell her more, not with the blood-vow binding my lips. Not with the promise I had made—the one I'd sworn to our mother. The one that hung around my neck like an albatross.

"You *failed*. Just like you will fail your mate if you refuse to see the truth."

"And what is the truth? Where is Willem? Who are these people you are working with?" I pressed.

"You are not the only one bound by a blood-vow."

I went still. She couldn't possibly know about the blood-vow. No one did. Not even Thea. It was the one secret I'd been forced to keep.

Her eyes sparkled malevolently as if she, too, could read my thoughts. "I've always wondered what Mother made you swear that was so horrifying that you went to sleep for decades."

I had no idea how she knew, but it was clear that she didn't care.

"I visited once, you know," she continued. "Came to the island, stood in your room, and watched you sleep. So, when I say that I have no wish to kill you, believe me."

"It would mean more if you'd stop killing everyone around me," I snarled. Even as I tried to process what she was telling me—and what she wasn't—I hadn't forgotten Paris. I hadn't forgotten Hughes or Han or the innocents at the opera. And I had certainly not forgotten her attack on Thea or the marks she'd left on my mate.

"There is a price for freedom. It's *death*," she told me.

"Is that what the people who attacked the opera thought? That they were freeing innocents?"

"Things got out of hand. Unfortunately, the Mordicum attracts a fair number of angry, turned vampires. The ones the Council and the purebloods try to keep under heel."

The *Mordicum*. Now I had a name. It was Latin perverted for modern use, but its meaning was clear. *Biting*. But not just the simple act of doing so. No, this was a violent bite—a tenacious, primal tearing, ripping, rending. "And this Mordicum is better than the Council?"

"They aren't afraid of what they are. They simply want to be vampires," she said fiercely, her eyes lighting up.

"And that's what you want?" I shook my head. "That's bullshit, and you know it. You've been free for decades. Why come back to start a fight?"

"You think I'm the one starting the fight?" She blinked, and the light vanished, the whites of her eyes darkening. "What do you think happened while you were sleeping? Why do you think The Rites have been enacted? The Council only wants to control you."

"The Council doesn't even approve of compulsion anymore."

"For *switches*," she said, and I blanched. "Don't look so surprised to hear me use such language. I'm not the virgin you sent off to the slaughter. The Council's rules don't apply to everyone. The old bloodlines still have power."

"You forget that they threatened my mate," I hissed.

"Yes, because you're ruining their plan—ruining *his* plan," she said meaningfully.

"Who?" My blood ran cold in my veins.

The corner of her mouth turned down, her eyes shutting, but she shook her head. "I can't tell you—not until you choose a side."

But I already knew. There was only one person who could have drawn Camila out of hiding—only one person she hated enough to join with these butchers she called the Mordicum. The person who made her into this monster sitting next to me.

Willem.

CHAPTER THIRTY-THREE

Julian

The city whipped past the tinted windows, cast in shades of night. Through the dark glass, it was as murky as the thoughts swirling in my brain. Even if Camila was right and Willem was alive, he couldn't hide behind the Council.

"Impossible," I muttered. "Our family—*our mother*—would never—"

"What?" she cut me off. "Our mother would never what? Did you think telling me about her closets of clothes for me would magically soften me? That reminding me of her politics would erase what she did?"

"She would never ally with Willem again. If she knew he was alive—"

"That's why you think I hate her?" Camila interrupted. "I'm not mad at our mother for worshiping the Council. I'm mad because she's a fool. After everything, she's still blind to the real danger they pose. She's still too attached to the family name, the family reputation, and the *family bank balance* to admit what's right in front of her. Just like she was when she used me as bait to catch the Drake family name."

"You courted him," I reminded her coldly. "You fawned over him. We didn't know until it was too late."

She laughed, the sound like the tinkle of broken glass—sharp and alarming. "Yes, I was responsible for my marriage, wasn't I? Not the woman who brought a virgin to the season. Not the woman who said nothing when the snakes ignored me at the First Rite. The snakes that crawled up your mate's body—*why*...?"

"Because she was a virgin," I said, my voice soft with horror as I realized what Camila meant.

"Do you see now? Sabine *knew*. She knew Willem Drake had claimed me *before* the First Rite even took place." Her voice shook as she spoke. "She knew I was tethered."

It couldn't be true. In the years we'd spent fighting the Council to change the law, Sabine had never admitted that my sister had not been a virgin when she was married.

"Don't you want to know?" Camila continued, barely suppressed rage dripping in her words. "How he *won* me so quickly? He *didn't*. He took me without my consent and threatened me so I wouldn't scream while he raped me in a dark corner. One minute. That was all it took, and then all he had to do was tell me to love him—and *I did*."

My stomach turned over, bile rising in my throat, and a wave of new anger erupted inside me. Only this time the blood rage wasn't directed at my sister. I didn't know where to spend it or who to blame. Instead, it built.

And built.

She continued, adding fuel to the inferno I felt. "He never let me stop loving him. It was my duty. He built us a home to protect me, but it was a prison. He ordered me to never complain, to never tell anyone the truth, so that he would never be called on to uphold his end of the bargain. When he beat me, when he raped me, when he starved me— it was all a way to prove I loved him, he said. If I loved him, I would endure anything, and with that tether in place, I didn't know my own heart anymore.

"He kept me from my family so I wouldn't remember real love. He fed me lies. And I thought I loved him...until the children came. I knew then whatever it was that bound me to Willem wasn't love. So, I took that knowledge, and I used it—to protect them. He hated them because they were the reason he couldn't quite control me. They weren't Drakes. He knew it. He knew they were like me, not him." She stopped, her jaw tightening, tears forming in her eyes. "When the fire started, he held me back, made me watch. I thought he meant to kill me, and so I found the flames beautiful. I wanted to walk into them and be free. But fate had other plans, didn't it?" Camila turned sharp eyes on me. "Someone came, distracted him. I ran for the flames even as I heard my savior scream for me to stop. But I didn't."

Neither of us looked away.

"I never saw my savior. I only heard him. When I woke to find that witch had healed me, and there was no savior and no children, I died a second time and took her with me. But she said one thing—*a name*—before I drained the last drop of her blood. Do you know what name it was?"

I didn't speak.

"I suppose we both know what secrets our blood-vows keep for us," she said finally. "I suppose that's why you went to sleep—because you couldn't save me that night. I never came to find you—because I hated you...for not saving *them*."

The magic binding my blood-vow curled around my throat as if ready to choke any confession I might make. It was powerful magic— proof of the power in my mother's ancient blood that it held even as the truth unraveled around me.

"But then I found out Willem was alive, and I was free to hate him. That should have been when I realized why Mother made you take that blood-vow. I thought she was protecting her reputation—that she didn't want anyone to know you had interfered in my marriage— but she was keeping them a secret... Why? Why did it matter if they were dead?"

"A Rousseaux answers when duty calls," I muttered through clenched teeth.

But Camila pounced on me, her bare fingers sinking into my cheeks as she screamed, "Where are my children, Julian? What did you do with them?"

I couldn't answer her, and even if I could, could I trust her? Or would she drag them into her warped war? I had no choice in keeping this secret, but even if I did, I had not guarded them for years—from everyone—to risk them now.

"What if someone took her from you?" she snapped. "Took your children?"

"I have no children," I muttered.

"*Yet*. They will never be safe in this world. Not with the Council. Not with Willem pulling their strings. Maybe that's what he really wants with Thea. She has power inside her." Camila smacked me. She raised her palm from the wounds she'd left on my face as if she meant to strike again. "The kind of power they want."

"What are you saying?" I growled, shoving her off me. She landed with a laugh on the limo's carpeted floor.

"Maybe they don't plan to execute her at all. Maybe he just wants *her*. Her magic could breed powerful vampires. The kind Willem always wanted." There was no triumph in her voice, just that edge of desperation I'd heard over the phone. "At least she can't be tethered—*twice*."

"I freed her of that tether." But I began to pant as I considered what she said—what she meant.

"Willem would not have been so kind," she said, "but if I'm right, he will not be pleased to hear his prize has been sullied."

"This doesn't make any sense." The Council wanted Thea dead. My mother would never work with Willem. But what if Camila was right? What if Sabine didn't know? What if my mother had inadvertently delivered exactly what Willem wanted, thinking she was protecting innocents? What if the whole time Willem had wanted vampires to stay away while he searched for untapped magic and pure females? And what would happen if this was true and he found out Thea was my mate?

"The Mordicum has been looking for Thea, you know, for weeks. She just disappeared," Camila continued. "Like she didn't exist."

Like Kelly, the woman with no past, no friends, no life. A woman whose magic was eating her alive. A woman who would protect her daughter at any cost. And a woman who would take one look at the vampire in love with her daughter and know the danger that love would place her in.

A shrill ring broke the silence, and Camila reached into her pocket to pull out her phone. She lifted a finger as she answered it. I was too preoccupied to eavesdrop, still reeling from the terrible realization that Kelly Melbourne knew about vampires because she was *hiding* from our world—and dying to shield her daughter from it.

"Julian!" Camila's sharp voice broke through my scrambled thoughts.

I started to tell her there was nothing left to say. I knew enough now. I would protect Thea from the Council *and* the Mordicum. I refused to be a pawn when my job was to protect my queen.

But when I looked at Camila, her eyes were wide, her mouth turned down in flat terror. When she spoke, her voice trembled. "The Council issued a command to local authorities. They want Thea brought into custody—*tonight*."

CHAPTER THIRTY-FOUR

Thea

Now I knew why The Penthouse was famous. Yes, the food was incredible. I'd enjoyed dumplings filled with pork cooked in warm, deep spices dipped in a tangy sauce with bright punches of lemongrass and citrus. But it had been hard to eat while Olivia glared at me, refusing to speak to any of us. I supposed that was better than her announcing to Alexia and Tanner that I'd lost my mind as well as my virginity—I suspected that might happen before the evening was over. But as night swallowed the sky, the moon veiled by clouds, the atmosphere shifted from restaurant to private club. The bar where I'd dropped my bombshell revelation on Olivia filled with people. Clustering together in the chilled air, they drank until they were warm enough to spread across the rooftop. The kitchen closed, and the music started, changing the vibe altogether. Unlike earlier, there were fewer coats and even fewer people clustered around the tall heaters stationed around us. I was surrounded by people who wanted to be seen, searching for what I already had—someone to spend the night with.

Tanner moved behind me, dropping a fresh cocktail over my shoulder. I cringed as I took it. I was already feeling dizzy. It had been much easier to drink than eat after Olivia called me an asshole for making shit up and stomped off. I'd lost count of the times my champagne flute refilled, and now we were moving on to the harder stuff.

"What is this?" I shouted over the loud music as I stared at the murky concoction he'd brought me. I didn't know if it was the colored lights glowing around the roof's safety railing or if it was actually green.

"Death in the afternoon," he said, grabbing my hips and directing them in rhythm with the music.

I took a sip and nearly choked. "Oh my God, what's in it?"

It tasted like how *drunk* felt.

"Absinthe and champagne. It's supposed to get you fucked up," he said, maneuvering me to the cluster of people here for the music.

"I can see why." I took another sip, wondering why anyone wanted to combine the delightful fizz of champagne with the bitterness of licorice.

"Just drink it." He rolled his eyes. On their way back down, they snagged on someone dancing nearby. He nodded. "What do you think?"

I swallowed the drink, gagging as fire raced up my throat. Following Tanner's gaze, I spotted a few persons of interest. "Which one? Him or her?"

"Either," he said with a smirk.

I studied the pair. The tall blonde looped an arm around the man's neck, his hand skimming over her rear. They both looked like they had money. Her silver jumpsuit dipped nearly to her navel and, judging from how it draped across her body, was designer. He'd opted for all black, a precisely tailored jacket over a black T-shirt and jeans. The gold watch on his wrist popped against the ensemble. While I watched, she leaned up and whispered in his ear.

I sipped more bubbly licorice. "I think they came together."

"Even better." Tanner's grin widened.

He would make an excellent vampire. I made a mental note to never introduce him to Julian's brother Sebastian.

"So, your fight with Olivia went well, huh?" He whirled me

around as the music changed. Maybe it was the alcohol swimming inside me or the utter mess I'd made by confessing to Olivia, but I burst into a fit of giggles.

"Smashingly," I managed to say between laughs. "She really hates Julian."

"Yeah, she does." He laughed with me.

Something about him admitting it sobered me up—but only a little. "Do you?"

"Does it matter?"

I nodded.

"Nah. I don't know him, and you aren't the first person to get back with their ex."

He made an excellent point. I tried to file it away for the follow-up fight I expected Olivia to pick later, but my brain seemed to have trouble processing new data.

"He got you one, too." Alexia stuck her tongue out as she joined us. "Gross, right?"

"Hey!" He held up his hands, releasing my hips finally. "It's what the guy at the bar suggested."

Now I rolled my eyes. "You listened to a bartender? He just wants to sell you something expensive."

"No, this other guy. He asked me how I managed to have the three most beautiful women here with me."

Both Alexia and I pretended to gag again.

"What? It's a compliment to you. I thought it meant he had good taste, but who the hell drinks absinthe these days?"

Hearing the word a second time sent a fuzzy recollection of a painted sign to my brain, but—

"I need the bathroom." Alexia grabbed my hand and tugged me toward the door.

"I think I'll try my luck." Tanner winked at me and started toward the couple.

"Do I want to know?" Alexia asked. I shook my head.

The cocktail turned out to be more potent than I thought. I stumbled behind, earning snorts of laughter from her. "Hey, we're not all ballerinas!"

She continued to laugh and slowed a little. When we discovered the long line waiting to use the restroom, Alexia groaned. From the middle of the queue, Olivia looked over and frowned. But if Alexia noticed, she ignored it. Instead, she dragged me over, earning a few snarky comments from the others in the line. Turning a sweet smile on the naysayers, she took hold of Olivia's other hand and tugged her along.

"What the—" But before Olivia could protest, Alexia spun around quickly. I had to grab her shoulder to keep myself upright.

"Work your magic," Alexia demanded.

The words pierced through my brain fog, and my mouth fell open. "What?"

"Your VIP privilege. With Jax or one of the waiters. There has to be another bathroom."

Of course that's what she'd meant, but I drew my hand away from her shoulder all the same. Maybe I should have worn gloves tonight. Who knows what I might slip up and do?

We didn't have to go far before an overzealous server accosted us. "Is there anything I can get you, Miss—"

"Bathroom," I cut him off before he applied Julian's name to mine again and made things worse. "Please."

He showed us to one reserved for VIP guests, a fact that made Alexia preen and Olivia huff. It was only a single toilet with no stall, but we all went in together. Strangely, it was more comfortable to watch Alexia use it than to look at my former roommate.

When Alexia finished, she stood and glowered. "Seriously, you two!" She smoothed her skirt back down and moved to wash her hands. "We're supposed to be celebrating. What is up?"

"Go ahead and tell her, Thea," Olivia challenged me with a lifted eyebrow.

Alexia looked at me in the mirror as she soaped up her hands. "Tell me what?"

I tried to speak but found it difficult. The lights in the bathroom danced, and I angled my head, mesmerized by them.

I didn't realize my whole body had tilted until Olivia caught me.

"What did you drink?"

"Some absinthe thing Tanner bought us." Alexia frowned, shaking her hands dry. "It was strong but not that strong."

"Considering she's the size of a kitten, it might have hit her harder." Olivia kept her hand on my shoulder even as disapproval etched deep lines around her mouth. "You should have eaten more."

"She's mad because I'm getting married," I announced loudly, batting away her hand.

"That's not why... Well, it's not the only reason," she said in a low voice.

"Married?" Alexia clapped her hands. "When did he propose? I need details."

"Oh, no!" I flapped a hand around me. "It was a shitty proposal. He has to ask again. I'm making him."

"But you're going to say yes?" Alexia pressed. "We can be bridesmaids."

Next to me, Olivia went rigid. "That might be a problem. Will there be a church wedding if he's a—"

The door burst open, cutting her off mid-sentence. It rattled on its hinges, the frame splintering from the force of smashing past the bolt. A man dressed in black prowled inside. I was vaguely aware of my friends' screams, but I found my attention pinned on the stranger.

"You!" I pointed at him. "My friend thinks you're hot."

It was the man from the dance floor—the one Tanner had planned to hit on. He didn't smile, and as he lifted his head, his eyes were jet-black. Alexia's renewed scream tore through the air.

"Shut up," he snarled, and the sound died in Alexia's throat even as her mouth remained open. Olivia's own shouts shifted to hyperventilation. Her wild eyes met mine as she realized what was happening.

Maybe it was the absinthe, but I couldn't help but shrug a shoulder. *"Vampire."*

Not that I was gloating, because even in my champagne-drenched brain, I knew this was very, very bad. At least I didn't have to keep her from institutionalizing me or treating me like I'd been making things up...

"Look"—I poked him in the chest—"you are not going to want to deal with my mate."

He hesitated, and I couldn't be certain if it was due to my threat or my bare finger. Before I could touch him again and find out, a furious voice ripped through the air. "No, he is not."

Love and darkness swelled inside me as Julian stepped into view, the magic that linked us greeting my mate. His black eyes met mine, and I noted the dried blood smeared on his cheeks. I searched him for a sign he was injured, instinct telling me it was his own. Had he fought other vampires trying to find me? But there was no sign of a struggle. His black wool coat was pristine, cutting a dashing figure before he sprang forward, pinning the vampire to the wall. He lifted him several feet off the ground as the vampire struggled.

"Which would you prefer, my love? Head or heart?" he thundered, his fangs bared.

"I represent the Council," the vampire said in a choked voice.

We both ignored him.

"I had it under control," I said, nearly falling over as I tried to step toward him, holding my finger up as though it was a weapon.

"So I see." He squeezed the vampire's throat, rivers of blood trickling from where his ungloved fingers punctured the skin.

Behind me, Olivia whimpered, reminding me that there were witnesses. "Thea..."

"Kill him later," a feminine voice ordered, and I blanched, feeling my cheek throb when Camila stepped into the crowded bathroom. "Question him first."

"What is she doing here?" I flung my finger in her direction. The movement sent starbursts dancing in my vision. I moaned and pressed a hand to my forehead.

Julian's eyes narrowed, and a second later, he dropped the vampire to his feet. Before I could blink, his arm hooked around my would-be attacker's neck and snapped it, breaking the compulsion he'd placed on my friends. Alexia's scream nearly ruptured my eardrums.

"Quiet," Julian ordered her, and I managed a disapproving frown before the dizziness overtook me again. A rumble vibrated from him before he forced a terse, "Please."

"You've got to be joking." Camila shook her head at the show of manners.

He didn't respond. Instead, he tossed the vampire's unconscious body to her like it was a rag doll and shot to me with inhuman speed. He caught me around the waist, steadying me as the world shifted under my feet. "Whoa. What..." He grabbed my wrist, lifted it to his mouth, and sank his fangs in without warning.

"Hey!" I yelped, surprised he'd want to do something so intimate...here...even though the alcohol in my system dulled the pain. Julian drew back instantly—and spat my blood on the floor. "What...?"

Murder coated his words as he answered, "You've been drugged."

Someone was about to die. I prayed it wasn't me.

CHAPTER THIRTY-FIVE

Thea

I stared at a crack in one of the wall's black subway tiles, feeling something splinter inside me. I heard my friends' faint sobs and wondered if they were asking themselves the same question I kept asking myself. I tried to block them out, but in the cramped space, that proved impossible.

I forced myself to face what was happening. "Am I going to die?"

"No! It tastes like a mild sedative." But he gripped my shoulders tightly like I might slip away. "Just enough to make it easier…"

He didn't finish the sentence, and I wasn't certain that I wanted him to.

My throat slid as I digested this information, but my strung-out brain found a new thing to obsess over. "What is with vampires attacking people in bathrooms?"

Camila answered me. "No windows. Privacy. No escape."

One of the other girls gasped as Camila revealed this trade secret.

"Why is she here again?" I mumbled.

"Long story," Julian bit out as he looked me over. His hand cupped my chin, moving my head to help with his inspection. "Did he hurt you?"

I shook my head and then giggled. "He was scared of my finger."

Which reminded me… "I told you I had this under control."

Camila snorted, and something snapped inside me.

"I got away from you," I reminded her.

"Not pumped full of drugs and absinthe." She waved a finger over her nose with her free hand before hoisting the male vampire's body higher. "I'll take care of this."

"Wait." Some of the fog lifted as I realized what was happening. "You don't actually trust her?"

Their eyes met, and seeing them together like this, I realized how similar they looked. But that was where the similarities ended. Camila was a monster. I had no idea how she'd fooled my mate, but sensing the danger he was in, fire blazed in my veins. The hotter it grew, the more awake I felt, as though it was burning through the drugs I'd been slipped. Julian might trust Camila, but my magic didn't.

"That's the question we're both asking ourselves," she crooned.

No, Julian answered me silently. My shoulders sagged with relief to hear him in my head. I let it anchor me as the final dregs of the sedative cleared my system.

"Take him," he said to her, his eyes returning to their normal shade as the blood rage ebbed from him. "I don't care what his excuses are."

"I'll let you know if I find anything interesting." She left without another word, dragging the vampire along.

I raised an eyebrow.

"I'll explain later," he murmured. "Let's deal with this mess first. Can you stand?"

"Yes, I think I burned it out."

This time, he lifted an eyebrow.

"I'll explain later," I parroted him.

Julian hovered near me even as he turned his attention to my friends, who were still cowering by the sink. "Ladies—"

"You're a vampire!" Olivia blurted out.

"Indeed." He looked at me, a question on his face, and I knew he was asking permission for what he had to do next.

Had I really believed I could tell Olivia the truth only a few hours ago? Fate had delivered a swift response to that decision. I nodded.

"You both had a wonderful time. You're going home, a little drunk but happy," he said in a musical tone. I closed my eyes as he compelled them, feeding them a story about the celebration we were supposed to have had. "You won't notice anything unusual about this room or in the restaurant." My stomach turned over, wondering what waited for us out there. "All you will remember after you say goodnight to Thea is that this was one of the best nights of your life."

Olivia blinked when he finished, smiling dreamily over at me. Tears clogged my throat. Part of me wished I could remember tonight the way they would. Instead of a celebration, it had become a funeral.

For my old life.

For my old world.

For the human I no longer was.

"Will I see you on Sunday?" Olivia asked me brightly.

I swallowed back a sob and shook my head. "I can't make it—and Mom isn't going to be there anyway."

"But you have to come," Alexia added, her voice hoarse.

"I'll see what I can do," I lied. A plan was already forming in my head, and it involved keeping myself as far as I could manage from any mortal I loved. I would need Julian's help securing favors or money. Whatever it would take to get them as far away from here as possible. As long as Olivia and Tanner lived in that apartment, even without me there, they were at risk. But Julian would know someone. Someone who could offer Olivia a place in a ballet corps, a job programming for Tanner, and my mother… An ache split me down the middle, and I shoved away my plans. I would deal with it later.

"I'll give you a minute," Julian said softly, squeezing my hand once before he stepped outside.

I went to Olivia, grateful that her final memories of me would be happy—even if it was all a pretty lie planted by a vampire.

"You two seem really serious," she said knowingly, adding, "just be careful there."

Julian's compulsion had already rooted, revising her recollection of the night. She didn't remember anything I'd told her about vampires or mates or marriage proposals. It was for the best, but still, I didn't trust myself to speak. I nodded, managing two broken words: "I will."

She wrapped me in a tight hug, and I thought of morning pots of coffee waiting for me, emergency ice cream, and weekly visits to the hospital. I knew I had to let her go—to protect her—but something inside me shattered. We would always be friends, but it wasn't the same. Only I knew that, though, so I forced a smile as I pulled away. Turning to Alexia, I blinked back tears.

"Maybe he'll propose," she said conspiratorially.

"They barely know each other," Olivia said, but this time she grinned.

"We should find Tanner." It took some effort to get the words out as pain consumed me. "I think Julian wants to get home."

"Yeah, he does…" Olivia winked at me. "By the way, call me. I feel like you need to confess a few sins."

"More than a few." I felt hollowed out, but I did my best to hide it.

We found Tanner lounging in a chair in the dining room. I looked around, expecting to see carnage, but the restaurant was empty. Outside the glass windows, I saw the bar was closed. A few staff members remained, sitting in unnatural silence—*compelled.* The party was over. The row of guards standing like statues near the elevators drew my attention. Between the unnatural stillness and their protective stance, I knew they were Julian's security team. I counted them. Five guards—there had been five vampire bodyguards here. How had that Council vampire gotten past them?

"I lost the blonde," Tanner told me as I approached him to say goodbye. "She just vanished along with the hottie she was with."

"I saw them leaving." I did my best to sound apologetic.

Is he talking about the vampire from the Council?

I nodded, wishing for the hundredth time that this reading-minds thing worked both ways.

"And then there was some medical emergency. I didn't see it, but they made everyone leave. They let me wait for you, but it looks like I'm going home alone." Tanner sighed heavily as if this was a fate worse than death.

"Come on." Olivia threw an arm around him. "You can take me home, and I'll even let you rub my feet."

"Me too," Alexia offered. "It will be like a threesome."

Tanner cast a despairing glance my way. "The night is young. Tell them we can go somewhere else."

"The night is old," Julian grumbled under his breath, and I bit back a laugh.

"We're going home." I nuzzled closer to Julian.

We finished saying goodnight. I barely stopped myself from crying as the elevator shut. But as soon as it did, Julian snapped into action.

"Are they compelled?" he asked a tall, red-haired guard.

The guard tipped his head. "Yes. We gave them a cover story and saw to the other guests before we released them."

"Good." But the edge to my mate's voice cut. "Now explain how the hell you let a vampire attack my mate!"

A muscle twitched in the guard's neck, as if he resented being questioned. But he drew his shoulders up and looked coolly at Julian. "Council orders supersede yours. In fact…" He paused for just a moment before he grabbed my hand and yanked me to him. Despite his lack of gloves, I felt nothing as I tried to twist away from him. He must have been turned. Had he been sired by a Rousseaux?

"I'm afraid I have to take her into custody," the guard said firmly.

"*Try.*"

How could one word contain so much violence?

The guard regarded him a second, his grip on me tightening. Magic pounded inside me, and I grabbed the back of his hand and let it flow freely. He jerked, releasing me, and stared. "How—?"

He only got one word out before Julian closed the space between them and ripped his heart out. The guard managed one blink— some delayed nervous response—then crumpled to the ground. His colleagues stared. Not one of them moved.

"Would anyone else like to question the hierarchy of my orders?" Julian asked, holding up the vampire's bloody heart.

None of them spoke.

I felt sick. Both because of how close I'd come to being taken to the Council for execution and because I couldn't take my eyes off the heart in Julian's hand.

"If anyone else is concerned about the Council, you can inform them that I will bring Thea to them myself. We're hiding from no one. Are we clear?"

Every head nodded. Julian lumbered toward the body and dropped the heart next to him. When Julian finally looked at me, his eyes were black again. His lip curled, revealing his fangs, and a single icy finger raced up my spine.

"Leave! All of you!" His command boomed through the room, and he pointed at the vampire corpse at his feet. "And take this piece of shit with you."

I moved out of the way as one of the vampires came to gather the remains. Straining to see his face, I found it blank. Did he care that one of his own had just died at Julian's hands? If the vampire did, he knew how to hide it. The remaining staff walked toward the elevator, following the vampires into the cabin, pressing closely together. When the doors slid shut, Julian rounded on me.

I had never seen his eyes so dark, except…tiny flecks of gold swam in the black orbs like stardust in a midnight pool. But it wasn't limited to his eyes. Darkness curled around him, beckoning me—calling me. My heart raced with his. Beneath it all, in a place only he had been, hunger, like nothing I had ever felt before, awakened inside me.

Death stood before me, and I answered it.

"Tell me what you need." I spoke softly, aware of the savage beast prowling behind that star-flecked obsidian.

With his jaw tight and his shoulders squared, he forced out an answer. "I need *you*."

"Take me," I urged, and he lifted me off my feet in a flash. A second later, my back was against a glass window. But he didn't kiss me. He didn't hike my skirt up. Every inch of my body longed for him to rip my dress off and fill me with his tongue, his cock, his fangs.

But Julian left me pinned, his breath ragged. "Not just me," he grunted. "*It* needs you."

That fragment of him that lived inside me bellowed in response, calling to its master. Magic to magic. Darkness to darkness.

His throat slid, and he licked his teeth. Anger rippled through his words as he spoke. *"He touched you."*

My lips formed a ring as I realized what had triggered Julian's bloodlust and, most likely, his tether.

"He felt your magic." Every word was strained as if he was barely clinging to reason. "This thing inside me…it wants out."

I didn't dare try to explain that it was a tactical move—and that it had worked. Not with that beastly magic clawing through him. Not while his tether choked him.

Reaching up, I pressed my palm to his face and felt warm power seep from me—a gift to him. "Let it out."

"It won't be gentle," he warned me. His eyes flashed, anguish in his voice, as he corrected himself. "*I* won't be gentle."

I looked into his eyes, past that black abyss, and said to the soul tethered to my own, "I'm not afraid."

And then…he bit me.

CHAPTER THIRTY-SIX

Julian

Blood as sweet as warm honey spilled over my tongue. Thea gasped, stretching her neck into a long invitation that I gladly accepted. Her pulse was stronger here, and it beckoned for me to continue. With each swallow, my self-control returned until I finally broke free. I reared away, my body and hands pinning hers against the window. Moonlight spilled through the glass, glinting ruby in the hair that fell around one shoulder. We stared at each other for a moment, and I knew a line had been crossed.

I'd promised her respect, and at the first test of our new mating bond, I'd succumbed to the primitive monster inside me. My control had slipped, and now this beautiful, intimate gift was laid bare for the world. I started to draw farther away, but she hooked an arm around my neck and pulled me back to the spot. Her other hand reached to fumble with my pants, and a moment later, I fell hot and ready into her palm.

"Don't stop," she pleaded, her other hand closing around my cock. Her magic sparked in interesting ways as she stroked it.

It was dangerous territory.

"I shouldn't," I grunted.

"*Please* don't stop," she said, licking her lower lip. "I want your cock." Her eyes were bright, even in the darkness. A faint color stained her cheeks as she made her wicked confession—the dirty words new but hungry on her lips.

"Where?" I coaxed in a low voice, pleasure guttering through me as she stroked my length. "Tell me, my love."

"Inside me," she whispered. Her lashes fluttered down shyly as she added, "I want your fangs. I want you to feed while you're fucking me."

How the hell was I supposed to resist that?

I clenched my jaw to keep from sinking those very fangs back into her delicate neck and forced words through my tight lips. "There's already a mark. It will be worse—everyone will know."

Her lashes lifted, her glowing eyes meeting mine. *"Good."*

So much ownership in one word, and a reminder that I belonged to her as much as she belonged to me. My marks didn't just stake my claim; they were proof of hers.

"I don't deserve you," I gritted out.

The hand on my cock tightened and dragged up my shaft as she smiled. "Then earn me."

Maybe whatever magic flowed in Thea's veins was sexual, because the woman pinned to the window wasn't a mortal. She was a goddess, and she had me—quite literally—by the balls. Not that I would have it any other way.

My head fell back, my mouth opening as I let my fangs fully lengthen. Darkness seized control of me, but even in the abyss, when I brought my face back to hers, she was there. Her magic glowed like a halo around her, welcoming me home. Thea twisted her head, offering her neck once more.

"You're forgetting one thing," I said in a low voice that belonged more to the night inside me than to myself. Reaching down, I rucked her dress to her waist. Thea bucked against me, the lace of her soaked panties rasping across it. I plucked the elastic waistband with my thumb and forefinger. "These are so unnecessary. Why do you bother?"

"So you'll tear them off," she said sweetly.

"Wish granted." I snapped the flimsy band with one tug, then the other side before pinching the center of the lace and drawing them slowly up her swollen seam. Pleasure gurgled from her lips at the exquisite torture. I loved the little noises she made almost as much as I loved watching her squirm with anticipation. I shoved the ruined underwear in my back pocket. "Did that feel good?"

She whimpered, and her teeth latched onto her lower lip as she nodded.

I reached between her legs, parting her just enough to find the center of her desire. Circling it slowly with my fingertip, I crooned, "I want to be sure you're ready. I want to know what you taste like when you come."

Her mouth parted, her breath coming in staccato bursts as her hips moved in rhythm with my finger. "I'm ready."

"Ready for?" I prompted. "I want to hear you say it."

"I'm ready for you to fuck me," she said softly, the plea reaching all the way to her round, hungry eyes.

My balls tightened just hearing her say it. I ran my tongue over my top teeth. "And?"

Her eyes rolled back, a little shiver of pleasure coursing through her petite body as I continued to massage the soft wetness between her legs. "*Bite* me."

I groaned, unable to wait a minute longer. Seizing my cock from her warm hand, I pushed it between her legs, thrusting into her with one possessive stroke. Thea arched against me, her head dropping to reveal her throat. My bite marks glistened with newly spilled blood, and I angled my head, sweeping my tongue over them, unwilling to waste one drop of her. Her breath caught, and both our hearts stuttered once before I sank my fangs back into her neck.

Thea grabbed hold of my hair, moaning loudly, and I gave in to the beast. The window rattled as I pounded inside her. That wouldn't do. I wanted to fuck her harder—needed to fuck her harder—but I wouldn't risk sending us through the glass. Cupping her ass, I spun us around, drawing my head up just long enough to spot the nearest table before my fangs were back inside her. Careening blindly to it, I held her against me as I swept one hand over it, sending the fine china crashing to the floor.

She didn't release her hold of me as I braced her against its edge.

"Don't stop." Not a plea this time. An order. "Don't fucking stop."

She tightened around me, pants turning into gasping cries as I moved deeper with each stroke of my cock. The sweet honey of her blood blossomed into midnight violets laced with absinthe—dark and mysterious and addictive. Somewhere in the back of my mind, I realized my mistake. I would never be free of my want for her pleasure-laced blood now. Even worse? I didn't care.

Because one taste had changed me forever.

I reared away, her blood dripping from the corner of my mouth, and brought my lips to hers. Thea whimpered as the kiss deepened, each sound a quiet encouragement, urging me toward completion. Breaking the kiss, our eyes met, and I snarled, "You belong to me."

"Yes, yes, yes," she repeated, her gaze never leaving mine. "And you belong to me, so I want to feel you spill inside me." The final wicked request undid me, and I released with a thunderous groan, filling her over and over as she clung to me.

When the last drop of pleasure was wrung from me, I gathered her against my chest and held her, listening as her breath returned to normal and our hearts gradually slowed to their shared rhythm. After a few minutes, I scooted her onto the table.

"What are you doing?" she asked suspiciously as I bent to sort through the pile of dishes and silverware I'd sent crashing to the ground. "I think it's too late for those."

"I'm aware of that, pet." I grinned at her as I lifted a napkin. After a quick inspection to determine it was free of any broken china, I shook it free of its decorative fold. "But I made more than one mess tonight."

"Indeed," she said with a smirk that I couldn't help kissing.

Thea watched me quietly as I carefully cleaned her. "Well, now I'm *definitely* sure we violated every health code."

She wasn't wrong. I shoved the ruined napkin in with her panties before I tucked my cock back into my pants. But there was one more matter to see to—her wound.

"Let me look."

She hesitated before she turned her head and allowed me to inspect her neck.

The puncture wounds were perfectly round. Despite my frenzy, I'd taken care to avoid tearing her skin. They'd stopped bleeding, but it would take a while to heal—time we didn't have.

"May I please?" I asked her.

"But your marks…"

"The scars will remain," I said gruffly, uncertain how to feel about that. Part of me hated what I'd done. But Thea had asked for this—my mate had asked for this—and there was no pleasure I would deny her. How could I be angry at my lack of restraint if that's what she wanted? But rules would have to be established, and boundaries needed to be redrawn. Given how often I needed to claim her, I couldn't feed from her every time. I would drain her.

For now, I waited for her permission. After a second, she nodded. I lifted my wrist and bit into it, puncturing a vein. It would heal any second, so I offered it to her quickly. There was no hesitation as she took my hand and drank. Just watching her share my blood made me harden again. If she were a vampire, "forever" would mean it…

I shook the thought from my mind. We had other things to worry about, but somewhere the fear I'd felt earlier when I heard about her mother tugged on my thoughts. It was a conversation we needed to have.

And soon.

CHAPTER THIRTY-SEVEN

Thea

Wind whipped my hair into my face, strands sticking to the tears coating my cheeks. A single shaft of sunlight broke free of the clouds, illuminating the gravestones around me. As if cued by the break in the rain, birdsong began, the world returning to its natural rhythm after the storm. I closed my umbrella and bent to remove some fallen leaves from the marble stone along with a bouquet of shriveled peonies someone must have left. Who would still bother to come here after all this time? If it was up to me, there wouldn't have even been a grave. It felt so unnecessary, even if I couldn't place why. It just felt…*wrong*.

Still, I'd wanted to see it. That was normal, right?

"Are you happy now?" Sabine appeared at my side, pulling her fur coat tighter to ward off the biting wind.

"I suppose." I strained, trying to see the inscription past the mossy dirt that caked the stone. No one had bothered to clean the grave for a long time. Maybe the old flowers were from a stranger passing by. Maybe there was really no one left who remembered.

"It's morbid," she pronounced. "Why would you bother? It's not like you're actually down there. You're a vampire now."

Frowning, I squinted harder and finally made out what the

tombstone read: Thea Claribel Melbourne. I stumbled back a step as I saw the dates listed under that name.

My name.

I looked to Sabine, but she'd vanished. My foot caught on something—a rock. No—a skull. Screaming, I tried to turn and tripped, falling not to the earthy dirt but into a deep well. Blackness swallowed me. I kicked my legs, my arms lashing out for something— *anything*—to grab hold of, but my fingers met only air.

I was going to die.

But I was already dead.

Dead.

Dead.

Dead.

The word smothered my screams, forcing them back down my throat as I fell.

And then my finger snagged something in midair. It felt like fabric against my skin.

"Thea!" The darkness rippled as though commanded by that voice.

"Thea!" It cracked, unable to withstand him.

Lips met mine, and electricity roared around me, shattering the remnants of the abyss. I clung to the kiss like an anchor until I felt the sun on my face again.

"You were dreaming, my love," Julian murmured against my lips, brushing another kiss.

"What?" I blinked, my eyelids weighted with sleep, and found my mate's face inches from my own. "I was…"

He waited, moving just enough so that I could sit up. I glanced around the sleek cabin, tugging the sheet over my naked body, even though the privacy door was closed to the rest of the jet. Outside, the sky had lightened, and the plane's wing sliced through gauzy white clouds. It had been an endless night when I'd fallen asleep.

"It was just a dream," he said gently when I failed to finish my thought.

I nodded.

"We're nearly there," he said, and I was relieved that he hadn't asked me what I'd been dreaming about. I wasn't certain that Julian would be happy to know I was dreaming about being a vampire.

I studied him for a second, allowing my lips to fall into a frown. "You got dressed."

Not that he didn't look good. I just preferred him nude. He'd opted for a black button-down shirt, worn loosely at the neck, and charcoal slacks. His shirtsleeves were rolled just to his wrists, and his hands were bare. I reached for one, weaving my fingers through his as I realized that soon we'd both be wearing gloves a lot more.

"I couldn't sleep." He pulled back a corner of my sheet and peeked under it. "But, trust me, I'm regretting my choices. Maybe I should have stayed here and kept you awake."

My core clenched as flashes of his skin and hands, fangs and lips came rushing back to me. I didn't even remember falling asleep, but now I found myself wishing he'd stayed. Not only to ward off my nightmares but because I also had no idea when we'd be alone together again.

"You're here now," I purred, reaching for him and letting the sheet fall to my lap.

Julian's lips cruised along my jawline and trailed down my neck, further chasing away the bad dream with each sensual kiss. He stopped on my shoulder and sighed. "Unfortunately, I came to wake you up. We're starting our descent."

I screwed my face up in annoyance. "Can't you compel him to forget we're in here?"

Julian snorted, kissing the tip of my nose before he stood from the bed. "I feel I've been a bad influence on you," he said, shaking his head. "There's a lot of turbulence around the islands. It wouldn't be safe."

"But would it make for a *bumpy* ride?" I asked suggestively.

"I'm afraid that you are slightly fragile," he reminded me, offering me his hand.

And he wasn't. That was the whole problem. We both knew it. I'd heard him think it back at the restaurant—along with another thought.

About me being a vampire.

He'd kept that thought to himself, and I hadn't worked up the courage to ask him about it yet. Not after what had happened the last time I brought up the possibility of him turning me.

I let him help me to my feet. His hand tightened on mine before he yanked me against him.

"I made a mistake," he admitted softly.

"Oh?" I lifted an eyebrow.

"Hmmm." He nodded, his blue eyes sparkling like light on water. "I forgot you were naked, and now I'm having second thoughts about compelling the pilot."

"Ahhh. I see." I smiled brightly, fluttering my lashes before I shoved him away playfully. "Too bad I'm fragile cargo. Remember?"

He took a step closer, a growl rumbling in his chest, but I held up a hand.

"I need to get dressed."

He froze, his eyes narrowing with ire at my choice of words. "Shall I wait?" His voice was strained, confirming I'd unintentionally activated his tether. I sighed and shooed him away, wondering if I would ever get the hang of dealing with an overly protective vampire. He was trying, and it would have helped if the first time I'd gone out without my mate, I hadn't been attacked by the Vampire Council. Since then, Julian had made a show of acting casually, which was a little stupid considering I could feel his magic prowling inside me, pacing back and forth like a guardian.

"I'll be out in a minute."

He stomped out of the small private bedroom, closing its door behind him. Grabbing my garment bag, I pulled out the outfit I'd packed carefully for our arrival. I had no idea if his family would be there to greet us or not, but I wasn't taking any chances. Celia had helped me choose the right ensemble for facing his family. As I unzipped the bag, the plane hit a pocket of turbulence, and I stumbled onto the bed. I righted myself quickly, hoping Julian wouldn't return to check on me. Taking out the ivory silk pants, I was relieved to find that they weren't wrinkled. I sat on the edge of the bed and carefully pulled them on. They rose high on my waist. I buckled them and then eased a cropped cashmere sweater over my head. Darting into the cramped bathroom, I checked its high collar, pleased to see it covered the two small scars Julian had left on my neck.

Thanks to his vampire blood, they were completely healed, but the last thing I wanted was to show up in Greece, newly mated, with bite marks in plain sight. I fussed with my hair for a moment, opting to pull it up in a neat ponytail, since it was a little messy from falling asleep—and, well, hours of sex.

There was a knock on the door, and I opened it to find Julian standing with a blue box about the size of a piece of paper. His eyes swept me from head to toe, but they lingered on my collar.

"You look beautiful," he said in a thick voice. He blinked hard and tapped the box in his hand. "I guess you don't need this."

"What is it?" I asked curiously, trying to grab it from him. He caught my hand and pulled me toward the main cabin.

After we were buckled into our seats and the attendant brought me one last glass of champagne, he handed the box to me. "I was concerned about your scar," he explained as I opened the lid and gasped, "but you had a more practical solution."

Inside the box was a choker made up of several strands of diamonds, woven together in an overlapping pattern. Smaller stones were set around larger ones, giving the appearance of flowers, and each gem was utterly flawless.

"I like your solution better," I admitted breathlessly. "Is this... real?"

Julian shot me a harried look and pulled the box away. "You can wear it on other occasions."

Translation: when I wasn't wearing a turtleneck.

As gorgeous as the necklace was, my stomach tightened as I realized what he meant. "I love it, and I can't wait to wear it," I said softly, "but I'm not going to cover the scars all the time."

Julian looked away, shadows spreading on his face. "I should never have bitten you there."

It was the first time he'd admitted he was upset about the

location, but I'd felt his frustration—his anger—even though it had been directed inward.

"I don't care who knows that you feed on me," I said firmly, meaning it. "I want everyone to know I belong to you."

"We belong to each other," he corrected me, then sighed. "Are you sure you don't mind?"

I shook my head. "And you shouldn't mind, either."

"I suppose you're right," he admitted, taking my hand. "We are breaking all the rules, and it's not like we won't scandalize everyone in other ways."

I swallowed, my stomach knotting as I recalled our plan. Once we landed in Greece, we would be near the Council's home court. Every move we made had to be thought out, but it wasn't the Council I dreaded facing. It was his family. Both the Council and his family had no idea we were coming early, which would give us time to get his family on our side before we faced The Rites.

"It will all work out. Sebastian and Benedict will be there," he said as the pilot announced that we had begun our final descent and would land momentarily.

"Is that supposed to be comforting?" I asked. I was never sure if his brothers liked me—and I wondered how they would feel about me when they discovered we were mates.

"They aren't your enemies," Julian promised, but I doubted they'd bought us matching family T-shirts.

"And your parents?"

He hesitated. The plane jolted as its wheels hit the tarmac, jostling my thoughts from my question. We remained silent as the jet taxied for a minute.

"You're a Rousseaux now," he said as the jet finally stopped.

"I'll be sure to start ordering people around, then," I joked, trying to lighten the mood, but his hand tightened on mine.

"Don't let anyone make you feel unwelcome. You're my mate—my equal. Well, maybe my better," he admitted, "and someday they will all bow to you."

"You think so?" I asked doubtfully, not really wanting the latter.

"I swear it." His words left no room for doubt. They soothed the ragged nerves that threatened to overwhelm me. At least they did until we stepped off the jet and found a long, black limousine waiting for us.

Julian cursed under his breath as he offered me his arm.

"What is it?" I asked as we walked down the jet's stairs toward the waiting car. "Is that for us?"

"I guess so," he said through gritted teeth, and I realized he hadn't arranged for it to pick us up. "It seems someone knows we're here."

CHAPTER THIRTY-EIGHT

Thea

Late morning in Greece was a cheerful affair despite it being December. Overhead, the skies were an unbroken blue, and, although the weather was cooler given the season, the sun warmed my skin as we approached the limousine. An olive-skinned man jutted from the driver-side door and greeted us with a tip of the head as he opened the rear door for us. I glanced up at Julian and found his eyes narrowed. Was it from the sunlight or the driver?

He said something to Julian in what I assumed was Greek. My mate responded in the same language, his hand moving to the small of my back as he guided us toward the inside of the car. I shouldn't have been surprised that he spoke Greek, given how many lives he'd lived before we ever met. But sometimes, I wondered how many more layers there were to peel back.

"My family is expecting us," he explained carefully as he joined me in the back of the car.

I exhaled, feeling relieved that we were facing them and not the Council. But the relief was over almost immediately, my stomach hollowing out when I realized that we'd be facing them soon. Julian seemed to be thinking the same thing.

"It's not too late," he murmured as the limousine left the private airfield. "We can check into a hotel, and I can arrange to speak to my family privately."

My hand tightened around his, and I shook my head. "Ride or die, remember?"

"As you wish." But his frown deepened, carving lines of disapproval around his mouth.

"What?" I asked.

"I was just thinking that death is more likely, in Sabine's presence." He lifted our joined hands and kissed the back of mine. "Just promise me one thing, my love?"

"What?"

Julian faced me, his eyes locking with mine. "If this gets violent, you'll stay behind me."

I waited for him to laugh. He didn't.

"You aren't serious," I said with a half-hearted giggle.

He didn't even smile. "I am deadly serious. Vampire families have gone to war over less."

"Why?" I burst out. Maybe I was glad that Julian didn't want to turn me. Apparently, becoming a vampire meant always having blood on your hands—even your own family's.

"Long lives and longer memories," he said darkly. He took a deep breath and smiled, but it didn't reach his eyes. They remained stormy as though occupied by thoughts of the past. "But our family hasn't gone to war with one another for a long time."

"I wish I found that reassuring," I admitted. "It won't really come to that, right?"

His silence was all the answer I needed.

"I think I'm going to throw up." I rubbed my churning stomach.

"Fresh air will help," he said softly, and I knew it must be as bad as I feared if he wasn't trying to soothe me. He rolled the window down, and sunlight cascaded over us, warm and welcome as a promise. Cool air rushed toward me, and I gulped it down, trying to get control of my breathing. The last thing I wanted was to face Sabine smelling like I'd just been sick.

Whatever we were about to face was bad enough that Julian wasn't attempting to calm me. Maybe it was because he couldn't lie to his mate. Or maybe he was just preparing me for the fallout. Either way, my dread increased as we drove through the picturesque Greek village.

"It's not like I expected," I said, eager to change the subject from our impending doom. The buildings we passed weren't sun-washed white like the pictures I'd seen of Greece. Instead, they were brightly colored and majestic. They looked more like a collection of palaces than a seaside village.

"Venice controlled the city for a long period of time." Julian leaned over and pointed out the window. "They built a lot of Old Town. But Corfu itself has a history that stretches back to the gods. The ancient Greeks called it Korkyra. Some say Poseidon named it after a water nymph he fell in love with and kidnapped."

"Is that why vampires are always trying to kidnap people?" I teased. "Because the gods used to?" Or had humans always been writing about vampires and mistaking them for gods?

"I didn't kidnap you. I saved you," he corrected me, planting a kiss on the top of my head. "And aren't you glad I did?"

I was, but there was no way I'd admit that to him. Not when I could tease him about it for a lifetime.

"And how long has your family had a home here?" I asked.

"As long as I can remember. The vampires were here before the Venetians." He winked at me, and I relaxed against his shoulder. "Most of the old bloodlines keep a residence nearby."

"Because this is where the Council resides?" I guessed.

"Yes, because they all need to stick their nose into Council business as often as possible," he said grimly. "My family included."

"Julian." I searched for the right words to ask the question weighing on my mind. "If your family rejects me, will that influence the Council's feelings?"

"Perhaps, but if my family rejects *you*, they reject *both of us*." He spoke with a conviction that both thrilled and terrified me.

I'd chosen Julian over my own family. Even being here now with what we'd learned about my mother's condition was a choice I'd had to make. Part of me ached to be back in San Francisco hunting her down. I wanted answers. I wanted the truth. But mostly, I wanted to find a way to save her and make things right between us. I'd taken for granted that she'd always be there, supporting my dreams. I wished I'd had the chance to show her what he meant to me, to show her that I was loved and cherished. But I'd run out of time to find her, and the Council had left us no other option than to return to the season. Soon we would endure The Second Rite, and if there was any chance of convincing his family to stand with us as we faced the Council, we had to take it.

I was still preoccupied with the question of Camila. I hadn't dared ask Julian if he was going to tell his family, especially after he'd allowed me into his mind to learn the truth. Now that I knew what had really happened that night and the blood-vow he'd been forced to take, I saw how complicated revealing the truth about his sister would be for him. "What if Camila is right and—"

Julian kissed me swiftly, cutting my question off. I was so surprised that I softened against him, completely swept away.

It's better not to speak of her or Willem until we're alone. His voice filled my head, interrupting the breathtaking kiss.

When he pulled away, I muttered, "I guess that's what they mean by *shut up and kiss me*."

Julian laughed as he dropped an arm around my shoulder. I hadn't considered that the driver could hear us, but if he was a vampire, he might. We'd agreed to keep what Camila had said between us until we knew more. Julian wanted to do a little digging, but if I was being honest, I wasn't certain I believed his sister.

She had threatened to peel off my skin, after all.

We traveled in silence for a few minutes, my fingers hooking around his and tugging his arm more tightly around me. The coastline was a jagged puzzle of sandy beaches, cliffs of cypress trees, and rocky hills. The main road was quiet and barely wide enough for the large limousine to navigate as we climbed the ever-shifting terrain. As we rounded a sharp corner, Julian whispered, "There it is. *Paradeisos*."

He didn't have to translate that word for me, because even if the meaning weren't obvious, I would have called it paradise at first sight. A large villa comprised of several white stone buildings was built into the side of the cliff ahead. It jutted out, seeming to hang dangerously off the side. As we drove closer, I spotted stone-paved paths connecting the network of houses to one another, each building set at a slightly different elevation.

The limo paused at a security gate flanked by olive trees. Glancing up, I spotted multiple security cameras perched along the stone wall that protected the estate from the street. I shrank back, fumbling to raise my window. It was silly, seeing how it was impossible our arrival might still have an element of surprise remaining.

Past the gate awaited manicured wilderness. More olive trees lined the paved drive, surrounded by tall grasses and shrubs. Eventually, the natural greenery gave way to a thick lawn of plush grass that wrapped around the circular drive leading to the main house. The limo pulled to a stop in front of a portico held up by two stone columns. Massive oak doors were open, revealing a glimpse of the airy, sun-drenched living space beyond. There was no one in sight.

"It seems our welcoming committee is late," Julian muttered.

"I'm not complaining," I said as the car door opened. I accepted the driver's gloved hand to help me out of the car. When I turned back to Julian, his face was a mask of stony restraint.

I held up my covered hands. "I had gloves on," I reminded him in a soothing voice. He bobbed his head, but the tension lingered around his eyes. I wondered if the protective instinct he felt would lessen over the years or if he would always have to fight the urge to attack any man who touched me.

"I'll see to your luggage," the driver said.

"Shall we?" Julian asked, taking my hand in his. I felt its warmth and looked down to find it bare.

"*You* forgot—" I started.

"Nothing," he cut me off meaningfully, and I understood what he meant before I heard him in my head.

I'm prepared. That's all.

For a fight. He was prepared for a fight, I realized, my heart sinking. Gloves might slow him down if things became violent. I knew he would defend me, but at what cost to his family? At what cost to himself?

"Should we just go in?" I asked, staring at those open doors. "Maybe they're out."

He shot me an incredulous look. "I forget how optimistic you are."

"Well, no one is here," I said flatly.

"They're here," he murmured. Squeezing my hand, he led me inside.

The foyer was as grand as the entrance, opening to a view of the sea. Overhead hung a chandelier made of carved mother of pearl, and on either side, white doors with brass handles were closed to other parts of the house. But what stopped me in my tracks was the sunken living room just a few steps away. A circular coffee table was the centerpiece of the room, a crest carved into its marble top. Surrounding it were two oversize linen couches filled with pillows and cushions positioned parallel to each other and two pairs of low-slung tan leather seats. It might have been the most beautiful, welcoming space I'd ever set foot in if it weren't for the seven vampires glaring back at me.

But it was the look on Sabine's face that made me take a step back—instinct screaming at me to run. I'd expected fury. I'd expected hate.

Sabine wore neither. Instead, her face drained of color, her nostrils flaring as she beheld her eldest son. All around her, the others began to murmur as they picked up on the changes we'd chosen not to hide—the proof of our mating bond.

Julian cleared his throat as she continued to stare, her face slack with what could only be described as horror. "I see *everyone* is here. Everyone, this is—"

Sabine's voice pierced the air, shattering any semblance of calm. *"What the hell did you bring into my house?"*

CHAPTER THIRTY-NINE

Julian

"You remember my girlfriend, Thea," I said conversationally, ignoring my mother's outburst. "Although you haven't met my other brothers."

I turned to discover my mate staring at Sabine with eyes as round as a full moon. Clearing her throat softly, she tore her gaze away and blinked before adding a numb, "Hello."

Mother continued to stare daggers at us, even as Lysander and Thoren rose from their seats.

"Thea," I said gently. "This is Thoren, and that's Lysander—my younger brothers."

"It's a pleasure to meet you," Thoren said. His copper hair brushed his broad shoulders as he bowed slightly at the waist. Thea's mouth opened slightly as she processed the large Viking's introduction, but all she could manage was a nod.

Lysander smirked as he bowed to her. His black hair was cropped, unlike the last time I'd seen him, and his shirtsleeves were rolled up, showcasing his tattooed forearms. His olive skin was a deep, rich tan, and I wondered what bit of earth he'd been digging up when he'd gotten the call to meet the family in Greece. "I can't believe you finally found someone willing to put up with your ass."

"Don't encourage him," Sabine muttered, glaring at her son. "Things have already gone *too* far."

Before I could return her biting remark, the only truly friendly face in the room swept toward us. Jacqueline had beaten us here, and I was grateful she'd agreed to come at all. Her blond waves swayed over her shoulders as she threw her arms around Thea in a tight hug. "I made him pull his head out of his ass," she whispered. Thea giggled, and relief washed through me that she'd finally snapped out of her daze, even as Jacqueline cast a sharp look over my mate's shoulder and mumbled, "You two know how to make a helluvan entrance."

She released Thea and moved to hug me.

"Has my mother been behaving?" I breathed to her as we hugged.

"Define behaving," she said softly. "She gave me a room, so I think *I'm* welcome to stay. You two, though? I think she knew why Benedict gathered the whole family."

Finding my other brothers here had been a surprise. If Benedict had tracked them down and called them to a family reunion, he must believe they'd be on our side. Or he was having reservations about his previous commitment to helping me win the family over regarding Thea. Either way, it was done, and I hoped I could count on my brothers to back me up.

"I should have had you hide the weapons," I told Jacqueline, my gaze snagging on a display of ancient Greek spears and swords. My mother loved to decorate with items that could be used in a fight.

"Stop whispering," Dominic ordered us. His eyes darted to his wife, who remained so still that even I was beginning to worry about her. "Your mother is on the verge of an aneurysm, and you need to explain yourself."

Jacqueline shot us an encouraging smile before releasing us. She didn't return to her seat. That had been part of our arrangement. There was only one person in this room I knew would take our side if things became violent, so I'd asked her to keep close to us.

"I do?" I said, meeting his gaze, stepping ever so slightly in front of Thea, who snorted at this show of dominance and immediately moved back to my side.

"It seems that she's a bit more than your girlfriend—or am I imagining things?" Dominic shifted in his seat and waited for me to deny it.

"You have to forgive me. We've been around humans too long." I'd chosen my words carefully earlier, sensing that my mother was already riled up. But it wasn't as if we could hide anything from them. They would have all sensed the changes in me the moment we stepped through the door. To be honest, I'd been dying to introduce Thea properly for weeks and had had very little chance to do so. "Allow me to reintroduce Thea Melbourne—my *mate*."

"It's been a long time since I've been around a mated pair," my father said solemnly. "I'd forgotten the effect the bond had. I suspect it will take some time to adjust to. Wouldn't you agree, dearest?"

Sabine turned her head, a flash of disgust twisting her mouth as she looked out on the unbroken view of the Ionian Sea. I grabbed hold of Thea's hand, tugging her closer to me. If she wanted to be at my side, so be it. But I needed her within reach in case things got out of hand.

"So, how did you two meet?" Lysander asked conversationally. He relaxed into his seat, his mouth twitching as though deeply amused to be in the middle of a disagreement between his older brother and his parents.

"We are not doing this," Sabine snapped. A flash of movement that even I barely registered, and she was standing dangerously close to the ancient weaponry. "Are we really going to pretend Julian didn't break the vow he made to this family? They aren't just mated. They are tethered. We can't trust a word either of them says."

"Things have changed," Benedict said smoothly, plastering his politician's smile on, "and the decision was presumably consensual."

I sighed at his choice of words. I wanted support, not a debate over my decision to tether myself to Thea.

"I don't give a fuck," Sabine bellowed, but Thea stepped between us.

I tried to push her behind me, but she turned a withering glare on me. "Stop. I need to handle this."

Her words locked me in place, but a growl ripped through my chest as my instinct to protect her fought against the order she'd given. Thea had known exactly what words to use to put a check on me through my tether. Normally, I'd find it sexy. But considering that I recognized the homicidal rage on my mother's face, at the moment, I did not.

"Look how casually she abuses his tether," Sabine hissed, pointing a finger at my mate.

I snarled in response. Both of them ignored me. My father's face remained unreadable as he watched this play out. Benedict and Thoren looked concerned, but Lysander and Sebastian shared a grin. More than ever, I wished I'd been able to introduce Thea as my mate to them individually.

"I'm only reminding him that I can fight my own battles," Thea said calmly, surprising even me. But the heart racing in my chest suggested she wasn't as relaxed on the inside.

"Get your pet under control," my mother demanded. "She needs to learn her place."

"Her place is at my side," I said through gritted teeth. "Thea is my equal—if not my better."

"So, you'll allow her to walk all over you?" Sabine crossed her arms but stayed close to the cache of weapons. "Is this your way of keeping your oath to never tether a virgin to you?"

I wanted to say yes, but before I could, Thea answered in a clear, strong voice, "He released me from my tether."

"Thea," I said softly, "what are you...?"

But she'd already accomplished her task. Her words fell over the room, silence following in a deafening roar as everyone tried to process this. My mate seized the opportunity to speak before they could start asking questions.

"Julian ordered me to do as I pleased regardless of his demands," she continued, earning impressed looks from everyone but my mother, whose anger slipped to show fear. Thea looked directly at her. "Your son is an honorable man. He had no wish to force me to do anything."

I ignored the fact that Lysander and Sebastian both heaved

with barely suppressed laughter at Thea's confidence. Even my dad seemed a little amused, but Sabine's fury rolled off her with a deathly calm that made me whisper in a strained voice, "Thea, my love…"

"I'm done." She shot a smile over my shoulder.

I exhaled and stepped to her side. "We've come to finish The Rites." I turned to my mother. "The Council wishes me to wed, and I have made my choice."

"Shit." Lysander sat up straighter, as if he'd finally realized how serious this situation was. "You're actually going to get married?"

A smile tugged on my lips. "If she'll have me."

"It's been discussed." Thea's emerald eyes danced as she looked up at me.

"But first, we intend to take The Rites. The Council made a move against Thea, so we will play by their rules, but I need your help allowing them to see reason."

"I know you think your participation alleviates this, but The Rites were enacted to see that the bloodlines are renewed," my father said with surprising gentleness. His eyes softened as he delivered what he assumed was bad news. "They won't approve a match with a human."

Thea and I shared a brief look.

Ready?

She nodded.

"Thea isn't human."

"What?" Sebastian asked as my other brothers added their own shell-shocked questions. There were too many to answer as they yelled over one another, each trying to be answered first. Even my father's face had gone pale. Only Jacqueline remained alert and focused, since she knew as much as I did about Thea's true nature.

"She's a familiar?" Dominic asked.

I started to shake my head—to explain that we didn't know or understand the source of Thea's magic—but my mom jumped in.

"She's no witch," she said coldly. "Have you figured it out yet?"

My eyes narrowed on her. She'd alluded to this before, but then, I'd thought she was just being overly dramatic. "Do you know?" I thundered.

Sabine rolled her eyes, flicking her red-polished nails impatiently. "You couldn't even wait to find out before you bedded her. What if this mate of yours is something even you can't live with?"

I heard Thea's choked gasp at Sabine's words, and pain flooded through me. I didn't know if it was my own or my mate's—and I didn't care. It was just like my mother to seize on the heart of her self-doubt and twist.

"I don't care what Thea is or what she is not. She is my mate," I roared, grappling to control the primal urge to convey this sentiment more violently. "She is everything I want and all I will ever need. Nothing else matters."

"So, you don't need answers, then. You choose not to *care*." Sabine emphasized the last word, shrugging her petite shoulders.

"We will find the truth," I said firmly, adding, "with or without your help."

"In that case"—my mother's mouth widened into a sharp smile— "allow me to help."

How? The question was poised on my lips when my mother flashed toward us and plunged a sword into my chest.

CHAPTER FORTY

Julian

The moment my mother stabbed me, two things occurred to me.
The first was that I should have told Thea exactly what ways a
vampire could die. The second was that my mother was a psychopath.

Thea screamed as Sabine twisted the weapon and shoved it in me
to the hilt. Blood bubbled from my lips as I looked down at the wet
stain spreading across my shirt. Chaos erupted around me. I blinked,
my head beginning to swim, and found my mother pinned to the wall
by Jacqueline. Dominic stood by, looking torn between intervening
on behalf of his wife and helping me.

Lysander and Thoren blocked the other weapons on display.
Sebastian was a few steps away, Benedict behind him, but they
hesitated. Lifting my head with the little strength I could muster, I
discovered my mate at my side—and what made everyone pause.

Power poured from Thea in a shimmering aura. Despite her size,
she was poised to attack as her eyes darted around the room.

I tried to speak…tried to tell her I would be okay if someone would
just pull this fucking blade out of me, but I couldn't. I suspected from
the amount of blood spilling from my lips that I had a punctured lung.

Thea. I reached for her mind, but she remained preternaturally still.

"We're going to help him," Sebastian said carefully. He edged closer, and Thea snapped.

The entire room froze—even me—as she lunged in front of me, her mouth curling into a snarl.

"Thea." Her name was all I could manage as crimson sprayed past my lips. I reached for her as the world went sideways, and as she turned, I spotted her *fangs*.

• • •

I sat bolt upright, wincing at the tender ache in my chest. My hand flew to the spot and found a clean shirt and a bruise that would probably take a few more hours to heal. The afternoon shit show flashed through my head, and I sprung from the bed with only one thought.

Thea had fangs.

I'd made it two steps past the edge of the bed when one word broke the silence.

"Hey."

Whipping toward the small voice, I nearly collapsed with relief to find Thea sitting in a chair by the window. Her knees were tucked beneath her chin, her arms wrapped around her legs as she hugged herself in the evening twilight. She didn't smile at me. She didn't even look at me.

"How long was I out?" I asked, wondering how long she had been sitting alone with her own thoughts.

"Five or six hours, I think," she muttered, her eyes cast to the choppy sea outside.

I didn't know what to say. I had questions—lots of them—but it wasn't as if Thea had answers. If anything, she probably had more questions than me.

"Do you think?" she said with an unamused snort, and I realized I must be blaring my every thought at her. In response, she nodded. "It's better than when you were out," she added quietly. "You were so quiet then. It was like you were…"

Dead. She didn't have to say the word. It was written all over her face.

"Vampires are hard to kill," I reminded her. "There was nothing to worry about."

Emerald eyes flashed angrily toward me. "Sebastian said you nearly died." Her voice shook with accusation. "You lost a lot of blood because they couldn't get the sword out of you—because *I* wouldn't let them near you."

Thea choked back a sob that threatened to tear me open again. With three long strides, I reached her.

"I lost a lot of blood because my mother stabbed me," I corrected her gently as I scooped her into my arms. She started to nuzzle against my chest but then pulled sharply away. "It's okay. You aren't going to hurt me."

My reassurance only triggered more tears. I held her against me as I settled into the chair. Thea buried her face into my neck and let go. For a few minutes, I let her cry, even though every second was torture. When the sobs racking her body slowed, I pressed a finger to her chin and lifted her tear-stained face.

"Tell me," I invited. I wouldn't presume to know what bothered her the most about today. I had my own list of complaints, but I suspected that while mine were mostly directed at my family, Thea was angry with herself.

"I thought she killed you," she whispered, her lashes heavy and wet. I brushed escaped tears from her cheeks in soothing strokes.

"I'm right here. I'm fine," I repeated, knowing she might need to hear that a few more times until she believed it.

"I could have killed her," Thea admitted. She tried to turn her head away, but I held it in place and waited for the rest of her confession.

"And?"

She sucked in a raspy breath, her eyes shuttering closed. "I *wanted* to kill her."

The agony as she spoke threatened to overwhelm me. Her pain grew inside me, tearing and clawing, and it took effort on my part to sound calm. "No one would blame you for that—not even Sabine." Her eyes fluttered, staring back at me with disbelief. "I promise. She knew what she was doing." Even if what she'd done had been absolutely fucking bananas. "She wanted to trigger your mating instincts."

Thea winced, shaking her head. "Well, she did a little more than that."

"Yeah, um…" How exactly was I supposed to ask her about what I'd seen before I blacked out? Maybe I had imagined…

"You didn't," she interrupted my thought. "You saw them. Everyone saw them." She raised a hand to her mouth and pressed a finger gingerly to her lips. A second later, she parted them to reveal two rows of normal, human teeth, but her gums…

Red lumps swelled over her canines, exactly where fangs would protract. I couldn't think of a thing to say, and I wondered if anyone had been able to—if anyone had comforted her.

"Jacqueline tried," she answered my unspoken thoughts. Tears glimmered in her eyes when she looked at me. "But no one knew what to say. Not that I can blame them."

"Thea, it might not mean—"

"What?" she cut me off with a small sob. "We know what it means. Julian, I'm a vampire."

CHAPTER FORTY-ONE

Thea

The confession hung in the air, waiting for one of us to pluck it down and deal with it. I'd been sitting in darkness for hours, waiting for Julian to wake up, repeating those words over and over in my head while I memorized the layout of the room.

I'm a vampire.

The king-size bed was nearly centered on the far wall that faced the ocean view, but it was ever-so-slightly moved to the left.

I'm a vampire.

There was a gnarl in the beech nightstand on the right.

I'm a vampire.

As the sun faded along the sea, it bathed the room in rosy shades that lingered now even as shadows crept through the glass.

And I'm a vampire.

I opened my mouth to say it again—to make it stick or force him to say something.

But Julian beat me to it. "You aren't a vampire."

I twisted in his arms so I could get a better look at him. Maybe I was expecting a smirk or a wink or some indication that he wasn't going to just ignore the fact that I'd sprouted fangs a few hours ago. There was no cocky grin—not even the hint of a smile. Instead, his blue eyes remained the same cool shade as the sea I'd watched all afternoon.

"What?" I blurted out. "You saw—"

"Fangs," he finished for me with a nod. "But that doesn't mean you're a vampire. Other creatures have fangs."

If his goal was to annoy me until I forgot the life-shattering revelation I'd had earlier, it was working. I stared at him. "Other creatures?"

"You could argue that werewolves have fangs...or really big teeth," he clarified.

"Werewolves?" I repeated faintly. "Werewolves are real, too?"

"There's a little truth in every myth," he said, reminding me of something he'd said when we'd first met. "Honestly, I doubt we even know what magical creatures still exist. Some have gone extinct. Others..."

I raised an eyebrow, too numb to speak. Of course other magical creatures existed. I don't know why I was surprised by that, exactly.

"Others have changed. They aren't what they used to be."

"They've evolved?" I asked.

"Did you think evolution extended purely to humans?" Julian's lips twisted as he relaxed into the seat and pulled me toward him. A stray shaft of fading daylight caught his face, and for a moment, I was mesmerized.

He didn't belong to this world. I'd known that since the first night I met him. I'd also known *I* didn't belong in *his* world. What world did I belong to?

"Tell me what you're thinking, my love," he said, his voice slightly strained.

"I'm thinking I have a lot to learn about your world." I swallowed and forced myself to confront the possibility that not only was I not human, but if he was right, I wasn't an immortal vampire, either. "What if I'm a werewolf?"

Julian remained completely silent for a minute—even his mind was a void when I tried to peek inside it—and then his damn lips twitched.

"You wouldn't da—" I started before his head fell back and he roared with laughter.

The bastard was laughing at me. I smacked his chest lightly—not that I could penetrate his thick skin or his thick skull, for that matter. "This isn't funny! A few hours ago, I practically tore your family apart—and you're laughing?"

"Sorry," he said, his voice still breathless with amusement. "I just imagined you as a werewolf."

I narrowed my eyes. "You were the one who suggested it."

"It was an example." He cupped my chin with his hand and tried to draw me in for a kiss. I crossed my arms and pulled away.

"Why is the idea of me being a werewolf so hilarious?" I bit out.

"Well, for starters, most werewolves are massive, and you... aren't."

Okay, that was a reasonable point.

"They're like, big dogs?"

He choked back another laugh but quickly smothered it. "Think of a dog the size of Thoren, and you'll have a good idea."

My eyes widened.

"Plus, they have fur," he added, "and thankfully, you do not."

"So, if I'm not a werewolf or a vampire or a witch, what am I?" I demanded.

"Whatever it is, it doesn't matter."

"Like hell it doesn't," I exploded. "Your mother just skewered you like a kabob to figure it out." I began counting the reasons on my fingers, since he seemed to be having difficulty keeping up. "You want to go to the Council and convince them that my magic is enough to allow us to marry. My own mother is probably dying from whatever magic is inside me, and..."

I couldn't bear to consider it anymore. It was already too much. Two months ago, I'd had a normal life. Meeting Julian was the craziest thing that had ever happened to me, and if he'd asked someone to erase my memory that night like I asked, we wouldn't be here going through an encyclopedia of magical creatures to figure out where I belonged in the world.

And maybe that would have been better. Not for me but for him.

And? The question in his thought tugged at me, wanting my attention.

"And maybe you wouldn't be in danger now. No pissed-off Council, no unstable sister." I frowned apologetically. "No freak of a mate."

Julian bristled at my choice of words, and I rushed on. "It's true. I don't belong here. We both know it. Your family knows it. Your mom *really* knows it." I forced a half-hearted laugh, but he didn't so much as smile.

A fire lit in his cold eyes, even as his face hardened into a stony mask. "You think you don't belong here?"

"Julian, I know I don't," I said softly. I'd known it since the moment I'd caught that vampire feeding on Carmen and realized Julian had been telling me the truth. "You have to know that, too. No matter how we feel about each other, we're just…"

"Just what?" Anger simmered in his words.

I couldn't bring myself to say any of the words that floated through my head. *Wrong?* No, how could I ever claim that? Julian was the only thing that felt right in my life. *Different?* Maybe we were before, but now…now we were the same soul split between two bodies.

"Doomed," I finally whispered. Not because I wanted it to be true—because, no matter how much I wanted him, I couldn't escape the fear that we would be torn apart.

And if we were, would either of us survive?

"You don't really believe that," he said hoarsely.

"Don't you?" I asked. "Isn't that why you were willing to die the night the Council delivered their threat in Paris?"

The arms that held me tightened possessively as if I might slip through them like sand. But even if it were true and our love was star-crossed from the start, I couldn't leave him. I wouldn't. I'd rather die—and these days, that was becoming a real possibility.

"I will follow you anywhere, even death," he said darkly. "In life and in death, I will be at your side."

"And if I said the same?"

He flinched, his upper lip curling as if to snarl before he stopped himself. "It's not the same."

"It's not?" I challenged. "How is that fair?"

"Because my entire soul is bound to protect you," he said through gritted teeth, his eyes flashing. "I am tethered to you."

My shoulders sank as my crossed arms fell limply to my lap. "So, you don't have a choice. You're stuck with me, and now you regret it. Is that it?"

There was a whoosh, and I found myself flying through the air. I hit the mattress gently, cushioned by Julian, who was already there. Before I could process that he'd just tossed me onto the bed like a doll, he climbed over me and pinned me to the bed. His strong body caged me in place as he glowered down.

"I had a choice, pet," he seethed, "and I chose you—tether and all."

"Don't sound so happy about it," I mumbled.

"I'm not happy." His confession sucked the air from me, but then he continued. "I'm not happy that my mate is hurting. I'm not happy that she suggested I regretted my choice. And I'm especially not happy that you would dare question what's between us."

"And what is that?" I asked breathlessly.

"Fate. Destiny. Whatever the fuck you want to call it," he snarled, revealing a glimpse of his fangs. "We're ride or die. We're mates. The only world that matters is the one we make together."

"And what if I'm—"

"I chose *you*," he repeated in a tone that brooked no further discussion. "I chose you, not just in that moment but for every lifetime. I chose you for eternity—and I will choose you every time."

"That's the tether talking," I whispered.

He shook his head. "That's not the tether. That's love. Because that's what brought us together."

We stared at each other until a sob broke free of my chest. "I'm scared."

"I know."

"How can you be sure?" I asked, searching his eyes for a sign.

His lips parted as he licked his tongue over his fangs, his eyes turning black as he spoke. "Let me show you."

CHAPTER FORTY-TWO

Thea

I grabbed a fistful of his shirt and yanked him closer. Our mouths met in a tangle of tongues and teeth, his fangs catching on my lower lip and drawing blood. I moaned as he sucked it into his mouth.

"I can never decide what I need most," he said with a rasp that made me shiver, "my hands on you, my fangs in your neck, or"—he nudged my thighs wider with one knee and moved between my spread legs—"my cock inside you."

"Why choose?" I bit my lip as our fully dressed bodies fought the restrictions of our clothing. Tasting blood, I released it and hoped he would come back for seconds.

Julian's mouth curved into a wicked grin that made my heart do a somersault. "You have a very dirty mind for someone who was recently a virgin."

"I have an excellent muse." My fingers strayed lower as I reached for the buckle of his belt, but he shifted to block my access.

"Slow down," he stopped me. "I'm not done making my point."

"I don't want a point. I want an escape," I said, ignoring him.

"If you're a good girl, you'll get both." He grabbed hold of my wrist and yanked it back over my head. The blackness of his eyes faded a little to reveal a glimpse of concern.

But I didn't want cautious lovemaking. I wanted to be owned in a way only he could possess me. I just had to press the right button. "At least we've learned one thing," I reflected.

"Hmmm?" His mouth cruised along my jaw, leaving a trail of fire in its wake.

"I'm not some fragile human," I whispered.

Julian lifted his face to study me. A muscle tensed in his jaw as if he was considering what to do with this statement. There was no smirk—no sign of amusement—when he finally said, "No, you aren't."

"Then stop treating me like it," I demanded.

His broad shoulders squared, annoyance flashing across his handsome face as my words jerked his tether. "Don't play with beasts, pet," he snarled.

"Why? Will you bite?" I asked with mock innocence. "Maybe that's what I want. Maybe I want the beast."

He growled and rolled off me. For a moment, we lay next to each other, each of us drawing shallow breaths.

"You want the beast?" he murmured.

I rolled to my side and looked at him. "I want the beast. I want the vampire. I want every inch of the male that belongs to me—and I don't want you to hold back."

"Take off your fucking clothes." His words hit me like an order, and without thinking, I found myself pushing off the bed. He'd never spoken to me like that before, but where shock should be, I only found arousal. I acted automatically. Every move was instinctual. Julian wanted my clothes off. I didn't care how rude he was. I didn't care that a dark energy radiated off him as his head turned to watch me undress. I drew my sweater over my head as it hit me.

He'd activated my tether.

There was a loophole to my freedom. I could refuse his demands *if I wished*—and right now, I wanted to strip away the barriers between us. I wanted to take my clothes off. I wanted to offer myself to him in every way possible.

"I didn't tell you to stop." He cracked his knuckles, as if preparing himself for what he planned to do to me.

My eyes met his as I reached behind my back and unhooked my bra. I let it fall from my shoulders to the floor. Julian swept a hungry look across my chest, and my breasts tightened under his shameless gaze. My nipples hardened into pebbles as I imagined his mouth on them—and his fangs.

Another crack of his knuckles as he raised one eyebrow. "Your pants?"

My mouth curled into a smile. Delighted to oblige, I unfastened them and let the silk puddle to the floor. I stepped out of them, my thumbs hooking the flimsy elastic waistband of my thong. "And these?"

"*Every. Thing.*" He took his time with the order, as if to remind me that he would take his time elsewhere, too.

I yanked them off me, realizing that not one bit of me was self-conscious about standing stark naked in front of a nine-hundred-year-old god. Instead, I swung my panties around my index finger in a circle before launching them in his direction.

Julian snatched them out of midair and brought them to his face, breathing them in. "Have I ever told you what my last meal would be?"

Oh my...

I swallowed and shrugged as if I had no idea what he was suggesting. Julian snorted as he tossed them onto the bed. I was practically a puddle by the time he beckoned for me to join him.

I dropped to my hands and knees, but he shook his head.

"On top," he ordered.

"But we—"

"On top," he repeated.

We'd never really managed to make that position work. He was so big—in more ways than one—that we usually switched positions quickly. But I had no choice as I prowled up his body, and I didn't want one. When I straddled his hips, he smiled.

"No, pet." Julian licked a full circle around his lips. "I'm *hungry*.

Come to me."

I hesitated before I kept crawling up his muscular frame, but I didn't make it far before I paused. "What do you want?"

"I want to feast on you." Shadows danced in his eyes. "Now, bring that pretty little ass up here and sit on my face before I have to take matters into my own hands."

Part of me wanted to discover what taking matters into his own hands entailed, but too much of me wanted to do exactly what he said to resist the call of my tether. Still, I trembled a little as I continued up his body, aware that he was still healing. But I wanted this—wanted him—so badly that my tether hardly mattered. Not when every inch of me longed to be claimed. Slowly, I placed one knee just above his shoulder. A second later, his hands grabbed my ass and hauled me over his mouth.

I nearly collapsed at the first hot lash of his tongue. Instead, I lurched forward and steadied myself with the headboard. Warm laughter tickled across my swollen flesh. Of course he thought torturing me was funny. He loved teasing me almost as much as he loved making me come. Almost. But before I could make a show of my exasperation, I felt the tip of his tongue slide deeper and circle around my engorged clit. I jolted, nearly smothering his face, and tried to lift myself off him. But Julian held me firmly.

He twisted beneath me, turning his head to kiss my thigh. "Is there a problem, pet?"

I choked out a "*no*," which was all I could manage as the blood rushed from my head and pooled in my core.

"I didn't think so. When you're ready, I want you to let go and give me everything," he said darkly before closing his mouth over me and continuing to tease with deliberate, languid strokes.

Our love was a storm, but Julian anchored me. Every part of my being centered around him, even as his sinful mouth coaxed me into rougher waters. When the first surge hit me—nearly dragging me under—I clung to the headboard. Julian's pace shifted from languid to rabid, and for once, the beast didn't beat inside my chest; it lay beneath and claimed me. He gripped my ass, rocking me faster and harder as waves of pleasure broke over me. I crested, crying out his name as he devoured me with relentless determination.

I collapsed forward, my body giving out as a hollow ache replaced my ecstasy.

Julian pressed a soft kiss to my tender flesh, and then in a flash, he was behind me. He moved with the ease of a predator. I heard his belt slide free of his pants as an arm snaked under me and urged me to lift to my knees. I kept hold of the headboard as the broad crown of his cock breached me. He held there and angled his head toward me. His hand slid to my throat and drew me closer.

"You are mine no matter what. I will never let you go. I will never stop wanting you. Nothing will change that. Our souls are bound together," he hissed, his breath hot on my neck.

I whimpered, unable to manage more than a nod.

"Say it," he demanded, and the words flew from my lips.

"I'm yours."

"Good girl." He kissed my neck as he seated himself fully inside me. I moaned and stretched my neck, earning a rough chuckle that grazed down my fraying nerves. "You want everyone to know you belong to me, don't you?"

"Yes," I practically sobbed. Because being his was all I wanted to be. Not a witch or a vampire or whatever the hell I was. *His* mate. *His* sustenance.

His.

"I shouldn't." He moved slowly in and out of me, each thrust deeper than the last.

I knew why he didn't want to bite me there, and I didn't care, because I didn't need some gentlemanly show of respect. I needed him—all of him. The beast and the male. I needed him to own me as much as I owned him. "Screw self-control."

Julian's groan told me I'd won, and when he sank his fangs into the scars on my neck, another climax ripped through me, another storm battered me, and I was lost to everything but him and us and this.

He pistoned faster, coming with a roar that probably shook the house before we collapsed together onto the bed.

We lay there for a few minutes, our shared heartbeat slowly returning to its normal rhythm. Knitting his hand through mine, he brought it to his lips and kissed each knuckle.

"There's something you should know—"

The door to our bedroom was knocked off its hinges.

CHAPTER FORTY-THREE

Julian

*P*rotect my mate.

Instinct kicked in automatically. I surged from the bed, dick still hanging out, and blocked Thea from the intruder. Or rather, intruders.

Several vampire guards wearing the insignia of the Council strode in, followed by my mother—who was screaming at them and brandishing the sword I was now all too familiar with.

"What the hell do you think you're doing?" she demanded. "Who sanctioned this?"

That bit caught me off guard, and for just a moment, my defenses faltered. When it came to vampires, one moment was more than enough. There was a flash of movement, and I whipped around in time to see a female I didn't know grab Thea and drag her from the bed.

"Take your fucking hands off my mate," I snarled, lunging for her, but hands seized me from behind. Rage erupted inside me, and I swung wildly at my attackers. I took the male on my left down with a single punch to the ribs. The other came at me, and my leg snapped out, flipping him off his feet. But even with two down, more rushed me. A moment later, another pinned me to the ground.

I struggled as the female shoved Thea to the floor and pointed to her clothes. "Get dressed."

Our eyes met, hearts thundering in our chests, as Thea scrambled for her modesty. I stared into her rounded green eyes, fear flooding me, and nearly vomited her blood on the floor.

"What is the meaning of this?" Sabine demanded with the sword by her side.

"Your son has broken the law and is being called before the Council," the largest male informed her without hesitation.

"Who ordered this?" she asked, her voice silky with venom. "I'll remind you that I am the head of this household. You cannot take my son prisoner without informing me of the charges and the petitioner."

The brutish vampire faltered for a moment, glancing at one of his companions. That was his mistake. When he turned back, he found the ancient blade at his throat.

"I asked you a question," my mother said, pressing the steel against his flesh.

"Katrine," he croaked. "She's charged your son with breach of the Anti-Tethering Act as well as consorting with a human during The Rites."

"Katrine is misinformed," Sabine seethed, then whipped her sword point in Thea's direction. "That *thing* is no human."

"Ma'am, we're only following or—"

The swish of a blade cut him off, and his head fell to the ground, blood splashing on the bleached wood floors. The guards pinning me fell back just enough for me to spring free. I jumped to my feet, shoving my dick inside my pants and surveying the room. I couldn't reach Thea without risking one of them hurting her, but I wasn't about to join my mother. Not until I knew what the hell was going on. Instead, I angled myself with the wall at my back, anger vibrating from me in primal growls.

Thea paused with one leg in her pants, her mouth falling open as she drank in the gore. But she wasn't a naive human anymore, and she quickly recovered, continuing to dress.

I would kill them. I would kill them all.

But before I could do that, my mother intervened again.

"Will anyone else dare to condescend to me?" she asked, looking around the room. "Or call me *ma'am*?"

The female holding Thea lifted her chin and glared at my mother, her dark hair swinging from a high ponytail that I planned to grab hold of when I bashed her lovely face into the wall. Her gaze darted to me, a smirk playing at her lips, as if she knew I was planning my attack. "Orders are orders. The Council expects an in-person audience with both parties."

"And who will vouch for their safety?" Sabine asked coolly.

"You have my word," the female said. "They will be delivered directly to the Council. No harm will come to them at *our* hands."

Thea paled across the room, and my heart raced in my chest. It wasn't much of a promise. Not with what the Council had threatened to do to her in Paris. But my mother lowered her sword.

"You will inform them that no action will be taken against *my son* without my consent."

"No!" I roared, charging blindly toward Thea. A guard jumped on my back, locking an arm around my neck. I thrashed against my captor until the female guard moved next to Thea. She didn't touch her.

She didn't have to.

"Stop fighting, or I will break her neck," she said casually.

I stilled instantly. I couldn't reach Thea in time, and we all knew it. The guard on me released me as another grabbed my arms and bound them behind my back. I only had one card to play, but it was a blind bluff at best.

Turning to my mother, I said hoarsely, "Order them to extend the protection to her."

She didn't speak.

"Please," I begged, searching her face for any sign of maternal instinct. I shouldn't have expected to find it there now. Not after its absence for all these years. "For me. Just until we have time to prove she's not human."

Cold eyes studied me, her imperious face remaining unreadable. She'd birthed me—given me life—and held our family under her thumb for centuries. In some ways, I knew her too well. But in moments like this, and ones like what had taken place earlier today, I realized my mother was still a mystery to me.

An eternity passed as we regarded each other. I'd asked little from her in my life because I'd always known she was unlikely to give anything. Finally, she turned her attention to the female guard. "You will not harm my son's mate, and you will inform the Council that I will be consulted before any punishments are levied against either of them."

"Madame," the female said carefully, her eyes on my mother's sword. "The request of a pureblood matriarch regarding her child is one thing, but—"

"Don't question me, or you will wind up like your colleague." Sabine nudged the decapitated head with the sword point. "Deliver the message. Extenuating circumstances. They will be wise enough to heed my warning."

The guard behind me shoved me forward with a sneering, "Let's go."

"Careful," Sabine advised the male. "My son is the heir to one of the original bloodlines."

The guard hesitated before nodding.

I strained to look over my shoulder, desperate to see Thea, but the security team blocked her.

Don't worry. I won't let them hurt you. I thrust the thought in her direction even as I forced myself to calm down. I'd made a mistake by letting my instincts take control, and it had cost me. I had to stay calm if I was going to get us out of this. I began studying the group as much as I could as I was herded up the stairs of *Paradeisos*.

This wasn't a novice crew they'd sent, meaning they'd learned their lesson from San Francisco. They'd likely counted on Sabine's cooperation. Even I found myself surprised that she'd championed us at all. Perhaps there was some maternal affection inside her.

But I doubted her concern would extend to Thea if the Council decided against her.

I'd anticipated a reaction when they learned of our arrival, but, honestly, I had expected an invitation for a formal meeting, not a raid. And where the fuck were my brothers?

I got my answer as we reached the main floor. Lysander, Thoren, and Sebastian stood in the entry, armed to the teeth with most of my mother's ancient weaponry. My father blocked the door. He hadn't bothered with weapons because he didn't need them. Even if the guards were seasoned, they'd never be able to take a vampire as old and experienced as Dominic Rousseaux. I glanced around, looking for a sign of Benedict or Jacqueline. A minute later, my best friend stepped into view, one arm hooked around my missing brother's neck. She shot me a grim smile that told me all I needed to know.

I lurched toward the traitor. "How could you?"

"You don't—"

Jacqueline cut off Benedict's excuse and shook her head, as if warning me to keep quiet. I had no idea why, but I fell silent.

"Going so soon?" Lysander stepped forward, twin daggers clenched in his hands.

"We are here on official Council business," the female guard informed them, but I caught the tremble in her voice. They were outnumbered now, and she knew it.

"Trespassing is trespassing, sweetheart," Sebastian crooned, flipping his blade between his hands. "Why don't you let our family go before this gets bloody?"

"Is that a threat?" she asked coldly.

"Would you like me to say please?" Sebastian said without blinking.

Sabine swept between us, sighing heavily. "Do you see why I tried to stop you?" she asked me. "Will you go to war for her?"

"Will I go to war for love?" I bit out. "I've gone to war for less. Love might be the only thing worth fighting for, so yes, I will go to war for love. And I will kill anyone who comes between us."

Sabine's nostrils flared, and for a moment, we all stood in silence. There wasn't a shadow of emotion on her face when she turned her attention to the guards. "Take them to the Council."

CHAPTER FORTY-FOUR

Thea

I'd expected a dungeon or maybe an interrogation room—someplace where all the sharp objects had been removed, and people watched from behind a fake mirror. Instead, I found myself in an opulent office with no idea how I'd gotten there. The last thing I remembered was Julian's brothers being told to step aside and let the Council take us for questioning. Then, *nothing*.

My memory was a total blank between that moment and finding myself in an oversize wingback chair, sitting in a room straight out of a novel. It was the sort of place you expected to find in a dean's office, except for the number of mysterious objects scattered on the oak desk and cluttering every surface. I resisted the urge to pick up a skull that looked to be either made of solid gold or dipped in the precious metal. I wasn't sure I wanted to know which. Behind the desk, surrounded by ceiling-high bookshelves, was a fireplace. The phases of the moon were carved into its mantel. Overhead, an iron chandelier flickered ominously, as if the wiring was shot. The faulty light sent shadows chasing through the room.

I had no idea where I was or how I'd gotten here. Was Julian nearby? Had he been taken someplace like this or...

A blurry memory of Julian grabbing a sword and swinging it

tumbled through my brain. He hadn't gone quietly. That wasn't surprising, but the recollection hollowed a pit in my stomach. I closed my eyes and searched for him inside me. My fingers circled my wrist, noting my languid pulse. Concentrating, I listened for him, wondering if I could hear his thoughts if I tried hard enough, but my mind was unnervingly silent.

"Where are you?" I murmured to myself. Deep inside me, I felt a rustle of dark magic respond, as if the part of him I carried with me was rousing, too. It wasn't much hope to cling to, but it was something. Julian was alive—for now.

That might be more of a consolation if I wasn't in the Vampire Council's custody. Exhaling heavily, I opened my eyes and found two coal-black ones staring back at me.

"Holy—!" I jumped a few inches off my chair, and the woman smiled. It was the female who'd captured me earlier. She'd traded the uniform she wore earlier for a ruby-colored sweater with a loose cowl neck that draped over one shoulder. Her clasped hands were covered in gold rings. Some were dotted with gemstones, and others were merely simple bands. But it was the way her dark eyes watched me that held my attention. "You…"

She didn't bat an eye at the accusation dripping in that one word. Instead, she lifted a bell and rang it. The door behind me opened, and I turned, my hands rising defensively at the potential of more danger. A squat male in a butler's uniform bustled in, carrying a silver tray.

"May I offer you something to drink?" she asked me like I'd popped in for a visit. "We have several kinds of tea and wine. I'm sure Theodore can scare up some sandwiches from the kitchen."

I stared for a second before shaking my head.

"Very well." She picked up a crystal decanter and popped its silver stopper off, tipping it. I watched the red liquid fill a goblet. It was too thick to be wine, and my stomach flipped. Her head tilted as she stared at me with naked curiosity. "I didn't expect to find you so squeamish, given the bite marks I saw on your neck. Do you allow him to feed from you often?"

My fingers fluttered to fidget with my high-necked sweater. Its collar hid the proof that Julian drank from me. I wasn't sure how to answer her question, so I remained silent. Was I being questioned now? If so, anything I said could be held against me and us.

"There's no need to be shy." She continued: "After our introduction earlier, I feel we're already intimate."

"Do you mean when you invaded my privacy and abducted me?" I asked her coldly.

"Good! You do speak," she said, ignoring my accusation as she sipped from her goblet. "That will make this easier."

"Make what easier?"

She smiled, revealing bloodstained teeth. "Having a conversation."

I shivered at the sight and wrapped my arms around my shoulders.

"I apologize. You must be cold. I'll have Theodore light a fire." She gestured to the empty hearth behind her.

"I'm fine," I said quickly. I wasn't about to sit here and waste time. "Who are you? Where am I? And where's Julian?" I shot off each question in rapid succession. She wanted to talk? Fine. I had plenty of things to talk about.

"You're quite demanding for a human. My name is Selah. I serve as a sort of specialist that advises the Council on issues relating to human affairs, shall we say. Given my expertise, they've asked me to speak with you."

"I'm not human," I said carefully. I wasn't certain if pointing that out would help or hurt me, but this was why we'd come to Greece in the first place—to lay to rest the Council's concerns. "Tell them that after you let me go."

"I see." She placed her goblet on the table and leaned forward, pressing her fingers into a steeple. "And why do you believe you aren't human?"

"Shouldn't I get a lawyer or something?" I hedged, wishing Julian was here. Where were they keeping him, and when would they let me see him?

"Vampire law is not terribly interested in due process." To her credit, she sounded almost apologetic. "I can assure you I am only gathering more information to help the Council ascertain the correct next step to take."

"Like how they should execute me?" There was nothing small or shaky about my question. It wasn't that I was ready to die—far from it—but I refused to let the Council—or their self-proclaimed specialist—terrorize me while I was in their custody.

She angled her head to study me with a puzzled smile. "What gave you that idea?"

"When they threatened to kill me," I said flatly. "Or was that just a joke?"

"Not a joke, but rather a misunderstanding." She flattened her palms on the desk, narrowly avoiding knocking into what I hoped was a really aggressive letter opener, and stood.

"A misunderstanding? You told Julian that I would be executed if the relationship continued."

"The night of the opera attack was traumatic for everyone involved. I assure you they *misspoke*."

"And now?" I took a deep breath and prepared myself for what I would say next. "I'm free to live my life?"

"Of course. However, we will need to compel you, and then there is the matter of your tether to Lord Rousseaux."

I'd heard him called this before, but this time it was different. There was something reverent in her tone that told me how important my mate truly was amongst his kind.

"Compel me?" I repeated.

"Before you return to your human life."

I held back a groan. Clearly, she wasn't listening to me, but why? "Why would I do that? My life is here with my mate."

Her eyes pinched together as I spoke, but her voice remained cloyingly sweet as she said, "Mate? I believe you are confused, which is perfectly natural. It can be difficult to adjust to the real world for humans."

"I'm not a human!" I exploded out of my chair. "And Julian is my mate."

"Lord Rousseaux is tethered to you," she hissed, giving me a glimpse of the fangs she'd kept hidden. "I don't know how you tricked him into believing you were anything other than a pathetic human—"

"I can read his mind. We both feel the magic." I thrust a hand out to her. "See for yourself."

I expected her to shrink from my bluff, but instead, she strode toward me, tugging her glove off one fingertip at a time, and grabbed mine.

Nothing happened.

I reached inside myself, searching for the spark that Julian's dragon guarded, but nothing happened. I couldn't feel anything. I ran my tongue over my gums, searching for proof of my fangs, but they were no longer tender. Any sign of my magic was…gone.

"Whenever you're ready," Selah taunted me.

I stared at our clasped hands, dumbfounded for a moment. Then I snapped out of it and glared at her. "Ask Julian. He'll tell you about my magic and our mating bond and—"

"Another specialist is with him," she cut me off. "It seems there's been some confusion. It's not surprising, since there is a tether involved, obscuring the truth."

The last of my patience snapped in two. "This isn't about the tether!"

"Of course it is." Selah raised a thin eyebrow. "What you perceive as magic is nothing more than the tether forcing him to protect and care for you—I imagine how intoxicating and magical it must feel for a human…"

"Julian released me from my tether." Doubt crept into my voice, and I hated myself for it.

"That's not possible." I opened my mouth to protest this, but she continued. "And this magic of yours is proof of that."

"I don't see how," I grumbled, but my heart began to race.

"You said you can read Lord Rousseaux's mind."

I nodded, rolling my eyes. "Please call him Julian."

"A tethered female does whatever the male wishes."

"I don't see how that proves anything." I crossed my arms, wondering how long she could drag this out.

"Perhaps he wanted you to understand him better, and this was how you responded—by being able to read his mind."

There was only one problem with her argument. "It happened before we were...tethered."

"It's likely a compulsion, then," she said with a shrug. How many excuses did she have lined up and waiting for me?

"Julian can't compel me." I found myself smiling. Selah might think she could break me—or whatever the Council had sent her to do—but I wasn't going to roll over.

"Of course he can." She faced me, leveling a serious gaze in my direction. "That is why you believe you have magic. It's why you agreed to go to bed with him. You've been under his compulsion since the day you met."

I shook my head. "Believe anything you want. Julian never compelled me. He can't. We're mates."

"Do you really think a centuries-old vampire would mate with a fragile human?" She snorted as if this wasn't a question. It was a joke.

"I'm not human," I whispered. Was this their plan? To wear me down until I said something I would regret? "Why would I believe anything you're saying?"

"I am not your enemy..."

Given that she'd dragged me out of bed while I was naked, I had my doubts about that.

"Fine," she said, sounding resigned. She walked toward the door. "If you won't believe me, perhaps someone else can persuade you."

I didn't know who I expected to be on the other side of that door—who she thought could persuade me of this version of events. She opened it, but it wasn't another guard or a familiar.

My heart leaped into my throat when I saw him, but something locked me in place.

He stopped, his gaze raking over me in a cold, removed way as he sneered. My blood chilled as he looked away with disgust. I closed my eyes, hoping that when I opened them, both he and Selah would be gone. But when I peeked out, he was still standing there with a look of pure hatred on his face—a look I recognized.

"Hello, *pet*."

CHAPTER FORTY-FIVE

Thea

It was the same look he'd worn the first night we met. A light in the hallway cast shadows over him, and he lingered in them like he belonged to that darkness. An ache split my chest, every inch of me longing to rush into his arms, but that murderous gaze held me back. It couldn't be directed at me. He was simply on edge, reeling from awakening to find himself a captive of the Council, just as I had.

But he didn't look past me into the magical office, even when I heard the rustle of Selah's movement behind me again. He kept his hateful gaze trained on me. I waited for his stony features to soften, but he continued to glower. Was this part of whatever plan he'd formed while they'd interrogated him? Did he expect me to go along with it or protest harder? Reaching out, I tried to read his thoughts, but I found nothing but dark silence. It was as if he was shielding his mind from mine. I swallowed, squaring my shoulders, and took two lurching steps toward him, my body simultaneously protesting the decision and propelling me to the safety of my mate.

"I wouldn't come any farther," he purred in a deadly voice, "unless you're planning to offer me a snack."

I stopped and studied him for a moment, but he turned toward the darkened hall as if he couldn't bear to look at me. "What did they tell you?"

"Oh no. You first, *pet*," he said. The word clawed through me, tearing me up with its poisonous barbs. It wasn't the sweet term of endearment I'd once treasured. It held none of the sensual promise I usually found on his lips. It wasn't even an exasperated reminder that he was a vampire and I was under his care and protection.

What rippled under his cold exterior clenched my stomach in knots I couldn't untangle: distrust. What had I done to deserve that? If I could hear what he was thinking, maybe it would be clear, but whatever they'd done to me had stolen that power along with the rest of my magic. I couldn't feel him even though he was close enough to touch. Pain wrapped around my heart and squeezed until I wasn't sure how much more I could bear. I couldn't take how he was looking at me like I was a stranger. Or worse, like I had betrayed him. It didn't make sense...unless they'd told him what they'd told me—that I was merely human. Even if they had, he couldn't believe them—could he?

There was only one way to know.

"They told me that I'm human," I confessed. "They said I have no magic. They said that we aren't mates. They said you compelled me."

I had nothing to lose by putting all my cards on the table. If he knew what they said and believed it, we had to face it. Maybe if I was honest—maybe if I was completely open—whatever anger he felt toward me would ebb and we could figure out what to do next. It was the logical move.

But it felt wrong.

Even as I spoke, I knew with absolute certainty that this wasn't just the tether. Julian hadn't compelled me the night we'd met. I had to believe that because if I didn't...I almost couldn't face what it meant.

It meant I was human. It meant there was no true magic in my blood. It meant that the Council would move against us; they would tear us apart. And if they did that, I wasn't sure how I would survive, even if they compelled me. Not just because they'd be taking away my mate and rending our joined souls in two, but because somehow, somewhere along the way, I'd stopped being human. I'd left that world behind, and no matter how hard they tried to erase it from my memories, I would never be the same person again—and I would never know why.

Fear seized me with such force that I doubled over and barely held down the contents of my stomach.

I couldn't go back. I wouldn't.

So, I waited for him to deny it, but instead, he laughed. The sound skittered down my spine like icy fingertips. I sucked in a deep breath, trying to calm my churning stomach. "Julian?"

"Given the circumstances, I think you should call me Lord Rousseaux." He prowled across the room and picked up the decanter of blood. "I guess our little gamc is at an end, then."

Game. The word echoed through the empty space in my heart he should occupy. Game? I flinched as he popped the stopper, my body tight with paranoia even as my brain tried to catch up. For a moment, I just stood and watched him. I watched those long, clever fingers that had caressed me only a few hours ago pour a goblet of blood. I could still feel them on my skin like ghosts, but now I wanted to get away from them—away from him—even as I craved the reassurance of my mate's touch. When I finally found my words, my voice cracked as I spoke. "What's going on? Why are you acting like this?"

He lounged against the edge of the desk and took a lingering sip from his cup. "Isn't it obvious?" he said with bloodied teeth. "Or have you really not figured it out? Did you think any of this was real? That our relationship was real?"

"It's not true," I said, but the kernel of doubt sprouted inside me. "They're going to compel me. They're going to make me forget you. *Forget us.*"

"Exactly why do you think I would care?" he asked coldly, and for a second, we weren't in some office in Greece. We were back in Paris, and he was breaking my heart. He was rejecting me. He was sending me away.

And that's when I realized what he was doing and why he was doing it.

"Don't do this," I said in a small voice, finally realizing what was happening. This wasn't my mate. This wasn't the male I loved. This was the Julian who had chosen me over us. The Julian who had chosen to break both our hearts to save my life. "I don't care what it costs me. I can't live the rest of my life with half my soul. Again."

Our eyes locked, and I dug inside myself, searching for the magic we shared. But the harder I looked for him inside me, the larger the void inside me stretched. He'd been here minutes ago when I'd woken from whatever spell or drugs they'd placed me under. I'd felt him then, but now? They must be blocking my magic because I couldn't feel the dark rustle of wings. No brutish energy paced inside me, readying itself to attack and protect.

He was gone.

If he was gone from me, then I was gone from him. But maybe my light wasn't all they had taken. I'd seen glimpses of the beast Julian caged inside himself. I'd felt him. Was that what stood before me now? Had they stripped every ounce of goodness and restraint from him and left nothing but this arrogant, smirking demon behind? A drug, a vow, a threat?

His head tipped back, and I braced myself for the full force of that wicked beast. Somehow, it was worse when he didn't attack me but roared with laughter instead. "Have you learned nothing about *my* kind? After all this time, do you honestly believe a vampire could love you?"

I didn't hesitate. "Yes. I know that you love me. I assume they've threatened me again or some other bullshit." I tossed a scathing look at Selah, who didn't hide her amusement from where she watched in the corner. She simply crossed her arms and smiled all the way up to her dark, almond-shaped eyes. She was enjoying this—enjoying how he'd ripped me open and laid my shredded heart before her. Hatred gripped me, and I clenched my hands into fists, wishing I had that dark pulse of his magic to launch at her. "Why not just be honest with me?"

"Oh, honey, I was honest with you," she said in a dark voice. "There have been no more threats. Are you certain you know him as well as you thought?"

"I can see how you'd be confused." Julian finished his drink in one long swallow. "I might have failed to mention we like to play with our prey. I believe you humans call it 'the long game'?"

"Stop," I ordered him.

But his mouth lifted into a lopsided grin. "You have to *mean* it. You have to believe that you need me to stop if you're going to use my tether against me."

"So, you are tethered?" I asked, my voice sounding strangely hollow to my own ears. "If this is a game, it seems like a dangerous risk."

None of this made sense. It couldn't be true. *This* was the game, but what was the prize?

"Yes." He shrugged one shoulder. "Thankfully, there are several simple ways to get out of that."

No. I shook my head, trying to unscramble my thoughts.

"And your sister?" I asked him. "If it was so simple, why didn't your family free her?" I provoked.

Was everything he'd ever told me a lie? It couldn't be. I'd met Camila. I'd seen how Sabine had reacted to our mating bond. Julian was lying to me now or…if this was a game—he wasn't the only one playing with his prey. They were all part of this evil charade. Every one of them had been toying with me, even Jacqueline and Celia and Bellamy—vampires who'd shown me kindness. Maybe if I'd never met them, I might believe that vampires were cruel, as Julian claimed. I might have lost the game we played now.

"My sister?" he repeated, his arrogant mask slipping for a second. "My family tends to be dramatic, but we all love the game, even Camila."

"Liar," I whispered.

Blue eyes flashed at my insult, and I found myself pinned against the wall. Julian's face was inches from mine, his eyes pure onyx now. His lips curled back to reveal his fangs. I waited for my body to respond, but where I should have felt love, I felt hate. There was no desire. Instead, disgust filled me. "What would I ever want with a fragile, useless human?"

"What would I ever want with a lying, sack-of-shit vampire?" I hissed at him.

"Careful, *pet*."

But I had him exactly where I wanted him.

I threw an arm over the one holding me to the wall, then ripped it back, sliding my naked fingers over his sleeve until I found flesh. I dug into it, and electricity snapped like a livewire where our skin met.

Then I crumpled to the ground in a heap. I looked up, not bothering to hide my triumph, and found him across the room. He crouched like a predator bracing for an attack, but I didn't move. Selah straightened, the smile on her face fading to a frown.

"You aren't my mate," I said calmly.

Selah stepped forward, dredging her fallen smile back into place. This time, it was brittle. It wouldn't take much to shatter it, but that didn't stop her from continuing to sell her lie. "That's what we've been trying to tell you."

I wasn't buying it. Not anymore.

"No. This is over." I shifted to face her as I rubbed my bruised neck. "That's not *Julian*."

CHAPTER FORTY-SIX

Julian

There was only darkness.

I reached for Thea, searching for her light, but where she should be, there was only darkness—and then everything came rushing back to me in one horrifying memory.

Thea knelt at my feet. Blood soaked across her cashmere sweater, pouring from a gaping wound at her neck. She'd begged me to continue to feed, offering herself with total submission even as she bled to death. And then...

She died.

I twisted, the cot's springs groaning under my weight as I hauled my upper body over the side of the bed and vomited a thin mixture of blood and bile. My body heaved, my stomach contracting violently even after I felt hollowed out and empty. But the images remained seared in my brain.

Thea is alive.

I spoke the words to myself like an incantation. I hadn't hurt her. I hadn't attacked her. The memories were lies. It was all some sort of game or test. Even though I knew that, it did nothing to soothe the ragged panic I felt. My tether had gone into overdrive, my body physically rebelling against my inaction by expelling the last blood I'd consumed from her. Now that my stomach was empty, nausea gave way to a splitting headache that made me wish someone would chop my head off.

I fell back onto the cot and tried to get control of myself. I could do nothing to help my mate by lying around. I needed to come up with a plan. The thought was rewarded with a stabbing ache, as if my brain hated this idea. I rubbed my temples, torn between soothing the pain and trying to listen for clues as to where I'd been taken.

There was only one path forward: getting out and finding her. So, I strained my ears and winced as I felt another hot stab. Ignoring the pain, I tuned my ears to my surroundings. My eyes finally adjusted to the black room, and I realized that the reason it felt like there was only darkness was because there *was* nothing else in this room—save for me and the cot I'd woken on moments ago. No windows. No other furniture. The walls were painted some neutral tone I couldn't make out without light, but they felt *beige*.

I swung my legs over the side of the flimsy bed, careful to avoid the pile of sick I'd left, and got to my feet. My body protested each movement, acting abnormally sluggish. The Council must have drugged me or placed me under a particularly powerful spell, but that kind of magic was long gone. More than likely, they'd slipped me a potion or some witch's herbal sedative to calm me down.

Probably so I wouldn't kill them.

That had only bought them time. A murderous rage took hold of me again. When I had realized what they were doing—that the body lying at my feet was a glamour—my relief had been short-lived. An all-consuming fury seized hold of me. I'd called their bluff and then waited to pounce. I'd managed to take a chunk out of the first guard stupid enough to enter the room. But before I could kill my way free, whatever they'd given me kicked in, and I hadn't gotten a second swing.

A buzzing noise broke the silence, followed by the click of an electronic lock. An overhead light flipped on, and a female familiar— about the age of my mother, judging by the way she held herself— entered the room. Several guards flanked her. One of them cradled a bandaged arm, and his eyes narrowed on me, spite flashing across his face. At least I'd made the one swing I'd gotten count. I smiled wolfishly at him.

"Are you ready to proceed to the next stage, or do you plan on maiming another one of my men?" she asked with a flick of her gloved fingers.

"That depends. Are you planning to fuck with my head again?" I replied in a smooth voice. I'd acted instinctively earlier, too ravaged by guilt and grief to think straight. I wouldn't make that mistake twice.

"How you spend the remainder of your evening is up to you." Her long gown swished around her feet as she approached me. Several of her guards looked nervous as she closed the space between us, but they hung back. "I'm here to share your options."

"How novel," I gritted out. I could only imagine what punishments the Council deemed worthy of being called *options*.

"You can stay here and keep attacking my men until you give up. As you are a pureblood vampire from one of our oldest families, the Council will allow you to leave your companion, go home, and forget any of this ever happened—"

"Not fucking likely."

She ignored me and continued. "Or you can be reunited with Miss Melbourne to face punishment together."

"Take me to her now," I growled. It had to be a trick. There was no way the Council planned to let me near her, not after what I'd done to the glamour they'd used to test me. Not unless they planned to kill us both.

And if that was the case? Well, I would die holding my mate's hands.

I still wasn't sure what had happened here—why I'd lost control and attacked Thea's glamour like that. Was I really in control now? Or had that been part of what they'd done to me? Was I a risk to her now?

But if there was a chance of seeing Thea, it was a risk worth taking.

The witch's gaze darted to the mess I'd left on the floor. Her head swiveled to one of the men nearby. "Have someone clean that up," she said, then her eyes flickered to me. "And somebody get him a stick of gum or something."

"That's not necessary. Just take me to Thea." I didn't give a shit that my head was killing me or that the sour taste of sickness lingered in my mouth. Hell, I could be bleeding from the head and I'd refuse to stop for a bandage.

She snorted. "Nonsense. It's no trouble."

One of the guards released the hilt of his sword and reached into his pocket. A second later, a foil-wrapped stick of gum flew through the air at me. I snatched it mid-flight and begrudgingly unwrapped it to shove in my mouth. I chomped a few times before baring my fangs at her. "Happy?"

"Ecstatic," she said flatly. She swept an arm elegantly toward the door. "Right this way."

I paid careful attention to my surroundings as they led me down a cramped corridor, the security team following me closely. Portraits of prominent vampire families hung along the wall, punctuated by unmarked doors. I glared at them as I passed, knowing I'd found myself in the Council's private chambers. The headquarters were located in a secret spot in the heart of Corfu. I'd never stepped foot inside it. The only vampires that did usually didn't come back out. I couldn't bear to look as I passed my family's own portrait, which hung in a prominent spot at the end of the hall.

At least I knew who stood with us now.

Benedict had betrayed our arrival to the Council. He had better hope I never stepped foot outside this building again. My mother had allowed them to take us. She'd lain down her sword. Had she known what they'd planned to do? How they'd intended to torture me?

More importantly, had she known what they did to Thea? Something even I had yet to discover.

We reached an oak door at the end of the hall, and my captor rapped on it. I knew she wasn't leading me to Thea, but I hoped whatever was inside—whoever was inside—provided answers. I'd seen no way out in the short walk from where I'd been held to here. It would take a considerable amount of effort to take down this many guards, especially while I was still foggy from whatever they'd done to me. If I could only get a clue—just find out where they had Thea…

The thought vanished from my mind as the door swung open, revealing her sitting in a large chair that nearly swallowed her petite body. Her knees were tucked under her chin, and her arms wrapped protectively around her shins. She lifted her face, revealing cheeks wet with tears, and we stared at each other. There were no signs of injury. No bruises. No blood.

Just *my mate*.

No one stood in my way as I dashed for her.

I felt her magic first. The golden light that I had searched for since I'd woken spread through me like a warm hearth fire welcoming me home. I smelled her next, and I drank in the spicy, sweet jasmine-laced-with-cloves scent that belonged to us.

It was her. It was *really* her.

I nearly collapsed with relief. Instead, I dropped to my knees in front of her, reaching out cautiously. Green eyes watched me warily for a moment before a heart-wrenching sob slipped from her lips. Thea threw herself at me, and I caught her as her body crumpled into mine. I held her, counting each heartbeat shared between us. I circled one arm around her waist to hold her steady as she sank her fingers into my shoulder as if she needed to prove that I was really here, too. Our other hands found each other, and I moaned with relief as her magic pulsed against my palm.

For a fleeting second, I forgot that we had an audience until someone cleared their throat politely. Thea went rigid in my arms, which tightened protectively around her.

"So, you have both chosen to face your fate together," someone said as she moved into the periphery. It was the female who had broken into my family's home to haul us before the Council. I snarled at her, but she merely blinked. "That is what you choose, is it not?"

I turned my attention back to my mate's tear-stained face and found her answer there. She nodded as if to seal it, but my own answer was already leaving my lips. "Yes."

"I told you, Selah," the witch said. "They are truly mated."

"So you did, Agatha." Selah's nostrils flared with annoyance. Clearly, she didn't like being proven wrong. "Try not to let it go to your head."

"You've caused quite the stir," Agatha said, striding across the room. She picked up a decanter and popped its top before wrinkling her nose. "Don't you ever serve wine?"

"I was hungry," Selah said with a slight shrug. "I'll send for something recreational."

They continued to bicker over the refreshments like any of it mattered—like we were having tea instead of facing the prospect of execution.

"Why not get some sandwiches, too?" I thundered. I pressed Thea closer to me, wishing I could spare her from hearing the question I asked next. "How long do you plan to string this out? Just tell us what our punishment is."

Thea's fragile hand gripped my shoulder tightly, but when I looked back at her, her face remained resolute. We would face this together. We would face anything together. And, more than ever, I knew I was ready to die for her.

"Oh, *that*." Agatha waved her hand dismissively. "Must you always be so dramatic?"

But the question wasn't leveled at us. It was directed at Selah.

"I wanted to be sure," she said with a serpent's smile.

"You just enjoy torturing people." Agatha turned gentle eyes on us and spread her hands. "Congratulations. You've passed The Second Rite."

CHAPTER FORTY-SEVEN

Julian

"This was The...Rite?" I asked through gritted teeth. Thea sagged in my arms, an almost hysterical laugh bubbling from her. I wished I found it amusing. Instead, I focused on more important matters—like trying to decide which one of them to kill first.

"Please have a seat," Agatha said rather than answer me. She picked up the decanter in front of her. "You must be hungry."

"Not really," I seethed as I guided Thea onto her feet. I wouldn't accept a handshake from the Council anymore. There was no way I would take whatever blood they were offering.

She turned her soft eyes on my mate. "Do you need anything? Water? Something stronger?"

Thea shook her head. I waited for her to sit in the wingback I'd discovered her in, but she remained standing—just as I planned to. It was clear we were both thinking the same thing. Neither of us would sit quietly while the Council delivered whatever lecture they'd planned. I wrapped an arm around Thea's waist, taking stock of everyone in the room and their positions in relation to my mate.

"I see we aren't going to be civilized about this." Selah sniffed, looking at the empty chairs.

"They're still in shock," Agatha murmured. "They've been

through a traumatic experience."

But Selah rolled her eyes as she moved closer to the desk. I resisted the urge to put myself physically between her and Thea. My agitation must have been obvious, because Thea placed her palm over the back of my hand and ran her thumb over it with a soothing stroke.

I felt every eye in the room on that bare hand touching mine, but no one said anything about it.

"The *Kathréftis* has been used since The Rites began," Selah explained. Unlike her colleague, she didn't look the least bit apologetic for what we'd gone through. She was definitely the first one I should kill.

The Council member arched an eyebrow as if she knew what I was thinking and shot a too-innocent look at me. "You did come to complete The Rites?"

Thea glanced up at me and swallowed hard when she saw the murderous look on my face. "Yes," she answered for us. "We did."

"Then I fail to see what the problem is," Selah said breezily.

"The problem is that we received no warning," I informed her. "Then there's the little matter of drugging us, or whatever the hell you did to trick us into believing—"

"It's a simple spell kept in my family's grimoire for millennia," Agatha interrupted me before I could reveal what this *Kathréftis* had shown me. "The spell creates a mirror of this world, forcing you to confront your deepest fears. It was necessary to keep you in the dark for it to work, *and* there have been some questions amongst the Council regarding your relationship. Some questioned the validity of your mating bond since your brother informed them of the happy news." To her credit, she sounded like she believed it was good news. "How you handled The Rite suggests there is a very strong bond between you."

Selah, on the other hand, wrinkled her nose like she smelled something rotten in the air. "It is unlikely, though. You're probably under the effects of a tether. You were a virgin when you mated?"

Thea sputtered at the nonchalance with which the stranger broached such an intimate question. I wasn't surprised. I had spent enough time around vampires to expect bluntness, particularly amongst the powerful females that occupied the highest rungs of the Council. There was the question of how she knew such personal information, however.

"Did my brother tell you that, too?" I asked coldly. Benedict had a few things to answer for, and he'd be lucky for his head to still be attached when I was done questioning him.

Selah's mouth parted into a fanged smile, and I realized she'd lain a trap for me. "It was revealed during the Salon, or didn't your mate inform you of what happened there?"

It was another test. Thea *had* told me about the ceremonial ritual asking for Damia's blessing. She hadn't completed The Rite, technically, which meant she wasn't bound to secrecy like the other initiates. The Council knew all of this. I had no doubt my mother had told them. Before I could reach out with my thoughts and warn Thea of the game Selah was playing, Thea answered, "Of course I told him. I had a few questions about tethering after that night."

"He must have answered them to your satisfaction," Selah said in her snakelike voice.

"He did." Thea lifted her chin and glared at both women as if she was about to deliver a challenge. "I had no doubts when I accepted him as my mate."

Agatha sighed a little, and I got the impression she found all of this romantic.

"Tethered mates—*interesting*," Selah mused before continuing with a dismissive tone. "Being raised as a *human*, you couldn't possibly understand the danger you placed yourself in by tethering yourself to a vampire. Placing yourself under the control of a male might seem romantic, but it sets a bad precedent. There was a time when *some* families believed it would build stronger alliances to have tethered marriages. We know better now."

I wasn't sure if she was saying that for the benefit of my mate or her starry-eyed colleague, but I hadn't missed the subtle accusation in her words. My family had been one of those bloodlines, and we had led the charge to finally abolish the practice.

"I trust Julian completely," Thea said calmly.

It was impossible to put into words how much I loved the woman in my arms. She had trusted me with not only her heart but with everything she was. Even now, after facing the unimaginable, she wasn't swayed.

"Then you are a fool." Selah shook her head. "A vampire male's place is to produce heirs, protect his family, and meet his consort's every need. Instead, you gave him control over you. It goes against everything our society believes in to give away that kind of power!"

"But he gave it back to me," Thea said without missing a beat, effectively silencing her tirade.

"I'm not certain I understand," Agatha said gently.

Before I could say anything, Thea began to explain our unusual arrangement. By the time she finished, the two women were staring at me like they'd never seen a male before.

"And how did you know this would work?" Selah hissed at my mate.

"I didn't." Thea smiled as the woman took a step back like she'd slapped her. "But even if it hadn't, Julian would never abuse that power."

"Never is a long time." The words came from Agatha, who'd remained very quiet during Thea's story. "Especially when there's unknown magic involved."

"But there is magic involved," I interjected, seizing my opportunity to change the subject to something more important than their stupid tests. "Given that, the Council will recognize Thea has every right to participate in the social season and marry me."

Selah blinked and looked at Thea's hand, as if expecting to find a ring. "I had not heard that congratulations were in order."

"It's not formalized," I said, choosing my words carefully. I should have asked Thea weeks ago. I should have shoved the ring on her finger, romance be damned, and made this official. Would they see our lack of formal engagement as a weakness to exploit?

"Pardon my misunderstanding, but you spoke with such certainty," Selah said apologetically. She looked at Thea. "I would assume your family would be thrilled at the dowry a Rousseaux could bring."

A swath of crimson bloomed on Thea's cheeks. "I don't... I mean, the dowry isn't important to me."

"And your family? Surely *they* care. Tell me, what magical line do they descend from?" Selah asked.

Tread carefully. She might bite. But don't lie. My mate dipped her head just enough to let me know she'd heard me.

"I have no idea," Thea said truthfully. "I only became aware of my magic recently."

"Before or after you accepted your mating bond with Lord Rousseaux?"

"Before," Thea said.

"I don't see why that matters," I interjected, "and Thea will receive the dowry."

"Your mother must be thrilled at the prospect of some unknown, penniless creature becoming her daughter," Selah said darkly.

"She will be." I looked her directly in the eye.

Selah smirked as if she doubted this but said nothing else.

"Why did we have to face our fears for The Rite?" Thea asked thoughtfully, and I braced myself.

I never wanted to think about what had happened—what I'd done—again, but looking at my mate, I saw how it weighed on her. Thea's shoulders slumped slightly, and her thumb continued to stroke my hand—as if she needed physical proof that I was still here, too.

"Because most creatures never do," Agatha explained. "But you cannot know yourself until you face your fears. And no one should take another without knowing his own heart and mind. So, for those who are unprepared to make the commitment the final Rites require, this can dissuade them."

"So you just want to break people up?" Thea shivered, and I drew her closer.

"This is only The Second Rite," Agatha reminded her. "Which most vampires and familiars take without having a match in place. They face the fears they have carried with them their whole lives. We weren't sure what to expect of you two. It's interesting that your fears revolve around each other. I think it is a sign of an unusually strong mating bond."

My eyes shuttered at this revelation. So Thea's fears involved me, too. Had I attacked her? Had I tried to kill her? Is that what she feared the most? When I opened them, I found her searching my face as if wanting to know how she'd appeared to me.

Later.

But could I tell her? Could I admit that my deepest fear was that I couldn't protect her, especially from myself?

"Regardless, passing The Second Rite means hardly anything. There will be more questions for you," Selah told us.

"But you admit that we are mated?" Thea's voice trembled as she asked the question. Was that what she feared? If so, I would remind her just how mated we were the minute we were alone together.

"It hardly matters. Mating and marriage are two different matters," Selah said, ignoring Thea's squawk of protest. "The Vampire Council would like to know what kind of magic we are dealing with before granting you permission to marry."

"Permission?" I roared, finally losing the last of my restraint. "We don't need your permission. She has magic, which is all you bloody care about, and everyone knows it."

"As a matter of fact," Selah said coldly, "you do. The Rites are meant to ensure the strengthening of the bloodlines. Without knowing where she came from and what kind of magic runs in her veins, we can't be certain she can offer the pedigree needed—particularly to marry a Rousseaux."

"Her magic is strong," I said quietly, but I knew my word wasn't enough. Not if they were determined to push the issue. I'd hoped to avoid this. It wasn't as if Thea didn't know why vampires married familiars or other pureblood vampires. I'd been clear on that since the first night we met, though it wasn't something we'd discussed much since then. I had my own feelings on the matter. I'd been clear on that, too. But things had changed, and I couldn't avoid the truth forever. "It's not a pressing concern."

"Perhaps it doesn't seem that way to you, but our way of life is under threat." A current of anger thrummed in her words. "We can't afford to ignore our duty. No matter how strong the mating bond is."

It was clear Selah would never approve of the match. Not that I'd wanted her as an ally anyway. But it would have helped to have more allies on the Council.

"And you?" I turned my attention to Agatha. As a familiar, her opinion would matter less, but she might be the key to persuading them that Thea had the necessary magic to become my wife. "Where do the witches stand on this matter?"

Agatha's eyes darted nervously to Selah. "Unfortunately, she's right. There are situations that you are not aware of. Perhaps if you talked to your mother—"

"That's enough," Selah cut her off. "It will be up to the Council to decide if she's fit to be your wife."

"It's up to me," I snarled, "and she is—in *every* way."

"Touching." Selah practically spit the word at me.

"I'll prove it," Thea interjected loudly. She pulled away, stepping toward the women. "Just tell me how."

They shared a look. Agatha seemed impressed by my mate's audacity, but Selah appeared like she'd caught her in a snare.

"Are you prepared to take your place amongst the most powerful vampire family in history?" Selah's voice held a note of contempt as she played with her prey. "Do you think that you can rise to the example of Sabine Rousseaux?"

Thea snorted, and Selah's eyes narrowed into slits.

"I will grant you this one mistake," Selah warned Thea.

I took a step toward my mate, ready to place myself between the two women if necessary.

"Let me be clear," Selah added. "If vampires had a ruler, she would be it."

Thea's head whipped toward me, her shock unmistakable as she waited for confirmation. I grimaced, knowing I would hear about this later, and nodded once. Her eyes widened into full moons.

And she'll never let anyone forget it.

Her mouth lifted into a limp smile at the private joke. After a moment, she took a deep breath and turned back to them. "I believe I can. Is that all?"

"Hardly," Selah snapped. "That's only the beginning of what will be expected of you. There is something much more difficult. Do you think you can fulfill the most important duty any daughter of the Rousseaux name carries?"

Thea's shoulders squared, and she stared unflinchingly at her interrogator. "Tell me what I have to do."

Thea. I thought her name in warning, but it was too late to stop it. She was about to learn the truth.

Selah's smile spread like slow poison across her face as she answered, "Bear Julian an heir."

CHAPTER FORTY-EIGHT

Thea

Bear Julian an heir. Translation: let my mate knock me up.

There were only a few problems with that. The first was that Julian had been pretty clear on the whole not-wanting-kids thing. The second was that I was twenty-two. I'd just graduated from college, I was newly mated, and I had no idea if I wanted kids. I hadn't given it much thought. It always seemed like something for future me to worry about. The third—and maybe the most important of all—was that I wasn't entirely sure I could get pregnant. As a human, it wasn't possible. But now? Maybe it was. Maybe it wasn't.

The world tilted under my feet, and I took an unsteady step to keep myself upright. I'd been having sex for weeks. Lots and lots of sex. So much sex. And if I could get pregnant…

Acid shot up my throat, and I gagged. My hand flew to my mouth, but nothing came out. Still, everyone saw. The guards. Selah. Agatha.

And *Julian*.

"I'm not certain how to take that," Selah said, but the twist of her cruel lips said otherwise.

Julian stilled beside me, muttering, "Neither am I."

I shot a look that he didn't need mind-reading powers to understand. We needed to talk.

We'd save that very important conversation for another time when we weren't in the middle of being grilled by the Vampire Council's liaisons.

I had one question, though. Aiming my glare at Selah, I asked, "Why?"

"Why?" she repeated.

"Yes, *why*," I said irritably. "Give me a reason why I have to bear his heir."

I chose her words because they sounded a lot more sophisticated than the terms rattling around in my brain.

"Our kind is splintered. It's important to produce more vampires of good breeding." She tugged at the glove she wore.

"Breeding," I echoed with a hollow laugh.

"It is our best chance at protecting the little magic there is left in the world," Agatha added. Her eyes crinkled a little at the edges, and I realized she bought into this—all of this. If a vampire had asked her to cut off her arm for the sake of magic, she would do it. No wonder Diana had resented it when I'd called her a familiar. Their allegiance was a little…disturbing.

"Thea will choose for herself if she'd like to have a child. The Council has no business demanding such a thing from her," Julian said coldly.

My mouth nearly fell open. I turned to face him, aware of the fact that he seemed concerned about my choice in the matter. Maybe it was a ploy to make it look like I didn't want kids so they wouldn't order him to do it. But shadows fell across the sharp angles of his face and clouded his eyes. He looked torn.

Why? How?

"Can we go? Since we passed?" I asked him, not bothering to hide my impatience. With all the people crammed into the tiny office, it felt like I couldn't breathe. The longer I stood here, processing this revelation, the more it felt like the walls were pressing in on me. I needed to get out of here before I actually did vomit all over the fancy Persian rug under my feet.

"Of course." Selah snapped a finger, and Theodore appeared

with the speed of someone who knew better than to keep their boss waiting. "Have a car brought round to return our guests to *Paradeisos*."

But to my surprise, he glanced at us. "There's already a car waiting for Lord Rousseaux."

I didn't miss that I'd been left out of that statement. Someone had sent a car for him. Not me. Not us. *Him*.

It had to be Sabine. Did she expect her son to return home suddenly single? What did she think they would do to me? Or did she care at all?

I already knew the answer to that. She didn't. She had orchestrated all of this. She knew what the Council would demand. The real question was: Which one of us had she expected to crack?

"How convenient." Selah's smile revealed too many teeth. "I'm sure we will see both of you again."

"Don't sound so happy about it," I grumbled, but she ignored me.

"Perhaps tomorrow at the festival?" she asked Julian.

He jerked his head, his answer somewhere between a yes and a no. I raised an eyebrow. "What festival?"

"The Solstice," she said slowly as though I was an idiot. "Has no one explained to you?"

I started to shake my head but caught myself. When it came to the Council, there were no innocent questions. I had to pay attention to every word they said and even closer attention to every word I spoke. "Oh, *that*. I wasn't sure how long I'd been drugged and tortured."

Selah rolled her eyes before bowing graciously to Julian. "I hope to see you there."

She swept out of the room without including me in her farewell. I doubted I was on her list of people she wanted to celebrate with.

But Agatha rounded the desk and regarded each of us in turn. "I hope to see both of you there."

I mumbled something noncommittal, and she placed a hand on my shoulder. Even the squat older woman was taller than me.

"Have faith in your bond," she said softly. "I do."

I stopped myself from asking her why. I didn't have the energy.

She disappeared, leaving us with the guards who stood like statues along the wall. Julian cleared his throat before holding out his hand. "Shall we?"

I didn't move. "The car is for Lord Rousseaux."

"Pet." Warning edged his tone. "Come."

I planted my hands on my hips, refusing to budge. "So I'm your pet again?"

"I never meant it like that." He paused and sighed deeply. "Please come with me, my love."

"Are you sure there is room in the car, *my lord*?" I snapped. None of this was his fault. He wasn't the one who had picked up the world and turned it inside out. But I was tired and hungry. I had no idea what time it was or how long we'd been here. And I really, *really* wasn't looking forward to sharing a roof with Sabine or Benedict.

"If there isn't, you can sit on my lap." He thrust his hand out another inch. I narrowed my eyes at him before I finally grabbed it.

Julian led us down the corridor through a labyrinth of rooms and hallways that seemed impossible to navigate. I breathed a sigh of relief when we reached two forbidding steel doors. He paused, glancing up at a camera tucked into the corner of the ceiling. A second later, a lock clicked, and he pushed it open.

I stumbled back as sunlight burst through the open door. It was morning. We'd been here all night. It took my eyes a second to adjust to the burning light. When I did, I spotted a large town car waiting at the curb. The chauffeur blinked rapidly as we approached—not from the sun but from surprise. He recovered himself quickly and opened the passenger door. It was pretty clear that his orders were to only pick up one of us.

"Good morning," he greeted us stiffly.

I huffed a hello and climbed into the back seat. A moment later, Julian joined me.

The car didn't have a privacy wall between us and the front seat, so we fell into an uneasy silence. I stared out the window, watching the Greek waterfront whip by. A few minutes later, Julian's hand dropped onto my thigh. His palm slid possessively up, but I didn't turn.

I'm sorry.

I continued to stare out the window.

You don't have to do anything you don't want to do.

I wished I could shut him out like he could do to me. I wished I understood what this magic was inside me and why it let me hear his thoughts. But more than anything, I wished the emotions swirling like a tornado inside me would settle into something I could understand.

Things were happening fast—too fast. Suddenly, I felt like I was caught in the storm raging inside me. I couldn't see my future or my past. I couldn't even see who I was anymore. A small sob escaped my lips before I realized I was crying.

Julian slid closer, and this time, I didn't resist him as he wrapped his arms around me and drew me toward him.

"You don't have to have a baby," he whispered, but the words were brittle. It was almost like saying them made him…sad.

I had to be imagining that.

And for some reason, that made the pain inside me twist into something I'd never felt before—something I didn't quite understand.

He didn't push me to talk. He just kept his strong arms around me. Now and then, I would steal a glance and catch relief on his face.

What had the *Kathréftis* shown him to place him so on edge? I felt him teetering there despite everything. Had it given him second thoughts?

When the car pulled into the private drive, I didn't wait for the chauffeur or Julian to open my door. I pushed it open and jumped out. Julian caught up with me a few steps from the entrance.

"You're in a rush," he said, reaching for me.

I sidestepped him, shaking my head. "I want to have a little chat with your mother."

"I'm not certain that's a good idea," he warned, stepping in front.

I stopped in my tracks, torn between screaming and relenting. In the end, I took the coward's way out. "I *need* to speak with your mother."

His jaw clenched as my words took hold of him. It was a shitty thing to do—to use the tether against him—but I had a few things to say to Sabine Rousseaux, and I couldn't let him stop me.

"Do you know what you're doing?" he asked, falling a step behind me but letting me continue toward the house.

"Maybe," I admitted.

"That's not a very reassuring answer."

"It's not been a very reassuring morning," I told him. I didn't bother to knock. Instead, I went straight for the knob, pleased to find it unlocked.

"I can handle my mother," he began, but I was already walking through the front door.

Everyone was in the living room, looking like they hadn't lost a minute of sleep, except for Jacqueline, who closed her eyes with relief when she spotted us. She stood, but I held up a hand to keep her from moving closer. No one was getting in my way. Not now.

Sabine finally turned, her eyes locking with mine. She set her teacup on the table next to her as her mouth turned down in disappointment. That was one theory confirmed. The car had been meant only for my mate. She hadn't expected me to return. But I was going to surprise her with how *here* I still was.

"I can handle your mom, too," I said to Julian, and then I walked over and slapped her in the face.

CHAPTER FORTY-NINE

Julian

I was between Thea and my mother instantly, the need to protect her overriding the leash she'd placed on me outside. It was a good thing, too, because it wasn't Sabine who responded.

It was the angel of death.

My mother transformed, fangs protracting, her eyes endless pools of onyx. But it was more than that, and Thea had no way of knowing what she'd done.

"Get back," I ordered my mate. I needed to see her back out that door. The only other option was braving the steep cliffs that dropped to the choppy sea below.

But Sabine knew that, and she used it to her advantage. She circled us, slowly herding us around until she was between us and the door.

"No." Thea refused to budge. Instead, she tried to push past me. "I will not allow her to keep treating me like I'm a piece of trash."

"Oh shit," Sebastian muttered, looking up from his phone and nudging Lysander with his elbow. But my other brother was already invested in the show. I should have known they would be more interested in my situation for its entertainment value than some brotherly bond.

It was Benedict who finally said something. "Perhaps we should calm down and talk it out."

"Shut up," the rest of us said in unison.

I glanced at him, allowing every ounce of hatred I felt toward him to show in my scowl. "You've done enough."

"If you will let me explain," he began, but my father shushed him.

Only Dominic and Thoren had yet to reveal their feelings on the situation, but I hadn't forgotten that they'd taken up arms when the Council had arrived to take us to The Second Rite. It wasn't much, but it was something. And if they were willing to do that, if Sebastian and Lysander had stood with them and Jacqueline was here, that meant we stood a chance.

Standing against the Council was one thing. Standing against our mother was something else entirely.

I wasn't sure what would happen if it came to blows, but I did know one thing. Human or not, my mate was flesh and blood—and that meant she could be killed. "Thea—"

My mother cut me off. "You are expendable. I don't care about the magic inside you. I don't care what my son claims. I will not lose another child to a foolish tether, and I will not let our bloodline die!"

And there it was. The reason my mother had been acting batshit crazy since I'd brought Thea home. I almost understood. Unfortunately, understanding wasn't enough. Not anymore. We had a different problem now, and there was only one way to handle it. Thea had assaulted my mother. No one in this room could blame her for that, but she'd done it with her gloves off, which meant she had signed her own death certificate. I only had one choice.

"Our bloodline won't die," I announced loudly, "and you know it."

"Hush," my mother hissed, whirling on me. "You took a vow."

It was enough to give me time to grab Thea and shove her behind me. A tiny groan escaped her, but I didn't care. She could be pissed at me later.

Because she would still be alive.

"What vow?" my father interrupted, and that's when I realized I knew exactly how to sway this situation in our favor.

Please. Please. The thing I couldn't say out loud but you know. The story no one but me knows. Pain sliced through my body as the blood-vow tried to restrict my thoughts, as if it knew that I'd found a loophole it needed to close. It was still a gamble. It might not work. But as the agony split me in two, I knew it would.

Thea tipped her head to stare at me with puzzled eyes.

"What vow?" my father thundered again.

Understanding broke over her face like the sun breaching the horizon. I sagged with relief to see it there.

"Tell him," Thea demanded in a haughty tone. I'd pay for this later. My brothers would never stop teasing me about how she'd ordered me around. Not like I cared. Especially if it stopped what was about to happen. "I need you to tell him about the vow."

"How does she know about the vow?" Sabine asked in a chilling voice.

My mate smiled sweetly at her. "I can read his mind."

"What?" someone shouted across the room.

"I can read his mind," Thea repeated for clarity—or maybe she just enjoyed the shocked looks on their faces.

"Interesting," Lysander said thoughtfully. He shifted forward, his eyes sweeping over her in a way that kicked my protective instinct into overdrive.

"You told her!" My mother flung an accusing finger in my direction.

"No, he just accidentally thought about what you did," Thea said.

Dominic rose to his feet, the floor shaking a little under his weight. "If someone doesn't tell me what's going on in the next ten seconds…"

"Camila's children…" I spat out, earning a sharp pain as the blood-vow fought with my tether for control of me, "…are alive."

Silence deafened the room. No one spoke. No one moved. Sebastian didn't crack a joke. Jacqueline didn't gasp. And my father had gone so still he looked like he was made of stone.

After a few minutes, he cracked. "My grandchildren are alive?"

He'd pointed the question at his wife. "How could you keep that from me?"

"Sometimes difficult choices are—"

"Bullshit," Thoren said quietly, pointing to each of us in turn. "You shouldn't have kept it a secret, and you shouldn't have taken a blood-vow."

"I know." I rubbed my temple, the pain beginning to ebb now that it was out.

"Why?" my father asked, beginning to shake. Not like a leaf. Like the first tremors of an earthquake. Sometimes—like now—I wondered if he really did have the blood of gods inside him.

"To protect them," Sabine snapped, turning her attention away from Thea and me entirely.

Now was my chance to grab her and run, but running wouldn't solve our problems. There was nowhere the Council couldn't touch us. Nowhere they couldn't find us, even with all my money and resources. Benedict—damn him—was right. We needed allies. We needed my family.

"That is not a reason to keep this from their family," Dominic roared.

"Don't you see?" she demanded. "It wasn't an accident. Willem tried to kill them. I don't need to explain my actions. The children are safe and well cared for, and I will decide when they return to our world."

"But Willem is dead," Dominic said flatly. "Our daughter is dead. Why keep them from their family?"

Thea let out a small squeak next to me. Every head swiveled in her direction as she clamped a hand over her mouth, but it was too late. Guilt hung heavy on her face. She really was a terrible liar.

"What else do you know about that night?" Sabine asked her, advancing in our direction. "Is there something my son hasn't told me?"

"If you think—"

I could tell my mate was about to pick another fight, and this time, it wasn't her fight to pick.

It was mine.

"There's something else," I said loudly, and she stopped. "Someone else survived that night. Camila is alive, and she knows."

Sabine faltered, her form shrinking slightly. I'd never seen my mother look small. Even when we'd lost Camila, the fire inside her had kept her going. Then, she'd had a purpose: to stash the children where no one could ever find them. To keep them away from the Drakes, who would have tried to take them.

"You're lying," she whispered.

The rest of the room simply stared at me like I'd lost my mind.

"She can't be..." Thoren trailed away. He toyed with the leather strip he wore on his wrist, his fingers ghosting over a charm dangling from it. Although he was the largest of us, he was also the youngest. He'd taken her death nearly as hard as I had.

"He's not lying." Thea moved to my side and took my hand. She squeezed it slightly. "She attacked me."

"She what?" Dominic bellowed, rousing from his shocked stupor.

"But she helped save you," I pointed out.

"That's debatable," Thea murmured before shrugging. "I guess she changed her mind about me."

My mother sank down, barely catching the edge of her chair, as she processed this. She turned wild eyes on us. "Where is she? Where has she been?"

"That's the bad news." I took a deep breath and braced myself to deliver it. "She's with the vampires who attacked the opera."

Sabine closed her eyes and shook her head. "No. She can't be with the Mordicum."

All this time, she'd been keeping more from me. We had fought the terrorists together. Had she known then what name to give their threat?

"You knew what they were," I accused. I'd asked her before, after one of them had breached her security at the Blood Orgy. She'd skirted around a real answer, but something told me she'd known the whole time. Of course she had, because as Thea had learned earlier, Sabine was practically royalty.

"We don't know much. Only a name," Sabine continued, wringing her hands. It was like looking at a stranger. None of her self-possession lingered. She looked brittle, as though the last few minutes had aged her thousands of years. Maybe they had. "They're anarchists. They want to destroy vampire law."

"That's not what Camila said." I looked from her to the rest of my family in turn, knowing I was about to make this about so much more than me and Thea and The Rites. "She said that the Council has been compromised—that someone is pulling the strings."

"That is ridiculous," Sabine hissed. "She's gone crazy. That must be why she hasn't come to us."

"She came to me," I reminded her coldly. "Probably because she knew what you were going to say."

"She is my daughter. She can always come to me!"

But that wasn't true, and everyone here knew it.

"What possible reason could she have for aligning with those monsters?" Sabine demanded.

She couldn't see it. She loved Camila fiercely—just as she loved all of us—but sometimes, the ones who love us are the worst monsters of all. That was the problem. Every villain was the hero of her own story, after all.

Warmth seeped through me from where Thea clutched my hand. Her magic reached out and spread, soothing me like a balm. It was a reminder that everything would be okay, somehow. I gripped her hand tighter as I told them why Camila had made her decision. "She's with them because she doesn't trust the Council."

"That's understandable," Dominic said carefully. "She must blame them for what happened."

Sabine's eyes pinned me to the spot as if she knew I was holding something back. There was no point in protecting her from it. She didn't deserve that courtesy, and now that she knew Camila was alive, she would search for her. She needed to be prepared for what she found.

"No, she's aligned with the Mordicum to try to stop the Council from falling to an outside influence."

"Who?" My mother rolled her eyes.

"Willem Drake."

This time the room exploded, words flying like shrapnel.

"Is everyone fucking alive?" Sebastian grumbled.

"So it seems," Lysander said.

"If Willem Drake is alive, I'll serve his head on a platter by the next equinox," Sabine announced, "but there is no way the Council is under his influence. I would know." The finality to her tone told me that it was going to take more than one conversation to convince her it was true. Maybe if I could get Camila here, Sabine would believe.

"I'm not sure I'll survive both of them," Thea whispered in response to this unvoiced idea. The others continued to bicker and shake their heads and point fingers. My mate yawned, and I noticed the circles dragging at her eyes.

"You need to rest," I said, continuing quickly when she opened her mouth to protest. "And we need a minute alone."

Her eyebrows shot up, but she pressed her mouth into a thin line that told me she agreed—but that it wasn't going to be pretty.

I was in trouble. Big trouble.

CHAPTER FIFTY

Julian

Morning sun poured into the living room, completely at odds with the argument happening. My family yelled across one another, each shout more emotional than the last. Now was the perfect moment to make our escape. I tugged Thea gently toward the hall. No one seemed to notice as we tiptoed across the polished marble floor.

We nearly made it.

"Where do you think you're going?" Sabine called in a lofty voice that rose above the others.

"So close," Thea muttered.

I stopped and turned to regard my mother, tightening my grip on Thea's hand. "We're both exhausted from being up all night playing the Council's games," I told her, "and I'm still a little sore from when *you stabbed me.*"

It was a long shot that she would care about either of my reasons. Unsurprisingly, her face remained stony, not a hint of emotion leaking past her guarded features. That was my mother. I didn't know which was worse: that she had stabbed me or that she wasn't the least bit sorry about it.

"Your mate issued a challenge. I simply want to know the time and place," she said, completely ignoring what I said.

I winced. I was afraid she would see Thea's slap as an invitation to more violence. "She didn't know—"

"It doesn't matter," Sabine snarled at me.

"That can't be the first time someone's slapped you," Thea said, yawning again, which made the retort worse. I closed my eyes, wondering if my mate suddenly had a death wish. She was picking a fight she couldn't win.

"No, it's not, but it's the longest I've let anyone live who has," my mother shot back. "Name your time and place."

I stiffened, knowing she meant her threat, but Thea rolled her eyes. "For what? I don't need a chat about this."

Sabine's eyes narrowed at her glib tone. "For our duel."

"Come again?"

"You challenged the head of a household to a duel," my mother explained.

"I *slapped* you," Thea said.

As much as I respected her right to fight her own battles, it was time to intervene. She had no idea how serious my mother was about this. And if she did...

"Thea is family. I think we can overlook this," I argued, but Sabine scowled at me.

"She's not my family. She insulted me, which I don't take lightly, and she attacked the head of this household. Our law says that is a challenge, so she will name a time and place. I will even let her choose the weapon," she said as if this was a benevolent gesture.

"Mom," Lysander called. "Think about this."

"Weapon?" Thea said blankly, as if she was just processing what my mother was suggesting.

"It's a duel. We could go hand to hand, but I suspect you'll feel better with a weapon." Sabine smiled.

Thea blanched, but she squared her shoulders. "What counts as a weapon?"

"Anything you think you can wield between those fragile fingers, my dear."

Panic constricted my throat. "You can't—" I started, but this time it was Thea who interjected.

"Fine, but I'm taking a nap first."

She stomped off, disappearing down the hallway. I threw a beseeching look at Jacqueline, who was peeking at me through her fingers. She nodded, looking as tired as I felt. I didn't know what magic she could work or what loophole she could find, but if anyone could, it would be her. My eyes turned to my father, who lifted one corner of his mouth to let me know he would do what he could to sway his wife.

In the meantime, I would try to talk some sense into my mate— or give defensive tips.

I started down the hall after her, catching her in a few strides.

"Don't even try to talk me out of this," Thea snapped. "I can finish what I start, Julian."

"I didn't say anything."

She tapped her forehead. "But you thought it."

"Do you really think I'm going to let you fight my mother?" I asked with a sigh.

She kept walking. After a few more steps, she paused and looked around her. On one side was a glass wall looking out over the Greek countryside. On the other hung a collection of art that would make curators swoon. But if Thea spotted the Monet or the Picasso or any of the others, she said nothing. Instead, she stared down the never-ending hall.

"I don't know where our room is."

"Come on." I took her hand, deciding to argue with her later. She needed to sleep. I felt her exhaustion in my bones as if it was my own. Maybe it was. Usually, I didn't require much rest, but at the moment, I wished I could slip into a nap for a few years.

"No!"

I faltered at Thea's panicked voice. "What…"

One look at her face told me she'd caught that thought.

"I won't, my love," I said, realizing she thought I was being serious.

"Even if we don't get married?"

This time I froze. Questions lined up in my mouth, but I clamped it shut and started swiftly toward our quarters, Thea struggling to keep up. We weren't going to have this conversation with vampires just down the hall, where they could eavesdrop.

This was about what the Council had told her, and if she was about to tell me that she not only couldn't but *wouldn't* have my child, I'd rather she did it in private.

"Julian," she panted. "Slow down."

I spun toward her and picked her up, throwing her over my shoulder.

"This again?" She sounded like she might laugh. I was less amused.

Our room was on the lowest level, and I took the stone stairs two at a time. When we reached it, I carried her inside and shut the door, but I didn't put her down.

"Ready to talk?" I asked.

"Um, can you put me down first?" Her voice was slightly groggy, as if she had already started to fall asleep.

"I'd rather keep hold of you." Maybe it was the last twenty-four hours or knowing how serious my mother was about dueling or the edge of panic gnawing at me. I only knew that every ounce of me needed her as close as possible.

But she groaned. "Put me down, Julian."

I had no choice but to comply. I took my time, however, allowing her body to slide slowly through my arms. She glided over my hard chest, her soft body molding against mine when I tightened my grip and left her feet dangling just above the ground. Her breath snagged as our eyes met, and her tongue darted over her lower lip.

"You're giving me ideas," I warned her.

"You haven't put me down," she said breathlessly.

My eyes slanted, a low growl rumbling through my chest as I let her slip to the floor, but I didn't let her go. I'd done as she'd asked, but I wasn't about to release her while she was talking foolishly about our future.

"You're going to marry me," I told her.

She sucked in a gasp, pausing for a heartbeat that lasted an eternity. "I know."

I fought the urge to take her immediately to bed and put this argument behind us. "Then why say otherwise?"

"You know why." Her voice shrank, hurt trembling in it. "You know what the Council demanded."

"Who cares about what they want? We're pretty good at breaking their rules." I forced my lips into a smirk, my eyes pleading with her to put this to rest.

"Julian, we can't ignore the demand. What if..." She trailed off, her eyes finding her feet.

I wished I could read her mind to know where that thought was going. Instead, I waited for her to finish it on her own terms. Reaching up with one hand, my other arm locked around her, I cupped her face and tilted it back up. Thea turned into my touch, her eyes closed and her breaths deepening.

"What if I can't have your children?" she whispered.

"I don't care."

Her eyes opened and found mine. "What if I can?"

That was the real question. The one we both needed to answer.

"I've never wanted children," I said slowly, noting the slight glide of her throat as she swallowed these words. "I've never felt the need to continue our bloodline or the desire to have an heir. I've never hung my masculinity on that. To me, having a child proves nothing."

"I understand," she murmured, pulling back from my touch.

"But," I added before she could break free of my arms, "I never expected to find *you*."

She bit her lip, giving me even filthier ideas before she released it. "What does meeting me change?"

"Everything." I brushed my thumb over her cheek and dragged it down to her swollen lip. "Meeting you changed *everything*. I didn't know I was incomplete until I saw you."

"And children?" She was breathless as our hearts began beating faster.

My own mind might be changing, but we hadn't dealt with the

more important issue. "How do you feel about it, my love? What do *you* want?"

The tether between us tightened, my words reaching out to demand the truth. Because I didn't want her to tell me what I wanted to hear. I wanted to know how she truly felt. This could only be her decision now, even if it wasn't what I wanted.

"I don't know," she admitted, our bond remaining taut. She didn't slip from it. She wanted to tell me how she felt, and my demand had freed her to do so. She took a deep breath and plunged forward. "It feels like the world is spinning faster every second and if I take a wrong step, if I stumble, I'll never get myself back up."

"I won't let you fall," I soothed her. "I'll be right here."

She nodded and continued rapidly. "Your family hates me. My mother hates you. We're mates. We're tethered. I'm some sort of unknown magical creature who may or may not be able to pop out babies as the Council demands. I'm only twenty-two, and I've never even considered having kids until about five minutes ago. But now I'm supposed to know how I feel about you knocking me up. Oh, and your mom wants to duel with me. Your sister possibly wants to kill me. I'm still not sure what's going on there. And you...you won't tell me what you want!"

She stamped her foot slightly, her cheeks immediately coloring as her brain caught up with her mouth.

My lips lifted without permission at her exasperation. Mostly because she was adorable when she was this angry. "I want you."

"You have me," she said, her shoulders slumping. "Julian, do you want an heir? I mean, a baby?"

"That is for you to decide."

But she shook her head. "I don't know how to make that decision. I *need* to know what *you* want."

Our tether strained, coiling painfully around my heart, and I couldn't deny her. "I want to take you to bed."

We stared at each other for a moment as my answer was processed by both of us.

"That doesn't answer my question," she whispered.

"I think…it does."

Her lips rounded. "Oh."

My heart kicked up as it beat against its cage, as if it wanted to escape and bury itself inside her. "Let me take you to bed."

"We don't know…" She gulped. "What if I can't?"

"What if you can?" I challenged her gently. "Tell me. If you could, would you want that?"

"I'm only twenty-two. I'm not sure I'm ready…yet." Shyness crept into her voice at that final word that changed everything. I saw the answer on her face—saw the hope and the anxiety, the fear and the want. I saw my own answer reflected back at me.

Because I had never expected to find her, I had never known what I wanted until I touched her.

"We can practice," I told her.

She panted a little. "Practicing sounds like fun."

"Oh, it will be," I promised her.

"Should we practice now?"

I groaned with relief, scooping her into my arms and flashing toward the bed. She giggled as I laid her across it.

"I guess that's my answer." Her hand fisted in my shirt as I climbed over her.

"Shut up and focus. We're *practicing*," I teased her as I angled my mouth over hers. I devoured another giggle, my tongue slipping past her lips and coaxing her mouth open wider. I could live in this kiss, die in it, be buried in it. It was all I ever wanted. *Her.*

So, there was only one reason to break it. She squeaked with protest as I drew back enough to look in her eyes and ask, "Will you marry me?"

CHAPTER FIFTY-ONE

Thea

Will you marry me?

It wasn't the first time Julian had asked me this question. Staring into his eyes—an endless ocean blue in the dim room—I knew it would be the last. My fingers remained clenched around his shirt, my breath hanging on his words.

In the last twenty-four hours, I'd faced my deepest fear: I was not some magical creature meant to be at his side but rather a leech that had sucked the magic out of him somehow. That I'd stolen it from him when we tethered our souls together when we first made love. The Julian that had confronted me in the Council's chamber still tormented me, along with the demands they'd made regarding our future.

Because part of me—a part of me that was buried in such a deep and secret place I hadn't known it existed until recently—thrilled at the idea of him and me...and a family. Something permanent. Something tangible. Proof that we were the mated pair others seemed hesitant to acknowledge.

Julian cleared his throat, his eyes searching mine as if he might find my answer there. The blinds had been drawn in our absence, allowing only streaks of light to cast themselves across his sculpted features. The sunlight danced over the sharp planes of his face, his regal cheekbones and the full bow of his lips. His weight pressed me into the soft mattress that might have lulled me to sleep if it weren't for the heart banging in my chest and the answer poised on my lips.

I'd asked him for a romantic proposal after his impromptu proposition in San Francisco. I hadn't known what that meant at the time. I'd only wanted something other than an attempt to end an argument. It had become a running joke, and now…it was here.

The moment. This perfect moment that was filled with absolute certainty. We had faced our deepest fears. Julian had yet to tell me what torturous illusion the Council's ritual had shown him. I only knew that, like mine, it had involved us. Maybe someday we would share those horrifying moments, but not today. Today, it didn't matter.

We had chosen each other. Again. Just as we would continue to choose each other for the rest of our lives. There was no reason to believe I had anything other than a mortal lifespan before me. Perhaps it would be cut short like my mother's inevitably would be, but every second of this one would be spent by his side.

So, I knew my answer, even if there were so many questions left to consider. "Yes."

Julian released a ragged breath before lowering his mouth to mine with aching slowness. The kiss was surprisingly sweet, soft, and almost hesitant. It was the kind of kiss he might deliver on our wedding day when the gesture was being observed by an audience, and my heart soared alongside his into the promise of what our future held.

"I was beginning to wonder if I needed to beg," he teased when he finally broke it.

I couldn't help but smile at the boyish grin the centuries-old vampire wore. "I didn't know that was on the table."

"It's too late. You've already agreed." His hand reached for my wrist, coaxing my fingers to relax. I released his shirt so he could twine his fingers with mine. Light and shadow pulsed between our palms—a searing reminder that we were already joined in the most intimate way. Our magic fused together by our mating bond. He brushed another kiss over my lips. "Would you like your ring now?"

I raised an eyebrow. "Ring? You have the ring with you? Were you planning this?"

"Thea," he said, sounding exasperated, "I've had that ring for... I had it before we mated. I've been waiting to find the right way to ask. I'm not sure this was it, but it felt..."

I understood what he meant. And somehow, knowing that he'd had it this whole time made the proposal more romantic, although I wasn't certain why. Maybe because it proved that even after the darkest night, the sun would rise again—that we could face any challenge as long as we did it together.

"I want you," I said thickly, hooking my free arm around his neck to urge his body against mine. "The ring can wait." After all, it had been waiting all this time.

Julian's chuckle sent goose bumps rippling across my skin. "Are you sure?" He nuzzled my neck. "It's a *very* nice ring."

I didn't doubt that. Truthfully, I was a little worried about how nice it would be, given his wealth. It wasn't the ring that mattered. Not really. He could have looped a rubber band around my finger, and I would wear it proudly. All that mattered was what it represented: I belonged to him, now and for eternity.

"Weren't we supposed to practice?" I mumbled, my body beginning to grow frantic to feel more of him—to feel our mating bond stretched tight between us as he claimed me.

Another laugh skittered over my sensitive skin, and I found myself reaching for his shirt. My hands slipped beneath it, and my fingers traced the dips and ridges of his abdomen and danced lower, reaching to unfasten his pants. But Julian stilled, rearing back to meet my curious gaze.

I had never wanted him more than I did at this moment. The need I felt roared inside me, pounded in my blood, and demanded to be met. He had to feel it, too. An emotion this intense would be felt through our mating bond, so why did he hesitate?

"What if we're too good at practicing?" he asked seriously.

Oh, *that*.

I took a deep breath and considered his question. Finally, I released it. "Do you have any condoms?"

Julian blinked, his expression momentarily puzzled before he roared with laughter. I glared up at him, and he fell silent with an apologetic smile. "If I had any, they would be long expired, pet."

"Well, as long as you aren't likely to change your mind," I said a bit sourly.

The amusement dropped from his face. "I will never change my mind about you or our family—if and when it grows."

Damn. That was a pretty good answer—and he knew it.

"But if you..." He trailed away, giving me the out that made it that much easier to know exactly how I felt about the situation.

"I will always feel the same." I locked eyes with him. "Whatever comes."

And there would be more challenges to face. Neither of us was foolish enough to believe otherwise. There would be more Rites, and then there was his family—I'd meant it when I'd agreed to duel with his mother—and the unknown magic inside me. But this? Us?

I would never have any doubt.

His mouth captured mine, whispering love across my lips, speaking it with his tongue. Julian left no part of me unexplored as his fingers freed me from my clothes. My own hands pulled and tugged until there was nothing left between us, and when he nudged against me, I closed my eyes to savor the sweet agony as his cock filled me.

"I love you," he murmured when he was sheathed to the hilt. "I will always love you, always protect you." Pure masculinity strained his face as he rocked deeper, pushing us slowly toward our future.

It didn't matter that I could fight my own battles. The desire to protect and serve went beyond reason. It was written into his very nature, binding itself to me as his mate. And I would protect him, too. I would worship him with my body, my life, with everything that I was and would become.

We etched our promise to each other with hungry lips and trembling fingers, and when the darkness crept across his eyes, I welcomed it and his fangs. My muscles tightened as he drank deeply, his venom filtering into my blood. It erased the slight pain of his bite and left only pure and total ecstasy. He groaned as I clenched around him, driving my release from me as he filled me with the heat of his—his body giving and fangs taking in a perfect, unrelenting circle of life. Our life.

When our rhythm slowed, he lifted midnight eyes and a crimson-stained mouth. His tongue swiped slowly over his teeth with relish. Without a word, our bodies still pinned together, he raised his wrist to his mouth and sliced it open. Blood welled across his skin as he brought it slowly to my lips. Not a test. An offering.

My gums swelled and pulsed as I breathed in the scent of his blood—rich with smoked cloves—and a moment later, my mysterious fangs broke through to accept his gift. I moved on instinct. There would be time to question this later. Now? His eyes shuttered as I closed my lips over the wound and drank from him with a shy, shallow pull that deepened hungrily at the first taste. And when I finally released him, his mouth crashed into mine, our blood mingling on our tongues as if to seal yet another promise between us.

When he finally rolled off me and drew me into his arms, I reached to check his wrist and found it already healed.

"Still convinced I'm not a vampire?" I asked quietly.

"Yes." He kissed my forehead. "If you were a vampire, you wouldn't be able to stop—no vampire can stop the first time."

"But..." I shook my head, trying to understand what he was saying. "Wouldn't that kill..."

He hesitated instead of answering my question.

"What if you were wrong?" I choked on the panic mingling with a surge of anger. "I could have killed you."

"I'm over nine hundred, remember? I could have stopped you," he said simply.

That didn't make me feel better. It only made me more confused than ever. "But I liked it—the blood." Heat rushed to my face as I admitted it. I already found myself craving him again, and with that desire, the same question I'd asked myself again and again leaped from my lips. "If I'm not a vampire, what am I?"

"About that. I have an idea."

I turned my face up to study his, finding his eyes tight with his own thoughts. "I'm listening."

"It's a hunch, but I think I might know who can help us find answers."

My mouth fell open. "You're just telling me this?"

"I was slightly preoccupied with more important matters and crises." His finger traced the curve of my breast lazily as if he hadn't just casually dropped a bombshell. "It can wait."

But I was already pulling out of his arms. I jumped off the bed and began searching for my clothes. I found his first and tossed them to him. "I can't."

I was ready for answers.

CHAPTER FIFTY-TWO

Thea

Julian grumbled as he untangled his pants. All I caught was a swift mention of "priorities" while I picked up my discarded clothing. My frown deepened as I surveyed them. They were beyond wrinkled from being on the floor and from being dragged through my ordeal.

"Something wrong?" Julian asked when I remained silent.

"I should change." I didn't feel like wasting time on something so unimportant, but I knew that every moment I spent in this house, I was being weighed and judged by Sabine. "I don't even know where my suitcases are."

Julian snorted as he stood and tossed his own worn jeans on the bed. "I'm sure someone put them away—unless my mother burned them while we were gone."

He strode past me toward a set of doors, sending his smoked honey and clove scent rippling over me. Ignoring the ache in my gums it prompted, I followed him. He opened one door to show me an en suite bath. Behind the other was a walk-in closet where all the outfits Celia had purchased for me hung neatly across from a number of Julian's suits. Our luggage was stored in a neat stack in the corner. A sharp thrill raced through me to see our things waiting for us. I'd only just gotten used to having a few drawers at his place in San Francisco, feeling guilty for the garment bags that Celia had shoved into storage. There was something so official about the way my dresses and his suits mirrored and complemented each other, as if each was matched to the other.

Just like we were.

I tried to ignore the fact that my engagement ring was probably in here somewhere. Instead, I stalked inside and looked at my options, acutely aware that his eyes followed my ass the whole way.

I groaned when I saw what Celia had packed for me. Fingering the hem of the silk gown, I took in my options. Where were the jeans and T-shirts? She didn't expect me to dress in haute couture every day, did she? I thought of Sabine and Jacqueline, and my stomach sank. Actually, she probably did.

"What's wrong?" he asked.

I twisted the delicate fabric between my fingers. "Just wondering if I should wear cocktail attire or gala attire?"

"Story of my life," he said with a low chuckle that made my knees weak. He took a step inside, filling the space with his immortal presence. It darkened around him as if shadows themselves longed to be near him. He pressed a button near the rack, and the smooth surface next to it split to reveal several drawers.

"Oh! Surprise!"

He smiled at me, undoubtedly amused by my delightfully human reaction, but the happiness fell from his face.

It was my turn to ask what was wrong.

"Nothing," he said with a shrug. "I just realized I made a mistake. I showed you where your underwear was."

I rolled my eyes and plucked a lacy white pair from the drawer. "You wouldn't have really let me think I had none to wear?"

His answering smirk told me I might be wrong about that. "I'd much rather prefer you wore none."

"Is that so?" I fluttered my lashes as I pulled a pair of breezy linen pants from another drawer along with a cropped top. Although I'd read the temperature was about the same as back home, San Francisco would be covered in misty fog and completely gray. I planned to make the most of Greece's sunshine. Before I closed the drawers, I dropped the lace panties back inside. "In that case…"

Julian looked positively feral as I pranced past him to put the rest of my clothes on.

"You're giving me ideas again."

"Nope," I called, even though I was unable to resist giving him a little show as I pulled the pants on. "I want answers. What's your plan?"

"I think there's someone in this house who knows what you are," he confessed.

My fingers fumbled as I drew my bra on. "What? Who?"

"My mother," he said with a grim smile.

· · ·

It would have been considerate for my mate to advise me of his theory before I'd started a feud with Sabine Rousseaux. Now I'd not only pissed off the one person who might be able to help us, but I was supposed to duel her as well. I had managed to dodge Julian's questioning about said duel on our way up, reminding him that I knew what I was doing. I was sure of that until we found Sabine holed up in a beautiful, covered sun porch—polishing a terrifyingly impressive array of ancient knives. She held one up, allowing it to catch the early afternoon light, and ignored us.

"Mother," Julian greeted her, his voice laced with warning.

The blade reflected her warped smile at us. "You never told me what weapon to prepare, so I thought I would prepare them *all*."

Knowing Sabine, she probably had a few swords, rifles, and a dragon stashed around here just in case. I willed the fear I felt to roll off me and shrugged.

"I doubt you'll need those," I said sweetly.

She huffed as she threw the freshly cleaned blade onto the stone table before spinning toward me. "Hand to hand, then?" Her eyes traced over me as if taking my measure. "That would be interesting."

"Neither of you—" Julian started.

"Wouldn't you like to know?" I said, mimicking the lofty voice she always employed when speaking to…well, *anyone.*

Sabine bared her teeth at me before looking toward her son. "Your pet needs a leash. At least put that tether to good use."

"Thea is free to say what she pleases," he said, although his voice sounded a bit strained, "and fight her own battles."

"If you're willing to let her fight me, perhaps you aren't as committed to her as I feared." His mother's crimson lips twisted.

She didn't think much of me. I was just a weak, scheming human in her mind.

I couldn't wait to prove her wrong.

But for now, I was more interested in finding a way to get her to talk. If Julian was right, if she knew what I was, I might have to play more nicely with her. My stomach soured at the thought.

"On the contrary." Julian shrugged, his eyes glittering. "We came to ask you a question and deliver good news."

My traitorous stomach nearly bottomed out, and I stared at him. He wasn't really going to—

"Thea just accepted my proposal."

Sabine's stillness felt deadly, like the moment before a rattlesnake might strike. Fighting her didn't scare me—not when she'd allowed the terms of our duel to be so vague. But I hadn't been prepared to tell her that we were engaged.

"Thanks for the warning," I mumbled.

Sorry. I heard the sincerity of his apology in my mind, but on the surface, he maintained a smile that was pure male arrogance.

Finally, Sabine snapped out of her trance and shrugged. "What do you want? A parade?"

"Congratulations would be nice," he said through gritted teeth, and I heard the hurt in his words.

"You don't expect me to be happy about this?" she spat back. "Or to give my blessing?"

"We don't need your blessing. The Council made it clear that if Thea can provide me with an heir, they will approve our marriage," he said more easily.

That wasn't entirely true, and we both knew it. It had been mentioned—along with the other Rites.

"If you think you can bluff me into a blessing, you are mistaken." Sabine picked up another knife and pressed it against the tip of her index finger. A drop of blood welled in the spot, and I felt my fangs cutting against my gums.

I clamped my mouth shut. There was no way that I was going to show her my fangs again. But—and this was way more important—I wasn't about to drink a drop of Sabine's blood. *Ever.*

"Look how she suffers." Sabine laughed. "My guess is that she's nothing more than a pathetic dhampir—and if that's the case, your union will produce nothing but sorrow."

Dhampir? The question must have been on my face, because Julian quickly explained.

A dhampir is the child of a vampire and a human.

"A vampire hasn't sired a dhampir in centuries—not since the curse." He brushed her off with a dismissive wave of his hand. "And dhampirs have no magic outside some bloodlust. You know that—*and* I think you know more about Thea's magic than you're letting on."

Sabine's lips spread into a cryptic smile. "I'm as *intrigued* as you are."

Julian exhaled heavily, shoving a hand through his hair. He paced across the room to stare at the ocean outside the window like it might be willing to give him answers.

We should have known that coming to Sabine was a mistake. If she did know, she would never tell us. But either way, she would enjoy torturing both of us. It was so different from my mother, and yet, somehow, I felt the sting of Sabine's dismissal as much as my own mother's refusal to accept my love for Julian. Was this some twisted Rite of its own? Did we have to reject everyone we loved for each other?

It was a price I was willing to pay for everyone's safety. I just wished I didn't have to.

"If you came to me for answers, I regret to inform you that I have none." She returned to her knives. "Perhaps you could consult a book."

Julian had opened his mouth, his face contorted with rage, when a drawling voice called from the door, "Or you could ask the family expert."

I whirled around, blinking to find Lysander standing there, holding an apple and a knife. He carved a chunk of the fruit away and popped it into his mouth with the blade's tip. Geez, what was with this family and sharp objects?

"The family expert?" I repeated blankly.

He shot my mate a look that said *seriously?*

"My brother is a world-renowned archeologist," Julian explained, adding, "and a famous pain in the ass."

Lysander's dark eyes gleamed with laughter. "I'm afraid he's right on both counts. Now, tell me what these powers I keep hearing about do." He prowled into the room, cutting up his apple with the unnerving, practiced ease of a serial killer.

"I felt nothing when we first met, except being drawn to her. I assume that was the mating call. Her magic came later. It's light magic—golden, almost," Julian told him, earning a nod. What did that mean? "She's unusually gifted at music."

"Unusually?" I repeated, on the verge of telling him exactly how many hours I had spent on that unusual "gift." Lots. There was nothing unusual about it. I'd earned that.

Sabine stood and marched from the room, casting furious looks at her sons. "Believe whatever you want. You'll only be disappointed— both of you."

Julian ignored her and pressed on, even as my own stomach dipped. "And since I met her, it feels like her magic is growing stronger. It calls to me."

"Before or after you two..." Lysander waggled his eyebrows suggestively.

I feigned a gag.

"Not that it's any of *your* business, but before," Julian said curtly. "And she can read my mind."

Lysander froze, a piece of apple falling off his knife. He caught it with the tip of his blade before it hit the ground. I stared, unable to deny that it was a bit impressive. "Well, that seals it," he said when he'd recovered.

I processed what he was saying. "You know what I am?"

Lysander's smile was devoid of any cockiness as he glanced at his brother. Actually, he looked apologetic, and when he turned back to me, his voice was soft, as if delivering very bad news. "It's obvious. You're a *siren*."

CHAPTER FIFTY-THREE

Julian

*S*iren.

The word echoed inside me, as distant and fleeting as the idea itself. Thea couldn't be a siren. They were...myths.

"Vampires are *'myths,'* too," my brother answered with an air quote. I hadn't realized I had spoken the thought out loud. "It all adds up. The music. The mind-reading. The looks."

My lips curled into a snarl, his words stroking some primal, jealous side of me. I caught myself quickly and bit back the possessive show. But glancing at Thea, I found her staring out the window, completely unaware of my slip.

Her green eyes glittered like the water outside, but it wasn't sunlight dancing in them. It was shadows.

Thea. Are you okay? I stroked the loving thought through her mind with gentle claws.

She jumped, casting a surprised look in my direction. "Siren?" Her mouth handled the word with care. "Like a *mermaid*?"

It was obvious what she thought of that idea.

"Totally different things." Lysander continued carving up his apple, but the casual charm he usually wore faltered. Whatever he knew that led him to believe my mate was a siren wasn't good. "Sirens go back in collected literature for several millennia before anyone started giving them fins."

"Okay," she said slowly. "That makes more sense, because I'm a shit swimmer."

Lysander chuckled, and I forced a hollow laugh, aware that Thea was watching me for clues.

I couldn't claim to know nearly as much as my brother, but what I did know...wasn't good.

"So, you're talking about the creatures that lure sailors to their deaths," Thea said flatly.

"Yes and no," my brother said calmly, as if trying to mete out the right amount of information to give her at once. "Honestly, I've never met a siren, so I can't say what's legend and what's real. If you'd asked me a week ago, I would have said your kind was extinct."

"Then how do you know that's what I am?" she challenged him.

Despite her flashing eyes, I caught the slight quiver of her chin. A moment later, I found myself at her side, gathering her into my arms.

"Sirens were renowned for their musical ability. It was more than talent; it was magic. If what Julian says—"

"But they were singers," I said quietly.

"In the stories, but the most ancient lines were gifted with music that mortals found irresistible." Lysander shrugged. "You're a vampire. You know how reliable stories are."

He had a point. There were plenty of ludicrous ideas about our kind in stories and folklore.

"Or maybe I just spent three-quarters of my life practicing my cello. Maybe I just worked for that talent." Thea's tone was as cold as her answering glare. My brother had struck a nerve.

But would she have reacted differently to being told she was anything else? I wasn't sure.

Lysander tossed me an apologetic look before he gently continued. "I'm sure you are, but there's...um, your *cantatio*."

"My can-ta-tio?" She repeated the word with stilted syllables.

"Your blood-song," I said stiffly, turning to my brother. "Other creatures have blood-songs—even humans."

"Yes, but—"

"Excuse me," Thea interrupted. "When you say blood-song, you don't actually mean…"

"That your blood sings," I finished before nodding. "That's exactly what it means. I heard it the first moment I saw you, but your scent was so strong…it distracted me."

"I *smelled*?" Thea's mouth tipped into a frown at the thought. "But you can actually hear my blood?"

"Every moment," I confessed. "Your music is my own personal symphony. It shifts with your scent, your mood. I crave its melody in your absence."

"And it's loud as hell," Lysander said around a mouthful of apple.

"So everyone can hear my blood singing?" Her voice pitched up an octave. "And no one told me?"

"Julian is right," my brother said, jumping to my defense. I appreciated it, since he'd thrown me to the wolves on this one. "Blood-songs are common enough. There's something about magic that tends to reveal itself as music. Yours is just unusually strong. It's likely why you were drawn to studying music."

Thea's face fell, her shoulders shaking, and for the hundredth time, I wished I could get inside her head. She'd wanted answers. We both had. I hadn't expected her to react so strongly to getting them.

"I don't remember my life before music," she whispered, her body tense as a live wire in my arms. It took me a moment to realize what she meant, but Lysander paused, his eyebrows lifting in curiosity. Thea sighed. "My mother pushed me into music. I've been taking lessons for as long as I can remember. I guess that's probably not a coincidence."

"Probably not," Lysander agreed softly.

Thea twisted away from me, and I was shocked when she turned glowing eyes on me. It wasn't trepidation in them. Instead, they were full of unfiltered rage. "Why, though? What was the point? Is she a siren? Is it just some siren thing?"

"Siren magic would be passed through the female line," Lysander confirmed. "As far as the lessons? Maybe she just wanted to put your magic to good use."

Thea barked a laugh that fell like shattering glass through the room. "My mother never told me about magic. She never admitted to knowing anything about the real world until…"

Her breath hitched as she choked on the memory.

"Until she met me," I said grimly. Until a vampire had walked into Kelly Melbourne's hospital room and forced her to confront reality.

"Not too happy about it?" Lysander guessed, and I nodded.

That was an understatement.

"There's another possibility," he said. "When was the last time you played cello?"

Thea's shoulders tightened before she answered. "Not since my final performance. Not since…"

We mated.

She bobbed her head, disappointment flooding through her eyes. It hit me like a riptide, the sudden violence of her despair threatening to pull me under.

"That's probably why your blood-song is so loud, then." Lysander didn't seem to notice her shifting mood.

Thea steadied herself. "Why?"

"Think of magic like a resource," he explained. "The more you use it, the less you have until you refill it somehow. If you tapped into your magic while you played, it would dull the magic in your veins."

"Okay, say you're right," Thea conceded, albeit hesitantly. "What about everything else? The glowing magic he feels, reading his mind?"

"Sirens were rumored to be mind readers because of their other kind of magic." He shifted uncomfortably, and I wondered which one of us he was about to piss off.

"Other kind?"

"There are different kinds of magic," Lysander said. "Vampires are generally considered dark magic, or dead magic if you ask the witches. Nearly everyone believes our kind is the result of some type of necromancy."

She nodded. "The witches believed vampires were created as familiars."

I blinked, surprised she knew that.

"Jacqueline," she murmured.

Of course my best friend would have happily repeated any gossip she knew about our origin.

"You told her to." Thea sounded annoyed on Jacqueline's behalf.

Lysander was studying us like he might some specimen on one of his digs. "Were you reading his mind then?" he asked, earning another nod from Thea. "Fascinating."

"Something tells me he finds it more frustrating," she said.

Lysander looked to me for confirmation, and I shook my head. "I don't mind."

There was nothing I wanted to keep from my mate. Maybe that was my own biology being reprogrammed to unite with hers. Or being accustomed to my inability to lie to her from the moment we'd met. Either way, I meant what I'd said.

"So if you're dark magic…" Thea said, steering us back to the conversation.

"You're light magic. Living magic. There are different kinds of that, too. Yours would be celestial."

"Celestial?" Thea blinked. "Like angels and stars? Why would that help me read his mind?"

Lysander shot a nervous glance over her, but I already knew where this one was going. I should have known all along. Thea's magic had never felt like the magic familiars carried in their veins. It was older—ancient, even. Lysander was right. It was all adding up. Had I just been too blind to see it or too desperate to ignore what was staring me in the face?

"Beings gifted with celestial magic tend to be…um…"

I watched my brother twist for a moment. It was unusual to see Lysander Rousseaux looking so awkward. His eyes narrowed as if he didn't need to read my mind to know what I was thinking.

"Ask your mate," he suggested.

I glowered at him. He'd thrown me under the bus *again*.

"I commented on her looks, and you nearly ripped my throat out," he said defensively. "I'll leave this one to you."

"Celestial magic is tied to beauty. Beauty like yours." I brushed my index finger down her cheek, struck by how very true that was. Thea wasn't just pretty. She was breathtaking. Every moment, she became lovelier—like a rose slowly blooming. I'd seen how creatures responded to her. It wasn't just the haunting melody of her blood-song. Everything about her drew attention. Was that why her mother had kept her in hand-me-down, faded clothes? Why she had forced her to dim the music in her blood by siphoning it into a challenging career most would give up on?

Kelly Melbourne had found another way to hide her daughter from our world.

"What he means is that you are obviously not human... You are far too pretty." Jacqueline's amused voice interrupted my thought. "And I think you've gotten even more beautiful since you two finally got it on."

My eyes closed at my best friend's choice of words. When I dared open them, she'd joined us in the room. Jacqueline pushed herself onto the desk.

"I heard my name. What did I miss?" she asked, fiddling with a loose strand of hair.

"I'm a siren," Thea said flatly. "Although I'm not quite sure what that means."

Jacqueline blinked rapidly. "Oh. That makes sense."

"I'm glad it makes sense to one of us," Thea grumbled. She poked my chest with her finger. "And he was about to tell me what celestial magic is."

"Was he?" My best friend bit back a smile, but it sparkled in her eyes. "Don't let me stop you."

I groaned. At least Lysander had the decency to act mildly uncomfortable about it. Jacqueline was enjoying herself.

"Celestial magic is linked to sexual magic. It's a gift of the fae," I said swiftly. "A celestial being could read the mind of her lover to... uh, please him."

"Seriously?" Thea looked around the room at each of us. "This is a joke, right?"

Jacqueline shook her head with a merry smile. "Nope. I don't know why I didn't see it before. I mean, I thought you were hot." I glared at her, but she shrugged. "Just stating facts. Keep your gloves on."

My mind went back to that earlier question. Kelly Melbourne must have known. She wouldn't have pushed Thea toward music if she hadn't, and if she'd known that, was it possible that she...

The color drained from Thea's face, and I knew she was following my train of thought. Had she reached the same conclusion forming in my mind? The slight shake of her head told me she hadn't. But maybe that was merely her survival instinct kicking in...or shock.

"You said she's prettier now." I pointed my words at Jacqueline.

She nodded. "It's probably the mating glow."

She did have a glow, and while every male instinct in me wanted to take credit for it, it was more than that. And the magic—the abilities—had started to surface before I'd taken her to bed. They had started...

"After my mom left," she whispered. Tears cracked her voice and leaked down her cheeks. "She didn't just push me toward music. She... She hid me."

I shook my head, drawing her closer as her pain shattered inside my own chest. I wished I didn't have to share it. I wished I could take it from her—free her from it completely.

"Hid?" Lysander repeated thoughtfully. He snapped his fingers as he arrived where we already were. "A glamour. She shielded your magic, and when you met my asshole brother, he blew that to hell."

"Thanks," I said drily, wishing I had it in me to laugh this off.

"The glamour... That's what was eating her alive. That's what the doctor meant when he said..." she croaked, falling apart.

I held her to my chest, knowing she was right. It made sense. Kelly Melbourne had spent her life trying to hide her daughter's true nature. Was it because Thea's gifts were stronger? Or was there some other threat? Was it the reason Kelly had begged Thea to turn away from me? Because I would undo what Kelly had sacrificed her own life to give?

"But why?" Jacqueline mused, her voice infused with gentle warmth. "Why hide her from this world?"

"Sirens aren't just rare. They're unheard of. Even I would have thought they were actually myths until I met Thea," Lysander reminded her. "And if their magic is that strong without grimoires and potions, they would attract a lot of attention."

"But my mother didn't have any special powers. She never played an instrument." Thea swiped at the tears on her cheeks, turning to face the others. "Why me? Why did I get powers? Maybe I'm not a siren?" The desperation in her voice killed me. "I mean, I have fangs."

But Lysander dismissed it with a wave. "Who knows how sirens evolved? Maybe you always had fangs or it's a recessive gene that was triggered in you. I mean, sirens used to have wings, according to mythology, and you don't, right?"

"She doesn't." I rolled my eyes.

"The fangs are not just decorative," Thea said with a huff, her lower lip jutting out in a particularly kissable pout. "Ask him. I just drank his blood in bed."

"Kinky." Lysander smirked.

"Or," Jacqueline said dramatically, forcing all our attention to turn on her, "something triggered the recessive gene. That's how that works, right?"

But she already knew. She had at least ten different doctorates from universities across the world. And if my best friend was right... we'd only been considering half of the equation. It wasn't possible. I almost couldn't consider it and the implications.

"Holy shit," Lysander said, voicing my own thoughts.

"What?" Thea demanded. "Finish that thought, old man."

But Jacqueline did it for me. "Your father. Thea, what if your father is a vampire?"

CHAPTER FIFTY-FOUR

Thea

There was far too little of this dress. I frowned as I turned in the mirror. I'd never worn something this revealing before. The nude mesh made me look mostly naked, save for the intricate beadwork that fanned like angel wings from my torso over my breasts. The delicate golden feathers swept across my hips and rear end, stopping just below the rest of my assets and draping into a sheer chiffon skirt.

Sirens used to have wings. It was all I could think as I surveyed my reflection. Were these supposed to be mine? Was this my siren song? It was a silly idea. Celia had picked out the dress and sent it along in a garment bag with a note marked *Solstice*. I'd questioned wearing it since unzipping the bag. I had never dressed like this. I'd always faded into the worn gowns I'd purchased secondhand. This dress? It was a statement. One I wasn't positive I was ready to make— especially in a ballroom full of vampires.

I was reaching for the hidden zipper under my arm when someone rapped on the door. Sighing, I swished over, the gown trailing behind me, to see who it was. Opening the door a smidge, I discovered Jacqueline's amused eyes peering through the crack.

"I came to see if you needed help."

"I was about to change," I told her.

"Sounds like I'm just in time."

Stepping to the side, I let her into my bedroom. She stopped halfway through the door and stared at me.

"That bad, huh?" I tried to cross my arms over my chest.

Jacqueline had opted for a velvet gown in a rich purple hue that was so dark it was nearly black. Twin straps crossed over her décolletage and draped over her shoulders. The dress hugged her curves tightly before flaring at the knees to puddle around her feet. She'd paired a set of matching elbow-length gloves with it. Her hair was swept to one side with an amethyst hair comb, curls cascading like a waterfall over her shoulder.

"What?" She stammered before shaking her head. "No! You look gorgeous."

I raised an eyebrow. "I feel naked."

"So?" She shrugged, grinning impishly at me. "You'll make quite the entrance."

"I just…" I twisted to the mirror again, trying to see what she saw. The gown was beautiful. I couldn't deny that. In fact, it wasn't about what I was wearing at all.

Yesterday, I'd finally gotten answers. Some answers, at least. But they'd only raised more questions. Not just about the possibility that Lysander was right about me being a siren, but also about their other theory.

Was my father a vampire? Was that why my mother had reacted so vehemently toward Julian when they'd met?

"I know that look," Jacqueline interrupted my thoughts. She squeezed my upper arm gently. "Want to talk?"

"There's not much to say." I paused and stretched my neck, studying the pearly scars from Julian's bite. Playing with my hair, I tried to decide if I needed to cover them. I didn't mind, but he would. The scars were for him alone. He'd made that deliciously clear. A shiver raced through me as I remembered how it felt to have his fangs in me while he claimed me.

"Wear it up," Jacqueline said. "Do you want me to style it?"

I nodded, emotions swelling in my throat. I was grateful that she'd come. Not only because I knew she had our backs, but also because I missed my friends. If I were back in San Francisco, would Olivia be helping me get ready?

I pushed the thought away, afraid I might cry off the makeup that had taken me an hour to apply. Jacqueline found a collection of bobby pins in the bathroom and set to work. Something about the soft touch of her hands slipping through my hair relaxed me.

"I can't be a siren," I muttered absently.

"Oh?"

"I definitely don't have any sexual powers," I told her.

"Julian might disagree with you." She winked at me in the mirror. "I've never seen him so satisfied...or happy."

I swallowed her words, knowing I felt that way. But that wasn't what was bothering me. "I know what they said about why she did it, but I wish she could explain it to me."

She nodded as she pinned and tucked my auburn hair.

"I keep thinking of how angry she was when she met Julian." I gulped down the panic I felt just recalling it. "Maybe you're right. Maybe my father was a vampire."

It would explain her hatred of him, as well as my fangs.

"She never told you who he was?" Jacqueline asked, reaching for a can of hairspray.

I shook my head. "She told me he wasn't worth knowing."

"There are a lot of vampires that fall into that category." Her lips pressed into a grim line as if remembering a few mistakes of her own. "Would you want to meet him?"

"I don't know," I admitted. "But I'd like to know what I am, and if these fangs are going to keep coming back, and if I'm more siren or more vampire and what that means. Sorry, I guess I have a lot of questions."

"Who wouldn't?" She stepped away from me to survey her work. "Can I give you some advice?"

"Yes," I said, letting some of my desperation show.

She leaned closer. "The questions will be here tomorrow. Tonight will be a memory. Enjoy the Solstice with your mate."

My absentee mate? I stopped myself from saying it out loud. Julian must have had a reason for staying away today. I just hoped that it didn't involve cold feet. He hadn't brought our engagement up again or given me the ring.

"And what should we do about these?" A velvet-tipped finger brushed the skin near my scars.

"Julian gave me a necklace." I moved to the dresser and opened the top drawer.

Jacqueline's eyes widened when I popped open the lid. "Maybe I do want a mate," she teased.

"I believe there are a few eligible Rousseaux brothers."

She lifted the diamond choker carefully out of the box and gestured for me to turn around so she could fasten it around my neck. "No way."

"Come on. We could be sisters," I coaxed. I felt lighter talking with her like this. I hadn't realized how much I needed time away from talk of the Council and secret magical powers and mating.

"Sebastian is too much trouble," she informed me. "Lysander is too hot for his own good. Thoren? I've known him for a couple of centuries, and he *never* talks."

I didn't miss that she'd left one brother off her list. "And Benedict?"

"Absolutely fucking not." She snorted. "We...don't get along."

Now that sounded promising. Except for one thing. "Fine. He betrayed us anyway."

Jacqueline fell silent as she smoothed the diamonds into place. When she finally spun me around, she stood in the shadows. "I'm not sure that he did," she said carefully. She held up her hand when I opened my mouth to protest. "Believe me, I am not Benedict's biggest fan, but I think he knew telling the Council would force them to give you The Second Rite."

"He could have warned us." If she was right and Julian's brother had knowingly delivered us to the Council, I wasn't certain that I cared about his motives. Especially since I'd spent the last twenty-four hours turning to find Julian watching me with haunted eyes. He still hadn't told me what he'd experienced during the *Kathréftis*.

I was beginning to wonder if he ever would.

"It would have undermined the whole thing," she murmured, "and you have to pass The Rites to get the Council's blessing."

I locked eyes with her in the mirror. "And if I don't want the Council's blessing?"

"Your life will be infinitely harder." She sighed, taking hold of my shoulders. "Trust me."

I hesitated a moment, trying to stop myself from asking the question that kept popping into my head. But curiosity got the better of me. "Why aren't you taking part in The Rites? Is it because you only like women?"

"I like everyone. Males. Females. Familiars. Werewolves. Vampires." She smirked at my surprise. "I like them all too much. After Camila got married, my parents and Sabine started getting ideas about Julian and me."

Sabine had mentioned something about them before—about an arranged marriage. My throat closed, making it hard to breathe. I could only nod.

"I was not about to marry Jules." She rolled her eyes before quickly adding, "No offense."

"None taken," I said wryly. "So, how did you get out of it?"

"We both tried to talk sense into our families. Julian had no interest in marrying me either," she said in a *don't-you-worry* voice. "I told him I would take care of it."

"Do I want to know?" I asked with a grin. Of course I did.

"They were going to make an announcement at the Solstice Ball, so I conveniently showed up with a werewolf, both of us drunk off our asses, and informed them things were getting serious." Her eyes sparkled as she finished her story, but somehow I knew there was more.

"I take it they didn't like that."

"They disowned me," she said casually. "I believe the words 'disgrace' and 'whore' were thrown around."

My stomach hollowed out at this twist. Jacqueline laughed it off, but there was no disguising the grief in her eyes. She had done what she'd had to do, but it had cost her. That was a pain I knew all too well.

"And that's why you don't participate in The Rites?" I asked softly.

"Technically," she said, "I'm not invited."

"Why not?"

"I'm not considered 'marriageable.'" She pantomimed air quotes around the last word. "Not without my mother's blessing, which she'll never give."

"I'm sorry."

"Why? I'm not." She giggled. "I've never met anyone—male or female—who's made me want to give up my freedom."

"It's not so bad," I murmured.

"You got one of the good ones," she reminded me.

I couldn't help laughing. "That good one could have been yours, it seems."

"Oh, you're right. I must learn not to be so picky."

We both giggled at that.

"What happened to the werewolf?" I asked, wondering if I'd met one of those creatures yet.

"Him?" She blinked. "I don't know. I picked him up in a bar down the street. He just went along with it."

"Even when you announced things were serious between you?" I wished I had half as much nerve as she did.

"We were really drunk, but don't worry, I made it up to him later," she added suggestively.

What was sex with a werewolf like? The question must have been written on my face, because Jacqueline's wicked grin widened as she fussed with my hair one last time. "Let's just say if I was Beauty, I would prefer the Beast."

Enough said.

"We should get going. Your mate will bite my head off if I keep you from him any longer," she informed me, checking the time on her phone.

"I think he's avoiding me," I confessed to her, telling her how he'd been gone when I woke up and I hadn't seen him since.

"Well, let's go find him," she suggested.

Jacqueline told me more stories about her various shenanigans, all of which she attributed to being a persona non grata at Council events, on our way upstairs.

"And tonight?" I asked, suddenly worried that she wouldn't be allowed to join the Solstice celebration.

"Tonight, I'm on the Rousseaux guest list—and no one questions your family's list," she whispered as we reached the foyer.

My stomach flipped at the idea that I was a Rousseaux. Not because I didn't want to marry Julian, but because I wasn't sure that I was actually a member of his family. How could I be, without Sabine's approval? And when she found out I might have been sired by another vampire, how much more would she hate me?

I was about to tell Jacqueline this, ready to get it off my chest, when she led me outside. The evening air bit at my bare skin, but I was too distracted to care. A trail of rose petals had been left down the drive, leading to an awaiting black Mercedes.

Jacqueline dragged me along to it, ignoring the questions I peppered her with as we walked. When we reached the car, the driver opened the door to reveal an empty back seat.

"This is where I leave you," she said pointedly.

"What are you up to?" I asked. "Where's Julian?"

"Just go with it." She winked, nudging me toward the open rear door.

I swallowed, looking to her for one more reassuring nod before I slid into the car. My heart hammered against my breastbone as the car pulled away from the estate and turned away from the city. Instead, the car wove along the rugged coastal road into the night. Darkness simmered outside my window, stars blinking in and out of focus as we continued higher and higher.

When we finally pulled onto a small overlook that jutted over the sea, I was out of the car before the driver could open my door. I made it two steps along the rocky cliff before I halted. A path strewn with white rose petals led to the farthest point of the cliff. Glass lanterns lined either side of it, but it was what was waiting for me at the end that stole the air from my lungs.

Or rather, *who* was waiting.

CHAPTER FIFTY-FIVE

Julian

Thea started toward me, and the world stood still. I was dimly aware of the rolling waves that crashed against the cliff below, of the sliver of moon that hung in the indigo sky, of life that existed beyond her. None of it mattered to me.

There was only her.

She smiled, wrenching her thin wrap around her shoulders as a draft of wind cut across the cliffside. The gust snuffed out a few candles and shook me out of my reverie.

I hadn't considered that we were too far from the town's magical center to fall under its protective shield or that she'd be wearing... Dear gods. What was she wearing?

I drank her in as I dashed toward her. She was trying to kill me. The dress looked to be made of silken air. The nearly invisible fabric might barely cover any of her delicious curves if it weren't for the embroidered wings that hugged her chest and hips. I whipped off my tuxedo jacket and wrapped it around her slight body.

I was about to apologize for my stupidity when she lifted her starry eyes to mine. "What is this?"

"Romance," I said hesitantly. "With a side of wind."

She laughed, and the sound chimed in my ears. Perhaps she was a siren. How could I tell? She had already captivated me, body and soul.

"I already said yes." Her hand slipped into mine, warm and soft. Neither of us had donned our evening gloves. She squeezed my hand as if she'd been waiting to feel it against her own for one stolen moment.

"You did." I tugged her toward the edge of the cliff, along what remained of the windswept petal path. "But there is one very important matter left to see to." I paused when we reached the end and turned toward her.

"Oh?" Thea didn't move, except for swift flicks of her eyes around us. "What is—"

Her question died on her lips as I sank to one knee before her. With her hand still clasped in mine, I offered her a small velvet box with my other. "You already said you would marry me, and I'm not going to give you a chance to take it back by asking again."

She laughed softly, her eyes twinkling like the stars overhead.

"All I am, I give to you. I swear to be your protector, your lover, your best friend as long as we walk this earth. For over nine hundred years, I sought some meaning in this world, and now I've finally found it. You. You are the meaning. You are the reason. And you are the answer. I am honored to be your mate, I am honored to tether my soul to yours, and I am honored to become your husband."

Thea's throat slid in the moonlight as she released my hand and took the box with both hands. Her fingers trembled as they pried it open. She gasped as she saw the ring inside.

"Julian, I—" She started to shake her head.

I'd expected that. She'd grown up with so little that I suspected I could have given her a ring from a vending machine and she'd try to refuse it.

"Nearly a hundred years ago, I was purchasing a sculpture for my mother at Christie's," I said. She blinked at the change in subject before finally nodding for me to continue. "I happened to be closest to the auction house, so I got stuck with procuring it. And while I was there, I saw this ring on display. They were showcasing it for an upcoming auction, and I remember that I just stopped when I saw it. I knew I had to own it. They tried to resist selling it to me, so I offered them an amount they couldn't refuse. I never knew why I bought this ring until the first time I kissed you."

She swallowed, still staring at it. "The first time?"

"The first time," I confessed. "That night, when you revealed you were a virgin, it took every ounce of self-control I possessed to walk away. I very nearly didn't, but I couldn't stay away."

"Thank God," she mumbled, tears spilling over her cheeks.

"Agreed." I took the box from her hands and stood, not bothering to brush off my slacks. There was only one thing I cared about. Plucking the ring from the box, I reached for her hand. Thea's breath caught as I slid it onto her finger.

"It fits perfectly," she whispered, staring at it. In fact, it looked made for her. Part of me believed it was—that magic itself had whispered to its creator to craft the spectacular ring just for her. The center stone was a flawless, nine-carat natural emerald—practically unheard of in the jewelry world. Its Belle Époque platinum band swirled gracefully around it, studded with diamonds.

"I had it sized in Paris," I murmured.

Her eyes lifted to mine, widening with confusion. "Paris? When?"

"While you were shopping with Jacqueline." I grinned at the open-mouthed shock on her face. "I told myself it was merely a present, but I always knew why I wanted you to wear this ring."

"So, you had it before you even met me?"

I nodded. "I would have given it to you sooner, but someone demanded romance." She giggled, her black lashes fluttering to her tear-soaked cheeks. "Did I do okay?"

"Perfect." She raised her face to mine, love reflecting back as endless and beautiful as the starlight shining on the sea beyond.

Cupping her chin, I brought my lips to hers. The kiss was a vow itself that promised a lifetime more, but it wouldn't be enough. Eternity couldn't sate my desire for her.

When I finally managed to tear myself away, she watched me with swollen lips and bedroom eyes. I cursed under my breath, earning a raised eyebrow.

"I wish that we could skip the Solstice Ball," I said.

"We could," she purred. "But what will we do instead?"

A growl ripped through my chest, the sound promising that I would find many interesting ways to fill our free time. But now, more than ever, we needed to make an appearance. It was part of my plan— part of the reason that I'd wanted to give her this ring tonight.

"We should go," I said, my voice rough with want as I crooked my arm for her.

Her lower lip jutted into a pout that sent my mind back to imagining better uses for our time. "Do we have to?"

"Unfortunately," I said, leading her toward the Mercedes I'd parked nearby. "But there will be plenty of dark corners for us to make use of."

She shivered as I helped her into the passenger seat. Judging by the flush on her fair cheeks, the reaction had nothing to do with the cold.

When I climbed behind the wheel, I found her admiring her new ring, and my heart soared. It was all I could do not to get back out of the car and shout from the cliffside that she was mine. I hit the ignition switch, knowing I had something much more fun planned,

"What's that smirk for?" she asked, her eyes narrowing as she leaned across the console and ran her delicate fingers up my thigh.

"Nothing."

"Why don't I believe you?"

"Just trust me." I braced for a fight, but she simply relaxed into her seat.

"Okay."

Maybe she'd already heard what I was planning in my thoughts. I hadn't trusted myself not to ruin the surprise by accidentally thinking about it near her, so I'd kept away for most of the day. Now that she was next to me, her candied-violet scent filling the small cabin, I wished I hadn't. Maybe I wouldn't be so on edge now. Maybe I wouldn't need to touch her so badly.

But, somehow, I doubted it.

"Where is this party, anyway?" She twisted her ring as if checking that it was real and not a figment of her imagination.

Later, I would strip off this tempting dress. I would unfasten that diamond choker from her neck. And when she was wearing nothing but my ring, I'd fill her with my cock and my fangs until...

Thea spluttered in the passenger seat, and I turned toward her in concern, only to find her fanning herself.

"Being in your head is almost as good as being in your bed," she admitted, her lips twisting into a sheepish smile.

Something rumbled in my chest as I turned the car toward the oldest part of the island. "Later, I plan to disabuse you of that notion."

"Promise?" she asked wickedly.

Fuck, she knew what buttons to press. If we weren't so close—if tonight wasn't so important—I might stop the car and take her on the spot. Part of me wanted to arrive with her smelling of me so that every creature there would know to whom she belonged.

She laughed as she pulled her gloves from her bag. The thin satin stretched just past her wrists. Once they were on, she slid her engagement ring over her gloved finger. "I want to show it off."

Another surge of male pride burst inside me. It was stupid to care about a human tradition like marriage, especially considering how we'd bound our souls together. But modernity be damned, seeing her wearing my ring made me want to beat my chest.

I took her hand and brought it to my lips, savoring the pulse of her magic that responded under the thin fabric. I was so preoccupied that I was on autopilot, driving the old roads by memory rather than sight. I only had eyes for her. My future. My fiancée. My mate.

"Julian!" she shrieked, snapping my attention to the road just in time to see the car drive off the edge of a cliff.

CHAPTER FIFTY-SIX

Thea

"Julian!"

I grabbed his broad shoulder as the car went over the edge, my stomach plummeting in expectation. But there was no weightless fall, no fiery crash—nothing happened at all. Digging my fingers into his shoulder, I stared out the window as the world shimmered and blurred before turning into a new one altogether. Before us and under our tires, the street continued into a bustling neighborhood. Despite the late hour, people dashed out of shops carrying strange objects, families walked down the sidewalk, and friends lingered under flickering strings of lights at open-air bistros. Each and every one of them was dressed like it was the middle of summer and not winter.

I glanced over my shoulder, eyes fluttering as rapidly as my heart, and saw the edge of Corfu's Old Town swimming behind me as though it were behind an airy screen.

"Probably should have warned you about that," my mate said with barely suppressed laughter.

I scrambled to get ahold of myself, pasting a glare on my face. "You drove us off a cliff!"

"Yes."

"We could have died," I snapped.

"I knew there was a street there." He reached for my hand and took it in his own again. Moments ago, he'd held it, kissed it, and then he'd nearly given me a heart attack. "Will you forgive me if I told you I was so distracted by my beautiful mate that I forgot to tell you we were heading into the *Mystikos Synoikia*?"

I raised an eyebrow.

"The Veiled Quarter," he translated.

"Let me guess. This is a magical oasis like *Île Cachée*?" With a ragged sigh, I rubbed out the stress in my chest. I should have known a place like this existed in Corfu. Julian had taken me somewhere similar in Paris. There, the streets were quiet and nearly empty save for vampires and familiars visiting shops that catered to the magical elite—and others with more dangerous tastes. Corfu's hidden world was packed.

"This city is beloved by vampires," he said with a nod. "Mostly because they've enchanted it to be a perfectly sunny seventy-three degrees year-round. Our kind comes from all over the world to visit."

"Wait. Are you telling me we're basically at vampire Ibiza?" I could only imagine the amenities that were on offer for holiday-goers here.

Julian's lips twisted as he maneuvered down a busy street, narrowly avoiding a group of girlfriends having the time of their lives. He slammed on his brakes and beckoned for them to pass. One of the girls, a leggy brunette, blew him a kiss, her friends laughing next to her—until they caught sight of me. I narrowed my eyes possessively, allowing whatever fearsome magic flowed in my veins to rise, and they all hurried quickly away.

Turning, I caught Julian's bemused expression.

"What?" I demanded.

"I love it when you go all alpha on me," he teased. "It's super sexy."

"Oh, shut up." I rolled my eyes. The truth was that I knew exactly what he meant. It wasn't that I wanted Julian to follow me around like some brute, but when the occasion called for it and his primal side came out…it was beyond hot. "What did you call this place?"

"*Mystikos Synoikia*," he repeated. "The Veiled Quarter. It was the first neighborhood built on this land by local covens. Its edge extends all the way to Old Town."

"The area we just drove through?" I gestured behind me. Thanks to his family and the antics of the Vampire Council, we'd been too busy enduring mortal wounds and mind games to do much exploring. "It's connected to that medieval fortress, right?"

He nodded, his eyes darkening a shade. "The Old Fortress has been almost entirely under vampire control since before the Venetians modernized it."

"Almost?" I hadn't missed that slight qualification.

"The Nazis captured it for a bit. It was a dark period." A frown pulled at his sculpted lips as he recalled its history. "We will never allow that to happen again."

I squeezed his hand, wishing I could share the memories. I would have to settle for shouldering some of the sorrow that seeped into my bones and seized my heart. Julian forced a faint smile, but it was full of regret.

"Sorry. I didn't mean to ruin the mood," he said. "I still forget you have to suffer everything I'm feeling."

I shook my head. "I will never mind it. I carry your heart, and you carry mine." I smiled as brightly as I could manage while still feeling the enduring sadness. "Ride or die, right?"

"Right," he agreed, his face slightly shadowed even as the grief ebbed away. But the shared joy we'd both felt driving into the Veiled Quarter didn't return. Instead, my skin felt prickly—almost tight. I found myself wanting to move, my body full of nervous energy. Looking over, I spotted Julian's thumb tapping the steering wheel restlessly.

He'd gone from sad to anxious, and I'd come along for the ride. Feeling each other's strongest emotions was one thing we hadn't anticipated when we'd officially consummated our relationship. It wasn't clear if it was the result of being mated or the tether that existed between us, but it was something to which we were both still acclimating.

"Nervous about something?" I asked.

"I wish we didn't have to go to these bloody events," he confessed. "I've made a match. We shouldn't have to bother with the rest of the social season."

"It will be over before we know it," I said, running my hand down his arm, "and then it will just be you and me."

His grin was forced, and I knew he was thinking about what I was thinking. That if the Council had their way, it wouldn't be just the two of us for long. As much fun as practicing making babies was, I understood his hesitation. I wanted us to spend more time alone before I had to share him. Maybe that was selfish, but he'd lived nine hundred years. I'd only had twenty-two so far.

It didn't matter where we were going as long as we were together. I'd dreaded going to Greece and attending the Solstice Ball and contending with more curious vampires and jealous familiars. But now I stared at the ring resting over my satin glove. Though it was beautiful, it wasn't the flawless emerald or its antique setting that made it so lovely. It was what it represented. A future.

Our future.

Julian reached for my hand and lifted it to his lips as if he was thinking the same thing. For a moment, it didn't matter that we were headed toward a ballroom full of potential enemies. Or that I was still grappling with learning I was a siren and all the questions *that* raised. All that mattered was him and his hand in mine as we drove under the clear evening sky. And maybe it wouldn't always be like this. Once The Rites were over and we were married, maybe we would find ourselves driving along the Grecian coast for no other reason than to hold hands.

It was all I could wish for. The rest of my dreams had already come true.

I glanced out the window, looking for a star to make one more wish.

We finally made our way out of the busiest part of the quarter, the streets widening into impressive boulevards lined with spectacular ancient mansions. It reminded me of the photos I'd seen of buildings in Venice, although beyond these stretched the sea, rather than canals. On a whim, I pushed the button to lower my window. Balmy evening air kissed my cheeks and caressed me.

"It really is like summer!"

Julian laughed at my astonishment.

"Hey," I pouted. "This is really cool. You can control the weather."

"Pet, I love seeing the world through your eyes," he said, and I softened. "But I don't control shit. There's a lot of residual magic here, so it's easy to create glamours like this. There's so much that entire veins of magic run all the way through Old Town."

"Outside the quarter?"

"You have to know where to look, but yes." He glanced at me with a grim look. "Most of it is the kind of thing that the Vampire Council and the High Coven don't sanction."

"So I shouldn't go snooping around for it?" I asked.

His jaw tightened as his blue eyes hardened into sapphires. "I'd rather you didn't."

"I won't," I said quickly. He was on edge enough without me making him worry. "So, what's this High Coven?" This was the first time I'd heard that term.

"It's the equivalent of the Council. They govern the laws surrounding the use of magic and oversee the politics of it all. Some say they guard a secret library of grimoires and histories that date back to the beginning of time," he said with a lowered voice, as if his words might carry on the warm wind. "The witch present at The Second Rite—Agatha—is a member."

"I guess I thought the Vampire Council oversaw everyone," I said.

"They like to act like they do." He snorted. "Believe me. The High Coven is just as powerful in its own way, but I wouldn't say that in front of my mother."

"Thank God you warned me. You know how much she and I like to sit around and gab," I said drily.

Better safe than sorry, my love.

Hearing his voice in my head made me smile, and I relaxed into my seat, enjoying the view out the window. Only a minute later, the car began to slow, and I felt my heartbeat tick up a notch.

"We're here," Julian announced as he turned down a private drive.

Huge olive trees, larger than any I'd ever seen, lined both sides of the path and twisted overheard. Their branches grew together to form a gnarled canopy, plump olives hanging off them. They continued as far as I could see. Swinging under them as if held by an invisible thread, golden lanterns lit the dark tunnel.

"*Lianolia*," Julian told me. "Corfu is known for them. The people saved the trees during the war. Most of the ones on the island are hundreds of years old—these have been around longer than I have. They're spelled to never stop producing fruit."

"Just one of the many amenities when you visit Vampire Island," I mumbled.

Julian remained thoughtful as we continued down the drive, but his thoughts remained veiled like the world around me. I looked down at my hand and the ring I wore over my glove. As much as I wanted to wear it, maybe tonight wasn't the best time to show up with it on. I moved to quietly slip it off, but he caught my hand before I could slide it free.

"What are you doing?" The deep timbre of his voice, laced with possessiveness, sent heat surging between my legs.

"We didn't really discuss this. Tonight probably isn't the time for me to wear your engagement ring. We haven't even told your entire family." No, we'd been too focused on other news, like finding out that I wasn't nearly as human as we'd first thought.

"I'd rather you never take it off again, except to change gloves," he said, his tone brooking no further debate. "Is that a problem?"

The truth was that it was all up to me. Thanks to most vampires adhering to a matriarchal order, Julian had been raised to not only respect a woman's wishes but defer to them. While some males, like his former brother-in-law, desired control over their partners, Julian actually respected me. Even when he'd had the chance to bind me to his will after we found ourselves tethered, he'd given me an out by ordering me to never follow his orders—unless I wanted to.

Which was one request I was happy to oblige.

"And your family?" I left the ring on my finger.

"Leave them to me."

Darkness smoldered in his words, and I focused on the more tempting possibilities the evening held. He'd promised we could find a dark corner, and now that I knew how pleasant the weather was in the Veiled Quarter, it seemed I might suggest we find a secluded spot under the stars.

An estate that rivaled any I'd ever seen waited at the end of the drive. It rose like a grand lady into the night. Enchanted candles lined the massive stone steps, welcoming us toward the light. We waited in a short line of cars until a young valet, clearly human, circled around to take the keys while another uniformed attendant moved to my side of the vehicle. But Julian opened my door, still growling at the valet's gall.

"Down, boy," I murmured as he helped me out. "He was just doing his job."

A muscle twitched in Julian's jaw as he fought his primitive urge to protect and possess me. I shivered at the shadows in his eyes as he watched me emerge. In the enchanted summer air, the mesh fabric of the intricate gown no longer felt so out of season. Julian's hungry gaze stripped away any lingering doubts I had about the dress.

"What big eyes you have," I said.

His answering look told me that he would happily devour me. His eyes flickered to the stone railing, as if he was considering hauling me right over to it and claiming me.

But tonight was important. We needed to show the Council that we intended to remain committed to each other—and only each other—regardless of their demands. We just needed to blend in so they stopped thinking we would undermine The Rites with our nontraditional match. So, rather than hoisting me onto the railing, he offered me his arm. With each step we climbed, my heart beat a little faster and my mouth grew a little drier.

It wasn't the first event we'd attended together, but it was the first one since we had officially mated. Would everyone know? Of course they would. Vampires had a supernatural sense of smell, and familiars also seemed to have an uncanny knack for sensing things.

At least everyone would be too preoccupied with the Solstice to notice us. I wasn't prepared to announce our engagement to the whole world. Not when it probably meant facing more interrogations from the Vampire Council—and Sabine.

We paused at the top of the stairs to wait for a man in livery to address us at the door. Beyond the great entrance, laughter and music drifted our way. My stomach tightened as I thought of the party waiting for us there.

"Lord Rousseaux," he said, bowing deeply.

I bit my lip to keep my mouth from falling open. Maybe I was just being dense, but it seemed like people in Corfu were even more in awe of my partner. I'd been told he was the equivalent of a prince, but in Greece, I'd finally been forced to process it.

Julian moved closer to the man and whispered something to him. I lifted an eyebrow when he turned back to me.

"They're announcing each guest," he said flatly. "We do love our traditions and formalities."

He led me to the small landing, pausing on the top stair as the attendant stepped before us. Below, the crowd quieted as if they'd been waiting for this arrival—*his* arrival. Curious eyes studied me, their owners wearing faces that ranged from interested to downright hostile. I shifted closer to Julian, my own gaze landing on Sabine's displeased face as the attendant announced us.

"Lord Julian Rousseaux and his fiancée, Thea Melbourne."

ACKNOWLEDGMENTS

I cannot believe the love my vampires have found in the world. Thank you for falling in love with this world as much as I have.

I couldn't do this without my agent, Louise Fury, and the Fury Agency team! Huge thanks to my foreign rights agents for bringing my words to readers all over the world.

Thank you to the entire Entangled Team for working to take this story to the next level. Thank you to my 1980s dream editor, Liz Pelletier, for always being there no matter what. Special thanks to Elana Cohen, Lydia Sharp, Rae Swain, Jessica Turner, Curtis Svehlak, Bree Archer, Hannah Lindsey, and Yezanira Venecia.

Thank you to the team at Tantor for bringing FRV to audio and to Stella Hunter and Teddy Hamilton for narrating!

Thank you to the teams at Blanvalet, Hachette, and Wydawnictwo Kobiece for bringing FRV to readers around the world.

I couldn't do this without my team. Big thanks to Shelby and Kai for keeping all my shit together. Huge thanks to my publicist, Graceley, for championing this book at every turn.

On the hard days, I can always go to my Loves for support. Thank you for being there through all my plot twists and cliffhangers in books and real life.

Thank you to Josh for being team vampire and the best editor a girl could ask for. Thank you to Shayla and Shelby for the eagle-eyed proofreading. Huge thanks to Ann, Jami, and Cristina for beta reads!

Thanks to my family for always understanding when Mom is suffering from word lag, for sharing me with fictional people, and for always having snacks at the ready. I'm so blessed to share my life with all of you.

And to my husband—every love story I write is because of our own love story. Thank you.

Filthy Rich Vampires: Second Rite is a steamy romance full of extravagance and an ending that will leave you on the edge of your seat. However, the story includes elements that might not be suitable for all readers. Violence, familial estrangement, blood rituals, beheadings, mind-altering substance use, and death are shown on the page, with sexual assault and discussions of cancer in the backstory. Readers who may be sensitive to these elements, please take note.

*Don't miss the exciting new books
Entangled has to offer.*

Follow us!

f @EntangledPublishing

⬡ @Entangled_Publishing

♪ @EntangledPub